D0375046

CALM SEA AND PROSPEROUS VOYAGE

# CALM SEA AND PROSPEROUS VOYAGE

*SELECTED STORIES*

# BETTE HOWLAND

EDITED BY BRIGID HUGHES
AFTERWORD BY HONOR MOORE

A PUBLIC SPACE BOOKS

A Public Space Books
323 Dean Street
Brooklyn, NY 11217

Stories from this collection appeared, in earlier forms, in *Blue in Chicago* (Harper & Row)
as well as the following magazines:
"A Visit" in *A Public Space* (2015)
"Aronesti" in the *Noble Savage* (1962)
"Power Failure" in the *American Voice* (1985)
"Calm Sea and Prosperous Voyage" in *TriQuarterly* (1999)

Significant support for A Public Space Books has been provided by the Drue and H. J.
Heinz II Charitable Trust, the Chisholm Foundation, and Justin Leverenz. This
publication is also made possible, in part, through a grant from the National Endowment
for the Arts, and generous contributions from the Amazon Literary Partnership, the New
York State Council on the Arts, the Sharna and Irvin Frank Foundation, the Strozier-Viren
Family Foundation, and other corporations, foundations, and individuals. We are grateful
to all of them.

Grateful acknowledgment to the Special Collections Research Center, University of
Chicago Library, for permission to feature "German Lessons." Grateful acknowledgment
to Scott Horton for permission to feature his translations.

Library of Congress Control Number: 2019933752
ISBN   978-0-9982675-0-0
eISBN 978-0-9982675-1-7
Distributed by Publishers Group West

www.apublicspace.org

9  8  7  6  5  4  3  2  1

FOR

THE ONES

BETTE

LOVED

## QUIET SEA

Deep quiet rules the waters;
Motionless, the sea reposes,
And the boatsman looks about with alarm
At the smooth surfaces about him.
No wind comes from any direction!
A deathly, terrible quiet!
In the vast expanse
Not one wave stirs.

## FORTUNATE VOYAGE

The mist is torn away,
The heavens turn bright,
And Aeolus unfastens
The bonds of fear.
There, the winds rustle,
The boatsman stirs.
Quickly! Quickly!
The waves rise up again.
The distant view draws close,
Land ho, I call!

—*Johann Wolfgang von Goethe*
*translated from the German by Scott Horton*

# CONTENTS

# A VISIT

I was driving an expressway through a large city. Interchanges, on-off ramps, bridges, underpasses. Traffic glittered, roadwork stretched ahead forever. I kept heading the wrong way. You know how it is: the wrong lane, the wrong turn, and you're stuck; nothing to do but just keep going, on and on, until the next exit. By now it was getting dark and the going was getting rougher. Flags, flares, sandbags, barricades. Not only was I lost—I was on a road not open. No road at all. A tunnel of rocks and mud, closed for repairs. That's why there were no more cars; other drivers knew about the mess and the construction work and had taken the detours.

But someone else must have been in the same fix, because out of nowhere a car came barreling past, exhaust glowing red in the taillights. I was almost expecting it: the skid, the screech, the crash and scream of metal and glass.

DON'T STOP. That's what they tell you. Drive, drive, even if you get a flat tire; if you break down, never get out of the car. It was night, it was no-man's-land, nothing around but burned-out buildings, black windows, brick walls scaled by steely vines of razor wire. On the smoking air drifted the distant whistles of sirens.

Still, I guess I stopped and got out anyhow—because the next thing I knew, I was on foot, picking my way clumsily over the rubble. My head felt fuzzy and my arm was smarting. Sticky. Oh, oh, I thought. What if it was me? I bet it was me! I must be the one in that wreck back there!

That made sense. I don't see well at night, and I was driving too fast. I do now, you know, ever since I noticed that cops don't stop gray-haired ladies in pickup trucks. So no wonder.

This was one of those Good News and Bad News situations.

I was lucky; shaken up, maybe, but scarcely hurt, hardly a scratch. By now the accident seemed to be the least of my worries. Because here I was, all alone, no one else in sight—who else would be dumb enough to take a road that was closed?—and not so sure I should hope for anyone to show up, either. Whoever did might not be coming to the rescue.

It was a pretty scary place, all right. The sort of place you have night-mares about.

An underpass, I had thought at first; but now I saw I was under-ground—a subway tunnel—and stumbling along tracks toward the sta-tion. Closed for repairs. No passengers, no turnstiles, no ticket takers. Planks laid across the potholed platforms. Crumbling ceilings, broken stairs. At the entrance, a makeshift door. Either the glass was very dirty, or—yes, it wasn't glass; it was that plastic stuff they staple over window frames for weatherproofing. That's why it was so hard to see through.

You may be sure I was watching.

And, sure enough, someone was coming. Through the plastic film the effect was of a form materializing—a uniform, stout, a badge on the chest. Then the door swung open, the man stepped quickly down the planks, and I saw he wasn't as big as I had thought—though big enough—and not in uniform. No badge, only a trench coat. Still, he had the manner of a man with a badge on his chest. A lot of shirtfront, thrusting buttons. The brisk pointy gray beard; the bristling gray hair; the neck short, rigid, under the collar.

He wore horn-rimmed glasses—angled, tilted, harlequin style—and under his elbow he clutched a portfolio, tightly, possessively, the way a woman might clutch a purse.

The Russians, he said. The Russians are driving me crazy!

Now that seemed strange, because he looked Russian to me. Maybe it was the glint of the glasses that gave his face such an Asiatic slant; his temples were polished and bulging and so was the bald ruddy bulb of his nose. And what about the raincoat? A uniform, after all: belted, wrinkled, that familiar shopworn look. A man from the KGB.

If not, what then? FBI? CIA? MI3?

He reached for his portfolio, which turned out to be a set of blueprints, and unfolded them with a rattle and snap of the wrist.

Well, it wasn't a threat, though not exactly a rescue. And it seemed time to speak up; my arm was burning. I sensed that he might be the man in charge around here.

Sir? I said.

He was inspecting the blueprints, holding them up to the light. Only a bulb—one bulb, in all this greasy darkness—one bulb dangling in a wire cage. What else could you expect on a construction site? Maybe he was the engineer for this project. But who was he working for? He still looked like a double agent to me.

Sir? I said. For I was catching on at last. The bad roads, the crash, the minor injury. This petty bureaucrat. This place.

Sir? I'm dead? Is that it? I'm dead?

He heard me all right—don't think he didn't—but he wasn't about to reply. Too busy squinting up at his blueprints, the beard stuck like a rabbit's foot on the end of his chin. I could wait. I had all the time in the world.

Does this mean, I said. Does this mean I have to be me for all eternity? I hate to be nosy.

He twisted his short neck over his collar and pointed his little stiff beard at me. For all eternity, he said.

What did I tell you? Just like I said: There was Good News and Bad News.

I was wondering what the chances might be of undertaking a crash course in self-improvement here in Eternity. Not so hot. Not so hot.

By now others were turning up, part of the crew, as far as I could tell—overalls, hard hats, welders' goggles. They didn't waste any time glancing my way, in case I was expecting the Welcome Committee. All of them standing around, their hands on their hips, gawking and goggling at their goddamn blueprints. It wasn't Hell, by the way, if that's what you're thinking. Only the next world, the netherworld—bad lighting, leaky sewers, busted gutters and all. So this was it! The Distinguished Place. A famous dump, that's what. Though that should come as no surprise: everyone knows the infrastructure is in terrible shape.

Look who I'm talking to! As if you need me to tell you. You must know all about it by now, don't you? You got there first.

That reminded me. Some people were going to feel bad about this, but only the ones I wouldn't wish to give grief. And now look what I've gone and done. They'll feel the way I feel about you. This is no time to reproach you, I know, but I wish you had cared more for your body when you were in it. I cared for it. When you were in it.

This made me think of the other question.

What about the ones I knew and loved? I said. Do I get to see them?

All the helmets crowding together, poking up under the caged lamp. For the first time he actually looked at me—the manager, the agent. I thought: Hard to be sure; but the slanted glasses glowed for an instant with a cloudy crystal-ball light.

That's what they all want to know! he said. But that's *the whole show*! I can't give *that* away, can I?

The light went out. Through the dark I came up. I was looking for you, I went looking for you. My arm was still aching.

# BLUE IN CHICAGO

First thing this morning, getting ready to leave the house, I heard on the news report that another University of Chicago graduate student had been shot and killed in a holdup in Hyde Park. I was holding my breath, but the name was not one I knew. I'm a graduate student at the university and I live in Hyde Park. I listened for details—the time of night, a number, a street. You always want to know how close these things have come to you.

There were two students. They were at a party and had gone out to get more beer. On the way back three youths wanted their money. One gave up his wallet and walked away. The other was a black belt in karate— he put up a fight. Five times the gun clicked and misfired; the sixth tore his side. The radio announcer went on to recall other such incidents in the college community, the last student murder only a few months before.

It was a dense dark morning. I live in a small studio on top of a high rise; it's mostly windows. A friend calls it a perch on a flagpole because I never draw the shades. Lately one visitor after another has expressed a wish for an apartment just like mine: "It's perfect," they say. From which I infer that they all want to climb up the flagpole; remove themselves. And there is something remote about my situation. For instance, I can see the helicopters surveying the morning traffic snarls, hovering over the city. On days like today they seem to be putt-putting about in thick gray gloom like outboard motors. The noise takes up the whole sky. Maybe because the details weren't more specific—because the victim was unknown, face-less to me—because I couldn't pinpoint the spot—all at once there were no limits. It was out there: I didn't have to know *where*.

One other thing. I was about to set off for a cousin's wedding, clear on the other side of the city. That's where all my relatives live. And it seems that every time I trek north for one of these family occasions (none of them would dream of going to see me), the subject is bound to come up: why I continue to live on the South Side of Chicago, with its high crime rate and race warfare. Almost inevitably something like this will have happened, played up on the news, plastered all over the headlines. Crime on the South Side gets the banner treatment. Everyone likes to know *where*, to isolate the symptoms. Only this morning I had a strange, obstinate reaction: I didn't feel like being hassled in this way, didn't feel apologetic about living in Hyde Park. Maybe it was just inertia. Or mulishness—a family trait.

My uncle Rudy's height and hulking shoulders filled the space behind the wheel. A huge man, six foot four, 250 pounds; crew cut, bulletheaded; the thick close-shaved folds of skin lay on his neck. Even from the back, in his checked gray suit, you could tell: a cop. I looked at the back of his head, wondering what he was thinking. Impenetrable. His head seems too small for the big body; his nose is a beak. When his nose got broken somehow, on maneuvers, the army doctors wanted to make it over for him. But Rudy wouldn't hear of it. Why kibitz with destiny? He's somewhat deaf, you know; he lost the hearing of one ear in the service. He could have an operation for nothing. But he never will.

"Who needs another hole in the head? One's enough."

It was April; the wind was blowing fresh tender soot, swirling papers fancifully in the gutters of Uptown—my grandmother's neighborhood. The sky was heavy and full of gloom, but here and there, a splinter, a gleam. Rudy pulled into the thick of the grimy, sluggish traffic—deaf or indifferent to our female conversation.

I couldn't believe we were going to talk about Roxanne's hair all the way to the wedding.

Roxanne is Uncle Rudy's young wife, a big handsome Southern girl, rawboned, rock jawed, her pale head dropped over her knitting. Peculiarly pale; translucent, like rock candy, and almost as brittle. It was stiff with spray lacquer.

"Oh, you did something to your hair," my mother remarked as we climbed in back.

"I don't like it," Roxanne said at once, without glancing round or lifting her head. Her bare shoulders were scarcely moving in their sockets as she yanked at her yarn and plucked at her needles. "I tolt her beige blont and she dit it silver blont instet." She spoke in her discontented mountain drawl.

"Go back and make them do it over," my mother said. "You pay enough, don't you?" Talk about needles.

"It smells pretty, though," my grandmother said, sniffing through the glitter of rhinestone frames.

Roxanne flicked the yarn irritably over her forefinger. "I don't like it." And so on.

But sometimes it seems that's all these occasions are really for. "Aren't you going to put on any makeup?" my mother asked as soon as I walked in the door. "Look how thin she's getting," my grandmother said, catching her lip between her teeth. "She's putting on weight," said my mother.

Even my grandmother is all dolled up. A little old lady, shrunken with age, gazing from between shoulders hunched with arthritis. Swollen crippled fingers clasping her coat, the lapels weighted down with dime-store brooches. She loves adornment. There was a pause just before, as we were leaving her flat; she wanted to retrieve her watch—a big Timex with a spandex band, a man's watch. The utilitarian chunk of nickel plating dangled from her fingertips. Her stiff fingers stretching the band, dragging it over her wrist. She's eighty-three and she's even more obstinate. Her children beg her to come and live with them, get out of that wretched neighborhood. Now their own children are marrying, they all have room—they'd love to have her. But she knows better. At her age, it's bad enough being mortal, without having to make apologies for it too.

"Hey? Which way you going?"

My mother sat up, suddenly erect, her striking white head looking all about. She was in black and white from head to toe, stark contrasts: dark mink stole, long evening skirt, pointed shoes. "I thought you were going to take Sheridan."

"Hah. We'd be there tomorrow, I took Sheridan," Rudy said, looking over his shoulder and showing the dark spaces in his teeth. He has a loud offended voice, the result of his partial deafness.

"You don't mean to tell me you're taking the Edens Expressway?"

"Nacherly. What do you think? I'm taking Edens."

"Edens. Who ever heard of anything so stupid? Taking Edens."

My mother was rummaging in her purse. She took out a mimeographed sheet—a map of directions to the church, in one of the northernmost suburbs; it had come with the invitations—and shoved it across the seat at her brother's big back.

"Here. Look. You go straight out Sheridan, you'll be there in fifteen minutes."

"You should of driven your own car, you wanted to take Sheridan." Rudy sat unmoved, eyes level, watching traffic in the mirror.

"I woultn't say nothing more if I was you." Roxanne turned sideways in her seat to view my mother. "We're liable to ent up in Milwaukee. You know how stubborn Rooty is."

Yes, and he's had riot training.

But my mother does not know how to desist. The irresistible force meets the immovable object. A routine encounter for her.

After a while she sat back, however, and began whispering to me, stating her case, thrusting the map under my nose. I had already been en route an hour and a half, just to get to my grandmother's house, and I couldn't make heads or tails of it. That displeased her. She got angrier with me, rattling the piece of paper in my face. Her own face startlingly sallow under her beautiful white hair. She must have seen I had no sympathy with her, either. I couldn't help that; my mother's panic is an old and potent enemy of mine.

It was now noon; the wedding was called for twelve thirty.

"And when they say twelve thirty they mean twelve thirty," my mother said, laying her hand to her cheek. "That's not Jewish time, you know."

As a patrolman on the city payroll, Rudy has to live in Chicago. My parents do too. My father hates grass; golf courses and cemeteries give him the creeps. But one of the reasons my grandmother would never consider moving in with her other children is that she finds life in the suburbs so dull. She likes to be able to see lots of people, to sit in a lobby somewhere and watch the world go by. All she asks for is a lobby.

In her neighborhood, with all the grim apartment hotels for the elderly, the shelter homes and halfway houses, there are plenty of lobbies. The one in her building is no good, however—too dark, off to one side, you miss everything—so she prefers to sit in the large plate-glass window of the A&P, resting her shopping bags. You see lots of old ladies sitting there.

Her next-door neighbor is confined to her room and keeps the door open, buoyed up among her pillows like a pile of life preservers. She has a darkened, pewter complexion; you feel the gleam of eyes on you. Though she's hearty enough—banging her cane against the wall to get your attention.

Today, when I had alighted from the elevator, both doors were open; my grandmother was going back and forth between the two rooms, keeping her neighbor company. She introduced us. "My granddaughter! My son! My daughter!" She was proud of her visitors, because we were dressed up for the wedding.

My mother, as it happens, was still getting dressed—presenting her back, all unzipped, to the wide-open doorway, her long skirts hiked up about her hips, fastening her garters.

"So what do you call this, Mother?" I said.

"Hmm," she replied airily, as she bent over her black stockings. "Nobody ever comes by here anyway."

And yet she is the first to complain about the suspicious types lurking in the elevators and passageways. They need encouragement. This is what you call flinging down the gauntlet. My mother was also taking the opportunity to announce that her charms were all used up. ("Who's going to bother with an old woman?") Not so, by the way.

Compared to other buildings in Uptown, this one is not all that bad: a tall, yellow-brick "elevator building," its roof rising high above the squat burned-out three-flats and boarded storefronts of Sheridan Road. The entrance, stripped bare, has the naked gleam of a ballroom; the dim narrow pier-glass mirrors hark back to its days of luxury.

As we were passing through today, my grandmother was suddenly reminded: last week, one of the tenants—a large old man, broad shouldered, one eye dim behind a smoked lens: I knew which one—got robbed on the bus. He had just cashed a pension check, eighty dollars. He sat in his shirtsleeves in the lobby, telling the others all about it. There wasn't much to tell. He had the money in his pockets when he got on the bus, it wasn't there when he got off. His fingers felt about his chest, still groping in his pockets for the money, as if it might turn up yet.

All at once he stiffened in his chair; his heart jumped beneath his shirtfront. He stretched himself out dead.

"So it turned out that jener"—the other, she meant; the pickpocket—"needed that money worse than he did," she said. That's what I like about the old lady; she's so sentimental.

By the time we got to the church, the ceremony had already started, the backs of heads gazing toward the altar. The church itself seemed rattlingly empty; row upon row of varnished pews and only the white sheet down the middle aisle to indicate the trappings of a wedding. I'd heard it would be small and simple, but there was something intimidating about such austerity. I crept into the last pew on the aisle in back, my mother and her mother following arm in arm. The old lady—well under five feet—shuffled along with her head thrust forward, looking both wary and determined. A few other latecomers hurried in, crossed themselves with a sprinkle of holy water, and—stooping quickly on the aisle—slid onto the bench at the other end.

It was the first I had realized that Millicent was Catholic, though I knew that her parents had objected to her marrying my cousin Gregg. (As they had objected when Gregory and Millicent traveled through Europe together. "If it was my daughter, I wouldn't let her go," Uncle Leon had reassured them.) I don't know what Gregory considers himself.

Long legged in his striped pants and frock coat, he was standing with his hands clasped in front of him, swaying lightly. I could just glimpse the edges of his swarthy mustache. Millicent looked very tall in her white veil, with her long black hair curling down her back beneath the train.

Rudy came strolling in with his hands in his pockets, the vents of his jacket split over his hips. It was broad daylight in the lofty empty church:

brighter than daylight, light spilling solemnly from the high arched windows. He looked like a monolith, wading through the pews. Glancing back and scowling at us over his shoulder—wondering what we were doing, of course, sitting all the way in back and on the wrong side; the bride's side.

The priest asked us to rise.

At once my eye was attracted to Uncle Leon's handsome white head—the same arresting white mane as my mother's. From the back, his figure seemed as youthful, as broad shouldered and narrow waisted in his frock coat, as Gregory's; and he was standing in the same way—his hands clasped in front of him, swaying forward on his toes; light on his feet. I don't know why I had never noticed the resemblance before. Women are always telling Leon how handsome he is: dark Latin features, bushy black brows.

"Ah, I wish they wouldn't," Aunt Irene will say, laughing good-naturedly. "There's no living with him after."

A robust, pleasing matron herself; brown haired, red cheeked, beaming, a bosom like a tea service; a Quaker from the Lebanon Valley. She met Leon at Valley Forge; he a wounded corporal, she a hospital administrator. For him she joined the WACs. In those days she could shake down her stoic braids and sit on her hair, all ripples and waves. Everyone knows that Leon raised the general level of intelligence, energy, capability, industry in our family several notches when he brought Irene into it. Yet after twenty-five years she is still the outsider. She's not Jewish. And everyone is sure that Irene, for her part, is still anti-Semitic. And why not? If our own prejudices are any indication.

Some crevices run deep. It used to be that at election time my uncle and his wife would make a pact: they promised each other that neither of them would vote, since their votes would only cancel out. Irene is a Republican, straight down the line; Leon is a party Democrat, one X in the box and that's it. But each would sneak off to vote just the same, so now they ignore politics.

Again the priest asked us to rise. By this time my mother had begun to whisper, leaning down in her dark fur. My grandmother couldn't negotiate these ups and downs and was staring ahead, biting her lip with concentration.

"Do you think she's *Catholic*?" my mother was saying. "No one told us she was *Catholic*."

Bride and groom turned around to accept the offertory. The bride's dark-browed face, broad in its headdress, suddenly, unexpectedly, shone upon us. It was burning, fiercely beautiful. *The Lord bless you and keep you and make His face to shine upon you...* For the first time all day I remembered what it was all about, felt privileged to be a witness. And everyone must have felt it. People came to their senses. There was almost a sigh of relief. The altar boy in his full black skirts crouched, quivering the brass bells; smoke fumed from the censers. Millicent lifted her veil to take Communion. Gregory did not take it.

"*Jewish?*" the ladies on the other side of me were whispering among themselves. "You really think he's a *Jew?*"

I had waited fifteen minutes for a bus and when it came it wasn't an express. The expresses weren't running. The express goes from Hyde Park directly onto the Outer Drive, and it takes twenty minutes to get downtown. The local takes forty, fifty minutes. And it meanders through the South Side slums. At this point I could have walked a block or so to the Illinois Central commuter station and caught a train as far as the Loop. But it was going to be a day when my inertia was great. I got on the bus and sat down by a window in back and opened a book on my lap.

I always take books with me on buses or trains. I never read them. Years ago when I was an undergraduate at the university, I used to travel three hours a day on these same buses, commuting between the South Side campus and my home on the West Side. "You can get all your studying done," that's what people would say. But I never got any studying done; I'd sit with the whole pile of books on my lap (I remember the thick green volumes of *The People Shall Judge*), looking out the window. Three hours a day, an hour and a half each way, staring at the same sights out the same windows. I was fifteen then; it's possible that all this travel was stupefying me. Still, it seems to me that there is something immoral—because inattentive—about reading when your body is in transit. And maybe I felt even then that I should be paying attention instead. But paying attention to what?

I glanced up the aisle. The thing I'd forgotten was how the bus kept turning. Up Fifty-First Street to Drexel; down Drexel to Forty-Seventh; up Forty-Seventh to Martin Luther King Drive; down King to Forty-Third...

Every few blocks it nosed onward, plunging deeper and deeper into the black ghetto. The coins clicked and rolled in the fare box.

The South Side has always been Chicago's black belt; these slums were here years before I was born. But in the past, when I used to travel back and forth this way almost every day, I never noticed if I was white and all the other passengers were black. Blacks had not yet pressed the issue. And it must be said right off that the fact that I didn't notice, that it didn't matter to me, did not improve the situation in any way.

I remember becoming fully aware of this discrepancy reading *Native Son*, when the rich girl and her Communist boyfriend think that their liberal sentiments will make up to Bigger for everything. The trouble is that these one-to-one solutions—I love you, you love me; you shoot me, I shoot you—are no good. Just no use. Still, this ignorance or innocence or whatever you want to call it was long gone—and I would have given a great deal to have it back again. Today I was very much aware of the color of everyone else's skin, and I was sure that everyone on the bus was just as much aware of mine.

This was manifestly not so. No one was paying attention to me any more than I was paying attention to the pages of the book lying open on my lap. As a matter of fact, almost everyone else seemed to be reading—the newssheets crackling, the murder black in the headlines.

The bus was getting crowded; passengers swayed in the aisle and grappled for the hanging straps. A girl was groping her way, arm over arm, along the rails, an unlighted cigarette in her fingers. Hot pants, vinyl stretch boots, turban. Her face flat, expressionless, artificially pale—an Oriental effect. She leaned her shaved eyebrows over my seat.

"Gotta match?"

I gave her matches.

This has got to stop. I've got to stop reacting to people according to color. This is what has been happening to me; happening to everyone I know. White and black. Race is a prominent fact of life in Chicago, a partitioned city, walled and wired. You can't help reacting in this way. Try it. Try it walking down the street some night. It's a reflex. Everyone is becoming conditioned. And for some reason I realized this all of a sudden, listening to the news this morning, realized that I've been allowing myself to become conditioned—letting this fear, this racism, run away with me. I'm not sure why a murder in the streets—even around the corner—should have had such a bracing effect. But you've got to come up for air sometime; maybe that's why I got on the bus today. I used to know these things.

The sign on the parking lot gate said Left Turn Only, so Rudy turned right. The rest of the cars had already gone off, leaving the church in a motorcade for the motel where the wedding reception would be held. But not us. Roxy was studying the map.

"It's right arount the corner."

As a matter of fact, we were at Fort Sheridan, the army base. I used to think it was much farther when I was a little girl and Rudy was stationed there. Now the low-lying motels all around were not that easy to distinguish from the barracks, the tracks of wire fences.

"Hey. How come you guys sat on the wrong side of the church?" Rudy asked. "The bride's side, dummies. How come you didn't come up front with the rest of the family? What's the matter with you? Don't you like to see what's going on?"

"All that standing and kneeling," my mother said. "I'm exhausted. Nuts to that. I didn't know it was going to be a *Catholic* ceremony."

"I coult've tolt you right away if I lookt at the invitation," Roxy said. "Only I never even lookt at the invitation." She's Immersion Baptist, I think.

I was wondering about this business of bride's side, groom's side. Partitions and more partitions. Why do we always have to take sides? How primitive are these divisions?

Roxy jerked a thumb at the window. "You turn right at this corner. Right at the stop sign."

Rudy went straight.

"Hey, you big jerk. You shoult've turnt back there." Roxy looked round, still jerking her thumb. "He't get lost for sure if I din't tell him."

"I think he must be doing it on purpose," I said.

"You don't say," my mother said, the corner of her mouth grim against her cheek.

In a minute the road disappeared, we came to a leafy dead end, a bower of branches, and Rudy had to back the car out through the trees.

By the time we got to the motel, the reception line had broken formation; the bride and groom were off having their pictures taken, and guests were milling around the pleasant blue room with its huge fireplace and shimmer of chandeliers. Gas flames licked and curled about the artificial logs; champagne glasses were being filled as quickly as they were snatched from the trays. When I have the chance, I always drink champagne.

I wasn't at the shower, so I hadn't met any of Millicent's family before. Her father was a slight dark man with a stiff highball splashing and jostling in his fist. Sober, a plumber with four daughters to marry off, footing the bill for all these bashes. His wife was elegant, blond, slender; and the four strapping girls, of course, are all bouncingly beautiful. So it looks as if Gregg, like his father, has done all right for himself. This was the gist of the intelligence report I had already received from my mother.

"You know me, one drink and I'm out," she said, tripping up in her long skirts and holding her glass aloft to show it was empty. It's true; usually she gets dazzling and giddy. But today she didn't seem at all light headed to me; and everywhere I looked I kept seeing her—my mother has a way of standing out in a crowd—her black-and-white dress grimly prominent, like the priests in their habits.

"Someone asked me who I was and I forgot my name," Aunt Sylvia said. My mother's younger sister: a helmet of smooth iron hair, earrings swinging at her cheeks. She had been on the Weight Watchers diet and her pretty face was thin, looked pinched, a little sour (the intelligence report from my grandmother)—and she was smoking; she never used to. Holding the cigarette at arm's length, tapping the ashes over the gold tips of her shoes.

"Guess what. Gary called up from school and told us to break out the champagne." Gary is her son.

"He's getting married?" my mother asked.

"No. He got a job."

The job was at Zenith Radio, where Sylvia herself used to work during the war years when my uncle Fred was in the service. They married on furlough. I remember very well—she lived with us at the time—her going off to work in her baggy-seated overalls, her hair bound in a turban with the black curls springing out on top. She was on the assembly line. Gary will have an executive position: fourteen thousand to start. A lot more than Fred makes as a printer.

My grandmother was sitting at an empty table, surveying the field of preparations, the white cloths, the busboys filling sparkling water glasses. She was waiting to be called by the photographer. She always says she hates to have her picture taken, but I noticed her slipping off her glasses and dropping them into her purse. Without the funny rhinestone frames, the iridescent lenses, she looks suddenly—bushy brows, coarse powerful white hair, and slanted cheeks—like a shaman. Her dress of some green wizard material, the shimmering jacket bunched under her heavy brooches.

As a younger woman my grandmother never used to have this personal vanity, she never cared for such things. But now her copyright has expired, so to speak; she has entered the public domain. She clutched her purse to her lap, smoothing back her strong hair with stiff misshapen fingers.

And now Millicent's grandmother was brought up for an introduction: two old matriarchs. A large woman listing heavily on a cane; vigorous, in her corsets, with the silver rinse in her hair. She's in her eighties too, her complexion darkened with age spots, tarnished, almost—like the neighbor with her pillow cushions. She had been opposed all along to the marriage because Gregg—or at least his father—is Jewish. The last holdout in the family; the wedding had been delayed to appease her.

"You must come and take tea with me sometime," she said, grasping my grandmother's hand. And then, hesitating—wondering about our rituals—"Or *coffee*," she added, shaking emphatically.

"When are *you* going to get married?" Uncle Rudy asked, towering over me. His hands were in his pockets and his gaze strayed automatically over the small milling groups—a head above the crowd—checking them out.

"I've already been; I don't have to," I said.

"So you wouldn't get married a second time?"

"Would you?" I said, sipping from the rim of the thin-stemmed glass.

He shrugged; his elbows flapped against his sides. "Huh. I didn't want to get married the first time," he said in his dull monotone, still peering all about. He looked like a hawk. That's the trouble with Rudy; you can never tell. You can't tell when he's putting it on, just pretending to be thick, slow, deaf, stubborn. Everyone knows he can't be as dumb as he makes out.

Now he seemed to have something on his mind. "How come nobody tells them?" he said. We were both looking toward Sylvia's daughter, Mindy—almost gravely pretty with her long, thin, exposed legs, long heavy hair. Hers would be the next wedding. Rudy took my arm, urging.

"Go ahead. Say something. Tell her."

"I know, but you can't," I said. "It's not fair."

"Oh. Uh-huh." And his head bobbed up and down. "It's not fair."

Uncle Fred had gathered a crowd. Telling dirty jokes again? Sylvia was fretting because they were to be seated at the same table as the Fathers. "I just hope he behaves himself." But this was serious. He was surrounded by Millicent's mother and aunts and scarcely glanced our way as we came up, going on in his tight-lipped, hissing whisper. It was Gary's job again, evidently this subject was of the most intense interest. I didn't understand the significance of this at first. The wedding itself was a sort of truce: it was the subject of Gary's job that really seemed to be uniting everybody.

Sylvia worked as a clerk to put Gary and Mindy through school; Irene has been waiting on tables for years. These blond aunts of Millicent's, with their freckled cheeks, must have done the same. Now the job market had collapsed; a college degree was almost a liability. Millicent is substitute teaching. Gregg was teaching driving, but has turned up something better—still temporary—with the welfare. Mindy has been looking for almost a year for a teaching position; her fiancé will be graduating this summer with another useless certificate. Wherever you turned, the story was the same. But now that the situation is so bad—so reminiscent—it isn't the kids who are worrying either: they are going to school, marrying, traveling to Europe all the same. It's the parents—the plumbers, the printers—the same class who have borne the brunt of things all along, who are still worrying about the future.

I noticed the contact lens over Fred's eye. An old shrapnel wound, quiescent for twenty-five years; all of a sudden it's starting to act up again. It gives his expression a peculiar urgency. All my uncles are damaged with war wounds. There's Rudy's deafness, his loud injured voice. And Leon—strutting among the white tables in his pleated shirtfront—is lame in one arm. Striking a match with his thumb, he lets it hang by his side. A funny thing about Leon. He's a scofflaw. He'll go out of his way to park illegally. He'll drive around the block looking for a No Parking sign or a nice little fire hydrant.

What was secretly depressing everyone was this: After seven years of a sacrificially expensive university education, Gary will be earning about the same money as Rudy—a city of Chicago patrolman, a "pig," who had to be trundled through high school in a wheelbarrow. Rudy makes a better living than any man in the family, and Rudy is the one who is supposed to be so stupid. It rankles. And—to top it all off, and as if to rub it in—he has nothing to show for it. A dilapidated apartment, a car that isn't paid for; the little boy is cross-eyed and they're saving up for an operation, there isn't a penny in the bank. (It seems that everybody knows their business.) And he and his wife don't get along either; there is rancor to go with all the squalor. No one can understand such a life. They feel sorry for, irritated with Rudy. Rudy and Roxanne seldom show up at these family occasions.

"Who's taking care of the children?" Sylvia asked, looking up at Roxy. Roxanne is six foot one in her stocking feet, statuesque, immobile, like a Las Vegas showgirl. But she complains she has no pep and goes to her doctor to get liver shots. My mother had already asked her that question; everybody kept asking her. It's an unwritten law: as soon as a harassed mother gets out of the house for a couple of hours, everyone has to ask her who's taking care of the children.

"They're olt enough to take care of themselves," she said tartly.

I still have custody, but since my two sons are older they have gone to live with their father, and now I'm the one who gets to see them only on school vacations. They had just gone back a few days before, and I missed them. It's not such a bad arrangement; I'm not complaining. In some ways it's too good, too rich—we are just skimming the cream. Only I believe that life—a real life—is lived day to day.

There is this to be said for it, however: at least no one asks me who's taking care of the children. Indeed, no one ever asks me much. I'm not married; my ID isn't validated, so to speak. Weddings are the worst; they don't know where to put me, what to do with me. Today I'm not even getting grilled about the usual topics—the crime and the "colored." I was glad to see the dishes being wheeled in, gleaming tiers on the service carts.

The best man—even swarthier than Gregg, with a more pendulous mustache—was offering his arm to my grandmother. Still time for one last picture: she was much in demand. She leaned on his dark sleeve. She won't use a cane.

"Oh, how little she's getting," Sylvia remarked, biting her lip as she looked after the old lady. A habit she gets from her mother. "She used to be as tall as I am."

The thing is, I don't feel sorry for my grandmother. I don't think it's a shame that she's so old. I love her with admiration, not out of pity. She's probably the only member of my family who doesn't wrench it out of me that way.

At the table, over fresh fruit cups and sherbet—the old lady with her back to the licking logs of the fireplace, her green jacket glowing in the flames—everyone started complaining about my father. He was in Israel, visiting my sister and the other set of grandchildren, and the postcards he was sending back were all identical.

"That's nothing," my mother said. It seemed she had just received two letters from him, and they were also exactly alike. "He just doesn't know how to write a letter, poor man."

Letters. Who expects letters? I'm supposed to be tickled he talks to me. But this is true, if I may judge from the five or six letters I have received from him in my life. Stilted, formal, almost to the point of illiteracy—all the more because he writes in a scribe's hand, slanting and fluid. Palmer method; he won prizes for his handwriting in grammar school. And it's as if someone had written them down for him, at his embarrassed dictation:

*Be a Good Girl. Apply Yourself. Obey Your Mother. Don't Disappoint… Your Dad.*

My mother was working in a summer camp then; my sister and I used to spend our whole summer away from home, and I would miss my father bitterly. Crouching homesick in my lower bunk—with its coarse army surplus blanket, the damp smell of rotting wood—reading these spartan lines over and over, his moralizing tone bewildered and bereaved me. What had I done wrong? What was I going to do? How did he know about it? But that seemed to be his prerogative; my father is a natural moralist. Almost as big as my uncle Rudy and far more powerful; he can fix anything, though his hands look thick and clumsy, capable only of brute strength. Once he lifted the back of a truck when a fellow worker was trapped under it. What I like about this story is its sequel, so typical of my father's fortunes, his outlook, his whole life. The man he had saved never spoke to him again, shunned his company, couldn't look him in the eye.

Last summer my father fell off a ladder while fixing the roof of a house (he's one of these obsolete men who maintain things). His size and strength added to the dread I felt in the hospital, observing his helplessness: a big broken creature, gray fleshed—the slick wet-mop grayness of internal bleeding—being lifted and turned by little Filipino nurses. How they accomplished this was a mystery, for they would pull the canvas curtains about his bed before they assayed such a task. When I heard the noises behind the drawn curtains, watched the blips on the heart monitor while he lay laboriously breathing—his heart was leaking—I felt something like the pangs I used to feel when I read his letters in summer camp. There was a persistency of tone. Reproach. I was wondering, if he left like this, how I would live with it.

His trip to the Holy Land was a pilgrimage after his Reprieve (his words, naturally). Passing silver sauceboats, baskets of crusty rolls, spearing icy butter pats (I always have trouble), I started thinking what it would be like to get a letter from my father. What if I tore open the airmail envelope—blue as distances—and confronted once again the same old phrases in the same sloping hand:

*Be a Good Girl. Tend to Business. Try to Make the Best of It. Don't Disappoint… Your Dad.*

The meal was excellent. Waitresses hovered, the photographer stalked, screwing the lens to his eye. He'd fling up one arm and stiffen suddenly, lifeless, dangling from it.

"Take off your glasses," my mother cautioned, knocking my arm with her elbow as he flashed our picture.

She was dissatisfied with me, and that's how it comes out. How well I know. Every time I have seen my mother for the last twenty years, she has made a remark about my hair. It's getting discouraging, to know this beforehand. People could get the idea we have nothing to say. And yet I found myself reacting to her in the same way—noticing all through the meal that she seemed to talk only when her mouth was full and her cheek was bulging like a fist. As if she were chewing a quid of tobacco and about to squirt. Alarming. Her sallow cheek. She was having a bad day. Bitter, discolored, dry eyed. I still wish I had been kinder.

The groom rose to make a toast. Slouched in his tux, rocking on his heels, like his father; a dark symmetrical mustache. "I guess there's everyone in this room who means anything to me," he began, lifting his glass. Everyone was touched; it was as if we had had to be reminded all over again: applause, murmurs rose gratefully from the white circles of the tables. There was a clatter of dishes being carted away.

My grandmother, of course, doesn't eat meat out; it's not kosher. And we had forgotten to order her fish. The waitress looked at her plate. "You finished?" eyeing the damp red slice of meat.

The old lady turned herself stiffly sideways to peer at the sound, since she can't move her neck. Her voice rang out. "Take it away."

She hadn't touched her food. She hadn't carried on, hadn't complained, though it was all in the script. She was watching them cut up the wedding cake, rapidly distributing slices over the scraps and crumbs of the tables.

"Wrap up a slice for me," she commanded my mother, pointing her big distorted finger. "I want to bring home for the goy." (She meant her neighbor.)

My children's father descends in a direct line from a Pilgrim who fell overboard during the voyage of the *Mayflower*. "A lustie younge man," Governor Bradford describes him, who held long and fast to the halyards, "sundrie fadomes under water," until they hauled him in out of the lurching sea. Since then the family had considerably loosened its grip. Papa was a medievalist, a prof at Indiana U., and they lived way out in a grand Victorian relic. I thought it was grand. There were raccoons in the attic— the shell-like claws left perfect tracks in the powder the exterminator had sprinkled; and in the bathroom—an afterthought, a cul-de-sac squeezed under the stairs, all eaves and crannies—you got the most delicious sense of privacy, as if all the world might forget that it and you were there. A grim reminder, however, was the mark painted about two inches up from the curved bottom of the bathtub, indicating the permissible water level. The same thing they did in the bathtubs of Buckingham Palace during the war.

The fact is, my in-laws were *tight*. Not the scraping, face-saving, working-class thrift I was used to; they were flagrantly, *shamelessly* stingy. The virtue of the faded WASP aristocracy. Papa would cook up a stew of beef and carrots at the beginning of the week, and start adding oatmeal and water toward the end. And he would follow you about, animated, talking (he was still greatly exercised over the persecution of the Albigensians), systematically switching off all the electric lights. This was a hazard, no joke, since the house was crammed to the rafters. He had to climb up a stepladder to fetch down his books; there was furniture on top of the furniture; my mother-in-law, still a porcelain beauty, without a chip or a crack, collected antiques. He kept magazines, newspapers, yellowed files in her cradle rockers and canopied cribs and native hammocks and even in the upright commode stools. And yet they were "only camping," she told me—this house whose every niche and shingle they had penetrated, occupied, swelling and expanding like the Rockwool insulation they had had pumped in, blown through a giant snorkel. Even at that time they had lived in Indiana over thirty years. But what's thirty years to a New England blue blood? They were ready to move back "at the drop of a hat."

Now there were only two sons left, the last of the line, and one a confirmed bachelor. This branch had lost most of their money about 1905— before any of my progenitors had so much as stepped off the boat. What the family needed was some fresh stock, "hybrid vigor." They were "sick of their washed-out New England blood." Thus Papa, thrilled at the prospect of having a Jewish daughter-in-law breeding with the race—for he believed that all Jews were cultured, cosmopolitan, intellectual, and rich. I had never run into this wacky Puritan Jew-worship before, for obvious reasons: I didn't fit the description, and I didn't know anybody who did.

What the dear old man thought when he took a half day off from his duties at the university (only time he *would* take; he had seven years' leave accumulated and untouched at his retirement, which had been forestalled through a special act of the state legislature), what he thought when he took his half day off in honor of the wedding and came up for the afternoon on the James Whitcomb Riley, what he thought when he finally met me and my family, I don't rightly know. I wasn't getting any bargain either. And it doesn't matter, because he was right about the "hybrids."

"Now listen, you guys," I said, as the automobiles were pulling up to the carpeted canopy. "I'd like to get home sometime today, so please don't go nagging Rudy anymore. Leave him alone. He's the driver—let him do what he wants."

"All right, all right," said my mother.

"She promist, I din't," said Roxanne, poking round in her bag for her knitting.

It had turned out to be a nice day after all; the sun had finally come out in the late afternoon, resting on luminous banks of clouds. The sky was blue as chalk. Rudy drove with exaggerated tenderness—like the Sunday driver he was pretending to be—taking Sheridan Road, the scenic route home, to please my mother. The road wound and dipped through wooded ravines, still rusty brown with winter's oak leaves. Here and there a glimpse of a cantilevered terrace, a glassed-in porch, a cathedral ceiling. We used to drive out this way sometimes on Sundays when I was a child, to ooh and aah at these sights, the half-hidden homes of the rich. These are the affluent North Shore suburbs.

A little red convertible, a Fiat Spider with the top down, cut in front of us. The driver had very short, shaggy, windblown yellow hair and the roots were dark as the center of a daisy.

"There!" Roxanne said, growing somewhat animated, for her, and pointing the bright tip of her knitting needle. "That's the color my hair was suppost to be."

The little car sped off in a burst of exhaust and lost us quickly on the winding road. Roxanne sank back, curving her spine and clicking her needles.

"Well, I'm just glad Pa wasn't there to see *that*," said my mother at last. "It would make him feel *terrible*." She shrugged her mink stole round her shoulders. "It just doesn't work out. It's much better when two people have the same background. It makes for a better chance in a marriage."

"Is that how come you get along so good with your own husband?" Rudy said, eyeing her in the mirror. "You got the same background?"

"I wasn't speaking *personally*," she said.

My mother always says what she is thinking; only what could she be thinking *of?* Rudy and Roxanne in the front seat, bigger than life; her own daughter sitting right beside her. And if you observe that my marriage was a failure, and that Rudy and Roxanne are no great success, that doesn't make her remarks seem more tactful. But it was a little late in the day for tact—it was sink or swim, every man for himself. And what bothered me was where she was at, what sort of world she must be living in. The fact is, with the exception of my sister (and *that's* a holy mess I won't go into), no one in my mother's family has married a Jew in the last thirty years. Which means that by now half her own relatives are not Jews. But never mind; she still sees her family as average, normal, the salt of the earth. Jewish.

Of course, I know where she was at. She was reliving the scene of her own greatest humiliation—the day of my wedding. Only now, each time this scene is repeated, she finds herself older, less resilient, stonier—more isolated. A ship in dry dock. She adjusted her furs, offended, while we stopped for a train crossing. Bells shrilling, lights flashing and winking back and forth. The heavy boxcars knocked and shuddered over the tracks; the hood of the car glimmered. We were staring straight into the flat red disk of the setting sun.

It dawned on me. We were supposed to be heading south and east— not west. And there are no train crossings on Sheridan Road.

We were elsewhere.

"Oh, for God's sake, Uncle Rudy," I said, shouting over the noise. "What is this? Don't you know I have to get back to the South Side yet."

Roxanne's face lit up. "You're the one that sait it, I din't," she said, turning round with a granite grin at the back seat.

After the student murder a few months ago, there were stirrings in the Hyde Park community. First-aid courses, an emergency switchboard service. It had taken almost an hour to get the victim to the hospital, with his fourteen stab wounds, and he bled to death. The purpose of first aid, switchboards, is to keep people from bleeding to death in the streets. And it makes all the rest of us, bystanders, supernumeraries, feel more effective. But these are, after all, only ex post facto, one-to-one solutions. It all reminds me, weirdly, of the fallout-shelter craze of the early sixties, when people were digging holes in backyards, sinking concrete blocks, stocking up with canned goods, flashlight batteries, shovels, rifles. The point is, these people were preparing for nuclear attack; they were accepting it as an eventuality—they were acquiescing. One questioned the quality of such survivors.

This was called civil defense. And telephones and tourniquets are obviously civil defense measures too; the similarity is no accident. The latest thing is a campaign to distribute whistles; you're supposed to keep them handy, wear them around your neck, blow them—after an attack.

None of this is going to stop the conditioning.

Now that nights are warmer—windows open to the darkness, artillery noises from the street—you sense it all the more. The fear is quicker. Besides, everyone knows that violence increases with fair weather. Numbers only assert, but at least a dozen women I know have been raped, beaten, and terrorized. The name of the crime is significant: we are a passive population under siege. This anarchy, the flashing of guns and knives, may as well be martial law; there may as well be curfew in the deserted streets.

You feel stranded after dark. The air is penetrating. Particularly in Hyde Park, with the ghosts of the old stockyards to the west, and to the south—very much alive, a red glow from my windows—the inner sanctums of the steel mills. Like the days after King's assassination—the odor of smoke and cinders blowing over the city. The slums were burning. The conditions I describe are only a dim reflection of the terror of that life.

"He wasn't a member of a gang or anything," a black mother is quoted in the papers after the slaughter of her son. "Someone at Ribs 'n' Bibs just thought David was laughing at him."

In the meantime all this is a topic of dinner table conversation. Our fear is becoming socialized. Moving is a constant theme. One friend who has been raped, burglarized, and had her car stolen (three separate occasions) is still considering leaving Hyde Park. Plenty of reasons for leaving. The rents are as high here as almost anywhere in the city, and the food prices are even higher—typical of slum communities, a captive market. No competition. There is only one movie house in all Hyde Park; indeed, for many miles around. Restaurants and businesses close early. More and more they close for good. There are no gathering places, no lively nightlife. How could there be? People are afraid to go out after dark. It is just an island surrounded by the defoliation of the slums.

And yet none of these are real motivations for leaving. The fact is that most people have come to Hyde Park in the first place just because of the things it did not have. (It doesn't have relatives, for instance.) And I realized this morning that "security" is not the main thing either. "Security" is an expensive illusion. We can't all climb into the fallout shelters. In my grandmother's neighborhood, Uptown, it's the notorious desolation, the poverty, that is the constant reminder of what the real facts are; in my neighborhood—so much more green and affluent from its rooftops—it is the tension between black and white. And I suspect that the real reason people want to leave is not so much that they think they will be "safer" anywhere else; or so that they will be able to go out to a movie: it is because they don't like their own automatic responses anymore. That's what they want to get away from. They want to halt the conditioning that is dehumanizing us.

"Aren't you going to come in?" Rudy asked, sticking his big head in at the window. We weren't planning to, had only stopped long enough to drop Roxy off so she could get back to the children. But Rudy seemed disappointed.

"*Her*," he said, lifting his chin at me. "I want her to come in and see my wallpaper."

With anyone else this might have meant that he had something he wanted to say to me in private. But not with Rudy. That will never happen; Rudy will never speak his heart. I followed his ponderous shoulders into the house.

The landlord lives upstairs, and his side of the front porch is even more sagging, swaying, and peeling than theirs. But the rent is cheap, and they have a sort of mutual nonaggression pact: they won't expect any repairs, he won't expect any raises. He's an old Swede, gaunt, bald, toothless, deaf, and he just doesn't want to be bothered. Something Rudy understands.

Rudy is an honest cop. When my high school sweetheart joined the force—"I wish I thought of it years ago; I'd a owned three apartment buildings by now"—Rudy told me right away he'd never last. "They don't want that kind no more." I'm sorry I don't know who turned out to be right; but the point is, Rudy is not a cynic. And anybody has enough brains to be cynical. He is immutable, incorruptible; that is the real truth of his nature. How could you buy him? How could you approach him? He has no greed, he has no vanity, no ambition. A threat would only provoke his obstinacy—the most powerful force of all. It would be like trying to bribe Starved Rock.

As soon as we got inside, Rudy pointed to the wallpaper in the living room, a crowded flocked pattern on a gold ground. "Roxy put it up." He stroked the wall.

"When was that?"

"It's been two years," Roxy said.

Rudy pulled my sleeve. "Come see the wallpaper in the kitchen." The vinyl pattern covered the ceiling. "Roxy put it up with a broom," Rudy told me, gazing up at the high ceiling from his gloomy height. Unmade beds, unwashed cups, cigarette butts, dishes in the sink; it's like a frat house. But Roxy is very handy, and she knits, crochets, sews to perfection—the handicrafts of her Kentucky hills. It makes the stuff you see for sale in expensive boutiques look disgraceful, I'm not kidding. Call that a quilt? Shame on them. They should see Roxy's patchwork, Roxy's coverlets, her shawls, stuffed animals. Her skill is the result of a long tradition, of which she is the end. Rudy showed off her projects. "Roxy did this too?"

The children in the meantime had gone out to the car to say hello. In a minute the little boy in his long pants and baseball jacket—his big glasses wider than his face—came dashing in, bursting with excitement. "Guess who's in the car?" he said, grinning up at us through thick dark frames, balancing their weight. One eye tugged at its inner corner. *"Bobbe! Bobbe!"*

He took off again. His shoes knocked with a heavy tread.

I was fetching a glass of water for my grandmother. Rudy shoved a book at me instead; a photo album. "Sit down and look at this. I'll bring the water."

It was no use, I didn't try to argue; I sank down in the wingback chair and the two tall girls came and stood shyly behind it, looking over my shoulder as I turned the pages.

Their baby pictures, snapshots of vacations, the grim isolated South. Several times a year Roxy goes home to her mother, who runs a gas station. In some of the photos I noticed a beautiful sturdy blond child with fat pouting cheeks and built like the baby Hercules. I asked Roxy who it was.

"Oh, that's the little daughter Rooty brung me." Rudy had found the child abandoned in a hotel room; he knew how she'd be shuffled about if he turned her over to the welfare people, so he took her home for Roxy to take care of her. In due time the mother showed up and got the child back.

Now the girls had sidled up on the arms of the chair, turning pages for me, showing me their school pictures, "Guess which one is me." The whole class lined up in the gym on wooden benches, hands folded in laps—just the way we used to do it. The same grins with the teeth missing. Only now the pictures come in color, and the girls giggled and squealed as I pointed to their faces.

"Hey, lookit—you wanna see Phoebe's report card?" Harriet said, waving the long manila envelope at me.

"Hey! No fair! Gimme that!" says Phoebe, snatching for it. I guess she's no scholar. So they started fighting, thumping and yelling. I was ready to leave, but Rudy insisted on taking me for a tour of the basement. His tall figure stooping ahead of me down the narrow steps.

As high as the ceilings are upstairs, they are that low in the basement. Rudy moved ahead of me in his slow wading way, his hands in his pockets, looking back over his shoulder; his head diving down and ducking the pipes.

I had seen it all before: the laundry room with washer and dryer; the storage room with the kids' new bikes; his own retreat—an overstuffed rocker and an old-fashioned floor lamp with a scorched parchment shade. I don't suppose he ever really uses the place. The basement is dry enough but dingy, raw cement. Rudy's eyes kept wandering, grazing all about, as if he had forgotten what he was looking for. His elbows shrugged and flopped against his sides. I was struck with the aimlessness of his wide back.

There was a workshop; but the high, rough-hewn bench, the rough shelves, were bare, except for an ashtray filled with stubbed-out butts. I wondered who had been standing in the corner, furiously smoking. "I don't know how to do nothing, so I don't use it," Rudy said, humbly, looking idly about with his hand on the light string. He ducked his head under the doorway as we went out.

Against the wall stood a bookcase lined with corrugated packages of light bulbs. If you pay your electric bill in person, you get them free. They caught his eye.

"You need light bulbs? Here, take some light bulbs," he said, catching at my sleeve. "What do you need? Forties? Sixties? Hundreds? They're all here; take what you want."

Turning over packages, examining them. "You need bigger ones? Here—here's one-fifty. Here's two hundred." I didn't want to take any light bulbs home with me on the bus, but he seemed very anxious for me to take some. "Soft lights? Three-way? You like pink ones? We'll get a bag upstairs." He piled the weightless packages up on me. I held out my arms.

Roxanne wanted Rudy to take her to Osco's—they had a sale on yarn. When I got into the car I saw that we had a stowaway: the little boy, squeezed between my mother's skirts and my grandmother's green coat— hiding himself, his feet sticking straight up in their dark thick-soled shoes. But before Roxy even stuck her face in, his smooth brown head popped up:

"Hi, Mommy! Hi, Mommy! Hi, Mommy!" he piped, poking his chin over the front seat and grinning up through his glasses with crazy cock- eyed charm.

My grandmother peered round, large faced in her babushka. I could see they were a little put out with me, wondering what had taken so long. "What have you got in the bag?"

"Light bulbs," I said.

I was feeling very sad. I think maybe it was the light bulbs. They made me want to cry. Once again I was looking at the back of Rudy's neck; thick, remote. For he is remote—my uncle is a blunt and mysterious man to me. His life flows in another direction; I shall never understand it. And yet I felt closer to him than to anyone I had seen all day. I felt that he had been trying to give me some message about his life; I sensed its powerless- ness—but it moved me. Rudy and I are both outsiders, as far as the family is concerned. Out of the mainstream. And we are made of the same raw material: even this unexpected surge of feeling for him was an obstinate, unpredictable force. I was wondering what role such forces must have played in my life. It always feels depleting to make these self-discoveries. Anyway, it makes a long day to go up north and see the family, and by this time I had realized that I was going to feel awfully tired when I finally got home—washed out, weary, letdown, empty. Blue. Yes, very blue.

# TO THE COUNTRY

It just so happens that my mother's oldest and dearest friend, Little Bertha, lives on a farm not ten miles from the summer cottage where my sons and I are staying in the country—and I haven't seen her in fifteen years. At least. My father can't be dragged out to visit the Elliotts again for love nor money. My mother says he's still angry because he loaned Little Bertha's brother Bucky a few hundred dollars many years ago and never got it back. That's no surprise; everyone knows Bucky robbed his own mother. Actually they say he made her mortgage the house in exchange for favors a mother shouldn't ask.

"So who tells you to go lending money to a crook like Bucky Klugman?" my mother will say.

"You did," my father says. "Aren't you always telling me what to do?"

"Since when do you ever listen to *me*?"

And they're off and running. Cheek to cheek.

I'd like to get a look at this Bucky, but he'll never show his face in Chicago again. Anyway, it's just an excuse; the truth is, there never was a time when my father didn't gripe about going out to see Little Bertha and Mark Elliott.

My father is a big, powerful man, almost inordinately strong, very handy. There's nothing he can't fix—or break, as the case may be. So wherever he goes, people always have something for him to do: "Wait till

Sam comes." They seem to sit around helplessly, pending his arrival. He even used to get calls in the middle of the night, like a country doctor; emergencies: a car stalled on the road, water pipes bursting in the basement and no one knows how to shut it off, someone in the john and the lock got stuck. It was nothing unusual. My father would zip up his pants and spit in the sink and off he'd go to the rescue.

But there was no end to the work at the Elliotts'. They regularly seemed to be starting from scratch, nailing up chicken coops in muddy backyards. Peg and Lynn were about the same age as my sister, Slim, and me; but no children of theirs were going to grow up in the city. They were determined to make a big break, become farmers, lead the country life.

This new farm is only the latest in a long series, beginning with that first, half-finished place in the sticks. Mark and Bertha both held down outside jobs—old Mrs. Elliott lived with them and kept house—and they were on the go from morning till night. They were building the house and the barn and their chickens were succumbing to a million diseases. You'd find poultry stretched in the mud like corpses hanging upside down in the butcher's window. Little Bertha would seize them by their scaly reptile feet, whirl them round and round her head and let fly at the trash heap. She wasn't much bigger than I was then, and she seemed fearless to me: they were dead dead dead. At the look in their glassy eyes my heart iced over.

The Elliotts were having a hard time of it. But I didn't notice it then; I thought a hard time was what you were supposed to have. And they kept my father busy from the minute he walked in the door. Hammering roofs, blasting tree stumps, mending fences. All in a day's work for Mark; but for my father it was supposed to be a day off. Besides, he hated the country. Not the outdoor type. It wasn't his dream. He'd mutter and grumble and blame my mother all the way home. The back of his neck red as a brick from the sun.

My father is nothing if not a man to carry a grudge (he has "no use for" me, either), and he hasn't forgotten that Mark almost talked him into voting for Wendell Willkie. But I think the real reason he seems so reluctant to have anything much to do with the Elliotts anymore is that their lives have become very different from his. Mark and Bertha have succeeded, in spite of all; they're farmers now—they have escaped the city. The transformation is complete. They vote Republican, attend church, go square dancing on alternate Fridays (how corny can you get?). And I gather they don't get into Chicago very often nowadays. Over the phone, Bertha was still full of some wedding they had been to the last time—a big event. "Don't let me forget, now. Be sure and remind me to tell you all about that wedding."

I get the strangest feeling driving through this Indiana farmland. The fields lie flat under cultivation, the trees seem stunted by distances. Then you come upon a rise in the road; you can't see beyond, the sun is striking the side of some lone whitewashed barn. And all at once the illusion is complete. A conviction. You're not inland at all; you're at the edge of the ocean. About to confront it, begin the descent to the wave-battered coast. The light is strong and solitary. You can even smell the salt water. People from the Midwest are crazy for the sea.

The two white houses sit out side by side, practically right on top of the highway; nothing else around but wires and posts and the white line on the blacktop disappearing over the crest of the hill. Lynn and the three granddaughters live next door; easy enough to tell the houses apart. A tire swung from shady branches in front of the big old place; the kids' wagons and bikes leaned about the yard, and an Irish setter pup with its red coat rippling like prairie grass started whining and licking at the fence when it heard the car.

The other house appeared to be still under construction. Black-tar insulation, sprawling rolls of chicken wire, the grass muddy and trampled down like coconut matting. Glazier's marks still scribbled on the windows. In other words, it was Mark and Bertha's house; like all the rest of their houses: I would have known it in a dream.

Inside, the same story. Even the furniture was the same as it had always been—Sears, Roebuck early American: spinning wheels, coffee tables, tieback chairs. Rockers, hutches, red rock maple. Though it seemed the furniture was new, and I was not rising to the occasion; for Little Bertha had to prompt me—looking up at me sideways: "I was glad about the rug."

It's because she's so short, she seems precocious; peering up at you perkily, her head to one side, her mother-of-pearl frames tilting inquisitively. Like a curious child. And she talks a mile a minute, doesn't have time to catch her breath. The words rush out with such force you wonder how come they don't knock her right over. I remember how vigorously she used to scatter the feed—the hens in the barnyard scratching and flapping, their plucky tails taking off in all directions. They seemed in a great hurry to get out of her way.

Mark and Bertha have gone back to their first love; the new farm is devoted entirely to the production of laying hens, thirty-six thousand of them in two long white windowless barracks. The slitted air vents gush and flutter. The farm looks like a small factory, with all its towers and power lines; all their acres are in corn for chicken feed. Not the tender sweet corn, white, almost transparent, wispily bearded, with even, pearly beads. These stalks thrust forth coarse flourishing ears, all scrambled and spotted and growing like wild. We could hear them rustling. There is a pond, a rectangular trough; you can see the teeth marks of the machinery that bit it out of the earth. A brown duck family skimmed its still surface; crows hung themselves on the hat rack of a dead naked tree. Flies snapped. Fields stirred in the sun.

Mark was in the chicken house, immunizing. He strode out in baggy overalls, square, true jawed as ever, a red bandanna knotted round his neck, stripping off his thick rubber gloves to shake hands. His rimless specs flashed. Right away I had a mental picture of him giving injections—reaching into the straw, feeling under warm flustered feathers (the way we used to, hunting for eggs), rubbing alcohol swabs on downy white breasts. But of course things aren't done that way, not on the scale of a modern chicken farm. Everything is automated, mechanized, industrialized. The vaccine is in high-pressure tanks, sprayed into the air.

Almost immediately, Jacob, my younger son, made some remark about the cost of living going up.

"Well, now, that's only relative," Mark began, settling his cap on his graying head, with its scraped, clean jaw. First thing in the morning, in the farm dark, you used to hear the most god-awful grinding whining and squeaking—Mark, cranking the handle of his razor-blade sharpener. Without further prompting, he launched into a speech that sounded just as familiar.

About growing up the sole support of his family, a widowed mother and unmarried sisters… About how they were poor, but always had enough to eat… About how you're not really rich if you haven't got self-reliance… About how it was the *standard* of living that had gone up, not the *cost*—for your real needs, your basic needs, are always the same… How that was what was wrong with the country today….

It was too sudden, a little embarrassing. We stood on the heated stoop, listening; flies, glittering in their mail, clung to the gravelly trenches of chicken manure. Little Bertha had lowered her glance as soon as he got started. She blinked and gazed behind her big white-trimmed specs. If *I* was well-acquainted with Mark's speech, she must have heard it a thousand times.

It was this rock-ribbed conservatism of Mark's that used to get my father's goat—a factory laborer himself, a union battler. I can remember him bundling up to march off to the picket lines: two or three jackets, a couple of caps, scarves, earmuffs on his head—padded against the cold and the baseball bats. He looked like the old lady at the newsstand with her apron full of change and her cracked red hands. In his thick-clustered hair there was a small worn patch where a rock beaned him; another scar on his back, where he'd been stabbed. My father wasn't imagining things. And yet at this moment Mark reminded me utterly of him. The real impetus for this lecture—the true nerve that had been touched—was one thing they had in common. It was Mark's longing for male companionship. Someone to talk to. Something I have seen so often in my father. Mark is surrounded by women, has always, come to think of it, been surrounded, outnumbered by them. And now here were the two alert, handsome boys—eyes alight amid sweaty thickets of hair—listening to him with upturned faces.

A steady muttering hum came from the exhaust fans of the chicken houses.

Twenty thousand chickens under one roof, without light or breeze. The air was suffocating; it snuffed your breath out. You could see white feathers stirring in dim wire cages. Row upon row, in long tiers, dark narrow aisles. They were keeping up a racket in their cracked bird voices, fussing and clucking, little chicken motors. A continuous stifled protest, a sort of treadmill of dissent.

The conveyor belts moved silently.

The birds spend all their lives in these cages; they never go outside. Ideally, they never touch the ground. They are fed by conveyor belts, watered by conveyor belts; eggs are collected on conveyor belts. The latest installation had been another belt, to haul away the manure we had seen piling up outside. Next—since one mechanical innovation begets the need for another—the manure will be chugged directly to the mill. Now it is being spread over the fields for fertilizer; then it will be ground up with the corn and fed back to the chickens.

Here and there a hen pecked tamely in the aisles, feebly almost, its red wattles trembling. Others roosted motionless, swooning under the stacks. The birds get no food or water at liberty—can't last more than twenty-four hours if they fly the coop. So someone has to go around at night, collecting all the strays and putting them back in their cages.

Bertha was railing off all this information, parts and prices, like a mail-order catalog. She always sounds as if she's reciting some lesson learned by heart. Her head tucked to one side, her fists clenched. In her gym shoes and ankle socks, no taller than her own grandchildren. All the profits are plowed right back into the farm, the largest in these parts. But they are on the verge of bankruptcy, the lip of ruin... Everything in hock, mortgaged to the hilt; the egg business in a slump, the cost of farm equipment skyrocketing... At that very moment disease was raging on the West Coast, flocks by the hundreds of thousands being exterminated, farmers wiped out.... An ice storm last winter had paralyzed the county, the power lines down. They carried buckets of water, feed, twenty-eight straight hours... prison wardens.

In other words, it was the same old story; the old continuous struggle, the day-to-day hand-to-mouth existence.

"Excuse me, and maybe I shouldn't ask this," Jacob began. I knew what was coming: his black eyes were clicking back and forth like the beads of an abacus, adding up all these figures in his head. "But how much do you think all this costs you?"

"You'll have to ask Father," Bertha said quickly.

Old Mother Elliott used to put on a spread like nobody's business; her table was literally heaped with food: hills, valleys, her own churned butter, hot biscuits to melt it, vegetables green from the garden, raspberries black from the bush. Her whipped potatoes were out of this world—not to mention her canning and preserves. She was a clean, smooth cheeked old lady who always smelled crisp and fresh. I don't know about the end. She had died a few years back, an uncomplaining invalid in an upstairs room. Little Bertha took care of her, driving home on her lunch hour. Bertha has never been the domestic type. She has worked all these years; now it's on the assembly line at a factory in South Bend, planting circuits in digital computers. You see a lot of aproned farmwives cashing their paychecks on Fridays in the supermarket. "It takes two working to live."

Everything on the table, with its Sunday company cloth, the paper napkins folded tricornered under the forks, was from the grocer's shelves; convenience foods, packaged, canned, frozen. Diet soda and lo-cal dressings. I had a sense of something diminished as we scraped out our chairs.

The packaged bread was still frozen stiff from the freezer, and Lynn's carrottopped twins—sitting at the card table with napkins under their chins, wide spaces in their teeth—were warming the slices tenderly between their hands as we passed the plate.

Peg, the older daughter, was the one I used to play with as a child; but it turns out that Lynn is the one who is my age. People always said she had a "heart-shaped" face; and there it was—just like a valentine. Grave gray eyes, pointed chin. The first day the family moved onto a real farm at last—horses, cows, tractors, the rough mangled roads of the country—Lynn fell out of the hayloft and broke both her arms. The next year she fell out of her bunk bed and broke them both again. So I remember her best as up to her elbows in bent plaster casts.

But in the meantime Peg and Lynn were learning to ride horses, to can, to bake, to sew. They belonged to the Girl Scouts, went to Sunday school, showed prize animals at state fairs. They were all-around 4-H champions. They rose in darkness; pulled on rubber boots to go off to their chores, wading in slippery barnyard manure. The big, soft-eyed, baggy cows, scarcely bothering to twitch their ears or glance behind them, stiffened their tails and shot out more. They talked in clear rising voices of mating, sires, dams, and foals, and actually got to watch the whole thing. (I was always being told to "just look away for a minute" when we went to the zoo. Once, driving through an alley, our headlights happened to pick out the figure of a man standing and urinating against a wall. The stream was hot; the bricks were darkening. Quick as a wink my mother pulled my face to her breast and covered my eyes with her hand. As you can see, the facts of life were pretty remote. Or, as my father liked to call it, "The Rude Awakening.") Mark and Bertha were getting their wish; their girls really were growing up on a farm. My sister and I were growing up in a more disorderly fashion; not to say haphazard. And I could never get it straight, what the fourth H stood for.

Oddly enough, we also lived in a house—for that time and place, a most unusual circumstance. Practically unheard of. Most of my school friends—whose fathers were chiropodists, dry cleaners, bookies, and jewelers—lived in cramped flats with Murphy beds in the living rooms. They had charge plates at Carson's and Marshall Field's. To me that seemed a mark of high civilization; unattainable; like speaking French or playing the violin.

Jews had been pressing west since the days of Hull House and Maxwell Street, and could not press much farther. We were west of Pulaski Road (a.k.a. Crawford Avenue) and within a mile of the city limits, the stalwart suburbs of Cicero and Berwyn. Here and there, amid the big brick apartment buildings, with their canyon-like courtyards, and the stone-fronted three-flats with heavy masonry steps, were small, neat, narrow houses; pointed roofs, painted porches; fenced yards, flower beds. Aluminum siding in patterns of herringbone or Harris Tweed. Long flights of wooden stairs. The ground floors submerged, below street level, in the style of fifty, sixty years ago. Actually it was the sidewalks themselves that had risen; in the summer they were black under the mulberry trees. These were the dwellings of the original Bohemian settlers.

Missionaries dropped by regularly, *Watchtower*s in either hand. It was embarrassing to get stopped on street corners and have little pamphlets shoved into your hand: "Take this home. Hide it under your pillow. Read it at night. Don't let your mama see." There was something exceptional about our position. Even our house seemed in between—squeezed on one side by Zeid's, a regular *Kesselgarten*, with tiers and tiers of rickety back porches, strung with squealing clotheslines; and, on the other, by Ko-varik's—the oldest, the best-kept house on the block. Mr. Kovarik hated unions and swept his sidewalk—these things seemed to go together—after he mowed the lawn, little green whiskers of grass. Mrs. Kovarik shopped on Pulaski Road; but my mother shopped on Crawford *Avenoo*.

Our house was the famous eyesore of the neighborhood.

My father—the fixer—loved to surround himself with broken things, things that needed his attentions. Now that I think of it, it was a rural scene; houses like this you see from the railroad tracks. At least one on the outskirts of every small town. The fence sags, the gate dandles from its hinges; the steps need paint; the very grass is rusted. Strips of plastic film flutter over the windows winter and summer. These folks keep junk as others keep pigs and goats. Drums, barrels, baby buggies; empty gas-oline cans of every description; bicycle frames without wheels, or wheels without frames—take your pick. Tires, inner tubes, wringer washers with deep round tubs. (An abandoned refrigerator is always a nice touch, but they get a bad press.) You see boards, bricks, cinder blocks, ditches, sand-piles, all over the place: evidence of a do-it-yourself project that the Lord in his infinite wisdom has seen fit to leave uncompleted. There will be at least one vicious-looking dog, barking its head off, lunging up on its hind legs—practically strangling itself at the end of a rope.

Nowadays, of course, such a collection would be bound to include a television tube or two, a power mower or motorcycle or snowmobile, keeping up with the times, the totems of a reckless civilization. My father, according to my mother, had "all the time in the world." On a twenty-five-foot city lot, his space was limited. This must be how come he never acquired the badge of honor, the Purple Heart—the stripped-down truck chassis overturned in the front yard.

You may be sure this was a fairly constant topic of conversation.

When was he going to fix the faucets, the light switches? (You had to screw bulbs on and off by hand and get your fingers burned.) Why couldn't our radio be made to work, the same as anyone else's? (On Sunday eve-nings, with much muttering and demanding to know "who the aitch had been fooling around with it," my father would unscrew the back of the cabinet, fiddle with tubes, touch a few wires together, and produce the voice of Walter Winchell: "Good evening, Mr. and Mrs. North and South America… ") When was my father going to take a look at my mother's washing machine, since he had just repaired the next-door neighbor's? Hadn't she been pleading with him for months? (My mother never asked; she *pleaded*. In the same way, Slim and I didn't exactly speak; we only *claimed*.) Why couldn't the girls have bikes, if my father—a very popular guy—had put together bikes from spare parts for half the kids on the block?

"A prophet is without honor in his own country," my father would say, frowning over the crossword puzzle without looking up. He always worked the crossword puzzle at the dinner table, sharpening his pencil with quick curly strokes of his penknife and sticking it behind his ear, in his thick curly hair. This was how come he spoke in dashes and aitches and absentmindedly asked for the s-a-l-t.

Well, how about throwing out the garbage?

In the back yard my father kept his dogs, a pitch-black pair with hides smooth as tar and chests shaped like gun barrels. They were of a litter that had been destroyed, the father turned killer. My father brought them home in a box.

I happened to be lying on the couch under a blanket, a wet washcloth across my eyes, a thermometer in my mouth—*claiming* some childhood illness or other. A smell of Vicks VapoRub; a dimness of drawn shades; a steaming glass of tea.

My father looked at me with a gleam in his eye, hugging the carton under his arm. It was moving; he had to hold the top down with both hands. "Puppies," he said, stepping back. The lid popped open. Out rolled two stir-crazy dogs, stumbling and tumbling over each other. You could hear their claws clattering like dice. Their tails were lashing. They came crashing over the table, splashed the tea, smashed the glass, knocked the thermometer out of my mouth, yanked off my blankets with a wrench of their jaws, and sank their teeth into my legs. I thought of sharks. Then they squatted down—looking contrite—and did their business in the middle of the floor.

After this they stayed in the backyard—had the run of the place—and my mother tossed them their scraps out the back window. They galloped round and round, digging up everything in sight, their tongues hanging out like slices of meat. Trophies of flesh. There but for the grace of God go I. This was how come my father had to throw out the garbage. Mr. Kovarik complained about "property values."

My sister Slim was a freer spirit. She'd cheat before your very eyes at cards. She liked to throw off all her clothes, climb out the bedroom window, and run around on the steep porch roof stark naked. Mrs. Kovarik's fat white chow, Chummy, was getting on; had a cataract in one eye and roving habits; and she used to watch for him from behind her curtains. Whenever she spotted Slim at it again, her fat white bottom bouncing up and down on the gutter pipes—which my father was still getting around to repairing—all the world knew how loose they were—she would call the police. Or better yet, the fire department. The hook and ladder would come wailing up, engines shuddering, and firemen leaping off the sides in their big gloves and boots, axes slung on their shoulders.

After the war began the wholesale migration of whites out of, blacks into, the West Side of Chicago; completed sometime in the midfifties. (Someday there ought to be plaques of bronze all over the city—the kind you see in scenic or historic areas—commemorating these landmarks and battle zones.) If I wanted to, I could probably fix the final hour, name the exact date on which there were no longer any Jews left in all of Lawndale. That had to be the day we moved. My father was a hard man to budge.

One night my mother woke to find a man bending over her bed. She could hear my father downstairs in the kitchen, stirring the spoon in his coffee cup. He was awfully fond of sugar. "Why, he's let someone get in and he doesn't even know it." She gave a feeble cry and tried to sit up.

My father rushed toward the stairs and snapped on the light.

At once the figure began to glow. He appeared to be a Hindu; he was little and frail, with nothing on but a turban and loincloth. She could see his ribs, distinctly outlined—a pale-green glimmer, like the spark of cigar butts or fireflies. He hesitated, wavered, and faded out of sight.

My mother said she had been hearing the same stealthy footsteps creeping up the stairs for years—only they had never made it to the top before.

"It's an omen," my father said. "Looks like it's time we moved. If the house is going to be haunted."

Naturally there were a few embarrassing questions.

"When are your folks coming out to see us again, it's been so long?" Mark and Bertha wanted to know. "And your sister Slim—we used to get such a kick out of her. What's her husband do?" (He locks himself in the bathroom and sits there in the dark till you leave, that's what he does. What my father calls "a character.")

But the conversation over the meal was mostly about farmers' dogs getting killed on the highway, a regular occurrence. Traffic has increased on these back roads; Lynn says she's afraid to let the girls ride their bikes. It's ever since they opened up I-94 and I-80. The green signs are everywhere. They used to say you could hear the corn growing; now you hear the truck tires, punching out the miles.

Every once in a while a pickup truck hurtled past and drummed the dishes on the table.

The very pictures hanging all about us were the same; oil originals, they had belonged to Mark's grandfather. Nature scenes, woods, mountains, waterfalls. The thick raised brushstrokes shone darkly in heavy gilt frames. I used to think the largest was supposed to be best, because it was biggest.

Mark noticed me looking.

"Guess I ought to take 'em in and get 'em appraised one of these days," he said, raising shining specs to the wall. "Maybe one of the artists died and got famous."

That was the joke he always used to make.

Jacob spoke up. "I hope you don't mind my asking. But how much would you say all of this is worth?"

"Well, now, that's hard to say." Mark tucked his chin over his plate. "I did most of the work myself, you know."

"Just an estimate, " Jacob said tactfully.

"I was going to tell her about the *wedding*," Bertha chimed in.

Mark looked up. "What wedding was that, Mother?"

"Why, the wedding we went to in *Chicago*." She sounded rather hurt.

That did it. All you have to do is say "Chicago." At once the conversation turned to crime.

The streets of Michigan City and South Bend aren't safe anymore, deserted after dark; business districts are dead. People go to huge outly-ing shopping centers, which have sprung up like oil rigs on the highways. Even social life has moved there: restaurants, cinemas, bowling alleys, cocktail lounges. Things have started happening that never used to occur in this part of the world before. Bodies locked in trunks, shoot-outs in gas stations, brutal murders that make even the Chicago papers—so you can imagine the big splash in the local press, with the news of church bake sales and false-alarm fires.

This is not the usual stuff: suicide pacts and exploding gas heaters.

There was the woman who went shopping in Kalamazoo. Her car was abandoned in the parking lot. A few days later a hitchhiker spotted a grisly blood-smeared infant sitting at the side of the road, prattling and pointing into the bushes. There they found the mother's body.

In Cassopolis, a man and wife were slain in bed—tortured, their throats slit. Once again, a pair of toddlers were witness to their parents' murder—standing in their cribs.

I could see Lynn took an interest in this gory fare; she dramatized, pointing her finger like the infant in her story, and her great gray eyes opened wide in staring childish horror. I must confess I take an interest myself. My aunt was murdered when I was a very small child, and my cousin—her daughter—and I discovered the body. She had been stran-gled, her apron strings knotted so tightly round her throat that they were hidden in its flesh. We thought she was fooling. We each grabbed an arm and started dragging, pulling, to make her get up. Her hand was limp, it offered no resistance. For many years after I could remember her heavy hand pulling on me, but thought it was a dream. My cousin moved away with her father; I never saw her again.

I know that evil is a great preoccupation of our life in the city; I am used to conversations like this, I am very much aware of being a woman alone. But it surprised me to learn that it's the same in the country, that people talk about the crime, they are preoccupied with crime—and all that goes with it. Fear and violence are by-blows of our modern life. They feel this life encroaching, closing in on them.

The fear of crime is profoundly a class fear: the fear of becoming a victim, of joining the ranks of the expendables—those spewed up by the system; of offering your neck to be butchered and slaughtered and laying yourself down with the rest. I realized the extent to which this has come to pass when we were pulling into the city one day, getting off at the Illinois Central station on Fifty-Fifth Street. The little red train from the country arrived at the rush hour. It was drizzling, passengers were alighting from cars heading in the opposite direction, coming out of the Loop. Steamy plastic raincoats, umbrellas, tired lines straggling toward the gates. The stairs were wet and muddy. The tracks are elevated here, tumbleweed blows off the railroad ties, down the steep embankments, rolls sweeping end over end through the ranks of housing projects.

Something was wrong. You could see the crowd halting ahead at the very bottom of the stairs. A snarl, a backup, something blocking the way. Two youths were killed, shot in the head at this station one recent evening while it was still light. So my first thought was "Oh, no." But what it was was a cat. A large, bluish, white-spotted animal lying on its side, all four paws stretched out. At first glance it appeared to be dead; then I saw its dark quavering gaze. It seemed to be trying to raise its head, glance backward over its shoulder. "Not for long," someone said.

As we went out past the gates I could see through the bars the last of the passengers still gathered round, looking down at the cat, helpless to express their concern. And as a matter of fact it is a rarity to see an animal on the city streets in this condition. People in a bad way you see all the time. You give them a wide berth.

All at once, through the bars, the cat became a man before my very eyes. I saw him lying on his side in the same stiff way, trying to lift his head up and look behind him over his shoulder with the same quaking motion. He was a black man in a black raincoat, with a bottle in his pocket; his fingers reaching, outspread. Was he supposed to be drunk? Having an attack of some sort? Had someone pushed him? Was he wounded? Had he stumbled and fallen? His eyes were shining and shivering like muddy pools of water. And the heels, umbrellas, were tap-tapping around him, passengers quickening their gait, avoiding his eyes.

Dawn, the oldest granddaughter, suddenly jumped up, pointing to the window. Her chair toppled backward, her fork dropped with a clatter.

"Flaming Molly got out! Flaming Molly got out!" Her hair was about the shade of the Irish setter's, and her little gold locket was rising and falling on her chest.

Sure enough, the big red dog came streaking past the window, its head between its paws and its tail like a brushfire. *Oh, no. Not again. How'd that happen?* Everyone was in an uproar. The twins shrieked and tore their napkins. I gathered that Flaming Molly was not long for this world.

Frank and Jake, all flushed with the excitement of the chase, ran out with Dawn to catch the dog. (Have I mentioned that she is a raving beauty?) Their footsteps jolted the bare unnailed boards of the porch. In no time at all the meal had disbanded; Lynn marched the little ones home across the lawn, Mark went back to his chores. I started to clear the table.

"Never mind all that," Little Bertha whispered, quickly wiping down her hands on her apron. "Now's my chance to tell you all about that wedding."

We sat side by side on the sofa, the scrapbook open across our knees. I saw I was in for a fairly lengthy and detailed description, not to say history. How many years Mark and Bertha had known the bride's family; what good time they had made driving into Chicago; how they got lost, circling all around, looking for the church… Okay, okay; so they finally made it. The organ was playing, ushers were taking guests by the elbows, leading them down the aisle to their pews. Programs were being distributed. *Programs?* Apparently this was to be one of those do-it-yourself scripts: a lot of quotations from Kahlil Gibran and Rod McKuen substituted for the vows and holy scriptures.

All of a sudden the lights went out, the church fell silent; a white movie screen dropped down in place of the altar. Onto it there flashed—a naked toothless baby on a bearskin rug. The groom. Over a microphone came a voice out of the darkness: the groom's mother, telling the story of his life. Accompanied by slides. The groom's first teeth, his baby shoes—dipped in plaster. The groom in a cowboy hat with strings round his neck and his little legs dangling from the back of a pony in Lincoln Park Zoo. And so forth and so on. Talk about history. Then the same with the bride. Her childish scrawls; her striped spelling papers with gummed red stars. She had had corrective surgery on her hip as a child, and even this was not overlooked—there she was on the screen, smiling and struggling in her casts and crutches.

Several of the groom's musical compositions were played on the guitar, and the bride's poetry was read aloud. It was announced that there would be a display immediately following the reception line—the newlyweds' arts and crafts.

I was stunned. I had been expecting a tale of hippies and flower children, bearded boys and braless girls, but what would you call *this*? What could you make of it? You go to a ceremony, and you get an exhibition. I had to say *something*—Little Bertha was looking up at me expectantly, her head perched to one side.

"It sounds like the bride and groom have a lot in common," I said.

"Yes. I'm sure they'll have a wonderful life." Her shoulders heaved a small sigh. "But I'm just not doing it justice," she said, shaking her head. "It's too hard to remember it all, it's been such a long time."

"Say, when was this wedding anyhow?"

Bertha flipped through the pages. "June fifteenth, nineteen s— Why, that's four years ago!"

She clapped the book shut on her knees and lifted her face wistfully, clucking her tongue. "My, my—how time flies," she said.

Let me tell you about this part of the country. At one time the southeastern shores of Lake Michigan thronged and thrived with summer resorts. My friends spent the entire summer vacation at Gottlieb's, Gettel's, Fiddelman's, in towns with names like South Haven, Benton Harbor, Union Pier. The towns still have the same names, but they don't sound the same to me. These were places of summer romance: they went to meet boys; they talked about Gary, Barry, Terry all winter. (The names of choice in my generation.) I didn't know anything else about life in the country, and I didn't care, either. I didn't grow up on the West Side of Chicago for nothing. I had no use for the outdoors; it made no difference to me— all I knew of nature was what dropped from the trees. What were those shiny, sticky things like black bean pods? Where did they come from? And the soft chains we used to call "caterpillars"? And what about the leaves? What did you call them? I never learned their names.

My proletarian family did not go in for that sort of thing. When I was very small we used to make our annual expedition to the beach—something of an ordeal. You took the Roosevelt Road car to the end of the line, forty-two blocks—Chicago blocks, long ones, and it ground to a halt at every other corner—and then you walked another mile with the blankets and thermos bottles. The bathhouses smelled of slimy timber; you had to race through them quickly, ducking the sniper spray of icy-cold showers. I wore rubber beach shoes, a rubber cap, a suit with no top(!). My father would scoop out a hole in the sand and crouch down in it—his thighs as thick around as tree stumps in his Charles Atlas trunks—trying to shrink and make himself look smaller, while someone snapped our picture with our black box camera. Otherwise his head and hairy shoulders would get lost above the rest.

On the long rides home Slim always fell asleep.

The streetcar was crowded; we had to split up. My father sat all the way up front with my fat little sister sprawled in his lap, his own big head nodding and dozing. It fell on his chest. My mother and I found seats in the back. The aisle got more and more crowded, people swayed from the straps; the car went slower and slower—dragging on, clanging, complaining. The long-drawn-out whine twanged the heart.

But it seemed to me that this was the way I spent most of my life: waiting. Waiting in buses, streetcars, automobiles; waiting on benches, stairways, laps, knees. Waiting in crowds, doctors' offices, clinics; waiting on beds heaped with rough coats at family parties. Waiting in the dark. Waiting alone. Waiting for nothing. This was the real tyranny of childhood. I wanted to be grown up and done with it—done with waiting—just so no one ever again would have such power over me.

I laid my head against the back of the seat and my gaze drifted toward the window. Suddenly I heard my mother let out such a shriek that every head turned the whole length of the car.

"Sam! She's asleep!"

That was *me*. I was looking at her too. Instantly I shut my eyes, dropped my head to my shoulder. And I pretended to be asleep (to be on the safe side) all the rest of the way home. My father had to carry both of us slung from his back.

So how should I have known that I would grow up with such strange longings, such a passion for "nature"? That I should have been asking questions all along? That I would want to tuck myself away in the country and learn the names of things?

The boys and I are sharing this summer cottage with a couple; we use it during the week, they come out on weekends. An ideal arrangement, except I'm sore half the time: someone uses your last clean towel, or eats up the leftovers you were counting on finding in the refrigerator. Or, departing, my friends go to great pains to lock up the place—draw all the windows, shut it like an oven—and forget to throw out their rotting garbage. It leaks all over and stinks to high heaven. The whole house swarms with fruit flies.

Unwelcome thoughts darken my door, enter my soul. They walk right in, make themselves at home. I could be put in prison for thoughts like those.

But I don't have to go into explanations. The case is simple. I'm jealous, possessive about the house—I don't want to share it. I don't want to share anything. I want to pack up my children and have a place of our own. This is my most persistent fantasy. I even subscribe to farm realty catalogs so I can read all about the Sportsman's Hideaways, Handyman's Specials, Sacrifices to Settle Estates. "The Land Remains." (It occurs to me that these catalogs are my equivalent of the rural scenes on the walls of the Elliotts' house—calendar paintings.)

It doesn't have to be the best place in the world, nothing special, no castle, no dream house. Riding along, I'll spot some austere and isolated shack—a roof, a porch, a weed-strewn path—and I'm ready to love it. To spring out of the car, fling my arms around it, twine myself, cling to it, sink my roots deep. If it will only be *mine*.

Too bad you can't feel that way about people.

Zimmerman's falls squarely into the category of Handyman's Specials. Mrs. Zimmerman and her husband staked out this land over forty years ago, and once owned all the cottages you see around here. Her husband is dead now, as she's sure to mention on every possible occasion, anytime she corners you—a tiny woman with frizzy gray hair and great big tiger eyes, magnified, welling up to the very rims of her thick glasses.

"My husband is dead now, you know. "

"Yes, yes, I know. "

The tenants try to evade the old landlady's tediousness. Though it's easy enough to understand. She feels diminished. She is not what she once was. This is not the truth about her—not the whole truth.

Most of the cottages belong to black families now, who live in them themselves and do not rent them out, and have put a lot of work into their places. Paint, shingles, cinder blocks; concrete patios, chain-link fences. Roofs straddled by TV antennas like Texas Towers—it still takes a lot of power out this way to get a picture. The rest—what's left of Zimmerman's Lakefront Villas (they're not on the lakefront, that goes without saying; you can't even see Lake Michigan from here)—are merely six or seven of the most leaning, the most dependent, the most run-down, crippled, and dilapidated. It won't be so easy to get rid of *them*. Which the old lady would dearly love to do, all right; she longs to soar away and be free. Help is so hard to get these days.

Missus Z. swears up and down by Mrs. Hodiak, the cleaning woman, who routs the cottages out in spring. Sweeps up the curled wasp corpses, the mouse pellets, the fly-speckled newspapers laid over the furnishings like wares in a shopwindow—three-legged armchairs, sagging studio couches, dressers with stuck drawers and sourpussed mirrors. Mrs. Hodiak is stout and fearless with her mops and buckets. Her hair is like a paintbrush dipped in lampblack, white at the roots.

It was cold when we first came out and I foolishly asked how to light the rusty old heater; I've always been skittish about holding up flaming matches to hissing gas. Mrs. Hodiak without a word dropped onto all fours and crawled under the buffet. That's where the heater sits, don't ask me why. I could see her big shaved legs and gym shoes sticking out.

"Never mind, Mrs. Hodiak, please, forget it," I said, as she crouched, her heavy back wedged in, scratching matches under her thumbnails.

There was a pop, but no explosion. Nothing lighted. No gas, of course. Mrs. Zimmerman seems to be the only one left who still expects the heaters to give forth, rise and shine; the toilets to shut their noisy traps for a change and quit dripping deliriously (no more graceful fountains);

the showers to do more than cough up a few drops of surly brown water, rattle their pipes and knock it off.

She seems so surprised and disappointed, in fact—the big yellow eyes sweeping up, trustingly, in her small wrinkled face—that you really hate to mention it. Like the hole in the boys' bedroom ceiling where the roof is caving in. What's the use? What can she do about it? Or the bathroom floor rotting away under the tub. The screen doors are a laugh.

"Mrs. Hodiak scrubs these cottages from top to bottom; she makes them *spotless*," the old landlady says with pride.

What it amounts to is this: Mrs. Zimmerman—by default—is a hold-out, a survivor. I made it up here twenty years too late. But she still thinks someone is going to come along and take all this off her hands. And you can always tell when something's up, she's got another prospect on the hook. An old man—another ancient faithful retainer, stooped, gnarled, with a spattered cap and overalls that hang drooping from their buckle straps—shows up, bright and early, and starts slapping white paint all over the place. He splatters the greenery.

The old guy must be stone deaf under his cap; his portable radio jumps and jangles and blares like a loudspeaker. The lawn mowers buzz, riding herd over the grass; the garbage trucks back up, groaning and grinding and gnashing their teeth. The neighbors' miniature poodles (all the neighbors own little white poodles with legs like pipe cleaners) sound off from their rhinestone-studded throats. Abused little yips and yaps. Even the woodpeckers get into the act—typing in the trees, hunt and peck; very unsystematic. In other words, life out here goes on—industri-ously. *And it's not supposed to.* It's supposed to stop, to hold still for us. Ev-eryone knows that. Isn't that the proper definition of life in the country?

The tenants wish she'd leave well enough alone.

This neck of the woods has always been a Bohemian stronghold in the summertime, and it still is. The old resorts still gang up one right on top of the other: Hspuda's, Redimak's, Sixta's. The restaurants with thatched roofs and stenciled shutters; the dark little groceries where they sell shriveled sausages and heavy black bread and display all the mimeo-graphed announcements—dances, raffles, bingo. They'll cash checks if they know you. Their strong community spirit definitely does not extend to outsiders. This is exactly the pattern the transition from white to black followed in the city—where all that dark bread comes from; husky loaves stickered with labels from bakeries in Bridgeport, Brighton, along Archer Avenue. These are the so-called ethnic neighborhoods—i.e., white working class. Inch by inch the ground is contested in classic style: you read about bricks and firebombs hurled through windows, crosses burned on lawns, parents picketing schools. Everyone knows that Czechs, Poles, Lithuanians, Irish are more stubborn than Jews.

At Zimmerman's, however, there are certain changes rung on these old stereotypes. Here it is the blacks who are the conventional, stable families; who own homes, who maintain them, who put up fences and fire up coals with lighter fluid on their portable grills. The whites are refugees from Hyde Park, university liberals—the other kind of bohemians.

At seven o'clock in the morning, Mrs. Bledsoe, sitting on her screened-in porch across the way, starts to give Byron his lessons in table manners. Mrs. Bledsoe is a round, brown, smiling woman who wears turbans, great dangling earrings wriggling like bait, long colorful robes. She looks like an African ambassadress—even when she throws out the garbage, the loose tropical sleeves flowing and fluttering as she slams and bangs the lids. She takes in children from the ghetto to board in summer, so they can taste the benefits of country life. "And because I never had any of my own," she says. (She pronounces it *get-toe*, in rich penetrating tones, to let you know it's not where she's from.) The little colony can be seen traipsing down the dusty path to the lake, Mrs. Bledsoe, her buttocks swaying in her long gown, forging ahead; the children scraping along in rubber thongs, striped beach towels over their shoulders. Later their wet suits hang on the line.

Byron is the youngest, the smallest, the puniest; the skinniest, blackest legs, the biggest ears; and his belly slopes and sticks out the most. He wears a yellow beanie with something like a windmill or weather vane on top. When the others tease him (they perpetually tease him), don't let him catch the Frisbee or take his turn at bat, he chases back and forth, frantic. I see the weathercock whirling on the top of his head.

I get very maudlin about Byron's yellow beanie.

"Don't slop your oatmeal, Byron."

"What you say when you ask for something? You. Byron."

"And what you say when you get it?"

I think she slaps his hands.

The light of the young morning creeps across the dewy grass. But this is not what I bargained for when I rented a house in the country. Not the twittering of boisterous birds in the trees. It makes me cringe. I feel it is partly on my account that Mrs. Bledsoe is making Byron's life so miserable, that he keeps getting it day after day like this. And it *is* partly on my account. Her voice rises, carries, sharp as a laugh—it means to be overheard. *Byron! Byron!* The other children titter—who can blame them? A moment of freedom for them. They're not even permitted to go barefoot, Mrs. Bledsoe's so strict: "It looks trashy." Whose world does she think she's making them fit to live in?

Our porch—we took this cottage for its screened-in porch, though it's in even worse shape than the house—is full of garbage. Belle and Emile save all our trash so they can take it to the recycling center at the Bethlehem Steel plant. That is their hobby. Recycling center at Bethlehem Steel—how d'ya like the nerve? That pipe organ on the lakefront. They belong to Zero Population Growth. They own two houses and three cars. (No, make that four. I gave my car to Emile on condition that he never mention it to me again. It was the kind of car you have fantasies of abandoning; the guy who sold it to me must have thought he had died and gone to heaven when he saw a sucker like me coming, with my great big smile.)

Our refuse isn't enough for them; they go around collecting from other cabins too. Tins, jars, soda bottles, beer cans, great green jugs of Gallo and Pio Vino. The stuff is stashed all over the place. Shopping bags buckle under their loads. Stacks of Sunday papers, comics, rotogravures. Then there are the ecological experiments: piles of browning corncobs (for fuel?); rheumy watermelon rinds. Belle and Emile know how I love to throw things out, so they leave notes for me:

*This is not garbage. Please save.*

That's not all. I nearly forgot the dishes of dog chow, boxes of kitty litter. They have three cats and two dogs. It would be no fun driving back to Chicago with all of them in the rear seat of a rusty Volkswagen, so the cats remain with us. Large, placid, easygoing Belle, with her big hips and pale ponytail, her long teeth like a rabbit's, straps herself in, stroking the old white dog in her lap. The young dog waves its lofty tail from the window. And out pops Emile's wedge of red beard, anxiously reminding us, just one more time:

"Don't let the cats get out. "

Don't let the cats get out. The cats are shy and strange and keep trying to run away. We have to shut them up whenever we attempt to leave; they hide from us, bound off, dive under the furniture. Their telltale eyes glare from dark corners.

One is black and white, fat and sleek and easy to catch. But Jacob spends a lot of time parked on his narrow haunches, lifting the edges of blankets, poking under beds—his thick shocks of bushy dark hair sticking out aft—coaxing the lean striped tabbies:

"Here, kitty kitties… here, kitty kitties…"

Frank and Jake are of an age and have always been close. Being shunted around—their father and I were divorced when they were babies—has made them closer. Frank is thirteen now, he's pulled ahead; broad shouldered, gruff voiced (Arf! Arf! Arf!)—almost hulking. His wrists protrude from the sleeves of his pajamas and the pant legs look as though they shrank to his ankles. Nobody notices these developments with more interest, more awe, than Jacob. "Holding Frank's hand is like holding a man's hand," he says.

Their father has married again; he has a new wife, a new child. I wonder if the boys feel at home there. Maybe they are on their good behavior, there are things they are afraid to say? Are they only guests in his house? And isn't it the same for them with me? Mine is a makeshift sort of life; I didn't plan it that way, I just don't have all the pieces. I'm sure they notice. Do they watch out? Do they bite their tongues?

"I'm always at home where Jacob is," Frank told me.

At first the boys played with Ralphie, a big heavy shuffling good-natured kid; a cowlick, calamine lotion smeared all over his fat red cheeks. He'd gotten into some poison ivy. His hand was in a sling, taped to the wrist, the thumb in a splint—just the fingernails sticking out; a firecracker had gone off in his mitt on the Fourth of July. He limped a little, lurched to one side—an ankle twisted in a fall from a tree. The boys assured me he was just accident-prone.

Then Jacob started asking, "Hey, Ma, is it all right if we sneak off after lunch and go fishing with Ralphie?... Can we have permission to sneak off after dinner? Huh, Ma?"

"Sure. But who sez you have to *sneak off*?"

"Ralphie does. His mother's punishing him. He's not supposed to leave his room except to go to the toilet. But he climbs out the window. "

Ralphie's mother is Gladys, a widow with an administrative job at the university; she comes out with her mother and five children. One son died in Vietnam. Gladys is a blond meaty woman with a ruddy thick-blooded face; the old mother is bony and scrawny and white as a ghost. And yet the two women are unmistakably of one flesh. It's the way they carry themselves—six feet tall, with heavy slouching shoulders, bison humps. It gives them a hangdog, defeated appearance; you can see they are used to being ineffectual.

Ralphie's "punishment" is typical; the threats fly thick and fast and no one listens to them anyway. "All right, I'm gonna leave you right here, then," I hear the old woman telling the baby, as it sits and bawls in a puddle in its diaper and pins. "You find your way back to Chicago all by yourself."

And yet it was Gladys who finally forbade Ralphie to play with my boys—because, she said, they used foul language. Then the three rosy little girls had to stop playing with their friends for the same reason. Very soon there was no one left who had not offended in this way, and Gladys's brood had no one to play with. On the beach she spreads their blanket far from the rest, and passing in the road she won't glance up, keeps her distance—humped, slouching, her feet pounding with determination, her chin hung forward with heavy pride.

You may be sure I enter into the spirit of things, narrow my eyes, set my jaw too. Hard feelings are so good for the arteries.

I was getting a patch put on a bicycle tire at the gas station on the highway. The temperature was in the nineties, the tar was melting. The light hurt your eyes. Every time a car whizzed past, shrapnel, all the signs started rattling and the colored streamers raised a dirty breeze.

The attendant came squinting up to me. He was drinking a warm Coke—the vending machine was broken. The brown liquid foamed and fizzed under his thumb.

"You see that guy that was here just now? The one in the suit and necktie. That was driving the blue panel truck."

I had noticed a truck standing at the pumps.

"Well, that's the deputy. He's got six colored boys in back he's taking up to the state prison in Jackson and they asked for a drink a water. Boy, you should of seen it. There's no windows back there, it ain't nothing but tin; I bet it was a hundred and twenty degrees sitting under that roof. The sweat was just pouring off them. They were *shining*. And the smell that was coming outta there could knock you right over.

"And the deputy," he said, shaking his head, "I seen him go in and give 'em their water. Some job he's got, huh? I wouldn't do that if you paid me."

Something knocks off the lids of the garbage cans and digs and scratches in the middle of the night. What can it be? A fox? A masked raccoon? Everyone is secretly pleased; proud of our possession of this wild creature (we hope it's wild). It is to us what the bears are to Yellowstone, ambling in under the tent flaps and eating up the peanut butter. Ambassadors. Ah, wilderness. It's official—we're in the country. When I hear it poking, nosing around, I jump out of bed and grab my flashlight, run to the door, shining its beam into the darkness; searching searching for two points of light, the pair of eyes burning at me like taillights.

Surprise. It *is* the country. How long has it been since I smelled summer nights? At that hour, the air is so sharply pure your breath cracks; the trees are creaking overhead like old weather-beaten barns. Mosquitoes sprinkle the grass, heavy as dew. And the Little Dipper, sparkling away up there, reminds me suddenly, forcibly of childhood... sitting out late on our front steps, gazing up, wondering at those same targets strewn over the summer night. The same? So they're still up there? Belle took her class of inner-city dropouts to the planetarium, and the kids clapped politely when the stars came out.

I haven't seen this animal yet. And it occurs to me: what if it's only a rat? A cat? Escaped? One of the neighbors' toy poodles with their jeweled collars and red ribbons? (No wonder they protest so much.) Or it could be Sadie, up to her scavenging and rummaging.

Everyone knows better than to start up with Sadie—hard enough to avoid her as it is. You wake up and find her face against the screen, her hand to her forehead, peering in. An old harpy head, streaked white bangs and beetling black brows. Always twitching.

"Just sniffing your flowers," she says.

Sadie knows every abandoned house for miles around—she's looted them all. She prowls the woods in helmet and slicker, galoshes, thick gloves, got up for the occasion like a welder or a beekeeper.

Sadie comes trudging down the loose rickety stairs to the beach—someone's going to do himself a mischief one of these days—her rubber galoshes flopping their tongues, swathed to the chin in a conspicuously striped beach towel. Very conspicuous—it's mine. I was wondering what happened to it.

It's wonderful, though, how everyone puts up with Sadie; the price you have to pay for a little fresh air.

Gladys lives on the other side of the same duplex (all seven in two rooms), so the women have been carrying on a running feud. Naturally you hear everything through the cardboard walls, and Sadie is forever thumping on them with (I presume) her broomstick.

I was talking to Sadie in back of the white frame cottage when Gladys came charging round the bend, her head lowered, very red in the face.

"All right, Sadie, I give up, I can't take it anymore. I'm here to beg you—is that what you want? Beg you to stop."

"Stop what?" says Sadie, not at all taken aback—as I was—but looking up and raising her glass to her lips. She was seated in a deck chair, drinking rosé from a shrimp-cocktail jar. All around us the smell of paint-spattered, fresh-scissored grass.

"Stop swearing at my children!"

"They swore at me first."

"Sadie. They're *children*." Gladys was choking back tears.

"They started it, I didn't," Sadie said.

I'd never seen her so composed. She sank back calmly in the arms of the striped chair, stretched out her legs—one ankle in its rubber galosh crossed atop the other—looking up at Gladys, her black eyebrows raised above the rim of her glass. And they weren't even twitching; her nervous tic had disappeared, stopped like a clock.

"I'm begging you, Sadie, leave us alone. What harm have I ever done you? We try to keep out of your way. I'm shushing my children all the time when you're at home. *What is it? What do you want from us? Why do you have to make my life so miserable!*"

Gladys's face was getting thicker and redder. All at once I understood—not a moment too soon, considering I'm in such a good position to appreciate—looking at her hunched shoulders, shaking angry jaws. A cornered creature, at bay. A husband dead, a son killed in the war, the children too much for her, the mother disappointed—a life of constant self-reproach. She was beside herself, leading a manless, unconsoled existence. The fear, the loneliness, managing alone. And of course pride.

Sadie smirked and sipped her pink wine.

I got up and took Gladys by the arm. "Come away, come away, Gladys," I said. "Can't you see she's enjoying this? She loves it, she thrives on it, this is what she lives for. You're no match for her. It can only hurt you."

"All I ask is a little peace," Gladys said. She had begun to cry in earnest and her big sunburned peeling shoulders were shaking. I put my arms around her, meaning to press her cheek to my shoulder. But since she's a good half foot taller than I am, that was impossible. I dropped my head on her shoulder instead.

"Why can't we have a little peace and quiet?" she cried. "Why oh why does it always have to be so hard? I come up to the country with my children to get away from all that. But it's the same here. Why do I feel like this? Why am I always so angry?"

She rocked and sobbed while I patted her on the hump, mindlessly, like burping a baby. Oh, yes. If not for Sadie, for the damned cats and the garbage and kitty litter. If Mrs. Bledsoe would just quit picking on Byron—in the tender hours of the morning at least. If only we could remove all these extra distractions… If if if.

And yet in spite of everything, the first thing that happens every summer is that everyone starts talking and scheming about giving it all up, moving out here altogether, living here year round. They've had it with the city—dirt, crime, crowding, corruption. To the country! To the country! It's only a matter of rearranging all the querulous details, our circumstantial lives.

So where is it, then? Where is the rightful life that is awaiting us? Where is that undiscovered territory? Where the air is clear and consciences are clean. How do we get there? How do we cut our path through this wilderness? How do we run up our flags and stake our claims? The tyranny, the tyranny of these dreams of peace and quiet.

# TWENTY-SIXTH AND CALIFORNIA

It is almost impossible to make out what is actually going on in a criminal courtroom, but you can tell at a glance, through the crack in the doors, what stage has been reached. If the benches are packed; if the air is thick; if people are moving all the time, going in and out—the heavy doors constantly creaking—then it is only the beginning. A bond hearing, maybe; prisoners being hauled in fresh from the lockup.

All the old-fashioned courtrooms look alike. The raised bench, the striped flag behind the chair. The clerk's desk with its green lampshade and batteries of rubber stamps. Manacles gleaming on the bailiff's hip. Calendar pages pasted on the wall. No Smoking signs. (You could cut it with a knife.) Flypaper shades—long tattered strips—buckling at the windows. The glass glitters between with intense prairie light. The big rotating fans are not stirring now, but you can imagine what it must be like in summer.

The name is called; the charge is muttered; a shuffle along the crowded rows—relatives, friends, rising to come forward and stand behind the accused. Court is above all a family affair. The benches are full of children, like eighteenth-century jails.

"This is Willie Monroe's mother, Your Honor. She has nine other children at home and she's on public aid. If the bond isn't lowered, she won't be able to raise the money to get him out."

To get out—that's the object. Everyone knows it; it's no secret here.

The judges also look alike, with their bent heads, bald spots, shoulders in black judicial robes. "If I set bond at three thousand dollars, you have to come up with ten percent. That means three hundred dollars. Think you can raise three hundred over the telephone?"

*Thud, thud,* the clerk stamps the papers. The turnover is rapid, more or less automatic; it seems to be the court's main business too. Meanwhile they're singing harmony in the lockup. Every time the clerk opens the door and sticks his head inside—calling a name into its barred depths—you can hear the notes escaping to a stomping rhythm.

"Hey. See that? See that there?" A bunch of little boys, growling whispers. Pointing across the fire escape at the grim bricked wall of the county jail. "That where you gonna end up, LeRoy." Holding their stomachs with laughter. "Hey, LeRoy. LeRoy. Your granddaddy gonna git hisself locked up with you?"

The big flinty block at Twenty-Sixth and California really does seem to stand in the midst of a prairie, open to the elements. The windows look far out over the vast industrial plain of Chicago. It shimmers with power; the mighty haze hurts your eyes. On the slopes along the front steps—the name, Criminal Courts, set in a mound—signs warn you: Keep Off The Grass. Though the grass looks tough enough to fend for itself. So do the matrons who frisk you when you enter. On the women's side, they do a land-office business in mace. The small black spray dispensers are dumped out of purses by the dozens. An old black man, bald as a crab apple, briskly snaps a rag at the shoeshine stand, an official seated before him, one foot mounted on the stirrup, briefcase across his lap. I don't know, maybe it wasn't such a hot idea to build a city on this site. There is too much energy here. Along with the power of construction goes a power of destruction. Tohu and bohu. Vacant lots, buildings condemned, neighborhoods decayed. Chicago isn't a city: just the raw materials for a city. The prairie is always reasserting itself, pressing its claims.

At preliminary hearings in felony court the benches are crowded with plaintiffs.

A young black woman in aviator glasses, a natural, a raincoat over her arm; flanked before the bar by two state's attorneys. On the other side stands a bushy-haired black youth, his red shirttail hanging out. Who is his counsel?

The clerk raises a rasping voice.

"Pub-lic de-fen-der? Pub-lic de-fen-der?"

A slim smooth-haired fellow in a light suit strolls up the aisle, head elevated, chewing gum.

"This yours?" the clerk says from the height of his desk, pointing down at the head of the accused. Who glances sluggishly over his shoulder, a gaze dull in dark glasses. It's as if you'd stirred mud.

"Please state your name and spell it... Where were you at eight fifty-five on the night of..." They have to caution the plaintiff to speak up. She raises her chin firmly, but her voice is still low.

A washroom on a college campus. She heard footsteps, someone entering, but she was washing her hands over the sink and didn't look up. When she turned to reach for a paper towel, shaking her hands, she came face to face with the defendant. He was standing at arm's length, a knife stretched between them. He told her not to scream, to keep quiet, to shut up. He backed her into a toilet stall.

"And what happened then?"

No one pays attention at hearings. It's too hard. Witnesses' backs are turned, you can't make out what's being said. People keep coming and going, infants smacking their pacifiers. Children stretched out fast asleep, the mark of the hard bench on their cheeks. Besides—no one has come to listen. They all have troubles of their own. Every time the door gives a scrape, all the heads go up row after row. But by now the whole room has sensed what's up; everyone knows "what happened then." You can even hear the plunging keys of the stenotype machine.

The public defender's eyes are black and bright in their cavities. "What time was your class over on the night of... And you were still in the building? At eight fifty-five?" His voice skeptically rising. "Speak up, speak up. The court stenographer can't record you nodding your head." He seems to move toward her, to crowd her. It's as if he too is backing her up, bullying, closing in; his chin thrust forward, rapidly snapping his gum.

She clasps her coat in front of her. He probes the details, over and over. *Toilet toilet toilet.* Every time he says it, people smile, cast glances over their shoulders. Comments are passing from ear to ear.

The defendant stands unmoved, neck forward, hands loosely clasped behind his back. He has said nothing; nodded only once, in response to his name.

Roughly speaking, there are only two kinds of people in a criminal court-room. Innocent, guilty have nothing to do with it. Plaintiffs and defendants are not on different sides; they are not opposing forces. They belong to the same category, are drawn from the same human mass. Almost everyone on the benches is black. And—although there are a lot of dragging fur-trimmed coattails, broad-brimmed hats, platform heels striking loudly in the corridors—they are, even more overwhelmingly, the bleak, unstylish poor. Drab winter coats cling like burdens to their backs. Children espe-cially are buttoned to the eyes, such stiffened little bundles they can scarce-ly move their limbs. Maybe that's why they're so good. They are bored and frightened and fall asleep from stupefaction. Glancing about these crowd-ed rows, men with hats on their knees, women rocking babies on their laps, one fact strikes you—you can't tell who is who, what they are here for. There is no special face of injury, no protest. No one seems to have any axes to grind. Nothing seems to separate outlaws from their victims.

In the other category—on the other side of the great divide—are the officials. The professional, administrative class. White men in business suits with important documents under their arms. That is where the lines are drawn. It is the only line. For everyone else, the impression is of a sort of soup kitchen; something being ladled, doled out—made to go around. The law is a tedious, passionless process, and they have fallen into its hands.

In violence court—murder inquests—something unusual: a fussing in-fant. The mother and grandmother are trying to keep it quiet. Mexican women, in mourning; their faces bend over the child and black lace drapes their cheeks. The matron, with her burly white sleeves, her vest and bai-liff's star, her great festooned wig like a silken lampshade, leans over the back of the bench to caution them. They pass the baby back and forth, thumping its back. There are circles of gold in its little dark ears.

A detective from homicide is called to the stand, and a man rises from the back row, cap in hand, to go up and sit at the long table. He is wretchedly dressed: dilapidated shoes, scuffed rubbers, a torn T-shirt stretched over a flabby belly, a matted jacket crushed under his arm. Small blood-shot bewildered eyes.

The detective had been called to the flat of Marvella Washington, late wife of Freddie Washington, and found a dead woman lying across the bed, sheets soaked with blood. She had been stabbed in the throat and shot in the stomach. The detective called upon her estranged husband; he denied any knowledge of his wife's murder and agreed to take a lie detector test. A couple of days later, the detective picked up Freddie Washington and asked him to come to the station for the polygraph. Freddie Washington changed his story. He said his wife had called him and asked him to come over to discuss child support. He told her he would but fell asleep instead and when he woke it was 2:00 A.M. He hailed a cab and went to her apartment. She buzzed him in. When he got upstairs, she went into the bedroom. He followed. She made straight for the bed, reached under the pillow, and when she turned to face him she was holding a knife in one hand and a revolver in the other. She brandished the weapons. He grabbed her wrists. She fell across the bed and he heard the gun go off. He turned her over. The knife was sticking out of her throat. The children were still asleep in the other room. He took the gun, wiped the knife, and went downstairs to get another cab. In the back seat he hid the weapons, shoved them down between the arm and the cushion. He got out at his apartment and went upstairs to bed.

The baby keeps crying the whole time, sucking and squeezing on an empty bottle. It sounds sick. Freddie Washington's counsel moves for dismissal on grounds that no crime has been committed. The charge will be involuntary manslaughter. Chairs thud at the table. Freddie Washington rises indecisively, fingers gripping his cap. What happens next? His brow is blunt, stunned, right between the eyes. So that's the meaning of their glazed pink expression. A steer slamming down the ramp at the stockyards. His attorney takes hold of him by both shoulders and turns him about, pointing him in the proper direction.

A woman sitting across the aisle nudges her companion. Time to go. The women rise and start shaking, waking, various children—heads popping up all over the place, staring round with shocked marvelous eyes. I remember all at once that I have been a child napping on these benches myself. There might be eight or ten of them, and they all seem the same age. The mothers scold them. Have they got everything? Boots? Mittens? They come wading up the aisle in unbuckled galoshes, half-awake, the women dragging two, three limp arms by each hand. They must have had something to do with the case; but you would never have guessed that was what they were here for. The two women had listened to the entire proceedings unmoved. Relatives? Whose? Were they with Freddie Washington or against him? And what about the children? Were some of them the couple's orphans?

The detective admitted that no effort had been made to locate the taxi Freddie Washington took home. You can't exactly blame him. They are mostly gypsy cabs, without radios, without licenses. Finding one that had traversed the ghetto at three in the morning would be like looking for a phantom ship in a phantom ocean. The address was on Sixty-Third Street. Woodlawn: the neighborhood is shell shocked, ravaged by slum fires. Abandoned buildings, jagged windows, blackened girders of the el tracks. Talk about the power of darkness. Children hunt cockroaches trickling through the rubble—spray them with Flit cans. ("I got 'm. I got 'm. Look how he curl up all his skinny little legs.") The elevated went up in 1892 to trundle ladies in bustles and whalebone to the world's fair. Now it comes pitching round the bend, shooting out sparks, eyeball to eyeball with smashed glass, bombed-out craters, curtains fluttering like torn stockings. At Stony Island, the terminus, it sits and shudders for a while. Nothing around but the prairie.

The farther along the legal process, the emptier the courtroom. That's axiomatic. The benches shine like church pews. There are fewer cases on the dockets but that's not the real reason. It's those calendar pages on the wall. Too much time has passed.

The bailiff is taking a siesta in the jury box, tilted back in the swivel chair with his feet up on the rail: a huge black man, powerful rolls of fat, his white shirtfront spread like a tablecloth, a feast. The clerk's green sleeves move under the desk lamp. The hands click on the clockface. A hat lies atop a folded overcoat in a corner of a bench; a shopping bag from Treasure Island is shoved under a seat. Could be someone's lunch.

This is a murder trial in its seventh week. Court was scheduled to reconvene at one thirty. At that time the jury, coming from lunch, emerged in a body from their special elevator—gates clanking in the silence of the corridor—and were herded into the jury room in back. A large diagram leans against an easel, the ground plan of the first floor of a house in the 5200 block of South Green Street.

All the houses on that block happen to be alike: solid yellow-brick lozenges; stone-step side entrances, fenced symmetrical front lawns. Grass grows in cracks in the sidewalks and small saints in grottoes stand in the yards. The neighborhood is just south of the now defunct stockyards where, once upon a time, most of the residents earned their livings. Like Mayor Daley's neighborhood, a couple of miles to the north along Halsted Street. Mayor Daley was a blue-collar mayor in a blue-collar town and that was his strength. ("Chicago *works!*") He got his power straight from the source: smokestacks, boxcars, steam whistles, steel mills. You call a wrong number and get the bridge over the Cal-Sag Canal. Choked waters, chugging tankers, smudged air, slag heaps. World without end. The bridgetender, friendly, is munching a sandwich. "Meat loaf and mustard," he explains over the telephone. The mayor was one of us.

But his personal protection did not extend to this block on Green Street. A few years back, black families began moving in from the south and east. Pressures were building. The summer passed without any special incident here though there was continuous rioting in Calumet Park— whites running down the beach, stoning blacks sitting on their blankets: "They've got everyplace else." That's the steel mills with their pipes and pumps. Lake Michigan has the look of a big dirty bathtub in the midst of all that plumbing.

One evening in late summer, just before school was about to open, a few grade school children—white—were standing on a street corner at Fifty-First and Peoria. Some older youths—black—came up and told them to make way. During the dispute over who was going to keep the sidewalk, shotgun blasts were heard. A thirteen-year-old boy, who had been looking on from a porch swing a few doors off, was killed outright. A girl, also thirteen, was hit in the eye and died a few hours later. Both were white. The prosecution contends that they were incidental victims of a gang war, that the shots fired into their midst were aimed at the blacks by a rival gang. The slaughter of the innocents. It created a sensation—at the time.

It is a quarter to three before the court rises, the men and women of the jury file in and amply take their places. Since we are talking about black and white: there is one black woman on the jury, and a young Puerto Rican, very slight and small in his chair. The alternate sitting in the side box is black, white mustached, hands stiffened atop his ball-headed cane. All the rest are white, more or less middle-aged: women in slacks, men in sport shirts, baseball jackets. A suggestion of leisure hours, domestic tasks; Saturday afternoon filling up shopping carts at the supermarket, trimming the grass. The defendants, at their table, return their glances with composure.

They are two slender young men, maybe twenty, twenty-one, dressed in high-heeled boots, vests, frock coats, satin cuffs, velvet collars. It's something of a shock. All their drama is in their dress. They look like something out of *Gone with the Wind*. In fact, they look like slave owners. You wonder how the jury, in the face of such incongruity, can form any impression of them. Ryan Murphy is handsome and bearded and props one boot casually on his knee. Cloyde Webb is serious and lean, his chin in his hand. The lenses of his glasses are like bubbles. They have been in county jail going on three years. The table is strewn with file folders, each six inches thick, stoutly labeled in laundry marker: *Murder*. Each of the defendants has two lawyers, and there are two state's attorneys. There are more lawyers than spectators in the courtroom.

After seven weeks the prosecution has rested. The defense has just completed preliminary statements and will now begin to present its case.

First witness is a personnel supervisor at Spiegel's Inc., where Cloyde Webb worked. A fair stocky man who has spent the last couple of hours on the pay phone in the corridor, feeding it dimes, looking at his watch. I overheard him promising a succession of auditors that he was sure to give his testimony today. "I've been waiting all week." Now he seems anxious to get down to business, laying out the documents he has brought with him to be entered in evidence. An employee attendance record, a punched time card. He leans toward the microphone, peering over his glasses. The stenographer lifts her face expectantly, her wrists bent above the keys. Both are eyeing the lawyer at the lectern.

"And now, Mr. Rizzo, will you read for the ladies and gentlemen of the jury—what is on that time card?"

The state's attorney looks up from the table. "Objection!"

The defense lawyer asks for a sidebar.

Apparently this is a conference out of hearing of the jury. The judge steps down in his robes. The four defense lawyers and the two state's attorneys go into a huddle with him in the corner of the room. The court stenographer follows, embracing her stenotype machine. She is a very short perky black woman in a purple pants suit. You can barely hear the murmur of their voices, but you can see her head poking sharply back and forth, her fingers sinking away.

They resume their places. The stenographer lifts her gaze, positions her hands.

"And now, Mr. Rizzo, do you happen to know where Cloyde Webb worked?"

"Objection!"

The judge thinks for a minute. "Objection… overruled."

"You may answer. "

"No."

"Is there any way you might refresh your memory?"

"Objection!"

"Objection… overruled. "

Now it is the state's attorney's turn to ask for a sidebar.

Chairs totter, feet scrape. This time they all march off to the judge's chamber, the little stenographer trotting at their heels. Light pierces the edges of the frazzled window shades. The men and women of the jury look at the defendants; the defendants look at the jury. Nothing passes between them. There is something about a courtroom that effaces emotion—expunges it. It's like a spell. Time has stopped. The courtyard of Sleeping Beauty's castle; the fires long dead in the hearth, the dogs and servants asleep. The large bailiff snorts a little, head nodding forward, arms folded on his chest.

The door opens, the lawyers file briskly to the table. They look angry, banging chairs, dropping pencils. As soon as they sit down they all start scribbling away at their yellow pads. The stenographer wriggles in her seat and loyally raises her eyes.

Mr. Rizzo is dismissed. He looks up: there must be some mistake. Is that all there is to it? He hasn't had a chance to utter one word of testimony. And the documents he gathers up—worthless; they will never be entered in evidence now. He grabs his hat and coat and edges toward the door, cautious, not exactly relieved. He looks as if he wants to run.

The defense calls the next witness. A heavy young black woman takes her place in the box, pushing up her specs with her forefinger. The clerk shuts his eyes; up goes his sleeve:

"…solemnly swear by the ever-livin' God…"

The state asks to approach the bench. The judge announces a short recess. It is half past three.

A journalism student was sitting up front, a spiral notebook on his lap.

"Hey," I said. "You have any idea what's going on?"

He nodded promptly. "Yes. It's called bullshit. The defense objected all the way through the prosecution's case, so now, it's their turn. That's how come this trial has been taking so long. The lawyers have used every delay in the book. And if that don't work they think up another. And with six of them—well, you can imagine. Someone's always late, or they don't show up altogether. I just feel sorry for the jury. You haven't seen anything yet. If you think this is something…"

A couple was sitting behind us. The woman leaned over the seat. "We thought maybe if they fined them," she said.

"Fines," her husband said, shrugging, without resentment. "Fines. Big deal. A lot they care."

They were the only other spectators. They belonged to the shopping bag. Both blond, roomy, blue eyed; he wore a zippered windbreaker, she wore stretch pants and red lipstick. They were younger than they looked. In other words, their affiliation was stamped. She dropped her eyes when she said that she had known one of the dead children. "Ever since she was a baby."

They had been discussing the chart in front of the judge's bench; they seemed familiar with the layout of the houses on Green Street. I asked if they lived there. "Not anymore," the husband said.

Chicago is the most segregated city in the country; that is its reputation. And it is true that to a great extent this is a matter of policy. Mayor Daley's neighborhood, Bridgeport, is a kind of museum; its composition, its crime rate—even rental prices—hark back to an earlier era. Practically the days of radio. It's that sort of dream. Urban life as a series of peaceful small towns: *The Aldrich Family, Fibber McGee and Molly, The Great Gildersleeve.* But that's the whole trouble; Chicago has never been integrated. Its constitution is basically suburban; homogeneous neighborhoods with well-defined borders; church parishes, company towns. When these barriers are breeched—when the dam bursts—when the bubble is popped— former residents flee. The great flat city tarred rooftops stretching as far as the eye can see—has an appearance of squat stability. It looks solid, stolid, permanent. What were the temples and pyramids to our stockpiles of brick? But there is no real strength, no welding force. A city isn't just a lot of people. Or is it? This is a city of migrations. Our covenant is weak.

Mayor Daley had his own idea for revitalizing the sinking city. Shopping centers. They would be built in the midst of various neighborhoods and equipped with all the things you can find in a *suburban* shopping center. Cocktail lounges, bowling alleys, barbershops, movie theaters. So people would never have to leave home. The solution to isolation is more isolation.

The mayor's critics cracked up. (They used to think he was *funny*.) His grammar was bad—that's always good for a laugh, right? As if his constituents didn't talk the same way. In newsreel close-ups, jowly, clucking, he resembled a mourning dove. But obviously Da Mayor knew his hometown—only too well. His scheme was true to its inner spirit. And his instinct was right; he put his finger on the problem. Where are our *sacred places*?

Now the diagram has been swung about to face the jury.

The new witness is Lotis Roche. At the time of the murders, she was employed as an aide by the Chicago Police Department and lived in the house on the diagram with her mother, her sister, her five-year-old son, her twelve-year-old nephew. Both defendants lived in the house next door, owned by Ryan Murphy's stepfather, "Mr. Bob" Tunstall. In all, eleven people lived in that house.

"Miss Roche, are you a friend of Ryan Murphy's?"

"Yes."

"Did you visit him in jail?"

"Once."

"Did you write him a letter?"

"Yes."

"Miss Roche..." The defense counsel's voice has been dramatically rising. He's not exactly stout, but his chest is high, his cheeks firm and ruddy. He has crinkly blond hair; rings glitter on his fingers. Just now he flashes them like a smile with gold fillings: "Miss Roche, would you lie for Ryan Murphy?"

"Objection, Judge!"

The state's attorney practically leaps to his feet, indignant, stung to the quick. He is what used to be called a *sheik*: pinstripe suit, pale jaws, slick black sideburns. It seems there is bad blood between him and the defense counsel.

It was a Wednesday. Coming home from work, Lotis Roche got off the bus at Fifty-Second and Halsted Streets at 5:00 P.M., and the first thing she saw was "Ryan Murphy and Leota Watkins ridin' around on a minibike." (Objection.) Ryan was wearing beige pants and gym shoes. (Objection!) As soon as they caught sight of the witness, they chased her home on the minibike. (Objection!)

After supper she went out front to mow the grass. It was 6:00 P.M. Ryan Murphy waved to her from his minibike. He was on his way to a baseball game. He took his feet off the pedals and signaled with both hands.

"Was he still wearing the same thing?"

"Objection, Judge! Can't you see how he's leading the witness?" The state's attorney flings down his pencil. The defense counsel turns to him

TWENTY-SIXTH AND CALIFORNIA

with exaggerated politeness, rubbing his hands. "I'm surprised at you, Mr. Irving. Really very—"

"Gentlemen," says the judge.

Lotis Roche waits, patient, pushing up her specs on her nose with her finger.

"What did he have on?"

"Nothing except his beige pants and gym shoes. "

Ryan Murphy grins, leaning back in his chair. Three witnesses have sworn they saw him holding a smoking shotgun. In police mug shots, with his face stiff muscled and the number plate hanging from his neck, he looked sufficiently desperate. The way anyone looks in a police mug shot. (Boy, I'm glad they rounded him up. What a hard character. Look at those eyes.) But this is the first you have any actual glimpse of him. Somebody's neighbor, clowning on a minibike. Showing off: Look, Ma, no hands.

This matter of what did he look like, what was he wearing, is universal in criminal cases. It has to be; a question of identification. But in a contemporary courtroom, in a city like Chicago with its divided population, the eternal class struggle boiled down to black and white, the theme takes on a more oblique significance.

Example: An armed robbery trial. The prosecution is grilling the defendant about his hairstyle. During the period in question he had changed it several times—from processed to braided to natural. The prosecution seems to think he was trying to alter his appearance to avoid detection. The defendant maintains it was only fashion. And as a matter of fact, you can see he's some dude. He has the good looks of a celebrity, a star athlete: tall, rangy, relaxed and lounging in the witness chair, the microphone intimately clasped in his knuckles. He exudes physical well-being, a natural superiority. He couldn't help it even if he wanted to. And for sure he doesn't want to. He seems patronizing, even a little amused, with the badgering questions, the pip-squeak lawyer. How often did he have to go to the barber with his natural? Every two weeks. How come he wore it combed some days, uncombed others? Because he felt like it. How long does it take for a process to grow out? Six weeks, maybe; all depends. (Hey, man, don't you know *nothing*?)

And the all-white jury. What are they supposed to make of this? How are they to judge? This is cultural shock.

"And what about that scar on your neck. You say you got it *on the tier*?"

Reticent—for the first time: "Someone scratched me."

"Someone stabs you. But you don't report it, you don't even go to the prison infirmary? "

"No, man. [Polite snicker.] You don't go reportin' every little old scratch you gits on the tier."

Example: Another armed robbery case. The lawyers are making summations to the jury. Two truck drivers, uncle and nephew, had parked their rig in an alley. They heard rushing footsteps, a man running toward them with drawn gun. One turned to the other: "Oh, shit, here it comes."

The defendant is the size of a twelve-year-old. He wears a mustache, and his hair is brushed stiffly forward—a horn, a tusk. He seems absolutely frozen; his elbows are stuck to the arms of his chair. He was picked up shortly after the robbery for a traffic violation, wearing a black raincoat, like the robber. Both uncle and nephew pointed him out separately in the lineup. They had seen the gunman for perhaps thirty seconds in a dark alley.

The prosecution contends this is long enough. "You get a good look at a man if he's shoving a gun against your chest." To make his point, he proposes to count off thirty seconds for the jury—to pace it off, in front of them—staring all the while at his watch. All you can hear are his shoes creaking. The silence is stifling; it seems interminable.

The prosecution rests. It's up to the defense. But the defendant hasn't been much help. Arrested for armed robbery, he was unable to recall three days after where he had been at the time. Nothing. No alibi. He just keeps denying the charge. This has been going on for three years. So this must be a public defender too—it's not likely that the accused, putting up no defense, has hired his own counsel. This lawyer seems inexperienced enough—clumsy, repeating himself, haranguing the jury.

"I submit to you, ladies and gentlemen of the jury, I submit to you… I don't say they weren't robbed in that alley. I don't say that. But, ladies and gentlemen, I submit to you…" If he says it once more! "I submit to you: How do you know this is the man?"

He is rapidly and seedily balding; a mustache, long hair (except for the crown), bell bottoms, platform shoes. To be sure, the client has not given him much to go on. What more can he do but question the identification? And his argument is more powerful than it appears. It goes straight to the heart of the matter—what's barely left unsaid:

*How do you know this is the man? How can you take their word for it? Could you be so sure? Come on—tell the truth. Don't they all look alike to you?*

Most judges snap out their rulings. Objection sustained! Objection overruled! This one likes to think it over. He pushes out his lip in a sort of half smile and rolls up his eyes. Very unnerving. I went to school with him; he was a staid and senior member of a friend's fraternity. It seems to me that even then he had the same small slow judicious smile. Here, in a courtroom, it doesn't make him seem fair. It makes him seem arbitrary. You get the feeling he's only guessing.

Lotis Roche cut, raked, and watered the grass. By that time it was getting dark. Some neighborhood boys were playing cards on the roof of Mr. Bob's white station wagon. (The state's attorney asks the stenographer to read back the names while he copies them out on his yellow pad. The defense counsel smiles down sardonically at the bent sleek black head—his hand on his hip; tapping his foot. His hair lifts and sticks out behind, same as his coattails.) Lotis Roche went into the living room and turned on the TV. The clock above the set said 8:00 P.M. She switched channels around, watching first a bit of a John Wayne movie, then settling for *Medical Center*. While she was watching, she heard a shot. She ran to the window.

She steps down from the witness stand to tap the diagram with a pointer, indicating the location of the windows on Green Street. Her habit—pushing her specs up—makes her look prim and schoolteacherish.

"As soon as you heard the shot, you ran to the window?"

"Yes."

"And what did you see?"

"I seen the boys jumpin' off the station wagon and takin' off in all directions."

"Objection!"

"We know that as a police aide you were trained to shoot pistols.

Now, was it a pistol shot you heard?"

"Objection!"

"Objection... overruled. "

"No. It was a shotgun."

"Oh, so police aides learn to shoot shotguns too?"

"Objection!"

"Objection... overruled."

"No."

"But you were familiar anyhow with the sound of a shotgun blast?"

"Yes, sure, I heard them lots of times. When we lived in the projects, why we moved to Green Street. They was shootin' shotguns day and night."

"Objection, Judge!" By this time the state's attorney is repeating it automatically, wearily, shutting his eyes, sulking in his seat. The defense counsel turns to the jury with a shrug, as if apologizing for a naughty child, holding up his hands.

"Gentlemen. Please."

Lotis Roche went into the kitchen. Her mother was at the back door, talking to Mr. Bob. He was saying she should call the police. Objection. The mother called the police. Objection. A few moments later a squad car appeared; from the window she saw her mother leaning down and talking to the police. Suddenly they switched on the revolving light. They backed up over the sidewalk, swung the car around, sped off in the opposite direction—going the wrong way—down Green Street. Lotis Roche went back to watching *Medical Center*.

Next thing she knew, there was more flashing. She went to the window. All of Green Street was full of squad cars with streaking blue lights. Policemen were jumping out the doors, running across the lawns, pistols drawn. They were heading for Mr. Bob's house. Lotis Roche ran into her sister's bedroom; that window overlooked the side entrance of the house next door. The policemen stood there, trying to kick the door down. One looked up and saw the two women's heads sticking out the window.

She quotes him: "'Niggers, you gonna get your heads blown off if you don't get back in.'"

"Did you and your sister go away then?"

"No; uh-uh." Shaking her head emphatically. Her large cheeks shudder. "We just went on hangin' out the window."

A few minutes later the police came out, dragging Ryan Murphy and pushing him along. He was wearing the same beige pants, "but only one gym shoe."

The judge declares a short recess. He calls the two lawyers to the bench. (Now they're gonna get it.) The jury files out, the defendants are marched away. The waddling bailiff brings up the rear, bangles of handcuffs dangling.

The two lawyers mutter with the judge. They turn away, cheerful. Two attractive young women have come in—thin, well dressed, smelling of makeup and perfume. They are the dates of the defense counsel and the state's attorney, and they all start talking about where to go for dinner, debating various noisy Greek restaurants on Halsted Street. They keep glancing toward the windows, as if they might be able to see and decide from here. Dusk lies radiant against the glass; the streetlamps are glowing like pearls in champagne. Lines of traffic spangle the expressways— nervous twitching lights, all glittering and struggling toward the same source, the same goal, drawn by some image of lurid beauty.

The two men lounge against the table, the one in his pinstripes and sideburns, the other with his rings and crisp hair, evidently the best of friends. It was all an act; they were putting on a show. Lawyers have a license to carry on—to get emotional in a courtroom. They're the only ones. You can walk through any door. "Mr. Rubinstein, you are the rudest man I ever…" "In all my years of practice, Your Honor…" Etc., etc. They wag their heads, click their tongues, look daggers, slump in the seats. It's all faked, staged—part of their job; part of the game. Like the slamming sprawling brawls in the Roller Derby, the grunts and whacking mats in a wrestling match. It's a kind of canned belligerence. They make their living off aggression, don't they? It's a substitute for the violence that has brought them here.

Because there is nothing sensational about a courtroom. Nothing emotional. All that is checked at the door. The violence is spent; even the grief. There is something more powerful than individual feeling. I can't say what it is, but you can see that everyone knows it. Everyone senses that impersonal force, undemonstrative, undramatic, in all these rooms, crowded or empty. That is the only thing that everyone feels. That is the only meaning in the passive faces on the benches.

Back in violence court, the baby is still crying; feeble whimpers. The matron, frowning, her fists in thick white cuffs on her hips, tries to look disapproving, as if that will make it stop. The mother has been called to the witness stand. She hands the baby to the grandmother and knots her black lace under her chin. In the box, her face is distant, pale, expressionless, looking from one official to another.

There will be an interpreter. They pass the microphone back and forth.

"Were you at 2515 West Eighteenth Street at approximately nine forty on the night of..."

The interpreter repeats the question. The woman answers in rapid Spanish. The interpreter repeats her statement simply.

"Yes, at the door of my house."

"Objection."

"Where were you?"

"At the door of my house."

"Did you see Xavier Nuñez?"

"Yes, he came to my house asking for my husband."

"Objection."

"Did he ask for your husband?"

"Yes, at the door of my house."

"Did you notice at the time that he had a knife?"

"Objection."

"Did you notice anything unusual about Xavier Nuñez?"

"Yes. He had a knife. And he asked for my husband."

"He asked for your husband, the deceased Alberto Ortiz?"

The face in the box turns indifferently toward the noise of the questions, then toward the face of the interpreter. The grandmother paces under the window, the baby in her arms, bouncing it up and down in her black shawl. It's night outside. Across the aisle sits a vast Mexican woman, helplessly fat, sprawling on the bench like a turtle on its back. She is as expressionless as the other women. Is there some connection between them? Does she have anything to do with the case?

Slowly, stammeringly, the story comes out. This is the way it must be in a court of law—arcane knowledge in the hands of professionals. It's all a question of what you get to put in or leave out. The whole story is never told.

The husband came down the street that very moment and saw his wife standing in the doorway talking to Xavier Nuñez. The two men started arguing. They crossed the street together. The wife stood in the doorway, watching to see what they would do. She saw Xavier Nuñez raise his knife. A car passed and she lost sight of the two men. When she saw them again, her husband was down on the sidewalk. Xavier Nuñez, astride him, the knife in his hand, was raising his arm again and again.

Objection! Objection! Objection!

Again and again the two men cross the street together, the wife watches from the doorway. Again and again the knife flashes, the car passes, the husband goes down. The witness turns her head this way and that, her voice as flat, unemotional, as the interpreter's. God knows what she makes of all this; why they have to keep asking the same questions over and over. Can't they get a simple story right?

"Mrs. Ortiz. Do you see the man who stabbed your husband in this courtroom today?"

The interpreter starts to repeat the question. Before she can even get it out, the woman has swung swiftly about. Her arm extends straight before her; her finger shoots out at the end of her hand. She is pointing toward the defense table with a classic gesture of accusation. A young man in a black suit stiffens in his seat, tosses back his hair. For the first time you see his handsome profile: hooked nose, sable mustache. It's as if a flash of lightning had struck a tree. So this is why she has come, all she was waiting for. Just this. To turn on him, point her finger, avenge her wrongs.

It's an archaic moment in the courtroom.

# PUBLIC FACILITIES

The most popular volume in the branch library was the medical dictionary. You had to ask. It was kept under lock and key in a glass case. Customers coughed behind their hands, trying not to look worried about their health. As if their troubles weren't plain enough. Watery sores, hoarse whispers, swollen legs, mackerel skins. One woman who kept coming in all winter long had something the matter with her nose. A hole in it; it was being eaten away. From her nose the condition progressed to her eye. The other eye—the one you could look at—twinkled and gleamed with classified secrets. At last she began to wear a bandage. That was too much. You couldn't help wondering what this bandage must be hiding—if it was still worse. Leprosy? The first thing I would think of. Our vocabulary of suffering is so limited. Maybe that's why these people were boning up.

But a lot of good. What was the use? It could only have sounded all the alarms, aroused fresh anxieties, deeper fears. The medical dictionary came back to the desk without comment. Miss Rose, the reference librarian, would seize the germy contaminated thing and lock it up again. Lock it up and then—she couldn't help it, kindly as she was, with her loud rude voice and knocking heels—she'd trot straight to the john and scrub her hands with green soap.

I lived in the neighborhood at the time, a few blocks' walk from my job at the branch, and saw a lot of this. There is more than urban poverty in Uptown. The population is largely Appalachian, American Indian, and they bring a special rural desolation. The streaked grime—melting snow—characteristic of the bricks of Chicago in winter, can be seen here even on the faces. Mexican, Korean, black, Puerto Rican, pensioned-off Jew: they get along more or less without racial strife. To tell the truth, that's the least of their worries.

Uptown lies a few miles north of the Loop along the lakefront, so it is bounded by high rises, motel architecture, rocky breakwaters, the twinge of lights on the Outer Drive. Lake Michigan spreads its deep blue rumor. Walls of glass greet the rising sun. First thing in the morning, salesmen are out cruising the streets slowly as cops in squad cars. Same thing goes on all afternoon—businessmen's lunch. These are the times when the younger and prettier girls work their shifts. Only the old warhorses come out at night. Bloated bare legs blue with bruises, plucked like turkeys in a meat locker. The bruises are like the bandage; it's no good guessing. But this is how you tell a whore in Uptown.

Public pay phones are always in use. You overhear the most personal conversations. "Oh, yeah? Who's threatening who?" a thin white woman in hair curlers says into the receiver. Her face is defended by pencil-trimmed eyes. A toddler with its thumb in its mouth clings to her slacks. "Suck my box, that's what you can do."

On Argyle, where the A train stops—a main drag—a couple of men and a woman are warming their hands over a fire in a trash can; passing a bottle in a wrinkled brown bag. The strip-mined faces of Uptown; drought; soil erosion; acts of God. The store windows are soaped, as for Halloween; the sidewalks look scabby; the fire smokes and snaps. The woman is wearing sunglasses, earmuffs, a fur coat split up the back. "This neighborhood is really going to the dogs," she is saying loudly, wanting people to hear. The undesirable elements, maybe? Who can they be? But all this means is that everyone is aware of degradation in Uptown. Everyone feels it. Everyone has the right to object.

"I'll drink to that," says one of her companions, tilting up his chin under the paper sack.

But Chicago winters are not all bad. We are a winter city, like Moscow; or, more to the point, Arkhangelsk, Vladivostok. Sometimes it gets cold, really cold; ten or fifteen below. An icy vengeful exterminating cold, sweeping down from the north like a moral force. Dung freezes in the street; germs drop dead; vermin starve. It strikes at corruption. Breathing seems less injurious. The air is pure and full of truth. Walking down Sheridan, Argyle, on my way to the library, I was in a position to appreciate this.

If not for the medical dictionary, there would have been hardly any traffic to speak of at our reference desk. Borglum Branch was not very busy. A sort of club of elderly gentlemen competed daily for possession of *Barron's* and the *Wall Street Journal*. Miss Rose kept the papers in her right-hand drawer, which smelled of wrapped mints. She was forever melting mints on her tongue; it made her look mischievous, up to something. Friendly, the permissive type. (Mrs. Speer, the head librarian, was the other—the watchdog type. Censorship by steely-rimmed stare. Hence the lurid books in locked cases.) If Miss Rose kept the papers tucked away, it was just an excuse, a decoy; so she could lure these shy old birds into a little conversation. "How are *you* today, Mr. Adorno?" She knew them all by name. A grittily poor neighborhood—despairingly poor; the most desperate, down and out in all the city; a terminal case; but the financial pages were in brisk demand, and the old men trembled when they asked—eyeing the drawer.

"You don't have today's? Yesterday's will do. "

Patrons—the regulars: the ones who showed up day after day and took the same places at the same tables—were familiar with our rules. Knew them better than we did. Any violation they took almost personally. They were very strict in particular about observing silence.

Something was the matter with the fan belt of the forced-air blower system. It made scandalized little noises. Tsk tsk tsk. The building itself was new: revolving glass doors, large plate windows—you could watch the icicles glibly dripping—but the reading room was the usual drowsy overheated affair: dim shelves, stacks of newsprint, tables of thick ugly honest oak and lampshades a suspicious green, like billiard cloth. And every time the heat went on it started clicking. The regulars objected to such distraction. This was supposed to be a library, wasn't it? People had a right to expect *quiet*. They knew their rights. Where else could they ever hope to enforce any.

But it was Miss Rose herself who was the heaviest offender.

I may as well get it over with—the whole description. The bright shy nearsighted gaze; the long cheeks puddled with rouge; the face dusted with powder like thick pink pollen. Miss Rose always seemed to be blushing. The glasses thumping on her nose, or—from a chain—on her flat sliding bosom. All this was loosely assembled. If she pushed in her blouse, her slip would peep out; if she hiked up her slip, a button would pop. Something had to give. You never could find a pencil when she was around. She stuck them all in her hair.

She hiked back and forth, lugging books—hugged to her chest, tucked under her chin—looking as if she was about to drop them. The only thing she never dropped was her voice. Even the regulars never got used to it.

Here was a new twist. The patrons telling the librarian to shut up.

"For shame, it's not ladylike," one gray-haired woman complained to me. "It's not *refined*. Who does she think she is? Anyhow? Acting like she owns the place."

Peevishly small; dainty; strings dangling from her plastic rain bonnet. Her gym shoes had no laces and her fur coat was fastened with diaper pins. "Her voice was ever soft, gentle, and low," she quoted, laying a finger to her lips. "Pass it on to Miss Rose, why don't you?"

Miss Rose had her admirers too. Mr. Herman had been after her to go out with him for years. He was another of our regulars: tall, bald, high-shouldered, stiff necked; rigidly polite. The back of his neck seemed very bare. His brows reached over the rims of his glasses. I think he had had a stroke at one time; the old man had a lip like a flat tire. It sagged when he smiled. He knew what hope was worth; a kite trapped in branches. Still he kept asking for the *Wall Street Journal*.

Miss Rose would hand it up, slyly sucking on her mint. But her voice reached all the way to the Zs. "You see? I was saving it. Just for you."

Armchairs were provided, sunnier spots before the big dusty windows. But regulars had no use for these. Wouldn't be caught dead. Too casual, maybe. Their habits were more rigorous. They were not here for browsing; that had to be understood. For them the library was an alternative to idleness. Lean men from the queues at the day-labor agencies on Wilson Avenue; old ladies speedy in sneakers, in fur coats fallen on evil days.

Pensioners poring over Moody's guides, Standard & Poor's, their hats at their sleeves. The fascination of the impoverished with the stock market reports seemed brutal to me, like the preoccupation of the diseased with the medical dictionary. Wouldn't they have been better off stuffing their shoes? But they were fans, like any others. For some it's sports, movie stars; for them it was the symbols of wealth and power. Age, failure, sickness, neglect; these were only temporary reversals. The utilities disconnected, the heat shut off. One could live with such interruptions. In the meantime, they dreamed of killings. The thin pages—*Barron's* airmail edition—rattled in their shaky hands. The reverence of old age.

Let us speak frankly. Where are people to go? People, I mean, who have no place to go. There are no clean well-lighted places. Bus stations are sorrowful, with all those black boxes that come to life if you drop in a quarter. The downtown movie houses which used to stay open all night—the ushers nudged you by the shoulder if you started snoring out loud—have changed over to porno flicks and charge too much money. I am thinking, of course, of the Clark Theater. The Clark was once the most illustrious of such institutions. It *was* an institution—a cultural crossroads. The Clark served art too. The odors of winos' holey socks mingled powerfully with the dust of Desenex in college boys' sneakers. This is Chicago, you have to understand. We are not in the same line of business as Paris, London, or New York. Though what our line of business is I'd dearly love to know.

What if it has something to do with places like the Clark.

It stayed open twenty hours out of the twenty-four. Tickets were cheap, the double bill changed daily. Another thing that changed very often was the seats. Patrons popped in and out of them with strange regularity. Watching *Grand Illusion, The Thirty-Nine Steps,* you couldn't help taking in all this restless activity out of the corner of your eye.

The seats squeak. Half of them are broken. Eyes slide—oily surfaces in the flickering light. Under folded jackets, in hidden laps, fingers are creeping. Hey. What's this? A hand on my thigh? Out of the dark your neighbor shoots a weasel-faced glance. Slowly, stealthily, with painful efforts at concealment—extra distracting—his zipper starts to creak. Just a little at a time. Same way the ladies in the balcony peel their candy bars.

The ladies gallery in the balcony is a special feature of the Clark. "For Ladies Only." This does not necessarily mean for the fainthearted. Some come to make themselves at home; straddle their seats boldly. Two seats, three seats, a shopping bag on either side. Even their wigs sit sidewise. The shopping bags get noisier as they get emptier.

Sometimes it happens that a man turns up in the Ladies Gallery— maybe he didn't notice the sign. A likely story. As far as the ladies are concerned, it's intentional. If looks could kill. All up and down the rows they are stabbing him with hatpins. Get a load of this guy. Sneaking down, trying to make himself look small; making off he just wants to watch the movie. Uh-huh. We know what he wants. Take advantage of your tired, your poor, your huddled masses, will he? The lousy bum can't even *read*.

Someday the worm will turn, the meek will inherit the earth, the righteous will be justified. But not yet. Is nothing sacred? A man is occupying the Ladies Gallery.

*Now* what's wrong with this fellow next to you? He hasn't stopped squirming for a minute. All of a sudden he stiffens in his seat—you can feel it jerk. His heels grip, his head flies back. A few small defenseless whimpers; then a grunt, a very minor satisfaction. The seat sags, the tension goes. He jumps up right away, his jacket limp over his arm. No rest for the wicked. Off to look for another seat.

His place is taken at once—at sixty cents a head the Clark gets crowded—but this time it's a more familiar type. A classic. The Clark Street panhandler: an old-fashioned, inoffensive derelict—upturned collar, jaw sugared with whiskers. Clothes brown and dusty as leaves in a gutter. He loosens his shoelaces, stretches his legs. His chin starts to sink, his head nods to his chest. With a loud snickering snore it drops on your shoulder.

Saturday nights it was the motorcycle crowd, like divers in wet suits in tight black leather. The sailors from Great Lakes, cheeks hidden in their collars. For all I know they're still there. Like the mirrors that seem to be blasted with buckshot; the toilets that keep running but never flush; the carpets that remind you of small animals flattened on a highway; no telling what they were once upon a time either. Though the management must have taken down the Fred Astaire posters. The Clark no longer serves the same mission.

On the last night before the change in policy, a brawl broke out. A drunk got rowdy, broke a bottle, started wielding its jagged neck. No one wanted to get near him. The audience whistled and stamped as if something had gone wrong with the soundtrack. At last a lanky shape detached itself from a seat on the aisle and pointed a gun. It was very dark, of course, hard to see. But all the movie aficionados recognized the weapon, the steely gleam. We weren't Humphrey Bogart fans for nothing.

"Hey, you. Yeah, you. You spoilin' my view. I'se fixin' to watch the movie."

It was an Orson Welles festival. *The Magnificent Ambersons.* Bustles, ostrich plumes, Joseph Cotten. The ushers arrived. The drunk left gladly. Other patrons followed him in droves—chased him through the lobby, swinging shopping bags and salvaged newspapers. They were the ones with the real beef. Just trying to get even. Who can afford three bucks? Who wants to watch dirty movies? Where would they go tomorrow?

At least the public libraries are still in business.

We had our flurries of activity.

On Friday afternoons, the barroom bets. On payday people get into aimless arguments. World records, batting averages; the age of the pope; the name of President McKinley's assassin. This would mean a delegation; three, four heavyset men, hot under the collar, elbowing and shoving. "This the reference?"

They fixed their eyes on the green blotter.

"We want to see a book. 'If,' a poem by Rudyard Kipling."

"'If you can keep your wits when all about you—'"

"It's *head*, stupid. "

"*Wits*, nitwit. *Wits*. "

"And I say it's *head*. "

"It's *head*," I said, looking up.

Wrong move.

They all glared down at me. Solid stares. What are you, a wise guy or something? Who's asking you? Even the one who had his money on *head* was against me, his lip lifting at the corner, his face redder than the rest. I couldn't help thinking of the social-protest films of the thirties—the ones they used to run all the time at the Clark—the scene where the gang of striking workers with hats in their hands confronts the big boss, smoking and swiveling. Did I expect them to take my word for it, just because I was sitting behind a desk?

"Talk is cheap, sister. Can you show us in a book? "

That was the catch. I didn't know where to find anything. Couldn't make heads or tails of the reference desk. I was a library *intern*—maybe they called it *technician*. Something scientific anyway. I forget. To me what mattered was that you could work halftime. And with the public library— nothing if not literal—half really meant half. Eighteen and three-quarters hours, half the thirty-seven-and-one-half-hour week. Half the vacation pay, half the sick leave, half the insurance coverage. And so on. Anyone who has ever had a part-time job will know that this was not a bad deal. Once again, I was in a position to appreciate. I've had a lot of part-time jobs in my life.

One of our patrons was on to me. He came in regularly with a quotation for me to look up. "Let's see. What'll it be this time? I know—how about Thoreau? That business about the distant drummer. That oughta be real easy for you. I'll even give you a hint. The odds are on *Walden*."

He was a big, red-faced, Sterno-breathed man in a peacoat and blond crew cut—picked rough rows sticking up—usually towing a little boy by the mitten strings. This kid was bundled within an inch of his life—a papoose on a board. He could barely move his legs, they were so stuffed in boots and leggings, and his hood, pulled down and puckered over his eye, made him look mad at the world. His nose was always running.

"How about this here book?" the father would say, tapping the glass. Our reference books also stood guard behind glass. Stooping and squinting at some cracked gold-stamped binding. "*Beloved Hymns and Popular Verse*. Hmm. On second thought, that's not so hot. Tell you what—don't mess around. You want to make things easy for yourself, just look it up in *Bartlett's*."

A friendly warning from your local vigilante. Did they make the rounds, visit other branches too? As time went by, he gave up on the introductions. He'd just march up to the desk, stand stock still, square his shoulders, hook his thumbs in his belt loops.

"'Shoot if you must this old gray head / But touch not your country's flag she said.'"

The little boy frowned at me and licked his clear shining lip.

But the one outstanding fact of life at Borglum Branch—the fact that so many of our patrons seemed to have nowhere else of any significance to go—was never mentioned. It was unmentionable. "She's very good with the old people," I heard Mrs. Speer saying into the phone. (A conversation about Miss Rose's everlasting promotion?) She meant the regulars. But she did not know that that was what she meant. Regulars weren't a category, weren't official. There was no way to count them, so they didn't count. Regulars didn't even have library cards. What for? Who needed cards? They practically lived in the library.

Popkin, a thin, scraggly, timid-looking soul with a scrawny neck and a military overcoat that dragged to his ankles—Russian Army issue—went tottering in and out of the stacks to a rapid shuffle. Toppling almost— pitched forward, on tiptoe—his eyes lifted in a startled expression. His white hair was thick as a cocoon and clamped in earmuffs, big black patches, that gave him the look of a horse in blinders. He always carried a book under his arm, pressed to his side. He was hatching it.

Miss Rose told me that he was a poet.

But what if you said, "But, Miss Rose, have you noticed? Popkin comes every day? All day? And night? In and out of the stacks—on tiptoe?" What would happen if you said this?

And what about Judge Brady? Not a real judge; he just looked like one. In the South they would have called him "Colonel." His profile plunged forward, his hair plowed back—stiff, erect, slick white goose feathers. His brow was polished and brown with freckles; his chin was doubled. The whole bust gave off a thick ruddy glow. Age had not diminished him; he loomed with it, powerfully, like a pile of rock.

It was a pleasure to watch him take his seat. First he unwound the long scarf from his neck, folded his coat, laid his hat on top of it over the back of the chair. He shook out his handkerchief, whisked it over the table, and laid his magnifying glass on top of that. He fished his watch out from under its flap and wound it with his thumb, consulting the clock on the wall. He put it back. He placed both hands on the table, lowered himself and scraped in his chair. At closing time the whole show ran backward. He pushed out his chair, raised himself up; two fingers digging his watch pocket—this wouldn't have been possible sitting down—looked at his watch, looked at the wall. Suddenly remembering another engagement. As if regulars ever left before closing time. Yes, what about him.

Or Mr. Adorno. At eighty, writing the story of his life. It was the story of his opinions, actually; he was against coeducation and in favor of the Kerensky government. A tidy little man, a baked-apple face, eyes enlarged inside his glasses. His teeth too; clamped like a vise. This gave him a fierce look when he came up to the desk and asked me to read back to him what he had written. "To make sure it's eligible." He used ruled notebooks, but his handwriting was too big to stay on the lines. And I think he just liked to agree with himself; listening, lost in admiration, his eyes lurking, motionless, in their depths. "Yes, yes. That's right. Right absolutely." His starched collar looked sharp enough to slash his throat. His fountain pen leaked—there was a spreading blue blot on his nice white shirtfront. "That hits the nail right on the head."

Of course, there were cranks. For instance, a tall straight old woman, dressed in gray from head to foot, like a Quaker or Civil War nurse, with a strange flat yellow face, with feet laced up in combat boots... she had been sighted all over the city; a familiar figure at downtown hotels during conventions. She just dropped in to use the plumbing. The toilet flushing continuously. It went on without letup. What could she be up to in there? Who was about to go in and look? You just had to wait until she decided to emerge, dripping wet, long, stringy, gray as a mop, slapping the key on the counter and sloshing out the door. Her boots tracking squishing puddles. It was the dead of winter.

This, I admit, roused a few eyebrows; glances were exchanged, wild surmise. But that was all. Our business was books; checking them in, stamping them out. Cataloging. Shelving. Minding our own business. At Borglum the level of tolerance for individual extremes was very high. It had to be—the facts were too peculiar. You couldn't let on, let the cat out of the bag. That would have meant acknowledging... all this other business. And that was the one thing that couldn't be tolerated. To have characterized the services of the public library in this way.

And what of the board of directors meetings downtown, at the main branch, the limestone white elephant on Michigan Boulevard? Guards, uniforms, badges posted everywhere; at the turnstile entrances, outside the public lavatories, on marble staircases with high carved mottoes. MCMXL... PRO BONO PVBLICO... Funny things go on in libraries; everyone knows that. It's got something to do with all those stacks; shelves and shelves of weighty books. Reason is a passion; an instinct, a drive. It's not so strange if citizens respond in its temples with primitive gestures; flashing switchblades, unzipping flies. Plans were being drawn for the expansion and remodeling of the old building—its crossed swords, draped flags, shimmering flocks of pigeons. It couldn't be torn down; it could only be surrounded.

Did anyone ever get up at these meetings and say: "Fountains, shmountains. Do you think the bums from Clark Street will go for this? After all, they're the ones who spend the most time here. And what about the little old ladies with the shopping bags? If we make the joint look like Marshall Field's or Saks Fifth Avenue, will they feel at home?"

There were two schools of philosophy in the public library. One was that it existed for the sake of circulating books. The other was that it existed for the sake of preserving them. This is what it all boils down to, eventually, with any bureaucracy in the public service. Mrs. Speer belonged to the Public Enemy school.

She was nearing retirement—with some relief. Harried gray braids, wisps escaping; pale eyes fused to glass. She wore tailored suits and frilly blouses and the ruffles rode and swelled at her throat. She had no chin; when her upper lip snapped down, she looked like a turtle. Even patrons trying to return books were challenged at Borglum. They had to show identification. "Just in case." In case what? "You never know." Mrs. Speer was proud of this rule—the only one like it in the city—but she knew I hated to ask; so she kept a sharp eye out whenever I worked behind the circulation desk. And as soon as she saw someone bursting through the doors with an armload of books, she'd come rushing out of her office, giving the ends of her jacket a smart yank with her knuckles.

"Don't you dare go letting them give any books back till they show who they are."

Borglum was losing customers steadily—but not so fast as it was losing books. Pasted above the checkout machine—where we could refer to it while stuffing pockets and stamping cards—was a list of delinquents: big-time offenders who owed hundreds of dollars in overdue fines and AWOL volumes. Names like Rockett J. Squirrell, J. Edgar Hoover, Hedy Lamarr. Books came back with bindings loose, pages ripped out, pictures defaced—mustaches, pubic hair, scratched in ballpoint pen. Some seemed to have been on a bender: dropped in hot bathtubs, propping windows. Greasy thumbprints, shopping reminders, telephone numbers, comments in the margins: "Bull." "That's what you think." "Proof?" "How true." These were the ones we got back—if we were lucky. The Public Enemy theory has its points.

Mrs. Speer's efficacy as a supervisor may have been rated in terms of circulation. But in her own heart she knew that her job—her sacred trust—was to protect the public from itself. There is a certain socialized insanity. (Once we start calling people cranks, where will we draw the line?) Schoolteachers used to be a prime example—I don't know if they are still. I recall a note pinned to the bulletin board in my high school principal's office—from a teacher who had retired to a chicken farm. I had been in her English class. We read *Ivanhoe*. That is, she read it aloud to us; sitting behind her desk, her cheek in her hand. A flowered smock, a crimped blue head. On her desk, under her desk, piled on windowsills, radiators, and from head to foot when she opened her closet, were stacks of colored notebooks. Theme papers. They were all on *Ivanhoe*.

You didn't get a grade if you didn't hand in a notebook. But everyone knew how grades were distributed in Miss Bozzich's class. Neat girls got E, girls who wore lipstick and blue jeans G. Short boys rated F. And boys who were tall, who had already outgrown the childish seats, whose long legs sprawled arrogantly in the aisle—i.e., bad boys—failed. Period. There was no appeal.

Each day, before Miss Bozzich began to read, someone had to get up in class and tell "the story thus far." As we progressed with the novel, these daily summaries naturally got longer. Besides, we were catching on; some of us could be long-winded. By the time we had finished with "the story thus far," and just about when Miss Bozzich—licking her fingertip, making a little light breeze of the pages—had found her place, the bell would ring. The nasty buzzer. Tin lockers slammed in the corridors. The heathens were on the march. We had reached an impasse. I remember the small stingy print, the crumbly paper—it broke off like soda crackers— pennants, visors, dark Rebecca. But we never got past page ninety-nine. Next semester it would begin all over again. English 1 2 3 4 5 6 7 8. No one ever finished *Ivanhoe*.

"My little chickadees are so nice and polite—so well behaved—so much more grateful than my thankless pupils ever were," poor Miss Bozzich had written.

Mrs. Speer already had her chickens.

These were the new books, stacked on a table in the back room in tall neat rows. On top of each pile a note: "Do Not Disturb, J. Speer." Mrs. Speer was cataloging these books, and whenever she got the chance she would shut herself up with them. Books on the shelves were marked-down merchandise—spoiled, soiled, grubby, touched by too many hands. Here they confronted her in their original splendor. New books don't smell as good as they used to—it must be the glue—but the bindings were still stiff and the pages fresh. Each and every one that came into Borglum Branch headed straight for the back. And it stayed there. When the table couldn't hold any more, stacks sprouted under the legs; then on filing cabinets, chairs. You didn't dare to move them. They were like that For A Reason. If things ever got mixed up, Mrs. Speer would have to Start All Over Again.

The thing was, the cataloging had already been done—at the downtown library. The books came carded, pocketed, and numbered, and all that was left were a few clerical tasks. Once upon a time cataloging had been the special responsibility of the head librarian. Now there had been a reorganization; the librarians had been freed from their musty cubbyholes, ordered—in other words—into circulation. The job had switched from archives to public relations. That was the idea—not Mrs. Speer's idea at all. She had put up with it at first. Then her husband died. It was a bad time for her. She resumed cataloging.

But there was too much for her to do; she couldn't make up her mind; she had lost the knack for decisions. Should it be 813? 973? You see? She talked about her "problems," the "tough nuts" she had "to crack." (Mrs. Speer loved slang; she was always pouncing on Miss Rose with a conniving sort of wink: "It's snowing below!"—Your slip is showing.) This was the secret of her mistreated glance and raveled braids.

It was the reason I had been hired; Mrs. Speer thought she wanted an assistant. She took me into her confidence—into the back room—and showed me the books mounting up, each separate pile with its own separate note. Weeks went by; no instructions. She put me to work typing file cards for volumes long retired from the shelves—"for practice." Then I arranged and rearranged stacks of yellow-bordered *National Geographics*. Once I came upon her, humming, floating a pink feather duster over the books. Up went her ruffles; down went her lip. She hid the duster behind her back. She wasn't ready to relinquish her task—that is to say, the books.

Maybe she was protecting them in this way. Why catalog? Why file? Why put books on the shelves? Why send them off to meet their fate—abandon them to the inevitable? Why start the whole damned thing all over again? She was weary of it all, the endless cycle, dreariness, decline, destruction. As I say, she had spent too much time in public facilities.

What with one thing and another, it was proving difficult to find a place for me at Borglum Branch. Regular employees were civil service; they had been fingerprinted at city hall. They already had their places, their allotted tasks, and did not wish to share them. Beebee, perched on her high stool at the circulation desk, hunched over in characteristic bad posture, was not less protective of her overdue notices than Mrs. Speer was of her new books. Beebee was a bookworm, always hiding some contraband in her lap—staff was not permitted to *read*, one of Mrs. Speer's phobias—and that was why she was always hunched over like that; glancing down possessively while her white fingers rippled the files. She was a lip-reader; the avid movements gave her away. A striking disorderly head; a thrusting nose; heavy Sephardic eyes. Her hair was coarse, crinkly, and black as the wire pins that—more or less—skewered her bun.

The bony ridges poked up on the back of her neck. The rich pink gums glowed when she smiled.

Beebee had a star-crossed love; her boyfriend, Henry, was not Jewish. It was supposed to be a secret. He met her at the branch—came to stand and gaze, leaning across the counter; her lips moving busily the while, her black head ducking over the files. He was tall, thin, in gym shoes and foggy glasses, and for a young man he was quickly losing his hair. After they said hello, that was it. They never seemed to need another word. From time to time, heaving a sigh, sinking her elbows onto her lap, Beebee would raise heavy eyes and gaze back.

Their romance was our current event; what we talked about over breaks in the kitchen while the teakettle whistled and the brown bags crackled. Should Beebee leave home and marry Henry? Defy her parents? Deny her faith? What if Henry converted? He looked convertible. Etc., etc. Beebee loved being the center of attention. Listening to advice, sipping sweet tea, her glance grew high crested and dreamy. Still, she was a private and secretive soul. Most of us kept our lunches in the refrigerator, but Beebee stowed hers in her locker—bananas and all—her head poking behind the tin door as sharply, jealously, as it darted over her files. Fines, overdue notices, all that privileged information. You'd think she had something hidden in there. Books. The worst thing you can hide—in a library.

The clandestine had a natural appeal for Beebee. But Miss Rose took an anguished interest in her story; Miss Rose had a story of her own. At college she had been engaged to a medical student. Drafted as a medic, he was killed in the war. And after Stanley was killed…

"Well, after Stanley was killed, I knew I'd never find another man as good. 'What's the matter with you, Dora?' my mother would say. 'Why do you have to be so *choosy*? Do you want to end up with nothing? Is that what you want? Isn't any man in the world good enough for you?' Well, that wasn't it, but I just couldn't help it. She wouldn't understand. Not after Stanley."

She held her cup in both hands, her elbows planted on the table, steeped in bracelets; these bangles had a way of sliding up her thin arms. Her light eyes, flush with the level of steaming tea, filled and dimmed with reminiscences. When Miss Rose took off her glasses, her face was defenseless altogether. After Stanley.

I used to urge Miss Rose to take Mr. Herman up on his offer. People were always urging Miss Rose. "Why not go out with him? He looks presentable. He seems to be a gentleman."

"Oh, he is, he is." Miss Rose would hasten to defend him; after all, he was a suitor. "He is a gentleman. A gentleman of the old school. A gentleman and a scholar. You don't know Mr. Herman like I do."

"So? How come? What's the big deal?"

It seemed that she liked to be teased in this way. She didn't mind it, on a cold night, waiting at her bus stop. The spaces were wide and dark between the arc lamps and she was afraid to stand alone. Safe to talk when your bus was coming.

Who didn't urge Miss Rose? If she took a certain exam and passed it, she could become a head librarian herself with a branch of her own, and her salary would jump considerably. Everyone wanted her to do it. But Miss Rose was afraid to take this exam; she shuddered at the thought of it. The very mention sent her fluttering. And it must have been mentioned with some regularity; it had been going on for years. Like Mr. Herman.

"I don't know, I don't know," she said, glancing up the street. The lights of the bus coming to the rescue, sweeping snow before it, threshing it like wheat. She peeled off her glove to get at her change. She carried the exact fare in her mitt. "After all. After Stanley."

"Oh, Miss Rose. Don't give me that. You know yourself it's all a lot of baloney."

She put her head to one side in her fluffy angora hat, with its jingling sequin chains. Her tongue tasted her mint. "Yes," she said. "Yes, I know it." And climbed aboard in her galoshes.

What hope was there for Mr. Herman—keeping an eye on IBM, Bunker Ramo, and Xerox but stuffing his money in a mattress, a shoe, the lining of his coat? It looked lumpy. What chance did he have against a dead man, a war hero, and a doctor on top of it? How disappointed he looked whenever he found me sitting at her post. Lifting his eyebrows and laying his hat against his chest:

"No Miss Rose tonight?"

It was not that Miss Rose needed or wanted my assistance any more than anyone else; but she was softer than anyone else. She gave in. That was how I ended up passing most of my eighteen and three-quarters hours at the reference desk—the one place in that moribund facility where there really was the least to do. This was the backwater of backwaters. The fan belts clicked, icicles dripped; Judge Brady focused the light in his curved reading glass.

It was Miss Rose's responsibility to lock up most late nights, and it worried her to death. She was no authoritarian; not a bossy bone in her body. But some people don't like to be waked from their sleep. There were always patrons who objected. "Whaddaya mean, closing time? It's only five to nine." We closed at nine. When Alphonse, the page boy, came rolling and rumbling his cart through the reading room, dumping books, clicking and dimming lights, it was taken as a personal insult. Regulars had squatters' rights.

There was one gaunt heavy-shouldered man who used to sit in the same position by the hour, his fingers bunched up, scooping his eyes. He came with a companion—another familiar type of the neighborhood: a mass of raw bones, dry hair, haggard fur. But she had been a beauty, had squandered great gifts; there was still a haughty distinction in her style. Her coat thrown open, her chair thrust back, her shins bare. When the time came she would reach out and shake him by the shoulder. Not everyone could be persuaded so gently. Shaken by the shoulder, they might not take it so well. Their sunken heads would lift with a growl. Their souls, off wandering, had not made it back.

Miss Rose could rise to the occasion.

"If you don't go quietly," she would say, her voice quavering and her eyes glittering a little above her rouge, "then—well, then—we'll just have to get the page boy here to throw you out."

Alphonse's dark eyes lustrously widened. He was a high school student, a tall black youth—very tall; stooping; dawdling, dreamy; shooting up so suddenly to such a height seemed to have exhausted his energies— who kept to himself and had no inclination for being drawn out, either. He looked for cover behind his cart. At such times we were reminded of our lack of manpower. Another fact of life in a branch.

Beebee had been followed to her el station by one of our patrons. We all knew who this was. A slight young man—probably older than he looked—in leather jacket and blue jeans, with a high white forehead and rough blond hair. The kinky ridges clinging, clenched tight. He sat at the table, a pile of notebooks open before him, fists shoved into his pockets, shooting out cunning sidelong glances. He had a tic of some sort, a muscle jumping in his jaw. It made him look as if he might be grinning, but you couldn't tell for sure—he kept it up all the time. One foot never stopped tapping under the table; one patched knee jerked constantly up and down.

As soon as Beebee saw him, she scrambled off the stool and hid herself behind the high hedge of the circulation desk. He looked her way, grinning. He slid his fountain pen from inside his jacket, crouched over as if to write; thought better of it; hid the pen again. Someone might be eavesdropping on him—stealing his thoughts—tuning in on his secrets. The world was watching him, wondering about him, trying to guess; he had to be careful, clever, and sly.

It was a dreary night, fit only for regulars. Darkness crowded the windows, Alphonse's cart rolled over the boards. Judge Brady, at the same table, was peering through his magnifying glass, his head reared back, his lips clasped in satisfaction. Someone snored under the green lampshade, a cheek on an arm. As for the gray-haired woman with the agile eyes and the diaper pins, it was Miss Rose as usual she was watching. What could that loud—that brazen—creature be up to now?

Miss Rose strode up, heels rapidly battering, her glasses on their chain pounding against her chest. No sooner had she leaned down to the young man—his head, half-hidden, seemed to be crouching behind his shoulder—than he was up with a bound. His chair crashed backward. His fist struck the table.

"Goddamn all you lousy Jews. Always telling people what to do. I'm not taking any orders from you."

"Please lower your voice," Miss Rose said thickly, her heart at once in her throat. "Please remember. This is a library."

"Don't have to fuckin' tell me what it fuckin' is. Full of fuckin' niggers and Jews. That's all you got. Think you're running the whole goddamn show."

There was a murmur throughout the room. The financial pages stopped rustling. "Such langwidge," the old lady whispered, clicking her tongue. Then all you could hear were the fan belts clicking. Tsk tsk tsk.

"If you feel that way—if that's the way you feel…" Miss Rose fingered her chain. The artificial color stood out in her cheeks. "If you're not going to keep your voice down…" But no one was listening. She wasn't listening herself. He had all the attention now. And he knew it. Glancing round craftily, his jaw clenching and grinning, taking it all in. All the shocked wrinkled faces, the Woolworth's specs pressing their cheeks like paperweights.

"Don't have to fuckin' tell me to fuckin' leave," he said, piling up his books with a thump. "I'm leaving, all right. I'm leaving. But I'll be back." He zipped his jacket to his chin and tossed his head. "I'll be back. And when I come you better look out. You better get ready for me, I'm warning you. Because I'm going to fix all you lousy creeps if it's the last thing I do."

"*Oh, yeah?*"

This was Mr. Herman, rising, drawing up his shoulders. "Why don't you start right now, then?" He slammed his hat on the skin of his head.

"*Oh, yeah?*"

Mr. Adorno. He kicked out his chair. His glasses had a dark sparkle. All over the room chairs were scraping. Pensioners rising; sleepers waking. The boy threw his books down and put up his fists. His elbows in leather sleeves gripped his chest. The old men too put up their fists, began moving in, waving their arms. They danced up and back and pumped up and down. Old-fashioned boxers with old-fashioned rules. Judge Brady stood firm, one foot planted forward, one arm doubled up in front of the other, his chin to his chest. His back was most honorably arched.

Miss Rose tugged Mr. Herman's sleeve. He shook her off. "He started it." The back of the old man's neck stood stiff. They were waiting for the other to swing first. He did. His arm shot out, snapped back; his jaw gave a twitch. The old woman gasped; this was for real.

Mr. Herman took his swing. His arm stuck out like a bat; it swung him halfway about. He missed by a mile. The boy rocked back and forth, his head dodging and ducking behind his raised knuckles.

"C'mon, c'mon. What's the matter? Chicken? I thought you wanted a fight. Hey, you old boys. You old bums. C'mon. How about it? What are you waiting for? Six against one. You're all a bunch of crazies, you know that? Misfits. That's all you got."

The situation was getting serious. I mean sensitive. It wasn't so much that we were afraid he was going to land a punch and hurt anyone—though his knuckles looked sharp, they could mark an old face. But what if one of the boxers should have a heart attack and drop right on the spot? That was the danger. All this dancing, hard breathing, crowding the enemy. Such excitement was too much for them. But who was going to say it? There are injuries and injuries. They were sick and tired too; sick and tired of being old, weak, damaged, done for, counted out. They weren't taking any more. They had had enough. The worm was turning, the meek were inheriting the earth. It wasn't the time to call attention to the facts.

"Isn't this the *limit*?"

The little old lady clasped her hands to her chin. She was in seventh heaven. Mr. Adorno was hopping up and down, thumbing his nose and baring his big teeth. Popkin was tiptoeing round and round, hugging his book tenderly under his arm. A punch landed. Oof. Whose? Where? They had him surrounded, they were closing in. A stringy arm hooked him by the collar, another by the belt. "That's right, boys," Judge Brady shouted. "The back of the neck and the seat of the pants."

"I'll get even—I'll get even." His heels were kicking; they had pinned his sleeves to his sides.

"Let's show him the door, boys."

They hoisted him up and hustled him out. All you could see was a head hanging forward, the shoulders of the leather jacket lifted like football pads. "Kikes. Crazies. Niggers. Bums. Look at you. All of you. They oughta lock you all up."

Pretty soon the police arrived, a low-slung pair in fur-collared jackets. They stood dripping and wiping their caps. It had started to snow and heavy clots were sliding off and melting all around them.

They settled their caps on their heads. "Now. What's this all about? What seems to be the trouble?"

It was past nine, but none of the regulars had left and no one expected them to. Now everyone started talking at once. Everyone seemed to have a complaint to make, an insult, an injury. They had been saving it up. Now was the chance. The old woman fastened the strings of her rain bonnet under her chin. What was the world coming to? You heard every-thing these days. Why just the other—Miss Rose, under compulsion, was forcing herself to repeat the threatening words. Beebee, still ducking be-hind the desk, was telling of the times she had been followed. Mr. Adorno had heard noises under his window. Someone had seen a knife. The cops, listening to all this, were more and more and more unmoved. They didn't exactly look at anybody. Their eyes grazed over the faces. The weak, the outraged, the indignant. *Big* deal. Hey, grandpa. Isn't it about time you were home in bed? Now and then they glanced at one another; you could see what they were thinking. Kikes. Crazies. Niggers. Bums.

They held up their hands. "Okay, okay. Cool it. Everyone. Pipe down. Now. One at a time. Let's have it again."

"And here's Judge Brady. And he'll tell you. He saw the knife."

"Judge?" said the cop, "Is he really a judge?" For the first time lifting his eyes and looking round with a flicker of interest. Judge Brady had post-ed himself outside to keep watch. He came in to report. His scarf was drag-ging, his galoshes unbuckled; he was hoarse with excitement and blowing his nose on his sleeve. His face was the color of a bowl of borscht.

"Snowing so hard you can't tell much," he trumpeted, and dashed out again.

The cop looked sleepy. He went to the desk and asked Beebee for the key; he wanted to use the bathroom. "Give us another call if this guy shows up again," the other said, taking a look around; a last browsing glance. Some dump. For the second time that night, the unmentionable had almost been mentioned.

The officers left and we locked up. Came a pounding at the door, a face pressed to the glass. It was only Henry, calling for Beebee. He had come to take her to her el stop. Patrons, staff made the rounds together; peeping in lockers, round doors, testing latches, switching lights. In the back room Mrs. Speer's books towered undisturbed. Ziggurats. When Miss Rose had locked the front doors, she turned around and locked them again, her fingers fumbling with the keys. Then she flung the keys down the mouth of the book depository. She never carried them off with her. What if she took that exam and passed it? That's what she was afraid of. Bad enough to have to lock up on dark nights.

It was snowing forcefully by now; not one of your fresh swirling fleecy snows. It wasn't going to be a white Christmas. This was a wet cutting sleet and the wind off the lake was blowing it all sideways. It seemed yellow in the lamplight, the sidewalks soaked. All those bare legs, gym shoes, cracked soles, creaking in the mush. It grappled with coat collars, clutched at necks. The streetlights were melting. Judge Brady and Mr. Adorno appointed themselves to escort the old lady. Others trudged off, looking back over their shoulders; remembering the late hour and the grimness of the neighborhood. As if such general misery were not a safe conduct.

Mr. Herman—trying to touch his hat brim in the slashing sleet—offered his elbow and asked Miss Rose if he might see her home. She demurred. Of course. She would always demur. But after all, tonight was different. It was time for a little charity. She consented to be walked as far as her bus stop. Her tinsel was shivering. He grasped her arm, she pinched his thick sleeve, and they bowed their heads to the snow.

# GOLDEN AGE

Old Mrs. Alonzo, in a voice that scared the daylights out of you, called and asked me to come and see her in the home. It was a gruff, deep billy-goat croak (male or female, you couldn't tell). I pictured her dark, lifted face, tarnished like a mirror; the light tilted in her glasses; her mouth open—as if that would help her to hear any better. The wire dangling from her hearing aid. So Professor Alonzo had finally put his old mother away.

I said, "Oh, Mrs. Alonzo," and she was flattered that I had recognized her over the phone.

I have an aged grandmother of my own, living on the other side of the city, so I used to look in on the professor's mother now and then. Feeling guilty; knowing it should have been the other old woman instead. The Alonzos' two flats perched one above the other in a deep court building, the yard bushy with trees. They were identical: grottoes. His furnished in books, top to bottom; leather library chairs, brass nailheads, the curdled fumes of cigars and whiskey decanters. The life of the mind was masculine turf. Hers was a matter of bric-a-brac, lace doilies, shaky-legged tables, and snarled faded carpets that reminded me of the worn hair on the back of her head. The TV set was often blaring full blast; which didn't distract her in the least—she couldn't hear it. She pressed her hand to her noisy bosom, breathing rapidly and loudly. You couldn't restrain a sense of alarm—as if something were breathing down your neck.

Now, the old lady loved to brag about her son—bald, stout, sixtyish, rough and scolding in manner, red in the face. With a great air of raking me into her confidence, seizing my arm and whispering, she showed me his clippings. "He's a famous man, you know." Well, he was, he was, much more than she thought. What could his dry-as-dust essays mean to her? What could she make of them? Written at white heat, in a hand that sent secretaries up the wall. Did you expect her to believe that anyone actually read such stuff?

In the dim light her glasses glittered—a mother's skeptical pride.

With Alonzo, alas, it was another story. He practically had to shout at her, at the top of his voice. She couldn't make out a word he said. I don't know; she always seemed to understand me. Of course, such commonplaces as we exchanged... Still, the great professor could speak commonplaces too:

"Mother, I'm going home now," he'd announce, rising, pushing thick fingers into pockets of tweed. The leather-patched sleeves smelled of Irish pubs and English fogs.

"What's that? What's that?" Opening her mouth, lifting her head. Her wires tingling.

He raised his voice. "I say. I'm go-ing home. Now. Downstairs."

"What? What? Huh? What's that?"

She lifted her face, he bent his; the two faces—so much alike, two swelling gourds, rimless specs stuck on the noses—pushing closer and closer. His was getting redder and redder—froggy eyed. I was afraid he was going to have an attack. But that's what I was always afraid of. Bluster was Alonzo's trademark; he shouted down everybody. His brilliance bordered on apoplexy. Its effects were famous on three continents. In the heat of argument, he actually seemed to lisp; his breath whistled between closed lips, and his hair looked like thistles. You couldn't help getting scared for him, once he got started.

His old mother croaked and cocked her head, her innocent specs flashing. She looked like Little Orphan Annie with the frizz of curls, the silver-dollar eyes. Meanwhile cowboys on the television were shooting off their cap pistols. Take that—and that—and that. You saw puffs of smoke.

This was a routine, of course. They were hamming it up. Burlesquing their relation, since it had become a burlesque. Doting mother, dutiful son. But their roles had been painfully reversed. Now it was her turn to play the slow stubborn creature who needed to be reasoned with, looked after, coaxed; now he was the one who had his hands full. At one end of life and the other, still the same gap. No understanding. So he hollered and lisped, she shook her deaf ear. They expressed their connection. There must be a better way of saying it, with someone you love, who won't be around much longer. But no one seems to have hit upon it yet.

Mrs. Alonzo was recovering from a heart attack. Then she started falling. The professor, at his desk, heard the thumps downstairs. She was supposed to knock on her floor—his ceiling—if she wanted anything. But no. She got out of bed by herself instead and groped her way to the bathroom. All the solid old-fashioned fixtures—painted pipes, grouty tiles, Roman faucets—waiting to crack her bones. He listened to every creaking overhead, and imagined her tripping on her shabby carpets.

She was giving him a hard time; people give what they can.

I saw for myself how things were going. A friend paid a visit with his son. The little boy took a look around—one room yawning into the other, the light receding, the brittle lace yellowing on armchairs and tables—and in a small voice asked Mrs. Alonzo how old she was. The old lady lied about her age—lopped off ten years. (Why ten? Why be stingy? Why not twenty?) Then she wanted to hold his hand. She reached for it, clawing—they were side by side on the boggy sofa—as if she meant to snatch it away.

"It's mine, it's mine. I'm going to keep it."

She wasn't kidding. Her voice was sharp, her fingers pinched. The child stiffened, but let his hand lie in hers. I watched this with very big eyes—almost as big as his.

"Actually I don't like old people," he told me. "They give me shivers up my spine."

I guess I'm talking about the shivers.

As long as this lovely spell of Indian summer holds, you see the old people sitting outside every day on the park benches by the underpass. A curving sweep of grass, squirrels pouncing on leaves, traffic wincing on the Outer

Drive. The blue blue shimmer of Lake Michigan. Beyond, the tall downtown buildings docked on the horizon, ready to sail on. At each bench sits a wheelchair, a "senior citizen" within; and on the bench—shackled like some familiar spirit—a sturdy black woman with her knitting or a movie magazine spread open on her knees. They come from the Shoreland, Sherry-Netherland, Del Prado, Windermere—hotels once famous for ballrooms, dance bands, steak houses, now providing package care for the elderly. My favorite of these couples is an old gent with a hooked back, a houndstooth check cap and plus fours and his young pregnant nursemaid. He likes to get out of his chair and push; she dawdles at his side. Her belly lifts the front of her coat; her legs look gray in white stockings. Meanwhile the great yellow maple is shaking its branches, squandering leaves. They scatter like petals. It's raining beauty; the air is drenched with gold.

Empty folding chairs were still standing out all up and down the front walk of the Woodlawn Nursing Home. A skinny, straggling lineup, as if the old folks themselves were sitting and staring. It had been another warm fall day; bright crab apples strewed the lawn and the leaves were swirling. Coming round the bend, I could already hear voices like Mrs. Alonzo's—raucous, growling in a drainpipe.

"Well, what about these teachers of yours?" a man was saying. "These Arthur Murray teachers? Were there any women at least?"

He was very small, very neat, with a tight white collar, a tight brown skin. His lip was stretched against his tight white teeth.

"Oh, no," from his companion, a woman leaning on a stick. "Only men. Two men."

"Men," he said. "Thanks a lot. Who needs that?"

The home is built in two wings—a tall one, where the inmates live, and a long low entrance wing with waiting rooms and administrative offices. The corridors were smooth, gleaming, done in Howard Johnson colors—turquoise and orange—and a sukkah stood in the lobby.

It was real. Red oak leaves, Indian corn, yellow squash, lemons, oranges, apples, melons. A woman saw me sniffing at the fruit and motioned for me to help myself. She was large and soft, smiling from cheek to cheek, and her lips squeaked, soundless, as if you'd squeezed rubber.

Take, take. But I didn't take.

Another woman, with a cane and dark glasses, was sitting sideways in her chair and asked for the time without looking up.

I stopped to read the bulletin board. There seemed to be a heavy schedule. Movies, cocktail parties, religious services, bingo, Arthur Murray. A woman was pushing herself along in a wheelchair and stopped to see what I was looking at.

"They keep you pretty busy here?" I said.

"No-o-o," she said slowly, thinking it over and gazing up at the board. She asked what time it was.

It was four thirty; getting close to dinner. That's why everyone was so interested in the time. Meals come early in institutions, remember—a matter of kitchen shifts. It was too early to go, but everyone was ready. All along the corridor, they were waiting in their chairs, asking each other the time. Some were already sitting in the dining room, at small tables with red-checked cloths. Steely carts. Prominently displayed was a juice machine, the sort you see in movie theaters, popcorn galleries, stroking and churning a thick purple froth.

The dining room was in the other wing. As soon as you stepped over the border, the scene changed in an instant. Everything was older, darker, glummer, more dingy. The corridors were dim and narrow and lined with chairs, like the gloomy hallways of a clinic. And there was the familiar clinging urinal smell. Leaky bladders? Old people missing the pot? This was where they lived, that's all. That was the difference.

I got into the elevator and rode upstairs. Same thing there; everywhere the old people were converging. Tapping down the halls on canes, holding onto the handrails on the walls, propping their shiny chrome walkers before them. They came rolling up in their wheelchairs, elbows lifted, working, gristly grasshopper wings. Passing open doorways, I could see women—they were mostly women—leaning over sinks, looking into mirrors, primping for dinner.

Mrs. Alonzo was not one of these. I knew she was bedridden, had brought her some books and a magazine that had just published a piece of mine—she liked to read. From the doorway, however, I saw that she was asleep; cranked up in bed against a pile of pillows, the rails raised on either side. Her head was back, her mouth was slack, and the string was hanging from her earpiece. Her breathing sounded as if a prowler had broken in, ransacking, rummaging round in her chest.

Just then the nurse came in to give her a pill. The old woman's eyes flew open behind rimless specs—a startled expression, a sort of angry surprise. Her head struggled up. She gasped something down from a little paper cup. The nurse went out, hips wagging in her girdle.

The home is in the thick of a desolate black slum. Burned out, bombed out, boarded up. Charred timbers, rubble, shattered windows. Through the slats of venetian blinds I spied children playing stickball in an empty lot. It was planted like a minefield with bricks, stones, scrap metal, squinting glass. In other words, what is called these days "the inner city." What a confession. Well, what can you do when civilization itself goes into competition with you—sets up its own spectacles of decline and destruction? Here was an old soul under the wrecking ball, undergoing the same kind of senseless assault. It was plain she had no idea who I was. (Who was I?) I pulled up a chair and sat down by the bed, my magazine under my arm.

The old woman looked over and stared at me, eyes wide open, as if something had her by the throat. She tried to lift her head. Her mouth munched. She was asking for something; thought I was the nurse. "What is it? Water?" I held the glass tube to her lips. She wouldn't drink. "You want your pillows straightened? You want to be turned?"

She kept trying to speak, straining her head. Then she gave a loud burp. Her throat rasped. I thought she was going to spit up the pill she'd just taken, and fetched the bedpan and held it to her chin. But that wasn't it either. I was getting panicked, ready to yank the bell for the nurse.

The fact is, I was frightened at being left alone with her, as I had been frightened my first time alone with a newborn infant. Not knowing what it wanted, what it needed. Its tottering head, its grasping fingers. I was frightened and ashamed of myself for not knowing what she wanted. Or, rather, for continuing to ask, to seek… as if. As if there actually were something—anything—a simple measure, word, gesture that would do. And that would be "what she wanted."

Her hand reached over the rail, feeling for my hand. The gesture seemed feeble, but the grip was strong. I remembered the way she had grabbed, grasped the little boy's hand. Her eyes were faded, the irises surrounded by dim thick rings. Aureoles. This truly reminded me of the newborn infant: two staring eyes, "clouds of glory." Some tenuous connection with the other world. I looked back, wondering and wondering. Is it a puzzle—or a mystery?

"Ma," she said. Then she sighed. "Oh, boy. Gosh. Oh, gee whiz."

My mother had just started to work for the Golden Diners Club, a program for "senior citizens" from the mayor's office. There are more than fifty throughout the city, where the elderly can get "hot, nourishing, low-cost lunches." They pay what they like; they don't need to pay anything. It isn't charity or welfare, it isn't only for the poor. But it is hard to convince people, especially the ones who need it most. The ones who are not used to taking, who have not much left but their pride. They don't owe anybody anything; they have paid their dues.

My mother works in a synagogue on the North Side, where they serve kosher food; so the customers are almost all Jews, from the old country, more or less religious. We were going to a funeral in the family and had arranged to meet there at lunchtime. In the meantime my mother sent me in her car to fetch her lazy old aunt, Yetta, who sometimes comes to eat.

Auntie Yetta lives only a few blocks away, in a terrace of brick two-flats right next to the concrete bunker of the el tracks. The trains go past like a rockslide. It looks like a munitions factory. Crabgrass shoots from cracks in the concrete, the bricks, the cement sidewalk. How heavy-hearted the smell of the warm autumn day, rising from all this mortar. So it seemed to me.

It took Yetta a long time to come to the door. Then I could hear her unfastening the many locks and chains. All my grandmother's sisters look alike—like their mother, the Bobbe. When I think of my great-grandmother, I see the scanty rusted grass on the slight mound of her grave, the tipping headstone. Then there rises before me the great leaning form of the Bobbe herself, pitching her weight heavily from side to side.

The old woman had trouble with her legs; thick, swollen, bowed—from ankle to knee it was a forty-five-degree angle. I'm not exaggerating. She went without a cane, but her walk was listing and broken. All her daughters have the same difficulty; it's an ethnic disease, like sickle cell anemia or Tay-Sachs syndrome, and afflicts women of the East European diaspora. A very exclusive Jewish disease. The thighbone softens and bends and drags you down like a fruit tree. Of course, I didn't know this as a child; their distorted legs were just them, the way they looked—how, I thought, they were supposed to look. Or, as I would say now, characteristic. Even more characteristic were their Slavic cheeks—wide, flat, heavy with bone. They seemed to peer at you over a ledge: above, you saw the glitter of eyes. They all looked like squatting idols, gazing at you from a distance. So maybe I am imagining the Bobbe, wide in her chair, filling it from side to side—huge, silent, her hands heavy on the armrests, and her terrible legs in front of her, wrapped in sleeves of flesh. Maybe.

She wore gypsy scarves, earrings, beads; she was, virtually, a gypsy. Her house was always full of her cronies, with their cards and tea leaves, rolling their little brown cigarettes with a flick of the tongue—all their gold teeth twinkling like loot. They cracked dirty jokes (according to my mother) in the Romany dialect. I do remember the heads together, laughing. But I can't recall that the Bobbe ever said a single word to me. I didn't speak any of her languages. Besides, it must have got boring after a while—all those descendants. Thirty grandchildren; so she must have stopped counting the greats. Give an old woman a break. It's thirty years ago now; she slipped and fell in the bathtub, cracked her hip, couldn't get out. The water turned cold. She died of pneumonia a week later. A series of events I regret to this day.

The door opened and there stood white-haired Auntie Yetta, more conservative than her mother—as who wouldn't be? but with the same prominent cheeks, flat barriers, the same legs sinking under the weight of her body. She gazed at me over her cheekbones. She was still in her slip.

"Oh, I can't go; I'm sick today, honey," she said. Whining a little. I could see this was a lot of hooey. She just didn't feel like getting dressed. Not in the cards. In that family they never cared to get dressed. As a child I used to love to stay overnight for a visit, so I wouldn't have to get dressed either. Behind her, the room was in a familiar mess; clothes, newspapers strewn everywhere, dirty dishes, bread crusts, banana peels, apple cores. It's always like that, since Yetta also doesn't care to clean. If you were a fish, you could swim through it. She wades; sidewise, clutching—a slow crustacean.

Yetta told me that another sister, Hodl, might be going to the Golden Diners today. Hodl had taken her husband to the clinic in the morning and they would be coming from the el. "You should keep an eye out; you might spot them."

It was actually hot; lawn mowers buzzing, spraying fine green dust. It was almost like spring, though the air smelled of leaf smoke. I didn't see anyone on the way. I was in the bathroom at the shul, washing my hands at the sink before lunch, when a white-haired woman came hauling herself in, lurching from side to side. She wore a cotton housedress zipped up the front; her legs were curved, her cheeks stone slabs.

"Auntie Hodl."

She put her fingers to her forehead. "Oh, I know who you are," she said. "I know who you are."

She was worn out. She had taken her husband to the clinic at 7:30 A.M. and they had just got back. "You know how they keep you waiting." He has dizzy spells, faints all the time, for some reason can walk only backward. So it would have been easy enough to "spot them" coming down the street, him toppling backward and her from side to side. In this manner, the two sick old people get themselves where they have to go. They climb the stairs of the elevated tracks and board crazed rushing trains. How does she shove him on? I wonder. This has been going on for years.

One hundred and sixty-seven had signed up for lunch today; only so-so. Fridays the turnout is better; then they can expect challah, wine, roast chicken. Today no one knew what was on the menu, and everyone was asking. A typical church function room: a platform at one end, windows narrow and high up, the dull gleam of linoleum and long tin-topped tables; the clatter of metal chairs. At each place was laid a slice of bread in a wax-paper pocket; a paper napkin, plastic knife, fork and spoon, and a slice of pineapple in a plasticized cup. The faces of the clientele too seemed remarkably standardized. It was the false teeth and the glasses: they lent a kind of artificial light. Their eyes looked so big, they seemed to explode behind thick lenses. The old people sat like a new race of children, lifting up their big blurred eyes. They were waiting for the prayer.

An arm shot up in the back of the room, waving a paper napkin. My father, signaling to me to show where we were sitting. So he's talking to me today. A great mauled-looking man in a dark-blue suit. It was the latest style, single breasted, narrow in the shoulders, belted in back, and every time he made one of his large gestures, I was sure he'd rip a seam. This Lord Fauntleroy stuff is not for him. I'd say Dying Gladiator or Laocoön. His skullcap sat on the back of his thick dusty hair like a lid; his shirt collar and tie looked to be choking him, and his eyes were a startling, smarting, blinking blue—like the eyes of a coal miner emerging from the pits.

My father always looks startled—you would too, if you'd been born in the wrong century—but today he looked stricken. There was a glare behind his glasses. The death was in his family—a beautiful child.

Everyone gets frightened, hearing of the death of a child. Everyone knows what it means: a puncture pain, a hook in the heart. We say "heartache," "heartbreak," the heart this and the heart that. But the strange thing is, that's really where you feel it. Wonder what that means.

One of my parents' closest friends, the companion of many years, had been murdered about a week before. Not even a robbery: two men walked into his store and asked for him by name. "You Zuckerman?" "Yes; what can I do for you?" So they shot him seven times. The period of mourning was just over, the widow wearing dark glasses to hide swollen eyes, talking slowly, tonelessly in a voice hollow with sedation, a chain of thick gold rings, bracelets, hanging heavy from her neck: the jewelry on her husband's hands when he died. Hal Zuckerman always went in for jewelry. Heavyset, bald, and round faced as Churchill, smoking big green cigars. (They seemed to me, as a child, to turn the air green around him.) Even in those days—he was not always as prosperous as he looked—he sported thick gold bolts on his fingers. I think my father would as soon wear a ring in his ear. But I guess you could say his "heart" was heavy.

Across the table were Auntie Hodl and Aunt Sylvia—it was her day off; she was going with us to the funeral. In the meantime, my mother had been putting her to work. "She always finds something for people to do." Sylvia, the younger, thinks her older sister is bossy. We both looked at my mother, dashing about, radiantly white haired in her light-blue pants suit. Her hair was whiter than anyone's here. Next to her empty place, a large, loose-jointed man leaned on his elbows, smoking. There was a No Smoking sign over his head, and his long-jawed face was wreathed in jolly fumes. Smoke poured from his hairy ears and spurted from his nostrils. He reached over and nipped my mother's bread.

The microphone gave a piercing bleat and whistled. A young woman stood on the platform, asking for "everyone's attention." But everyone hadn't come to give their attention. Their manner—necks stretching, fists on the table—said plainly enough that they had come to *get*. Where were the eats? They were growing impatient. Meantime she was announcing the day's activities and the circulation of a petition. A bill proposing abolition of the state sales tax on food for senior citizens. (In Illinois there is a tax on food.)

No one was listening, and the microphone seemed to pop with exasperation.

"If you don't care about yourselves, no one will care about you," she said.

I didn't hear the prayer, but someone must have said it, because people were chewing their bread. And the man with the fur in his ears ripped off my mother's pineapple.

Two women, evidently Golden Diners themselves, were pushing their way along the rows of chairs, one fearfully lifting a tray of little soup bowls. The liquid was trembling; you could see the golden *mandeln* bobbing up and down in the broth. The other functionary, following close behind, seemed to be doing nothing but scolding shrilly at the first one.

"Oh, no, not again," my father said, ducking his head. "Better watch it. Those two dizzy dames are always at it. Fight fight fight."

They slapped the bowls on the table; the soup spilled and ran all over my mother's chair. "Look what you did, you did," the loud one squawked, screeching and flapping.

"Don't yell at her so much," I said. "You make her nervous."

"Don't pay no attention to her, darling," the first one said, rolling her eyes at me over her shoulder. "You got to feel sorry; she's not all there."

So the little bowls slopped and splashed on the tables. Don't spill the soup, the soup. The microphone shrieked and hooted. My father bent down, mopping up my mother's chair with paper napkins. The old guy neatly snatched away her soup plate.

Sitting next to Auntie Hodl was a man who looked familiar. A beaming circle of a face, his napkin nicked round his chin. His eyes in big glasses stared owlish and unblinking. Out of the corner of my eye, I thought I saw Hodl twisting toward him now and then—giving him a sharp poke, a tap on the wrist, or swiping his chin. It dawned on me that she was "minding" him—that this must be her husband, Uncle Whatsisname. Now we were even.

I was wondering about something. My mother and her sister Sylvia are a handsome pair. Not smart, expensive women; they're working-class wives who get their hair done every other week, and manicures maybe once or twice a year, for special occasions. (Except they would call them "affairs.") They don't shop at Field's, let alone Saks, and they go in for shiny fabrics and bright colors—the pinks, purples, yellows, oranges, greens, preferably all at once—of their Romanian grandmother. Especially purple. *Nor spring nor summer beauty hath such grace / As I have seen in one autumnal face.* The two sparkling silver sisters get dressed up, go to weddings, and put the brides to shame. (It's true my mother has her grim, dark, liverish days, but I'm not talking about that now.) My mother is older by some eight or nine years and leads an even livelier social life. She's always stepping out. "Where's your mother tonight?" my grandmother wants to know whenever I call. She thinks I keep tabs. "Is that a Jessie! Always running."

Okay. My point is this. My white-haired mother could be one of those sitting and waiting at these tables herself—not working here. Auntie Hodl is only six or seven years older, and look at the life she leads. And how resignedly. A waddling old woman with a sick husband in tow, wiping his nose. She seems to have no complaint to make, no other set of expectations. Then what is the difference? What constitutes entry into the ranks of the elderly? Where is the dividing line, if it's not just years. Money? There must be more to it. Sickness? Senility? Being alone? But Hodl has children; grandchildren too. I bet they all do. The people at the Woodlawn Home have families: it's their families who put them there.

In my neighborhood I pass a certain basement window, Council for the Jewish Elderly. You see signs: Do you need a lawyer? A doctor? A visiting nurse? Information about Medicare? Medicaid? Hours are posted for the shuttle-bus service to Michael Reese Hospital. It looks like they've got troubles. The elderly are a subculture in our society of subcultures. That is, they have not so much a life in common as a condition. Who understands this condition? What can be made of it? Cut off, under attack, no retreat.

These people were all old Jews. Judging from the accents I heard around me, most of them had come over on the boat. They were not, as the jargon goes, assimilated. But there are places like this all over the city. Golden Diners—Golden Agers—are not just immigrant Jews. And yet their status is symbolic. This is no country for old men. All of them must be in the same boat; they are not entirely of America either.

Our party was attracting attention. Faces were turning on us enviously from all the other tables. Privileged characters. They didn't like to see outsiders here in the first place. And now we were getting served first, to top it all off, while they sat waiting. (My mother had told them in the kitchen that we had to go to a funeral.) The two bickering old biddies were making their way toward us again, bringing the main course—the trays held high, as if to keep them out of reach. The one was still timidly hiding her head, the other still yelling, stretching the veins in her throat. For once the buzz in the room died down; people stiffened into silence.

"Who's going to the fu-ner-al?" she was demanding, at the top of her voice. "Who's going to the fu-ner-al?"

Scolding, to the old, must seem a way of life. We all scold my grandmother too. How come she never keeps the chain up on the door? Why won't she use a cane? When will she let someone take her to the doctor? Etc., etc. She's eighty-five, crippled with arthritis, a widow on a pension of something like a hundred dollars a month. So who do we think we're kidding, with our canes and doctors and door latches? Who's she going to fool with that stuff? She ducks her head and lets us talk.

It's in Uptown, a large old elevator building. In Chicago, a city of the plains, built outward, low-lying, such vintage structures are not so common. This neighborhood, now so squalid, was once fancy: stone urns on the lintels, potted geraniums, doormen in gold braid. A mayor of Chicago used to live here. At least, every time we enter and traverse the vast lobby—a trackless waste; I feel like a camel plodding across the Gobi Desert—my father remarks: "Mayor So-and-So of Chicago used to live here." (I met this Mayor So-and-So once, was taken up to the dark wood-paneled offices with their swinging gates and swivel chairs, golden window shades, rich green blotters. I had won a grade school spelling bee. The mayor pushed out his hand—past his big, buttoned paunch—and, as we shook, asked me to spell "eleemosynary." I corrected his pronunciation. My God.) (I was wrong.) I don't know where my father gets his information, and I'm not sure what he means. But I have an idea. He means that every dog has its day.

And in fact this neighborhood will rise again; it's in the path of progress, so to speak. Heading north along the lakefront, the trail of the young, the fashionable, the singles bars, wine and cheese shops, liberal politicians, psychiatrists' town houses. The culture mishmash—propagandists for the good life in the city. ("Interesting people with complex demands," as one of the rental ads puts it. God forbid anyone should admit to simple needs.) First there was Old Town, then New Town; next will be Uptown. It's inevitable. And the drive must be very great—it must be all-powerful—to overcome even this. The decrepit old buildings with their jagged windows and smell of leaking sewer gas will come down; glass high rises will go up in their place; the misery will move elsewhere. That part is easy; it travels; it's footloose and fancy-free.

The lobby is stripped; just a few cracked mirrors, prongs in the chandeliers where the lights used to be. At one end a black-and-yellow sign: Fallout Shelter. It leads upstairs; that makes me wonder. Down at the other end, the glassed-in reception desk, a shirt cardboard leans against the counter, scribbled in pencil: Out to Lunch. Through the window you can still see the old-fashioned switchboard, plugs torn from the sockets; the empty pigeonholes that used to hold mail, telegrams, important worldly messages. The present tenants get mail once a month: pension, relief checks. The desk clerk has been out to lunch for fifteen years.

The pièce de résistance is the elevator. There are two, one reserved for the janitor's use. As you can see, someone has a sense of humor. Janitor? What janitor? And since none exists, do we need to invent one? The tenants are not here to complain about leaky faucets. They're on their last legs themselves, a condition they are used to. My uncle was trapped in this elevator once; it fell to the basement, the door wouldn't open, and the alarm didn't work. What else is new? He hollered and banged until the fire department finally came to the rescue. A cop, six foot four, padded with police fat; he didn't think it was funny. And what if it had happened to one of them?

The upper part of the door is a dirty gray slush color; through the glass, if that is what it is, you can see the light coming: rising like an acetylene torch in a mine shaft. The elevator clanks, creaks, rattles its chains, scrapes and lashes overhead like storm-tossed branches. This is it in a nutshell, a capsulized version of our city life—its paranoia, its guilt and dread. An ancient, corrupt piece of machinery, plainly a fire hazard, no sticker of inspection. Is it going to fall? Is it going to fail? Will the door open? And who will get in? Some drunk breathing fumes you could light with a match. A quarrelsome derelict. Or just someone so old, so broken down, so weary of the march, you hate to look. You drop your eyes. That's the worst part. I would take the stairs, but it's ten flights up and they're not always lighted. Groping my way down once, striking matches, I came upon a pair of broken glasses in a pool of dried blood. As for the freight elevator, never send to know....

This building is ten times better than the one my grandmother moved out of a few years ago.

At your knock, you hear her slippers shuffling to the door. The chain scrapes in the latch. She opens and peeks out, head thrust forward, peering from the hump between her shoulders.

"How many times do I have to tell you? First you look—then you take the chain off the hook. What good does it do if you take the chain off before you open?"

"I know, I know."

She knows.

Her feet scrape the floor, dragging along the big loose slippers. Big swollen hands dangling from her wrists. She flaps one. "Leave the door open for some air. It's all right now you're here."

Her voice croons. From Transylvania, she moved to Kentucky. It's not enough my grandmother is half-gypsy; she has to be a hillbilly too. But never mind family history. The bed is made, the table cleared, dishes are stacked in the drain rack. She's not like her sister Yetta. Still, you don't have to be nosy to see it's not so clean either. The dishes are greasy, the floor could use sweeping, there's a smell from the bathroom like the odor in the corridors of the Woodlawn Home. A drizzle of soot from the open window, the curtains struggling and fluttering. A row of pickle jars on the sill, filled with cloudy water; sprouting sweet potatoes, wandering Jew—the thin strings of roots reaching in all direction—a cracked avocado pit thrusting up one scrawny shoot. No power on earth could keep these windows clean. Chicago lies before us in all its unfinished business. Brightness falls from the air.

"Well? How are you feeling?"

"I?" Turning herself, stiff necked, sideways. Surprised you should ask. "I'm all right."

"Then what took you so long to make up your mind?"

She chuckles. This is our form of communication, like Alonzo and his mother with their vaudeville routine. I can't say when we got into this habit, but after all, she knows what I mean. I guess she knows. I hope so. Because it's a little late, now, to start delivering messages. To bring up the one subject, the real subject. You have to begin that in time. Otherwise it sounds too much like last things. And I sometimes think she is a little afraid of me; that she senses, through the banter, that I might suddenly start talking in another vein. What then? She has never been the demonstrative type. Never one to volunteer information. She's not going to be the one to bring it up, sitting in her corner, her hands heavy in her lap.

My grandmother's fingers are bent—fused—in the shape of a priest making the sign of the cross. Pretty strange, huh, for an old Jewish lady with all her Jewish infirmities. With these hands she pries open tins, digging at the jagged lids with an old-fashioned puncture-type opener—the kind I can't use. The only kind she can. She has no grip. She carries food to the table, hot heavy pots practically dangling from her fingertips. Her shoulders pulled up, her head pulled down. Now, what would she say if she knew I was thinking all the while that she looked like the pope?

No sooner have we sat down, the door open, than in slinks a black cat, arching and rubbing itself along the wall. Presently two women approach, holding onto one another, hand in hand.

"Did anyone see a cat?"

Their voices quaver. They appear to be identical twins—is this possible? Two withered old crones, crooked backs, hooked noses. Even their chins are hooked, tipping upward—hoops. White hairs quiver on their chinny chin chins. To top it all off, they're dressed like twins; dolled up, perhaps, by some doting mother—knitted caps, crocheted shawls, thick woolen socks and Mary Janes with buckled straps. The impression is overpowering. This must be what is meant by second childhood.

"A black cat?"

"Look under the bed," says my grandmother.

That's what she always used to say whenever I asked her for a penny. She wasn't being facetious—not her style. Her husband, my grandfather, was a big handsome man, a storekeeper, careless with small change. It fell out of his pockets, got stuck in his shoes, his trouser cuffs, and when he undressed at night, rolled around on the floor. So if I crawled under the bed I could strike it rich. In those days my grandmother was big and handsome herself—pardon me for bragging—five foot nine, astonishing for a turn-of-the-century East European immigrant. She wore her dark hair divided in the middle, combed in two large flat rolls above her temples. With her wide-set eyes, wide impassive cheeks, it gave her a look of powerful repose.

"Sit down," my grandmother offers. "He'll come out when he's ready." The black curve of the tail was sticking out from under the bedspread. The aged twins, plucking at each other, steadying, holding hands—at the same time helping and hindering—tiptoe in and pull out chairs at the table.

I suppose I should say something about the furniture. It's in keeping. Junk. An enamel-topped kitchen table, scratched, like a bathtub; a dining room set; a couple of "upholstered" chairs—sprung, soggy stuff you wouldn't be surprised to find in an alley. Which is probably where my father found it. And by the way—where do all those busted, waterlogged sofas and mattresses come from, that I keep seeing on the curbs these days? Is there an epidemic?

In other words, this is not, as with Mrs. Alonzo, the accumulation of a lifetime. There is scarcely anything here from the past. My grandmother does not go in for souvenirs. Sylvia has told me many a time how, even in the old days, with a houseful of kids, the whole family packed up and moved every two years—without fail. So they could get the free decorating when they signed a new lease. There is a television set, of course, rabbit ears sticking up, and a telephone at last—a Christmas gift from Sylvia. Now we can worry when we ring and ring and get no answer.

The twins have a story. It seems they had found a pension check in the street, under the viaduct that leads to Foster Beach. (I know the spot—like a slaughterhouse with its feathers and pigeon splash.) At first, they had passed it up.

"But I told Sis right away, I sez, 'Say, if that don't look like a pension check.' Did I say that or didn't I?"

"I could of told you. Anyone could reckonize a pension check. It's the govverment onvelope."

"So we went back and picked it up."

Went back. That would be worth a discussion. It's not so easy to "go back"—to retrace such doubtful, painful, tottering steps. Each one takes so much effort. What if it wasn't a check? What if it was torn open, empty? But there it was, the address nearby. Trembling, all excitement, the twins looked up the rightful owner. A colored man named Jackson. He came downstairs in his overalls; he was working on the roof.

"You Jackson?"

"What do you want to know for?"

The story was getting exciting. My grandmother meantime listening, turning sideways, her shoulders lifted to her ears. Her glasses flashing with a candid light. The way she listens to everybody, keeping her thoughts to herself.

Jackson, for reward, gave them five bucks apiece. And oh, you should see what they bought with it at the A&P. More than they could carry. I'll bet. The elderly, who can afford it the least, buy the most expensive way—the smallest quantities. There are lots of reasons. Because they're alone, they're afraid they won't use it up, they have to watch their money, there's no place to put the stuff. And, not the least, they have to get what they can carry. No use picking out a five-pound bag of sugar if you can't lift five pounds. They have to think of that; a prominent fact of life in these parts. Once I arrived just as my grandmother was coming along in her bright-green coat—head poked forward in her babushka, her legs so bent they seemed dragged down by the heavy package weighting either hand. She was carrying a bundle for her neighbor. It occurred to me that anyone noticing her—if anyone notices anyone here, where they all have such grim preoccupations of their own—a stranger, passing, would think: Here comes a funny little old lady. An elf, a gnome. And not know. Know what? What am I trying to say?

And what was she doing carrying someone else's groceries?

Well, I could believe these twins had struggled with their miserable shopping bags, ten bucks' worth of food, putting them down and lifting them up and tugging at each other's sleeves all the way home. They went on talking.

I used to resent these gate-crashers. Every time I pay a visit to my grandmother, someone else shows up. It never fails. The next-door neighbor, for instance, picks just this moment to return the *TV Guide*. (Sylvia's husband, a printer, works for the paper and keeps the old lady in *TV Guides*.)

"Oh, I didn't know you had company," the neighbor will say, clutching and closing her wrapper. "I'll come back later on." Half-stooping, apologetic; ready to sit down, waiting to be asked.

"Stay, stay," from my grandmother. Then: "Well? What's new? You looked? Anything good on tonight?"

"Pooh. Same old junk. Never nothing good."

TV is another prominent fact of life. They all watch television—what else is there? Their heroes are the teenage idols of yesteryear. My grandmother loves loves loves Elvis Presley. (She probably imagines him in a yarmulke, with a shaved neck and earlocks. I'm only guessing.) The old folks observe the pop culture day by day—its soap operas, game shows, reruns, old movies; its commercials and more commercials. So they know all about us; you can't take them by surprise. After all, they don't have to make sense out of it; what is age for, if not to release you from such servitude? This is the modern world; anything goes; it's all in the script.

So my grandmother told me about a young woman she had seen while shopping at the A&P. The store was full of old-age pensioners of the neighborhood, timidly plucking their five-and-a-half-ounce tins of evaporated milk off the shelves, when in stomps this girl, briskly wheeling a cart and wearing—so far as I could make out, from the description—a cape, a nude body stocking, and hip boots. That was it. Give her a mask, she'd be Batwoman.

"Everybody looked," my grandmother said. "But we didn't say nothing. We know it's the *style*."

One of the things my grandmother likes about this place is that it is not "just for old people"; like public housing for the elderly—which would be a lot cheaper and cleaner, God knows. But she resents the category. I don't blame her. And she's right; this building, this neighborhood, are not just for the aged. That is not the lowest common denominator.

Uptown is the home of the displaced, the disinherited, the uprooted. What are called, these days, "internal immigrants." Appalachians, American Indians—aching with homesickness; the poor, the elderly, the halfway houses. They all find their way here by the same natural process, the end of the life cycle of a city neighborhood. That is why the bricks, cement, concrete pillars have the look of temporary shelters: tents, prefabs, lean-tos. Uptown is a DP camp; that is its secret.

So it is nothing to see people haggling with themselves in the streets, carrying on quarrels with unseen enemies, wheeling empty baby buggies, pawing through trash cans. They are more than old; they are outcast. They have escaped the net; they are outside every sort of social institution.

But why can't they come some other time, I would think—come when she's alone? She's alone so much. Why now? When I'm here. And—since it's no use if you don't tell the truth—who needs such visitors? Who wants them? I don't want to look at any more toothless mouths, black glasses, skinny arms, swollen livers. My grandmother is my grandmother—but who are they?

Which just goes to show: I didn't understand anything. Not the first thing.

My grandmother is one of the few in this building, in this whole neighborhood, for that matter—which is nothing but a vast reservation for the elderly—one of the very few who "has anybody." Family, that is; who love and care; who don't just "pay visits"; who feel more than duty. And these others come to be close to that forgotten feeling. To steal up next to it, warm themselves at the fire. My grandmother knows this, and that's why she always tells me to "leave the door open for some air."

Ah, here's the rub. If that's true, if that's true—then what is she doing in a place like this? A place for those who have nobody? Who are alone in their extremity—forgotten, spewed up, swept out with the sawdust and ashes. The "wretched refuse," the "tempest tossed." Refugees of old age, with their perishable goods.

Last winter the old lady tripped and fell in the house. Didn't we all tell her not to keep that crummy throw rug by her bed? She didn't break anything, but she was on the floor for seven hours, passing out, trying to pick herself up. Thinking of the Bobbe in the bathtub? I wonder. At her age, that didn't do her much good. It damaged her heart.

In the hospital, they doped her up; her mind wandered. I was afraid she would lose hold. Her lip curled back from the bright line of her teeth—a death snarl, a mummy. "Don't take any pills," I shrieked. "You know what pain is, you're used to it. Don't swallow anything; leave it under your tongue." Advice after her own heart; she's scared stiff of doctors, with their black bags, merchants of death. And hospitals: the smells, the sounds, the crack of light all night long under the door.

"You know how these old people are," the nurses kept saying, winking and tapping their foreheads.

All the old woman could think of was getting out, going home. She was still insisting, with a stubborn will—she could barely lift her head from the pillows—that she wasn't going to live with anyone.

But we all knew the time had come.

Everyone *offered*. Even I *offered*. She put up a fight. I live too far from the rest; she'd be stranded out there, no one would come to see her. Besides, she knows I work at home and don't want someone looking over my shoulder. Her sons' wives are not Jewish, though that's not the real complication. "How come they don't visit me, if they want me so much?" Aunt Irene has an old mother of her own, paralyzed, in a nursing home in Quaker Pennsylvania. This other old woman was also looking forward— passionately: it was the only passion left—to going home. But they had auctioned off her house and all her belongings in the meantime. "Let Irene take care of her own mother instead."

As for the two gay, pretty daughters, with their busy social lives— my grandmother was ready with her defense. "You're never home. What would I do alone all day?"

"But you're alone all day now. Why do you want to give us an argument, Ma? You know you're no trouble."

What's the use of talking? You see what a stubborn old woman she is.

No one heard what she was saying. That she wants to be taken care of, she needs to be; she's too old, too weak, she's ready to lay her burden down. But what good is it, moving in with someone, if she's to be "no trouble"?

My mother would have taken her as a matter of course. She quit her job to take care of their father when he was dying. She's the one who does that sort of thing in our family. But my mother was about to go on a cruise. She had put down her deposit; she was looking forward. Ten days in the Caribbean, a call in Venezuela. All her friends go on cruises. The poor woman had her heart set on it. And she didn't see why one of the others, the rest of us, couldn't take care of my grandmother until she got back.

This was cruel. My mother didn't deserve to be put in this position, not after all her faithful service. But her father died fifteen years ago. She has since joined the Great American Public. And she's fifteen years closer to the grave herself—that's what it's really all about. She has discovered that life is for having a good time—a recent discovery with her, as it is historically. Better late than never. Happiness has become a novelty item. Everyone's got to have it. Since when do the Lumpenproletariat take cruises to Venezuela? And the death of a child used to be an ordinary event. Now it seems terrible, the worst that can happen. Did it seem less terrible when it was common? I might ask my grandmother, who lost two of her own; but she's not talking.

After two days at Sylvia's, her husband said, loud enough for the old woman to overhear: "Why don't you put your mother in a home, where she belongs?" Well, everyone knows how he is. He was raised in a home himself, an orphan.

My grandmother couldn't wait until she crept back here, to her hole in the wall. A triumph of sorts. She heard the sigh of relief. Because she's so stubborn, so independent, she won't take anything, she won't become a burden to anyone. Because she's not senile—"Thank God"—and she never complains. Those seem to be the alternatives. It's nobody's fault. She knows it's *the style*.

So the subject was canceled; it will never come up again. She will live out her life here, stick it out to the end. It's too late to leave now. She has become attached to her belongings, her surroundings, her own stubborn independence—no matter how wretched. It's not for us to say. To her neighbors, tapping on doors with rubber-tipped canes. Checking up on each other, of course: they all have a fear of not being found for days. Roots? No time to talk of that. Barnacles, better. To cling or not to cling. She has found her last spar.

It's fiercer than ever now. If you go to the store for her, right away out comes the "pocketbook," her fingers prizing the clasp. "How much? Huh? How much?" Her big feet push her slippers across the floor, her hands drag the backs of the chairs. Her mouth is tight, as if she has suddenly thought of something she has forgotten to do. And her voice is getting rough; I find myself raising my own voice more and more. She peers round at the sound, turning her whole self stiffly sideways; an old white porcupine heavy with quills. She seems to be using all her senses at once, trying to make out a strange noise in the dark. Do you think she could be getting a little deaf in her old age?

# HOW WE GOT THE OLD WOMAN TO GO

"I'm coming into O'Hare at nine o'clock," I said.

"Why?" my mother said.

Some answer. I held the phone to my ear, feeling a little foolish. What do you mean, why. What kind of question is that. "Why not?"

Her voice was resonant; I thought she had been crying. I imagined tears blazed on her cheeks. It still scares me to hear my mother cry; the way it used to whenever she started talking Yiddish in front of me. I didn't understand and wasn't meant to. Something inside tightens its grip.

"And you want Daddy to pick you up, I suppose."

"Well, yes."

"Better tell me again, then. I have nothing to write it down with. I'm in bed with an awful bad cold."

Looked like no one was going to meet me at the airport.

My grandmother had died the night before; the funeral was tomorrow. I was in New York when my mother called with the news. "No one expects you. You don't need to come." Hard to tell what this meant; after all these years I still don't speak her language. "You have your memories," she said. I do? I thought, worried. I couldn't think of any memories. All I could think of were a lot of No Trespassing signs. Private. Keep

Out. The woods were papered with them. The past is not such a good neighbor. It knocks when it wants, but it won't let you in. What good are memories?

This wasn't exactly news. It had taken almost a year. It was spring when she fell and broke her hip—I was away then too—and by now it was the middle of December. So it was an old story; the same old story. Nothing was spared. Everything she had been afraid of, holding out with such will. All that was no good to her now—her own worst enemy. "She could last a long time." I couldn't see myself strolling in Central Park while they were putting the old woman into the ground.

"It's Bette, Ma. Bet-te Lee. She's been a-way. She came to see you."

My mother bent her dark cheek over the pillow and raised her voice coaxingly. The old woman's eyes were shuttling back and forth, back and forth, in her close-mouthed face. Since when was it so small? And white as spittle. Her hair was bound in a wispy topknot. I thought of shrunken heads with the lips sewn shut.

"Don't she look cute?" Roxy said. "We showt her a mirror, so she coult see how cute she lookt."

Up went my mother's head, straight as a rifle barrel. Loaded, of course. I gave her a swift kick under the bed.

"But she din't like it. Dit you, Bub?" She calls her mother-in-law "Bub" for short. They are landsleit, in a manner of speaking. My grandmother spent her girlhood in Kentucky, bluegrass country; Roxy is from the eastern hills. Even her face is hilly. A lean whittled jaw, the eyes close together and fanatical. A cigarette quivered between two crossed fingers. "You're too particular for an old lady, aincha?"

The old woman's eyes were busy busy.

Well, what did we expect. Whatever made us think it was going to be easy. That one day she would just make up her mind, close up shop—lift her shoulders, bite off the thread. We all know how stubborn she is. Even now her head had a purchase on the pillow—like her hands on the sheets. Like her features on her face. Slanted back, steep, severe. Her brows were outthrust and her mouth was gripping. They would have to come and get her first. They would have to pry her loose.

Rudy came padding out of the bedroom, sliding his belt into his pants. He's on nights this month, he'd just got up. In fact, he had only one eye open, the other squeezed under his brow. It gave him a grousy look, frowning down at us—he has his mother's tufted brows—with one stinging eyeball. Rudy doesn't talk much. He doesn't listen either. The floor was thudding under his bare feet.

"Here's Rooty. We're going to get you up now, Bub. Want to show Bette Lee how we get you up? First you neet your collar, don't you? She don't like it neither," Roxy said, dropping a glance over her shoulder, snapping the foam rubber neck brace in place. The short crop of her ponytail bounced with rough enthusiasm: "You don't like nothing no more, do ya?"

The fall had also dislocated a couple of vertebrae—though they didn't find out till later.

My grandmother had shut her eyes and fastened her lips, offering her chin on a chopping block, in a noose. Her lids were flickering. She looked both timid and aloof. Now she hooked up an eyebrow and stole a glance out of the side of her head at Rudy—standing in the window, his arms wrapped across his chest. An obstruction, a beam. His hair is so short it bristles and glistens. A breeze was rattling the paper shades.

"Oh. It's the narr." Her lids sank shut. But her voice. Her voice. You could have blown it out. I felt something snuffed, extinguished.

I frowned at my mother. "Wha'd she call him?"

"You heard her. The narr. The fool. That's what she says, all the time now. Right to his face. It's the funniest thing." She put a finger to her lips. "But shhhh. Don't say anything. It hurts his feelings some-thing terrible."

When in Rome do as the Romans do.

Everyone knows that Rudy is his mother's favorite. No one begrudges him that. After all, what are a mother's feelings for, if not to make up for life's short rations? It's not just a preference, it's rapture; the undemon-strative old woman's joy in life. He was the child of her middle age. My grandfather used to blame it all on that.

He stood staring straight past us, over our heads.

Of course, it would be nothing for Rudy to lift his old mother. He weighs twice as much as she does—250 would be my guess—he's almost twice as tall. It's her tubes, her bags, her braces, her bruises, her bones. She's not sick; there's no disease. She's just broken. And she's no help, either. You can't tell if you hurt her. "She won't never complain."

Naturally. Not giving out her position to the enemy.

Rudy hauled her up under the arms. Her mouth shrank; her chin poked over her collar; her elbows struck her sides. For a moment she looked like something hanging by the neck, swinging from a hook. Her big blue feet dangled and dragged; so much deadweight.

"Her feet," my mother cried. "What happened to her feet?"

I stuck her in the ribs, but not in time. She had picked up her head—her white trademark. The rubbed red spots stood out in her cheeks. "Her feet look burned. How did her feet get burned?"

Awkward silence. Roxy knelt by the wheelchair, slamming the footrests; clipping the catheter bag to the rail. Its dark tea was swishing and foaming. Her cigarette twitched in her tightened lips. Rudy clings to the hope she will die of lung cancer. "That's right. Uh-huh. I burnt your mother. Dit it on purpose. That's the kint a care I take."

She looked like a teenager in her cutoff jeans, the little whip of hair switching on her neck. She stalked haughtily out of the room. Rudy stared.

"Now look what you done. She still ain't talkin to me from the last time." You've got to hand it to my mother; it's something to get a rise out of Rudy. His arms hung at his sides; his brows crouched in his face.

My grandmother had lowered her eyes; her lips were pressed together with firm intentions. She looked small, almost fugitive, perched over the wheels and spokes of the chair. This is the way she always gets when angry voices are raised around her. "Just look down, don't say nothing." That's her motto. One she recommends to her children, with such results as you see. I was beginning to understand why she has resisted going to live with any of them all these years. Maybe it wasn't just pride—shame for her own condition. Maybe she was more ashamed for theirs.

"Your mother," Rudy said, looking at me over his shoulder, thrusting his way past. "Why don't you tell your mother?" Behind her back he suddenly turned, pushed out his face, and put out his pickled white tongue.

"What's that for?" As if I didn't know.

"So?" He shrugged, his hands spreading his pockets. "That's what the doctor used to do. The one that took care of Ma in the hospital."

"That's a big recommendation." Copycat.

"Why not? What do you want from them? They're human."

That's what you think. Please don't tell that to my mother. Doctors are her natural adversary. They hold the franchise on life and death. And who gave it to them? And whose side are they on? She has fallen into their hands.

My mother has powers of her own. I had just got back; everyone was waiting to jump on me. "Your mother. You know your mother. Better tell your mother." Right. Tell her. Go explain that she feels guilty about her mother's accident, her agonies—the fact that she isn't taking care of her herself—that that's what's eating her; that's why she finds fault with every little thing, her hand against every man's, won't let up for a minute. She believes she is battling for her mother's life. Tell her.

"Oh, Mother," I said.

"What's the matter? I'm not supposed to say anything?"

Her skin was the color of an autumn leaf; the dark slopes contrasted with her bold white hair. Holding her tongue? Yes, she was holding her tongue. Like a dog with its teeth sunk into your leg—that's how my mother holds her tongue. My heart was not in this. I knew what she was thinking. *And when it's my turn—when my time comes—who'll put up a fight for my sake?*

Don't look at *me*.

The girls were sunning themselves on their elbows and stomachs on the back porch, portable radios fixed to their ears; waiting for Rudy to go to work. "What's taking him so long? Ain't he ever gonna get outta here?" The TV set was blaring in the living room; flies buzzed over the dishes in the sink. The little boy, Jordie, came stomping up the stairs—giving them a trouncing—soundly slamming the screen door. The other kids pick on him; he was fighting back tears. They seeped from under his big blurry glasses. He's like one of those foundlings his father is always bringing home. Home. Anyone can see Rudy has a soft spot; opinions differ as to where it might be.

From the glum bedroom, crammed with their two double beds, at right angles—there isn't room enough to turn around (their lives are separate, but not private)—we could hear Rudy's voice. Sullen, insulted. It always sounds that way. The voice of a deaf man. He's not that deaf. From Roxy ominous silence. Well, the old woman always liked a bit of life around her.

"The narr," she repeated, pinching her napkin under the hinge of her thumb. She was waiting for her dinner. Any day now.

My mother cocked her head at me. "Guess she knows something we don't know." Then her face changed. Her range was point-blank. "My God. How stupid can they be. Showing her a mirror."

In the kitchen a candle was smoking in a glass. Yahrzeit, in memory of my mother's father—the old woman's husband—who had died almost to the day, many years before. The little flame licked and lapped at the clear pool of wax. It reminded me not so much of the old man himself, may his soul rest in peace, as of the house I grew up in. The pantry was full of scorched glasses; we seemed so often to have them lighted in the kitchen, sputtering away. A gruesome effect; I knew what they were for. They cast such big shadows over the walls.

It was all a mistake. That's why no one met me at the airport. They thought I meant nine o'clock in the morning. "We wondered why you'd be coming in tomorrow morning."

She was in robe and slippers, her face shiny with cold cream, her straight cheeks shedding light; a crown or paper collar wound round her splendid white hair to keep its set for tomorrow. My mother is splendid—can she help it? A Noble Savage; a cigar-store Indian. About time I figured it out. But something was the matter with her mouth. It overshot the mark; puckered up like purse strings, an empty pouch. I keep trying to tell her that a bridge is not just for cosmetic purposes, but she can't wait to take her partial dentures out at night. On her little finger—her hands are large—she wears my discarded wedding band. Been helping yourself to my things again, huh? Finders keepers. Though it seems a weird choice of trinket—memento mori.

She intercepted my stare.

"Well, *you* didn't want it, *did you*?" She tugged her robe round her shoulders, her wide spreading bosom, and the rim of gold caught the light.

On the floor was a small neat pile of my grandmother's belongings they had given my mother at the nursing home. Half a dozen cotton nightgowns, laundered and folded; a pair of striped knitted slippers; a clear plastic brush whose lucid bristles reminded me forcefully of the old woman's hair. Oversize disposable diaper pads with blue plastic liners. It struck me as oddly like the collection you might take home from the hospital with a new baby. More like the beginning than the end of something.

"The end of an era," as my father said. So people really say things like that.

He was stopping the clocks. Otherwise I would never get to sleep. He has all these clocks, chime clocks; they sound like a church mission. People break them and throw them away; my father finds them and fixes them. "Only a little something wrong." They don't keep the same time; they are set to sound off one after another, so you can hear their voices, diagnose various frets and complaints. Your ear laid to the dark like a ticking chest. I say that walls should be seen and not heard, as we were forever told as children. As you can see, my father loves slogans. "Might Makes Right." "You can fool all of the people some of the time." "For want of a nail..." Why was he telling me all this? And I know for a fact he thinks this must mean I have a bad conscience. That is his opinion of a sleepless night. After all, he can sleep through anything; if he can sleep through his snoring. "Warm feet, cool head" is his surefire formula.

He was reaching his big hand inside the glass cases remorsefully, as if he were robbing their nests. A scholar's specs, a prizefighter's nose—flattened, mutilated, like a statue's—eyes like cornflowers in a crannied wall. Years ago, when we lived in a house on the West Side, he would come up from tending furnace in the basement with his thick-clustered head whitened with sawdust and cobwebs; from scraping the pipes. That's the way it looks now.

"No visitation," my mother said. "Sylvia and I decided. We don't want. It's all a lot of 'Hi, how are you,' and 'I haven't seen you in such a long time.' Phoo. Is that what they call paying respects? Leon don't care, you know him; he leaves it up to us. But Rudy wanted. He says policemen always have visitation. Sure, they're Irish. Them and their wakes. How many Jews have they got on the force? And all Jews like Rudy, I bet. But I want to get there early tomorrow for Rudy's sake. That's when the police are coming. My poor kid brother. What else has he got? And besides, he goes to all of theirs."

"I'd like something of hers," I said. "I know there wasn't much, there wasn't anything. Just something that belonged to her. Something she touched."

My mother thought for a moment. Then she looked pleased. Over the candles her features lit—a struck match.

"I know. Her clock."

A large blunt back rose in front of the room. It was Rudy, a black circle of a skullcap perched on his head. The back of it has more flesh than hair. He glanced over his shoulder—Oh, it's you—and lifted his arms across his chest. He was alone with the chairs and the long narrow blue box. It was open, the raised cover padded in Styrofoam packing material. Inside lying on wrappings and ruffles of starched stiffened gauze—was another box. This one was shut. A painted wooden lid. It was the figure of an old woman in a sunken blue bodice, with a bit of lace pinned to her transparent hair. Her eyes were stuck down, her mouth was fixed. Her glue had dried. I realized that this was supposed to be my grandmother. I realized that this was my grandmother.

"There," Roxy said, leaning down to the old woman's ear. It seemed to cling to the side of her head, her white nest, as in some chill wintry blast. "There. Now you got your bib on. Now you can show Bette Lee how nice you eat. She likes company to sit and watch her whilst she eats."

She does? She sure don't look it. Her head was clamped into her collar, a paper napkin bunched under her chin. Her stiff fingers plucked the spoon. But Roxy is the authority now on all my grandmother's likes and dislikes. Who would have thought the old woman had so many? I pulled up a chair and sat down close to the wheelchair. Too close. I was practically right on top of her. It was because my seat was so low—Jordie's, kiddie furniture. (I'd catch it for sure if he found out. Jordie is not only possessive, he's dogmatic. "It's not nice to… " "You must never… " He talks like one of Dickens's little orphans, his lip between his big ragged new front teeth.)

We were face to face, eye to eye. Our two heads were at the same level. I don't think this ever happened before. And I know she felt my gaze. A quick reckoning glance glimmered under her lids. My grandmother can't stand to have people watching her.

"Whatcha looking at? You?"

That's what she always says to me. "You-all? Whatcha looking at?" Clicking her tongue. She knows I get a kick out of her Kentucky Yiddish. What a combination. Clucking chiding cooing. A Jewish pigeon. "Go on. That girl. Always looking. She thinks she's gonna see something."

She said nothing now. She began to eat, silent and blinking. She seemed to have aged a hundred years. It wasn't any of the things I had been afraid of. No wrinkles, no trembling, no coarse threads on her chin. No munching lips. (She was blowing, cautiously, on her spoon.) None of the above. She just seemed covered with frost, like ice on a window. You could sense that her nerves took a dazzled concentration. All her movements were solemn and premeditated. Each time she took a bite, she gravely pressed the napkin to her lips—her fingertips brittle, pinching; starfish. Her lids grazed her cheeks. She was brushing my gaze like a fly off her face.

It was a new sensation. How often do you get to watch your grandmother eat? I've never even sat with her at the same table. That's a fact, if a strange one. What good is a fact without some strangeness? Even years ago, when we had dinner at her house almost every Friday night and always on holidays—especially then—my grandmother never sat down to eat with us. She carried hot pots from the kitchen, her apron hoisted, tied under her arms. I questioned this once.

Maybe it was a Passover seder. At my father's house—my other grandparents—these ceremonies went on well past midnight, the old man singing and swinging his glass; until he himself suddenly fell asleep at the table, just like one of the children: his head laid on the wine-stained cloth, his two hands clapped under his cheek. He had a mustache like a bale of hay on his lip. After he died (and his wife followed within weeks) there was one more seder on that side of the family. We sat down to the familiar table—the seltzer bottles, the blackened silver, my grandmother's dishes tinted the pink of the chambers of seashells; the sedimented wine, a sweet purple dye. We opened our books; the men felt their heads to straighten their caps. My uncles groaned, "Let's eat."

Here things fell somewhere in between these extremes. There was something hasty and droning about the whole business. Year after year they discussed what to leave out and what to leave in while my grandfather glowered over these territorial concessions. My father read Hebrew very deliberately—letter by letter—and the others were always after him to hurry, keep up, quit slowing them down. But he took his sweet time, rocking back and forth, his head smooth and shiny in his skullcap and his voice tolling out after the rest:

"...minayim shekol mako umako."

"...mako umako!"

It even sounded like an echo, hollow, reverberating. You could tell he didn't really know what he was saying.

I finally piped up. "Where does Bobbe eat? How come she never eats with us?"

My sister, Slim, had already drunk all her wine—she always did, first chance she got to tip up her glass—and now she was crabby, her cheeks flaming red, and my mother was holding her down on her lap with one hand, stuffing matzos in her mouth to make her shut up, and turning the pages of her book with the other.

"And this one with the questions," my mother said, smacking me on the side of the head and shoving my face in the direction of my plate. That was her name for me. "This One."

"Not in the head," my father said, in ringing tones. Even at the time, when I didn't know there was a word for it, I knew my father had principles.

"Look who's talking. The big shot," my mother said.

Words of Yiddish passed over the table like the Angel of Death. It was the language of bad news; bodily functions; the parts of dead chickens.

My grandfather brought his fist down on the cloth. Actually it was a bedsheet; who had tablecloths? He hated noise. Many were the times we seemed to leave the house rather suddenly, beat a hasty retreat, the way we would grab our blankets and towels and run from the beach when it started to rain. He was a large, impressive-looking man, broad jowls, broad shoulders, smooth iron hair. It had a solid luster, like the candlesticks. He rose, buttoning his jacket. He always wore a jacket and tie, not just on holidays. And there was something in his bulk, his hoisted shoulders, injured dignity, that makes me think of Rudy. He began to pronounce the names of the ten plagues of Egypt in a stern, almost angry voice. As much as to say, on both your houses. "Dom... Tz'fardea... " Vermin... Frogs...

We lowered our eyes and dipped our fingers in the wine. Like I was saying, it was an embarrassing question.

The old woman dropped her eyes and blew on her spoon. She seemed almost to be counting to herself; almost a ritual. I looked and looked. I will not say to my heart's content. How could that be? I couldn't learn her by heart; she wasn't going to keep. I was looking so hard and so long that she was almost finished by the time I caught on to what she was doing. It was a can of stew Roxy had heated up for her. My grandmother was systematically spitting out the chunks of meat and storing them in her fist. Not kosher.

*She thinks she's gonna see something.*

All right for you. You and your secrets.

There was a commotion in front of the room. A group was approaching, all together—hanging, holding on to each other, pushing, crowding. They all seemed to be talking at once. They looked like a conga line. They stopped abruptly in front of the box. Their voices were tensely lowered.

"Ma! Don't cry. Ma! If you cry... "

It was Auntie Hodl and her family—my grandmother's youngest sister. Fat matronly Theda and her handsome husband; little Sherwin and his tall stylish wife; the wife's parents; and of course Hodl's husband. The old man was twisting his head and staring all about the chapel as they yanked him along. His cap was on crooked. The rest were staring at Hodl.

She was the only one who was looking at the stiff horizontal features in the box. She seemed to be wearing half a dozen sweaters and her pants were stuffed into her boot tops. She resembled an old Chinese peasant with her smooth flat cheeks and slanted eyes. Now they were glittering. Her shoulders sagged; she let out a sigh.

"That's right, Ma. Keep it up. Just keep it up. After I told you—"

"How's she supposed to keep from crying?" I said.

"Doctor's orders," snapped Theda, without turning round—pushing out her face more threateningly at her mother. The old woman hung her head. She looked ashamed. "I got a bad heart, kiddo," she said.

She sat down beside me on the sofa, sobbing guiltily and popping little pills into her mouth. Her shoulders shuddered as if she had hiccups. The others piled into the next row, pulling the old man along—since he has to be propelled—and as soon as they sat down resumed staring hard at Hodl. Theda, right behind her, pushed up her sleeves and folded her arms.

Of all the Bobbe's grandchildren, Theda is the one who takes after that remote ancestor—the old gypsy. I wonder how many millennia it took to make such features: the wide impassive cheekbones and half-hidden eyes. But something pained in her expression spoils it. My mother says it's because Theda was raised according to some dictatorial method of child rearing fashionable at the time. No matter how hard the infant cried, no matter how the mother's nipples squirted and ached, it couldn't be fed—couldn't even be picked up—until the hand saluted on the clock. And as a matter of fact she has the look of a hungry baby, her eyes squeezed up and her mouth squeezed down; her face and her forearms prominently displayed.

Hodl kept sneaking backward glances at her husband. His face was beaming, smooth as soap. Hodl shaves him. "Listen, dolly, do me a favor—fix his cap, it shouldn't fall off." She doesn't know my name. "That's better," she said, biting her lip. She stuck her fist in her eye. "I wanted so bad to go and see her in the hospital."

Theda looked over. "You're starting in again? Fine. I'm going to march you straight home."

"And now they won't let me go to the cemetery."

"Ma! What did I tell you? There's nothing to see."

"Maybe we could take her," I said.

"No. She's not dressed warm enough. She hasn't got enough pills."

The funeral director was hanging around. "Oh, no, I wouldn't recommend that," he said, worried, rubbing his hands. His hair was as black as his paper skullcap. "No, not if she's not well. I wouldn't want to take such a responsibility."

"You see," Theda said.

Out of the corner of his mouth the funeral director addressed me. "Please, lady. I don't want no trouble. I got all the business I need."

A lot of people were coming by now. My mother turned up her face, tears streaming sideways across her cheeks like rain on a window. They closed the box. There was a hush. So it was time. I had a sinking feeling, a kind of stage fright. All right, old lady. You're on your own.

"Call your mother." That was the first thing my grandmother said to me when I came to her house. "Call your mother." She knew it was the last thing I wanted to do. There is something very peculiar about the relations between mothers and daughters these days. She wasn't criticizing, exactly—just letting me know. My mother is a hard person to live with; she won't live with her herself. Still, it was an unnatural situation. No good could come of it. Maybe she knew someone would have to pay. Maybe she knew it would be her.

My mother called. My grandmother was at her house. Rudy had walked out on Roxanne. For a change; usually it's the other way around. "He didn't expect Ma to catch on, sick as she was. He never thought she'd take in what was going on. That's the part he couldn't stand. It was too humiliating."

I had to come north immediately, rent a "two-bedroom apartment" and "hire a woman" so I could take my grandmother off her hands. My mother has been after me for years to move to the North Side. She knew it was my intention to leave Chicago altogether. That was why she kept harping on a "two-bedroom apartment."

"Why do we have to go through all that? Why can't she just come here?"

"No. That's no good. The family wouldn't be able to see her. They'd be afraid to go out there—in that neighborhood."

What did you think I had in mind?

I wanted to take the old woman; I couldn't take the family. But that was a contradiction—how could you separate them? She stood for the family. She was the family. Rudy thought if he had her in his house, she would make it a family too.

It was up to us; the others weren't even in the running. Sylvia said she "would love to have" her mother. But Fred had put his foot down. Fred can be counted on for that. Leon said she would be welcome to stay with him and Irene "if she could get up and go to the bathroom by herself. " As if that wasn't the problem.

We didn't ask much, did we; we only asked her to *get better*; we only asked her to be *as before*.

Anyway, they were going to Europe. I guess they got fed up with looking at Fred's slides. "Europe," my grandmother sniffed when they told her. Her head sank scornfully into the pillow. "Europe. *I've* been there."

I felt my mother was trying to use her mother—to trap me, to get me in her power again. Make me part of the family. I knew she wasn't going to let the old woman come to me; she knew I wasn't about to go there.

"Mother. If that's the case. You have a two-bedroom apartment. Why can't you hire a woman?"

"I? How can I hire a woman? You have nothing better to do."

What business did the old woman have, living so long? Her own children were too old for this. Time was running out on them too. How did they know how much they had left? "She could last a long time." It was her life against theirs.

I had told my mother that I would move in with her and help her take care of my grandmother. I didn't remind her now and she didn't remind me. She felt trapped too by the old woman's lingering death. It was in our feelings for each other that we failed her.

It's strange. The city has been built up so much in the last few years, distances have shrunk in the grip of the expressways. But Jewish Waldheim seems as far out as it has always been. The same long bumpy ride, the car horns, the curtains drawn in the back of the black and silver-gray hearse.

It still seems nowhere. A muddy brown pasture in the midst of factory fences, industrial waste. This is the new part, where the stones lie flat and they have something called "perpetual care." The mud was full of dried sticks of grass. I had forgotten that my mother's father is buried among my father's people. They were all around us, tarpaulins spread to protect the graves. All the same, a lot of mud was getting dug up and tracked. The ground was just iced over; glazed puddles. I went to stand behind my mother's chair.

Her cold was bad and she was all bundled up—like Hodl: boots, pants, sweaters, scarves. The more she had put on, the smaller she looked; stooping. She seemed to shrink before my very eyes. Now, when she felt my hand on her shoulder, she turned herself sideways to see who it was, her head poking forward as if she had a stiff neck; her cheeks bound in a babushka. It scares me how much she is getting to look like my grandmother. *Listen, Mother, don't do this to me. I'm not ready for it yet.* She reached up a mittened hand.

It seemed strange to me that my grandmother was at one and the same time carrion—garbage—that had to be got rid of, shoveled quickly out of sight; and something precious and tender, of infinite value, being laid away as if for safekeeping—sunk in a vault. These things seemed opposed, but they weren't; they couldn't be; because both were true. It was necessary to hold them both in your mind at once. That's all we were trying to do, standing over the open grave.

But it was very cold. You could see the rabbi's breath puffing in front of his beard. He was young, and the hairs spread brightly and ripely over his chest and almost up to his eyes. In the chapel, as soon as he had opened his mouth, I knew it was going to be all right. He wasn't going to talk like Dylan Thomas. And he was no sadist—he was making it quick. Of course, it would have been nice to prolong the services. A shame to waste such an opportunity. A raw windy day, a low sky, a box suspended over the straight steep sides; pinched faces somberly staring. Funerals are the only chance you get. Weddings and bar mitzvahs are practically useless. Happy occasions; people are thinking of the presents. At weddings they all want to write their own scripts anyway; be original; make up new words. For funerals the old words seem good enough.

But it was just too cold. The wind was goading. People couldn't stand still. Humiliating to be thinking about your fingers and toes when you knew your mind ought to be on eternity. The sky was as white as the trail of a jet.

Two workmen bent, releasing the tapes. The long blue box slid smoothly downward. I felt my grip on my own life loosen a little.

The four surviving children rose to say Kaddish. Fred, Sylvia's husband, standing behind her, lifted his head, a keen look in his eye, reciting the words with firm conviction.

"Yisgadal v'yisgadash shma rebo... "

It startled me a little. Fred is an orphan, the lucky dog; his parents died when he was small and a large family of brothers and sisters grew up in "the home." This sounded like a good setup; I would have been willing to take my chances. But people talked as if it was something catching: "He's from the home." "He got that way in the home." His children to this day correct his pronunciation:

"Daddy. It. Doesn't. Mean. An-y-thing."

"That's like I say. It don't mean nuttin."

A sly foxy glance, a sharp chin, shrewd lifting brows. White cotton pads of sideburns. His hands in fur gloves clasped to the front of his coat. For reasons of her own, my grandmother always called him by his last name, Solomon. She never called him Fred. He was her son-in-law thirty-five years. It was still Solomon. And if the world ended tomorrow, it would still be Solomon. She never said a word against him—she didn't need to. Everyone knew what she meant. We all pretended not to notice anything amiss.

Uncle Leon was knocking back and forth, rocking on his toes, just like the bearded old Jews in shul. Tall, bushy browed, ermine haired—a kind of smooth thick white fur slicked sidewise over his temples. He is the one who takes after his mother; it's not just the features, it's the expression. He looks as if he's keeping his thoughts—the best ones—to himself. I remember him once, when I was small, frowning down at me, shaking his head and wondering out loud: "What good are girls? What good are girls?" Now he was mumbling and ducking his head; it hung forward, red, shame faced. His lips shuffling mechanically. "Na na na na." It was nonsense syllables. He was only making off; imitating the fervent old men with their chanting and swaying.

Roxy and the kids were standing behind Rudy, looking at his coat. The girls with stung sullen faces, shrinking and shivering in leather jackets, hiding their fingers up their sleeves. The little boy, his glasses like a pair of obstacles, peering out from under them in his elderly way. Lost. Where does he come from? They're a bunch of giants and he's such a peanut. And Roxy, somber and striking in black, all six feet of her, her legs elegant in black stocking, a veil loose about her cheeks. She was entitled. She was the one who had done what needed to be done.

Rudy was standing stock still, staring straight ahead with his unfocused, unflinching expression. As if he could feel their eyes on him. His hands were behind his back. His lips were not moving. So my father was right after all. This was it. The end of the line. It was all over. The old woman's sons were not going to say Kaddish for her. They didn't know how.

"Sarah? Sarah?"

The lab technician smiled and clutched her clipboard to her hip. "How are *you* today, Sarah?" A smooth blond head, big smooth white teeth.

My grandmother was lying on her side, on her cheek, a handful of hair gathered to the top of her head like a scanty white beard. Her large hands clutched the sheets. Her lower lip gripped the upper; a tube was fluttering in her nostril. One eye turned inward, sunk in its socket. The other stared.

"Don't you remember me? Sarah? Don't you know who I am?"

The girl bent down, encouraging; her voice got higher. "Do you know what time it is? Do you know what day it is? Sarah?"

The old woman's lip kept gripping. Her shoulder was lifted to her ear as if she expected to hear a terrible crash.

The girl stood up. A row of ballpoint pens was clipped to the pocket of her lab coat. "How long has she been like this?"

"Like what?" We all said it at once. We all turned on her.

"Like this." She shrugged. "Senile."

"My mother is not senile," my mother said. "My mother was never senile. She's sharp as a tack, sharper than any of us. You don't know my mother."

"It's only since the accident," Rudy said.

"What kind of accident? Even after the accident. After waiting three hours for an ambulance. Sitting on an orange crate in the storeroom at the A&P. Barefoot—her shoes flew off—that's how hard she fell. And then the doctor has the nerve to tell me—"

"Let's not get started on that now, Mother," I said. You keep flaying yourself like this, there won't be anything left for the knacker.

"She couldn't. 'She couldn't—not with that hip.' That's what he said. I saw it with my own eyes, and he's telling me. 'She couldn't have been conscious. She couldn't have been sitting.' Well, they don't know my mother."

How often she must have gone over it in her mind. Even the words hurt. Crash. Smash. Hip. Splinter. Smithereens. A bottle of cooking oil got knocked off the shelf and shattered in the aisle at the grocery. They picked up the pieces but the floor was still slick. You could say it was bound to happen, what with all the old people shopping there, in that miserable dregs of a neighborhood. Someone was bound to slip and fall. Maybe even break something. What fragile vessels we put our feelings in.

For some reason, after all that had happened, all that had gone wrong with the doctors, the hospitals—and everything had gone wrong; I'm not going to make a list: who doesn't know, who hasn't felt, the arrogance, the indifference, the shameful neglect; everything gains in value with age but a human life—of all there was to torment herself with, this had made the strongest impression on my mother. This was what stood out in her mind. *They don't know my mother.*

And it is the sorest spot. It is the hardest thing to take. They don't know. They don't want to know. And now of course they will never know.

The girl stood with her clipboard under her arm and her pens on her chest. "She doesn't answer my questions."

"Why should she?" Rudy said. "They're dumb questions." He was standing at the foot of the bed, legs straddled, hugging his elbows in his blue uniform. His cheeks heavy, inert—as if he had a helmet strapped under his chin. I see what it is. He always looks on duty. "You think after all she's been through she cares what day it is? She'll think you're making fun of her, you ask her what day it is."

"But she has to care. You should talk to her. Orient her to reality."

"Oh, reality," Rudy said, with a deliberate, dumbfounded grin—jerking his head up and down and showing his jack-o'-lantern teeth. "Ha. Uh-huh. I see. Reality. "

Die with dignity. Die with dignity. I know what it means. It means without all this. Without the doctors, the hospitals, the tubes, the technicians—why are they still squeezing blood out of this turnip?—without the TV set tilting down from the top of the wall with no one watching and the lights and buzzers that no one can reach. I know what it means. But what if dignity is not our lot?

The old woman lay on her side, in her crib, the tube in her nose and her face to the wall. *Hear no evil. See no evil. Speak no evil.* Her skin was not so much wrinkled as twisted—wrung out. Her eye was sunk in its tunnel, her mouth clenched. She did not express apathy. She looked tenacious. She was hanging, holding on to something. Her lip. It was cracked and bleeding from the dryness of force-feeding. She had been hiding it from us the whole time: the lower lip defending it like a weapon.

A few days later Fred and Sylvia were sitting beside her bed for a long time. At last Fred got up and reached for his coat. "Come on, Syl," he said, raising his voice and pushing his arm into his sleeve. "We might as well go if she ain't gonna talk to us."

It would be Solomon who finally broke her silence. Solomon had always got her goat. The old woman lifted an eyebrow and rolled up an eye:

"What's there to say?"

"Just a little, three times," someone said behind me. The funeral director. Still hanging around. The nervous type. "Just a little, three times," the rabbi said. I struck the shovel at the pile of dirt. The earth was shockingly hard. The impact jarred me. It was all I could do to scrape up a few stones and scatter them on top of the lid.

The bulldozer bumped forward, gave a nudge; the whole pile slid and dumped in at once. Rudy ducked his head between his shoulders, stretching his neck out as if there might be more to see. His coat seemed too short for him, flapping at his knees. A good two inches of white sock showed at his ankle. It's not that his head is so small—it's that the rest of him is so big. He moved off, his hands digging his pockets, flicking a glance at Fred and me. Just a habit, professional; he didn't really see us. His back stiffened in the wind. I just realized; Rudy had lost his only friend. Nothing stands between him and his life. Only himself; a great seawall.

We looked and looked. Everyone else had hurried back to the cars; they were closing the curtained doors of the hearse. But Fred seemed reluctant to go, hesitating, his chin pressed to his chest; his fur gloves laid one atop the other against his coat. "She always called me Solomon," he confided—shyly, not looking me in the eye. Glancing about under his mobile brows as if someone might overhear. "If she would of just once called me Fred."

My father's two sisters and his brother were almost the last to leave—parked at some distance, making their slow way over the mud. They are heavy people and it was heavy going. Aunt Dee in her cloth coat and Aunt Flor in her fur; their purses trailing by the handles at their sides. They seemed to be laboring slavishly under the law of gravity. It was obvious when I caught up with them that they had been talking—conversation stopped dead. I asked for a ride.

Once, many years ago, I happened to see Uncle Arnie standing on our front porch sticking a note in the mailbox. It was a summer evening; the screen door was on the hook. I went and peered out. He was the baby of the family, his face still lumpy and purplish with acne. He brought it close. "Tell Sammy his father died," he said and ran down the stairs. His face is still lumpy and purplish, and whenever the family gets together he wants to know where all the good times went.

We stood beside the car, silently scraping barnyard mud from our shoes.

"Your mother," Aunt Dee said, turning on me. Her face was very close, puffy and pouchy, her teeth small and crowded. She looked like a chipmunk. There were creases under her eyes. I'm going to have that, I thought; I saw it in the mirror. Well well well; the rough with the smooth. Her eyes under her glasses were just like my father's—the same amazed blue specimens.

"Your mother."

As I have said, my mother's parents are buried in my father's family plot. There is a large stone bearing the name. Of course, today, there had been a lot of traffic; in spite of the tarps the mud had been trampled and churned on the graves. They were upset. "Showing no respect for the dead."

"What's my mother got to do with it? It's not her fault if the cemetery's getting crowded. "

"She wanted those plots. She insisted. I didn't want to give. But you know your mother. It's her own way or nothing."

Usually it's nothing. Aunt Flor looked embarrassed; Arnie looked away. Aunt Dee has been a widow many years; twenty, to be exact; it was a day much like this, a long drive to Waldheim, the air white with snow flurries. Her husband did not leave her in good circumstances. He couldn't bear leaving that way; had hung on long after the doctors had given up on him, pedaling a Good Humor wagon with a face that must have given his customers pause. I was not about to forget. Only—one at a time, please. To tell the truth, just at the moment, stepping on graves did not seem to me the worst thing in the world. Not even the most inconsiderate. It didn't seem to occur to them that they were "showing no respect for the dead."

The workmen were still banging down the backs of their shovels, flattening the earth on the top of her grave.

It was business as usual, the quarrels of the living. My mother has a reputation for going where she is not wanted. But why did she have to stick her poor parents where they were not wanted? Wasn't the plot in the old cemetery good enough? So what if it was all used up? That never made any difference before. They're all buried on top of each other there anyhow; especially the children, two or three in a grave. Headstones and weeds all over the place. My grandmother's family. They were always thick as thieves.

Rosie's husband, Herschel, was a fruit peddler, a little red-faced man with hard cheeks polished like apples and tiny eyes that seemed to be wincing and snapping with satisfaction. As if he'd just downed a schnapps. Ahhh. He often stopped at our house to take a glass of tea.

His clothes stank to high heaven and the fruit flies buzzed round him. His horse, Buck Jones, was madly in love with its master. (It was named for a cowboy star who perished in the Cocoanut Grove fire. All Herschel's children were named for stars, cowboys, and sirens.) Buck Jones was blond, blunt featured, with a white mane combed to one side and bangs hanging over its brow. Rudy loved to feed it apples he stole from the cart, just to see the creature swallowing them down whole—gulping them like yawns. Patient in its blinkers, flies scaling its lashes. Lifting one hoof at a time. But when it felt that a sufficient interval had elapsed, Buck Jones would come climbing up the front steps, clipping and clopping and dragging the cart. Scales tipping, brown bags flying; rotten apples rolling in the street.

They say Rosie nagged Herschel to death. He got his revenge. All thirteen children looked like him. My mother told me he didn't just kiss the babies—he licked them; dragged his tongue over their faces like a cat. Rosie was something of a battle-ax, with her bowed legs and straight hair and a set of false teeth that looked as if they had been made for Buck Jones. She was always getting up packages to send to "the poor people." Naturally we all wondered who these poor people could be—with such a benefactor—and where she ever found what to put in her packages. Same place Herschel found his apples.

There are only three sisters left of all that tribe. Rosie is a cripple in California; Yetta has taken to her bed—not to rise and shine again, I fear. Hodl was the only one who could come to the funeral. And I couldn't get over her family—scolding the old woman, staring at her like a prisoner in a box. I happen to know that she babysits for them, often weeks at a time; takes care of their houses, their children, their pets—she hates pets—with her sick husband and her bad heart. (What's the matter with the in-laws, I'd like to know. They look to be in pretty good shape.) And now all of a sudden they were so worried about her they couldn't take their eyes off her for a minute. Of course they were worried; they were scared stiff. People have a funny way of showing these things.

It was time. Funerals are the last outpost of family life—the last stronghold of such feelings. That is why they bring out such strange behavior. My father's family, like Hodl's, were simply trying to express their sense of what was fitting to such an occasion. A public statement of continuity, solidarity. At the same time you could see they had their doubts; the most nagging suspicions. Their sacrifices were ready. But where was the altar?

"You have no regrets," Flor said to me as we were riding once more past dreary streets. "You went every day, every day." I felt as if she had slapped me in the face. What kind of person has "no regrets"? And who went "every day, every day"? I had plenty of regrets. And yet I was drawn to my grandmother—pulled to her. It wasn't a feeling. It was a force. The raw material of feeling. It was what had brought me back for the funeral. Surely it was worth something. Surely it was more powerful than these petty family differences. I knew I didn't have anything "better to do."

The family was sitting at Sylvia's. ("She keeps telling me, 'Tell people not to come, tell people not to come.' What did she want it at her house for, if she doesn't want people to come?") Fred belongs to the Skokie chapter of the Jewish Legionnaires, and in the evening they sent a minyan. The men arrived all at once, stood stamping in the doorway in earmuffs and galoshes, blowing on their hands, opening boxes musty with odors of prayer books and fringed prayer shawls. One had brought his son, evidently just bar mitzvahed—a pale boy in an embroidered cap. He looked scared to find himself in the house of death, with its baskets of waxy-looking fruit, the thick yellow sponge cakes, the sheeted mirrors. He stared at all the people wearing their ordinary faces.

They chased the women out of the room. What good are girls?

Sylvia wanted to show off her new couches in the den. It seems that Mindy and her husband had gone on vacation and left their cats with her; and the cats had clawed up the furniture. "It's all right," Sylvia said cheerfully. "I wanted to get new." Sylvia is good-natured. I think it's called happy. Not to say complacent. But she and Fred dote on their things; what they throw out is as good as new. Even Gary's toys, when they gave them to my sons; as if he had never played with them. Years ago, when they lived with us, it was a wonder to me to see Fred carefully hanging up his clothes (no one in our house ever hung anything up), brushing them out, sticking his shoes on shoe trees. Something else he must have picked up in "the home." It used to make me feel guilty whenever we came to their house, tracking in dirt—they watch your feet when you walk in the door; they say hello but they keep eyeing your shoes—throwing our coats on their bed, all bolsters and dust ruffles; using the little guest towels displayed in the bathroom. (I could never feel quite sure they were meant for me.) And that's the way it was now, as we all packed into the den and shut the door, taking our seats on the couches and folding chairs labeled "Weinstein & Sons."

A funny thing—some of the women were talking—the same thing had happened to them. Their children had gone on vacation, left them their cats, the cats had damaged the furniture. And they didn't even like cats. Couldn't stand cats. Who wants cats?

"Cats," Sylvia said. "That's what I get. Cats."

She stuck her fingers in the crooks of her elbows and looked at Mindy out of the corner of her eye. Voices rose against the wall; the men in the next room had started their prayers.

It was as if a gavel had been rapped—a meeting called to order. Sylvia had thrown the subject open to discussion. She was asking for agreement, for sympathy—almost, for justice. All the mothers were murmuring indignantly. They had a common protest. Their daughters were having cats instead of children.

Sylvia takes her mother's advice—she doesn't raise her voice, she drops her eyes. My grandmother used to hold her up to my mother as an example. Fred had the reputation of "making remarks" and "talking dirty," and in a family where the father always put on a clean shirt before he sat down to the table—and the mother never sat down to the table at all—you could see where that would go over big. So I could tell when Fred had said something; the blood would stand still in Sylvia's cheeks and her eyes would drop so quickly they seemed to clatter. These days she just glances down, briefly—the way she flutters her eyes over the rims of her Ben Franklin specs. And in a pretty matron, with a stunning silver tiara of hair, it's very effective.

It just so happened that all the mothers had sat down on one side of the room, the daughters on the other. So it was a kind of mock tribunal, a kangaroo court. The mothers were bringing a case against the daughters. There were about fifteen or twenty of us altogether, and except for Mindy and me, and Fern—Sylvia's new daughter-in-law, Gary's bride—the daughters were not necessarily daughters of these mothers. That was all to the good. There is safety in numbers. The condition was generic; the complaint was general. The mothers crossed their arms and stared. The daughters stood accused.

"No children and no plans for any," Sylvia pronounced.

"So they tell me." Looking from Mindy to Fern as much as to say, Well? What have you got to say for yourselves? Hmm? Why are you holding out on us? Where are our grandchildren?

Mindy was also looking down. You could see they had been through this before. Petite, almost breakable; her pliant hair hanging past her cheeks. Her face is so small—wedge shaped—the cheekbones seem too big for it. But that is her beauty, the bit of strangeness. She gets the cheekbones from our grandmother. And I was just noticing: her nose, delicately arched, is like the old woman's too. An exact replica. I know, because I had been studying another replica of my grandmother—the still features in the box—that very day. I didn't expect to see them ever again. And now here they were. We are her connection with the future.

You could picture the men swaying to their vibrating voices. The daughters said nothing. They had already spoken. What better way to tell your mother what you think of her than not to have children? That was what they had to say for themselves. Their silence was accusing. You could feel the weight of hostility shifting. They didn't need to state their case against the mothers. They had stated it so many times before.

Once again, the mothers were to blame.

Once again, it was all their fault. The burden of proof was on them; they were caught in the middle. Why not? It was a position they were used to. Has there ever been a generation more in the middle? They must have been sick and tired of rendezvousing with destiny. It seemed they had always been middle aged; between their parents who had belonged to the old world and their children who didn't want to grow up.

Well, to give you have to have. They were the generation that "didn't know any better." Someone actually said that now. "We didn't know any better." (Who was talking about *knowing*? What did that have to do with it?) The mothers—once again—were defending themselves.

"It was the psychology courses," Sylvia said. "That's what did it. We drove Gary to Champaign in September, and when we picked him up in December for Christmas vacation, he told us everything we did wrong."

"When you love a man, don't you want something from him?" Irene asked. She sounded worried.

"Children are just an extension of yourself," Fern said. "That's all. That's just as selfish." I guess she felt obliged to say something because she is a daughter-in-law. She's even tinier than Mindy, hips smooth in French-cut jeans. Thirty; older than Gary—who doesn't look very old, alas, in spite of his mustache and muttonchops, his baby features swamped in corporate hair. Between the two of them they are now earning forty-five thousand a year. Every time I see Fred and Sylvia it goes up. Nothing else is new. At first Sylvia was proud. Now she seems puzzled. What do they want it for, if not "for the children"?

There were a lot of spent bullets whining around the room.

I heard my father's voice rasping after the rest. At the cemetery when they said Kaddish he took off his glasses. His eyes looked smaller, weaker, unused to the light; the big sunburned nose emerging between. His skullcap trimmed with curly gray hair. He seemed to be peering over a fence, a wall.

The men were tending to their business; we were holding a little postmortem of our own. Because now—and everyone must have known this was coming—someone brought up a recent public opinion survey. It had run in a nationally syndicated advice column.

*If you had it all to do over again, would you have children?*

Eighty percent of the readers who wrote in in response answered No.

It's no use saying, So what, what does it prove, who cares about advice columns? My family are the readers of advice columns. And it's no use observing—as I was about to—that people who write in to advice columns are troubled souls, complainers to begin with—"Just a bunch of bellyachers," as my father would say. Because the same grievance was lodged in their hearts.

Now they tell us.

It was a revelation. It explained the whole thing. Explained it more completely than anything else could. They, themselves, had never wanted children. They should never have had daughters in the first place. No wonder it had all been so difficult. They had been bilked, conned, hoodwinked, swindled, sold a bill of goods. (Hadn't they always said they "didn't know any better"?) Now they saw what the daughters were saying. The daughters wanted just what the mothers wanted out of life. Only they wanted more. And they wanted it now. And they knew how to get it. They weren't going to run the race for happiness in any three-legged sack. No, thank you.

The mothers stared. Once again the hostility shifted. Only there wasn't time; it was too late even for that. They didn't have it all to do over again.

My mother and I were not taking part in this discussion. My parents have five grandsons, not a bad hand to draw when you've started out—as they seem to see it—with a lousy low pair. She was standing pat. It cannot have been a very familiar sensation. For once she had nothing to reproach me with. For once life had not handed her a rain check.

She was lying on the sofa, a blanket on her knees, a pillow behind her back. Her cold was bad; she kept dipping her nose into a fistful of Kleenex. I couldn't help thinking: There she goes again—the couch and the Kleenex. But I knew this was real. Even her hair was limp. Her beautiful hair. The set hadn't held; it's getting too fine—or too thin. Getting that blown dandelion look. You can see the pink scalp through the fibers. Soon it will be levitating.

From time to time we exchanged small smiles—a glance of complicity. We are veterans of these wars, battle scarred. We've fought over this ground so many times before. We've been at it so long we've almost forgotten by now what the fighting was all about. We were practically comrades in arms. It was a kind of truce. No whistles blowing, no white flags waving. But it had suddenly dawned on me: my statute of limitations had just run out. The old woman is dead. My own children are grown. Soon I will be forty. Move over, Mother. I'm in the middle now.

In the next room strangers had finished chanting prayers for our dead.

And now I see that this squalid little tale is a love story. Is it our fault that this is the way love shows itself—hides its face—and that these are the remnants of our rituals? Everyone said it was a bad end. She didn't die with dignity. I'm not so sure. For us, yes—we were weighed and found wanting. I was heartbroken for her suffering, her humiliation, which seemed so undeserved—as if that's any criterion. It was bitter to know we had let her down. Maybe bitterest of all to guess what it meant. But she outwitted us; she kept her secrets. She went out on her own terms; even to the end she would rather have had us believe that she didn't know us, she was losing her memory, than let on how truly defenseless she was. And she didn't ask for anything; she didn't take. She was always so afraid of taking. You'd think someone was giving.

After the small settlement with the A&P for medical bills—they sent back her shoes—there was just enough from her savings left over to cover the cost of her funeral.

The clocks were ticking. My mother in her reading glasses was looking up a number in the telephone book, licking her finger as she lapped up the pages. Usually when I'm around she asks me to do this for her; but I was just getting ready to leave, going back to New York. As usual I had deposited some of my junk in her closets.

"Aren't you going to take anything with you?" she asked, glancing up, rather resigned, her cheek moving up and down in her hand. (My God. Doesn't it ever end? Don't we ever get rid of them? Don't they ever grow up?) The glasses, I suspect, are from Woolworth's. Their depths are serene, a thick diffused light. They seem to smooth and calm the Great Plains of her face. They accomplish something I have never been able to, imaginatively. And I don't think old age will do the job, either.

My father was honking the horn outside. Tapping it—the SOS signal. He thinks he's the only man in the world who honks a horn that way.

My mother spoke quickly: "I can't tell you how glad I am you came," she said.

I know. That's what I came for. That's what this has been about.

I bent down with my bundles to give her a kiss good-bye.

"My cold, my cold. Don't catch my cold," she warned, lifting her face. It was suddenly luminous, her glasses brimming over with tranquil light. I can't live within ten miles of her; I dread the distance there must one day be between us. "I won't," I promised. So we turned our faces aside; our cheeks just touched. And we parted—yet one more time—forever.

# ARONESTI

Aronesti disliked the smell of the house. It flagged a cue card at him: Nostalgia; but when he sniffed—"What is it? What is this smell? What do I remember?"—his imagination dived and skidded, like a false start in a dream. That was the way that summer cabins smelled, that was all. This air of past summers trapped under the floorboards; the heat's furry embrace: Sham. Eight years he had been coming to this town on the dunes, renting this same cabin; he had brought furniture, he had left books. But nothing changed. Whenever he returned to walk through the four small rooms, to force the fast windows and to thrust open the doors—waking up the curled wasps that would begin staggering—he sensed that he was serving a notice of eviction.

A high school biology teacher, two months' vacation, a chance to break, every year, with routine; he knew that his would be considered a "nice life," but not for the reasons he had chosen. Why anyone should want to break with routine, he could not understand; change filled him like a keg of murky water. But he adjusted to his summers—ate rare hamburgers, spat watermelon seeds, set mousetraps, mended window screens (since something chewed them). And in the night, if he heard the click of a mousetrap, he would give a start of satisfaction. But also, often, he would lower his book, and look about for its companions: he felt lonely and constricted when he was not surrounded by books, and had no choice of them. He lived like a prisoner who must exercise in his cell to maintain his dignity.

Why, then? Ada had wanted it. Why now? His mother wanted.

"Phew," the old woman said, coming up to him with her nose buried in a pile of linen. "Damp; damp. This smell is bad for you. Take these sheets before I have to make the beds, and give them a hang up on the line."

"Miasma, miasma. Smells can't harm you."

"But the damp—the damp smell; it gets into your lungs." She held a sheet out in her fist.

"Why can't you trust me? I know about such things."

"Then go turn on light bulbs. I think we need some. I'm writing down a list for the store." She was not writing; she hated to write; it exhausted her. But it sounded busy.

So he went around the house switching on lights, crouching in dusty corners to plug in plugs. He went out to the car and brought in the sandwiches and lemonade left over from what his mother had packed for lunch. He opened the refrigerator—the little light popped on; he felt warm and happy, and then a plunging sadness; he had forgotten for a moment where he was, that he was on this side; and on that side was the past, everything. And on this side, only he; and all eternity would not fill the gap between. He nudged the door, but it slammed with finality. The motor throbbed.

Aronesti's mother would answer the telephone: "Who's that?" Or the doorbell, "Who's that?" She was still in a foreign country; she would always be. There were things she did not even care to get used to, the doorlock buzzer, for instance, which she always held down with her thumb (they lived three flights up, in the city) until the caller came right to the door. She could not believe that its only function was to unlock that door way down there.

Nevertheless, she answered their telephone. Aronesti did not like telephones: it was mere forgetfulness that he had had their summer number connected again. One night when he was ranging the house with a flyswatter, developing a style of swinging (with a hook), of sliding the dead beast off the flip end—the telephone rang. His mother was in bed. It was very late. Something imperceptible as the force of gravity pressed on his bowels.

"Hello."

A hesitation. "Hello." Female.

"Hello."

"Is Jack there?" She already knew that he was not.

"Jack who?" How senseless to prolong it; he knew no Jacks.

"Jack Bramer?"

"Did you say Bramer?"

"Listen—is Jack there?"

"No. I think you must have the wrong number."

Click.

It was not his fault. That some piece of machinery had summoned him. Rudely. He was ready.

Maybe eternity was like that. Disembodied voices. "Who are you? Who are you? Is that you? Where are you?" Nice thought. You could look a long time. If you wanted someone. Oh God, he wanted someone.

"Ada, where are you?" His elastic heart.

She once had taped a photograph of herself on their dresser here in the bedroom. It was her only beach picture, she said, that was why. He went in and in the yellow light, his hands on the high dresser and his bald spot tallow in the mirror, peered at her face. He often did this, for long times; there was something he was looking for that he was not seeing.

The picture had been taken when she was nineteen or twenty, and it looked like all old photographs, which seem not only to fade but to freeze. In a light now dim and wintry, six girls were sitting and posing on the sand, all smiling into the camera. Except Ada. She was holding up her hand to the camera, telling the photographer to wait a minute, probably. Her black hair was short and curly and her long eyes narrowed and confused, as if someone had just made a joke and she was waiting, with good will, to have it explained.

He tried unfocusing his eyes, to blur it, to make those faces melt in his vision. But they would not unfreeze.

To look at her caused him no pain; he saw not her face, but the photograph, and that he knew. When he had looked at the bookshelves in their apartment—at the neatly torn white paper markers that Ada had, over time, placed among the first twenty or thirty pages of so many, the markers sticking up all over like simple headstones in the graveyard of her good intentions; that he knew; he could smile. But when in this summer house he had found an old handbag—a good one, that she had, because it was good, hardly ever used—when he opened it and saw within a crumpled Kleenex; a comb with two teeth missing; a chewing gum wrapper—why enumerate?—when he saw what he would find in any woman's purse; when he smelled the sweet stale perfume rising out of it, and thought of her bending her head over it seriously, as women are serious with their purses; she seemed anonymous, a woman who had lived and died; and it pumped spasms through him that a defenseless creature, who had been endowed with the power to do such ordinary, inoffensive things as to acquire possessions and to keep them orderly, should have that power taken. If he had her here now; if he saw her standing in the hall, her chin on her chest, her knee slightly lifted to balance a purse and catch its contents to the light. Oh, now. Now.

Twice a day he went to the shul (a big, shabby house with a sign outside that said Zoned Commercial, so much frontage) where the old men from Feidelman's Resort nearby always formed a minyan. The old men smelled like wet, crushed cigars; their white beards were stained with yellow streaks of nicotine, and they coughed up white-yellow phlegm. Aronesti prayed loudly, the sweat erupting; no more mumbling; his pronunciation had got much better; he knew the service so well that he did not have to think about the words, and they blended in the bloodstream that pulsed in this dry room.

He felt relaxed when he left, soothed by a trance.

Then he would walk home, past the screened-in porches where, because of the insects, the people were sitting; rearing their heads to look at him, their eyes nacreous in the darkness. He knew how he drew their eyes: big, but potbellied, the shiny spectacles set in his eye sockets, the shiny dome of the skullcap, from which the globes of sweat were swelling. And a black suit: he felt like an old rabbit in an astrakhan wandering among these—among these? What were these people lizards lying on the beach by day; now, like penned-in cattle, hiding from the insects that were warming up in the grass and hurtling against the resilient screens.

Twice a day; visiting hours. No one in that hospital would look you in the eye; you could wander through it like a passenger lost on a jolting subway; and see no one to ask the way of, no one who was responsible for anything—only your fellow sufferers, who would glance away from your distress and uncertainty because it might get to them. And the lights and buzzers of the corridors, going on and off like the impulses of an outsize computer brain.

They called him up in the middle of the night. He heard the ringing; his mind parted in a smile of bewilderment, and a plume of steam spit through it. He did not have to answer; even the news of her death came from the impersonal machine.

"Mort, what's the matter, don't you go out or do anything?"

"What is it? What do you want me to do?"

"What I want? What matters? You can't sit around reading all your time."

"If I want to?"

"You're white like dough." She pinched his arm. "Every time you walk in the sunlight you look so pale you scare me; your face shines. I think you're going to faint from looking pale."

"People don't faint from looking pale."

"Go outside. Get out. It's hot in here. It's no good for you."

So he took his book outside, and a chair, and sat under the apple tree. On a branch he noticed a bag, an envelope of cotton candy; caterpillars, twisted like the burned-out wicks of candles, were writhing within. Two hundred maybe. He moved his chair; he could feel the caterpillars wiggling under his collar, and they might be crawling in his hair. Bits fell on his pages; bits of what? Animal? Vegetable? He did not know; he could not read. Birds yacked, dogs barked, women yelled, children cried. Nature. For the two hundredth time he rubbed his ticklish nose.

Every sound. Outside. In. These houses flimsier than the worst tenements of the city, more crowded. Shacks. Shanties. Overrun with kids. Everyone barefoot. The husbands show up on the weekends; the orphanage in the valley.

And the nights, too, could be noisy; teenagers walking up the road singing, a neighbor whistling for his dog—the sounds sudden and confused, as if they did not know what messages they carried in the darkness. Late at night, he had heard quarreling, the people next door: the man had a voice like an announcer, smooth and consistent, cake batter dripping from a spoon. Like the commentator for ERPI Classroom Films. Aronesti had to sit through a film, two showings in a row, once a month. The sound of student feet shuffling into the assembly hall, over the desperate buzz of the projector palpitating, a stream of light on the vacant screen, colors jerking. So, a bazaar in China. And then the voice, the voice that had introduced a canning factory the month before. "Why, this isn't the real thing," Aronesti would think, looking about with embarrassment at the sweet, young, light-suffused profiles; the voice was too clever, condescending; it would pretend excitement, but knew better. Awful, to be in an argument with a voice like that!

Two little boys walked in the dirt road, towels under their arms, their legs streaked with sand. One had a belly like an Aborigine. They stood at the screen door pounding and calling. Must be locked. He heard bare feet running through the house. Must be bare, bouncing. The mother appeared, a pale shadow, smudge of red lipstick, behind the door. She undid the hook and held the door open for them, stretching out her arm, the white inside blue veined, the bas-relief of a tendon.

That white arm. She looked like Ada. Ada, lying on the couch with those white arms behind her head. Ada, slowly smiling. Then her smile subsided, sinking back into her soul. "Ada," he had whispered. She turned her head. "What were you thinking, just now?" Her head lolled back; she shrugged her uplifted arms and laid her chin into her chest. It made no difference; it was not the explanation that he wanted: but the connection, the connection, the current of life that had passed through her and had passed him by.

It was the Fourth of July. Late, the sound of fireworks began in earnest, the explosions curiously soft, muffled in the absorbent darkness. Pale moths were fastened to the screen, like dull faces peeking in. His mother came wandering through, past her bedtime, making noise to show that she had no intention of disturbing him.

"How could I sleep?" she said when he looked up at her; and sat down at once beside him. "That fan is wasting its breath in here."

"Turn it off."

"That's an answer." Her hair was wet and she smelled of lipstick, which had been applied raggedly. And her breath smelled somewhat like lipstick—artificial, stale; close. Close, the smell of old people. Everything locked up in there all that time.

"You never try to be a help," she said.

Justly, too. A hot, noisy night; he knew she had not fixed herself up at this hour for nothing; so he gave in, and they went for a walk. It was pitch dark; the deep lights of the houses kept to themselves; the crickets were jittering like hot wires dropped in the grass. With warning tremors, a car approached, its beams of light thick and swarming, cutting a swath of pale leaves and black shadows. The hedges loomed around them, intricate, gleaming fretwork. The car rolled on, turned a corner. An explosion crumbled through the darkness.

The feeling the night gave you when these dense sounds diffused in it.

But the length of it. Nothing took time anymore. Take? Did he want them to take his time from him? There were moments when he could hear time going, as if a movie screen had filled with luminous significance, and he could hear the projector churning. The depths of silence. The depths of the night. Fireworks; thunder. Rain.

Rain in profusion, striking the bricks, the cement, the stone steps; teeming in the gutters. Spending itself for nothing. They were safe in bed. In the freak blind light of the window he would see her, sleeping on her side, her back to him, and her hand reaching over covering her shoulder; the naked hand; the one without the ring. He would lean over her, her hair swept up and the soft shiny underside of it exposed; her particular odor rising freely in the warmth of sleep; he would whisper—not to wake her; in the abundance of the night, no need to wake her; only to nudge some response from her as she repossessed her dream.

Rain, that very afternoon that she was buried. Scant—as if that made any difference. He stood at the window, watching the dark splotches erupting on the pavement, the stone steps slickening. So she had become part of that.

From far down the beach, from the pier decorated like a bandstand with crepe-paper streamers, the fireworks were shooting out over the water, bursting needles melting into the black lake. All along the shore there were people looking up restlessly at the sky. Their faces flickered with the colors—yellow, orange, red, purple—a special sigh for purple. Like the selections from Tchaikovsky the school band was always playing, this display; no one seemed to know how to end it. Long tails of firecrackers popping off, the rockets beginning all over again. On the stage, Mr. Riga, the conductor, turning his stiff chin to the audience. As if knowing their impatience. (How could he help but?) As if dragging things out just for spite. The players, mostly girls in sticky white blouses, planting and squirming their ballet-slippered feet. The music lurching on indestructibly, the audience asking with one heart, Now? Now? Now? When? *Pop Pop Pop Boom.*

It was a few moments before the crowd started to disperse.

His mother took his arm, took full possession of it, slipping her narrow elbow through his and clasping his wrist with her other hand. She did not lean on him, but he could feel the stiffness of her bones, the heavy pacing of her steps, the strange distribution of her weight. Now her expression had lapsed interest; she knew she was out of it.

So, who was not out of it?

It was no darker, no cooler, no quieter than it had been an hour before. It was not getting any later. The summer night was opening, opening, opening; porous and fragrant. And the restless crowd scenting it; hovering, swarming; ranging the darkness—for the center of it, the heart of it. The instinct for yearning.

He knew. He felt it too. The clumsy, cumbrous feeling, some old yearning rousing itself. Some old yearning that you had never had. Just some old impatience, this vague rousing nothing but impatience. And impatience with nothing, nothing but the night.

The traffic lights were set to blinking yellow late at night, but this was a holiday weekend, and the main road fed other resort towns north and south. So there was no chance of getting across; though people were gathering: the road was full, the cars moving gelatinously. Along the curb, the pedestrians collected, blinking in the headlights' long, sticky beams, which seemed to fuse to the eyeballs before they ripped away. Like the moths hooked on the screen, their faces—moist, white, sleepy; glittering and dull.

Everyone seemed to assume, however, that something would be done; they would not be left this way. Aronesti trusted, too; he felt awed by the spectacle and yet detached, as if it were the vast activity of some other form of life. When he shut his eyes, he imagined the noises (the honking, rattling, rumbling) feeding the remote air of some night swamp where wild cattle were herding. ERPI Classroom Films again. He saw too many of them.

On the other side of the street a girl of nine or ten (skinny, large nosed, a head of frizzy blond hair) was trying to get across. Maybe she had been sent to get someone; she kept stepping off the curb and stepping right back. Her face, turned into the lights, had a tense, semiconscious expression, like the close-ups of athletes on television; she was just calculating what car to take a chance in front of, anyone could see that. Several women in housedresses and hair curlers were discussing her ("tcching" and taking in the breath). Himself—though his tongue tensed and swelled each time that she threatened to make the dash—he could not call out. There must be some reason no one else gave a yell.

Then without even seeing, he knew she had darted out; tires screeched, screeched, screeched, sticking to the asphalt; a car horn swooned; his mother pulled on his arm. He heard the women say that was good, that had scared her—she could have caused a real accident, the little dummy. And there she was, back on the curb; her shoulders hunched, her face popping out from them, ghastly, and her eyes like reflectors. Not only had she had a good scare—she had almost got herself run over, in front of all these people; so she looked ashamed and turned her head from the lights that were whipping over her face.

He felt a swarming emptiness, a stray grief, as if the headlights, penetrating him, had picked up some straggling animal—the startled eyes like a stopped heartbeat. Death was a dark world, and she was wandering through it.

Sometimes before sundown Aronesti walked on the beach. It was filthy by then, full of ice cream sticks, dented paper cups, cigarette butts, empty squeeze bottles. From the bathhouse came shrieks, volleying in that wild, unearthly way of sounds in closed, partitioned places; catacombs, prisons. Zoos. Fat-thighed girls, their stiff sprayed hairdos glimmering like beetles' wings, plunged gravely through the sand. Teenagers; for the beach was theirs, mostly; the people without responsibilities. They smoked, they petted, they rubbed sun oil into each other's backs, they cracked gum; their portable radios blared at their knees. Most of all, they looked; they looked up at everyone who passed; they looked around. Afraid of missing something, someone. (It gave him a quick, log-heaving revulsion, to think of their puppy love.)

So why did they look so glum?

After all, he was a teacher. Maybe he wore some mark of it between his brows, and it was on that they fixed and followed? No, no sign of recognition; they might have been following an optometrist's flashlight along a wall.

No, why did they look so glum?

Over the loudspeaker, a throat cleared. "Attention. We are looking for a little lost girl. She is blond, about four years old; she wears her hair in a ponytail. Her name is Kathy Lynn Begoun. She is wearing a red-and-white polka-dot swimsuit and blue sunglasses. If anyone sees this little girl will you please bring her to the beach manager's office? Thank you."

Routine. At least six times a day, children turning up lost or children looked for; the clear young lifeguard voices efficient, good humored; the sunbathers looking up from their blankets to listen only because it was impossible not to listen. So the faces lifted; some frowned with the sudden input of sound and sunlight; no one paid any attention.

But it touched him, this unison of listening, these heads going up unconsciously, these faces—against the background of glinting water—frowning with some rudimentary recognition. Ada looking up, frowning into the camera—the camera, however, not waiting; the moment never explained. Preserved merely; intense, dilated.

Close to the pier, two little boys were throwing stones. They threw as if they were casting a spell, lifting their arms up over their heads and opening their hands; and the stones sprinkled out on the water.

It was cooler on the pier but the air viscous. He stood with his hands on the railing looking at the water. It looked tepid and dirty; the foam floated on it like spit. Surely, people who jumped off bridges and things like that would not choose this kind of water. Unless you were doing it for the principle. Nihilism. Like going down the drain.

Back from the pier came a slight, pale woman, trailing her hand along the railing. Was that his next-door neighbor. Then those must be her dirty little boys throwing stones at the waves. But the neighbors' boys were older maybe. Well, when she got closer. But she pivoted around on one hand and crossed her arms on the railing. He would not be able to tell now whether he knew this woman. She had given no sign of recognition.

Aronesti dreamed.

He sensed himself—some buttons on a coat, a weight; saw sometimes his shiny shoes against the cindered snow, now the hat on his head. And Ada too he hardly saw, but felt her—her arm through his, her black nubby coat, her small feet in high heels—bare, too bare for such a day—picking over the mushy ground. At last the train came. So they had been waiting for it. The el, blowing up the gritty dust in their faces. In spite of the blurred, smoky, yellow light inside, the car was cold. A window was open. No wonder. He got up and closed it. But then noticed another open. He got up and closed that too. There were people in the car, but nobody helped with the window closing; nobody even seemed to notice that there were windows open. More. No matter how hard he looked to be sure, there were more. And he had to get up—for the wind was bitter—though Ada was sitting patiently, turning her pale face to him and then back to the window; and he wanted to sit down with her. At last he noticed an old bum sitting right in front of them; a lean man, shirtless, in a dark colorless suit that he wore like a bathrobe, as if he had pulled it on only to answer the door. Dirty colorless hat; grizzled chin; bloodshot eyes. This man, he thought, is eyeing Ada. He sat down immediately and began looking out the window. Every time they passed a station, he tried to see the name of the stop somewhere; but they always pulled out too quickly, or he could see the sign but not make it out. Then it got darker; the yellow lights were strung in reflections in the windows. The old bum turned around and looked at them, only his eyes over the edge of the seat, dark and colorless, impossible to tell their expression as they slid to the corners, exposing the terrible bloodshot whites. Then in one sliding movement of the eyes, the head, he slumped to the window and died.

Aronesti heard the snap and recognized it instantly, even as he started; somewhere in the house, a mousetrap had gone off. He knew he had been dreaming about Ada, and did not want to think about it. He had been grateful at first for such dreams, but now they did not lend themselves to probing: the events had become incoherent, her appearance garish (rouged and powdered, covered with brown crumbling leaves), as if the dreams themselves, with time, were decomposing. So he did not want to lie in bed. He got up and turned on the light; his glasses were on the dresser, the lower half of the lenses thick and cloudy. He took up his flashlight and, sending the light along the edges of the moulding, went looking for the trap.

It was in the kitchen, right under the sink, the thumb smear of yellow cheese untouched, and a small dark mouse underneath the snap resting its head on its paws. You were supposed to be able to remove the mouse and use the trap again. What he needed, a pencil, pry the thing up; one handed, he rolled up his pajama sleeves, and then, tucking the flashlight under his arm, picked up the trap. The slim tail hung free. With a shudder he threw the mousetrap into the garbage can. What did they cost? Eleven cents? He took the garbage can too and put it outside; there was a cantaloupe slice of a moon. Covering the flashlight with his hand, he moved quietly back to his bedroom, his fingers glowing like bloody coals.

He put the flashlight back on the dresser and without expecting it, looked up into his face. He stared at the face in the mirror—the strange walls, the strange threshold. He remembered the dream. He sat down on the bed, numbly pulling the sleeves down over his arms. This incident had actually happened. Some years before, on a cold snowy evening, on the way to a party; some poor down-and-out soul sitting right in front of them on the elevated had glanced back at them and died. They had been held up for at least an hour, too; what with getting the body off, the police, the passengers from that train and from several successive ones knocking and squeezing together like molecules trying to keep warm. They had gone on to the party; walked into the heat of the room, smoke, laughter, lightly perspiring faces turned toward them as they stamped the packed gray snow from their boots; and in that instant, without speaking, agreed to say nothing of the man who had died.

Now Aronesti sat on the bed, his elbows on his knees and his chin thrust forward, trying to see back into his dream, to get a look at those eyes. But they would not keep still for him; there was the looking toward him, the sliding away—and when they had slid away, he had to force them to turn back, himself to stare, all over again.

He had wondered, often, what the look was for. The simplest thing, of course—for help. But the man had made no sound, no sign; and he did not seem in pain. In fact, the glance was if anything reproachful. But let anyone turn to look at you—just look at you—over his shoulder; it would seem reproachful. And what if he knew—looked back for one last human contact, or, with some instinct, to see what was overtaking him? But there had been nothing like that in the look. It had been—just a look.

And here Aronesti knew that he was lying. He could not tell what was or was not in the man's eyes or his mind; that he could never know. But he had always known what the look had meant. Why else had they waited on the cold platform, among the gum machines and defaced posters, shivering and turning away from the wind, until the dead man had been taken into other hands? How else had they known as they walked in on the party in the overheated flat, that they could not use this man's death as an excuse for being late, as if it were an episode in the newspapers, on the radio, in the public domain. What had he seen? Frowning faces in the bony winter twilight. Faces that in the next moment would be looking on his dead body. People who would answer whatever demands his death had put on them, and then resume their temporary destinies.

When he turned, he had been looking back on his survivors.

*Survivor.* The word seemed like some primeval amphibian dragging itself up from a swirling sea and gasping toward the sand. Ignorant, tedious, triumphant word: containing so much of the pain and necessity of living. And he felt that there was a further significance to this word that was not beyond his comprehension; a responsibility he yearned to undertake; a connection he verged on making. He got up and pressed his hands together, tensely took off his glasses and laid them down on the dresser, on the photograph. The young, smiling faces welled up in them. He stared at the blurred, grainy faces; hers was among them; she was there. He snatched up his glasses, held them to his eyes, thumbs laid against his temples, and bent his head over the face that was still looking out, almost smiling; the eyes that were still squinting in the weakened sunlight.

# POWER FAILURE

I was sleeping on the couch under a pile of blankets and coats and the fire scratched in the grate.

The power was out; one of those freak spring storms that bump off trees and knock down lines. The world was a snow-swamp, the Everglades turned white. Knee-deep drifts, floating branches, limbs bent low, broken and bearded with snow. Everything bowed with age and silence.

The only other soul I'd seen all day was the caretaker who looks after that place across the way—the one that used to belong to Colonel Somebody-or-Other. The heirs are in court, squabbling about who gets what and which was promised when; and in the meantime the house just sits there—a big pink elephant, gingerbread, jigsaws, doodads and all—getting picked clean by vandals. They would have walked off with the cannon that squats on the front lawn by now, only it's up to its cast iron neck in concrete.

The old man seems to have all this on his mind.

He comes by just about every day. I hear a car door slam, I look up, there he is, larger than life—green plaid lumber jacket and waxy yellow work boots—squeezing out of a low-slung hatchback. A Japanese make, which I mention because there seem to be so many in this neck of the woods. The local dealer must be one helluva salesman. The little cars go clattering up and down the patriotic landscape, almost a part of it; like the red brick and bow windows, the bumpy blue pyramids of the mountains, the white birches. (You think other trees are white, too, until you see birches again.)

So here he comes. Collar up, earflaps down, hands shoving into pockets over his stomach; pipe extending the angle, the purpose, of his stubborn Yankee jaw. His eyes have a nippy glitter inside his glasses; his breath in the iced air stiffens and staggers before him.

"How's the typewriter?" That's what he always asks, only he says "haaoww" and "typewrituh." It's his joke; he means me and my machine both. He's the one who delivered it, got down on all fours under my desk to plug it in. "Well, yuh've gawt noh excuse naoww," he said, scraping and grating his sandpaper hands together. "Gawt tuh get daowwn tuh wuhk naoww."

From his baggy pants dangle wires, pliers, clippers, black electrical tape. He's been busy rigging up traps and alarms, meaning to give the vandals a surprise: "Next time they get the shawk of their life."

I think he'll be sorry if there is no next time.

Today the house was safe; buried under a ton or two of savage bright stuff. You couldn't look at the snow for the pressure of sun on it. A blue jay flashed in branches, the colors of the wintry day. Black white blue. Trees snow sky.

Spreading its wings it became a miniature landscape, something painted on a fan.

I read by the fire in earmuffs and mittens. (Have you noticed? How hard it is to turn pages with mittens on?) When it got dark—whenever that was, the clock had stopped—I cooked supper over the flames. The hamburger dripped, smoking raw. The potato burned black; ashes blew into the coffee. I was getting good and mad at myself: too lazy to take the trouble to do things right. Just because the situation was temporary. Some excuse. What isn't temporary? If you want to get technical? As if that's any way to live. (And how long since I've been meaning to buy a kerosene lamp, in case of emergency, and replace the dead batteries in my portable radio.)

By the time I went to bed, I had fed the fire just about every scrap of paper in the house; and if there's one thing there's plenty of around here, it's scrap paper. All the same, the last thing I saw—turning my back to the fire, hitching up covers—the last I saw, in the red flickering glow, was the one scrap overlooked. A letter from my mother, stuck to the bottom of the wastebasket. The envelope raggedly ripped.

Even in my sleep I knew that this must be the reason for my dream.

Now please. Don't get me wrong. I don't mean to embarrass anybody. I get discouraged myself, when people start talking about dreams. Especially in stories. Because what's to keep us from telling lies? Making it all up? Are there rules? And besides, everyone knows that dreams aren't just dreams. Someone is trying to tell you Something—with a capital *S*. I don't know about you, but that makes me nervous.

All right. I apologize. But what can I do? I'm not trying to put one over on you. (I told you to begin with I was sleeping—remember?) This isn't really a story—and I was dreaming. And I'd just like to see if I can get things straight.

In the dreams my sons are just learning to walk; bold staggering steps and shy shining faces. One light head, one dark head, at the same level. My daughter is older (though that can't be right, can it?). Her short skirts lift and stick out in front and show her bare narrow legs, the puckered trim of her bloomers. What's odd is her hair; smooth heavy hair, straight-hanging, as if water weighted, and so long it surrounds her. She is mantled in hair; a dark shining cloak.

Some children are born that way; right from the beginning; come into the world wrapped in the mysteries of their own personalities. You can see my daughter is one of these.

My heart glares with gladness; as dazzling, as hard to bear, as the sun burning snow. Because I know what's going on—I recognize this dream. I've had it so many times before—though never in my sleep. It's here, this is it. I'm getting my wish. My children are small again. We have it all to do over.

I can't tell you if I had read my mother's letter or not; ripped open doesn't mean anything. I might have been looking to see what was inside. Lately, she has sent a few checks. "Go buy yourself something." "How's the money holding out?" This is something new; I'm not sure what to do. Maybe I cash them, maybe I tear them up. It all depends. No rhyme nor reason.

I see I have just confessed—and put it in writing—that I am the sort of person who opens a mother's letters in case there might be money in them. Good. Glad that's over. So now you know. Here we have a stock situation, the old antagonism. Mother and daughters. You've heard this story before.

But I'm not the only one, it's not just me. This condition must be very widespread. (There's safety in numbers. But is there truth?) Many friends tell me they can't read letters they get from their mothers, either. And who can blame them? Why open up a letter and read it when you know darn well, beforehand, what it's going to say? What has been written, predestined, foreordained, from time immemorial. A little reproach, a little punishment, a little guilt. My friends must feel the same way I do when I see my mother's handwriting on an envelope. The postmark. The wavy lines, the canceled stamp. About the way it feels to see my name on a bill:

Remit immediately or action will be taken.

And after all she is presenting the bill. It's that time. Payment is due, she means to collect. Only—only—it has been established by now that I am never going to come up with her currency. And she won't accept mine. So how can I pay up? What will I use for wherewithal?

Like they say: The letter killeth.


You know how it is when you try to recover a dream.

A tug on the line; a quiver, a gleam. You grab hold, you hang on; it struggles and squirms. Maybe you catch something, bring it to light. Maybe it sinks into the depths.

Splash! Gone for good.

That's how it is in my dream, only the other way around. In my dream I'm trying to recall real life, waking life. My own life. I have it, it's hooked, I'm reeling it in. Then the same thing happens. A wriggle, a flash, it slips from my grasp.

I reach for the past—and it isn't there.

I might have known. This dream was too good to last. My sons I can picture as infants; that means the past is there—somewhere. I could lay hands on it (couldn't I?). What's wrong is my daughter; she's the one. Looking closer, I see that she's not really a child at all. She is only reduced in size, in scale: a miniature. Except for her hair. It can't be any longer and straighter now. And that's another thing. I don't recall girls having hair like that, when I was her age. So lustrous, so lithe, a kind of raiment: an animal's coat.

Her eyes have the same liquid gloss.

Something tells me I am seeing my daughter in my dream just exactly as she has always been. A grave little image, a stand-in for her grown-up self.

But who got her ready for school, then? Who brushed her hair, who tied her shoelaces, who buttoned her blouses down the back? If I didn't? Who painted orange stuff on her cuts and stuck the thermometer under her tongue? (Don't tell me she never ran a fever, fell down and scraped and hurt herself?) Who kissed her good night? Who checked the covers? Who told her things a mother tells a daughter? Someone must have.

Who else could it have been? If it wasn't me?

The brightness fades; a bare white light seeps through me. No fair. No fair. This isn't my wish! Not what I bargained for, not what I meant. I said I wanted to live the past over again. I never said I wanted to lose it.

What made me say handwriting?

My mother prints, scrawled block letters. This is likewise something new. Maybe it's too hard for her to write? She has a touch of arthritis in her wrist, it could be acting up. (I ought to know, I have it too. I'm feeling it right now.) Maybe she thinks it's too hard for me to read? Her letters could be scribbled to a child:

TELLING YOU THIS FOR YOUR OWN GOOD

And she expresses herself, more and more, in a telegraphic style.

P.S. EVER GET THAT CHECK I SENT? BYE NOW. LOVE, MOM

Wait a minute. Just a minute. Whoa—hold on. So she calls herself Mom? Since when? How long has this been going on? Who calls her Mom! I call her Mother. And get introduced to her acquaintances—as all my life long—as my daw-ter.

No name, just the generic.

"Mother," I say. "Is that manners? Is that nice? Are your friends supposed to call me Daw-ter?"

She arches up her two little pinched eyebrows plucked, picked, singed like pinfeathers—the style of movie vamps of her youth. In that mode also, her thin wine-colored lips. You smell the perfume of her lipstick as she compresses them: "And what makes you think they'd care what your name is? If I told them?"

Otherwise her features are large, dark, and dignified; the profile of a coin. The head on a buffalo nickel.

So she thinks of herself as Mom. She wants to be Mom. That's news to me. What do you make of it? What's in a Mom?

And while I'm at it—that reminds me. Just where does she write these letters, anyhow? (The ones I don't read.) Since there's no place in the whole darn house where a person can sit down, in a comfortable chair, under a decent lamp, to read or write. Naturally not; she'd be a social outcast. This is a retirement village in south Florida—where the skies are as blue as the ocean, and the clouds are as white as its wakes.

Correction. That's at high noon. At sunrise the clouds are bashful pink, blushing, puffed-up flamingo feathers. At sunset they are gossamer—gilded—edged in radiance: translucent as an old lady's hair.

She must write her letters at the kitchen table. Stamps and stationery she keeps in the cupboard, hiding the bottle of sweet purple wine. (The grapes on the label sweat glassy beads of dew.) My mother doesn't drink herself, except for a drop in hot tea when she has a cold, but she does like to keep a little something on hand; just to show how broad minded she can be. And it's no use telling her I don't drink; even if strictly true, she'd never believe me. She knows better. I'm divorced.

HOPING YOU HAVE LEARNED YOUR LESSON

What is her currency? A life she can approve of, what else? What does any mother want? Why can't I be like her friends' children, acquiring things, habits, for a lifetime?

Go explain to your mother that there has been a breakdown in "personal relations"—as if she didn't know—and when that happens, when circuits short, fuses blow, lines come down, connections fail—you're on your own. You need a lot of luck, or a lot of character.

And I only said that, about the character. Just ask my mother. How would I know?

The caretaker told me they were fixing to get the paowwuh back on during the night, and I figured I'd be the first to know. This cottage has oil heat, but an electric switch kicks it on—and I do mean kicks. The first time, I thought a deer had taken a running jump into the side of the house. I was afraid to go out and see. Do deer look before they leap? They give a whistle, I know; and their little white tails stand up and stiffen and it's the last glimpse you get. There were deer here aplenty in the colonel's day, when this cottage was part of the colonel's grounds. Now no more deer, but it's still the colonel this and the colonel that. (The license plates say Live Free or Die, but oh how New Englanders go crazy for titles.)

Anyway, the furnace gives me a start. Even in my sleep I'm listening for a thud. The night is booming: snow plopping and thumping from all those pitched roofs and pointy firs, dumping down clods and clumps, blow by blow, like wet concrete. The fire is low; flames scavenge the logs, gnawing and sharpening red rodent teeth. That is what's real. And I want to wake up, throw off the weight of sleep and dreams and too many covers and snow loading down the backs of the trees. The burden will snap the young spring branches, with their clawing buds.

I know this is a dream. Only a dream.

Winter dusk. A pearly slush packs the skylight. Galoshes lean outside doors. Climbing stairs, I smell dinners getting cooked. Fat spits and spats in frying pans. This run-down building seems familiar. Have I been here before? People pack their bags, they move on, they leave no forwarding address. Window shades fly up with a clatter, clack like tongues. Frozen snow glazes the glass.

I'm looking for the person who raised my daughter.

The children were small, money was scarce, I got sick. That must be when my daughter was sent to strangers. That's how come the missing years, the missing memories. It wasn't me. It was someone else all along.

But who? Where? No one answers my knock. Streets, stairs, doors keep changing. Room after room is empty, and not just empty—deserted. No one lives here. The building is condemned. The doors are lined up like rows of fences.

I have found the past. I am in it. This is it—all that's left of it. Not even a memory. My daughter and I have no history; only the history of mother and daughters. I know just how she is going to feel toward me. I have forfeited my one and only chance.

I didn't tell you what it felt like when I saw that torn envelope. A jolt, a shock; it buzzed right through me. I thought the furnace had kicked, they'd got the juice going, thrown the switch. The force was so strong, I didn't know what to call it. And what difference does it make. Call it anything you want. It's all the same power, it all comes from the same place. So that's the way we're wired up.

I didn't know there was that much left in our connection.

But what about all those years, when my children were growing up, when we were alone?

WASH MY HANDS   YOU MADE YOUR BED NOW LIE AS FAR AS I'M CONCERNED NO DAUGHTER OF MINE

Mother Mother, why can't you be one way or the other? So I could feel one way or the other? Why have we wasted our time like this? Why couldn't we have called it something else? What good are checks and letters now?

Now she sits at a plastic-topped table, ballpoint pen in hand, gazing as if for inspiration at a row of newly planted palms. All lined up and wired, pliant grass-skirted utility poles. Flamingos shift on coat-hanger limbs. Her face is carved teak from the Florida sun, her lipstick glows in the dark; her eyes swim like goldfish in the cloudy depths of her glasses. You know those fishbowl lenses old people wear.

Old? Did someone say old? My mother?

The frames are mother-of-pearl, as white and luminous as her hair.

I'm numb; frozen stiff. The room is cold, the clock is stopped, the fire is out—powder and ashes. The windows are streaked in leaky gray light; cold sweat clings, a sheet wrung from the wash. It takes a minute or two for me to understand. I'm awake. It's all right. It was a dream; only a dream. No one is going to feel that way toward me. Still, it's not exactly a relief. Because who was she? Who is she? And what do I do now? I never had a daughter.

# GERMAN LESSONS

I.

To begin with the house: just an old wooden house. Sloping roof, shutters, smoking chimney. It stood on the hill, in the trees, almost a part of them, narrow, steep, its shingles like bark. But this was Bavaria, all was created perpendicular. Castles, churches, rigid fir forests, monuments, towers, and of course the Alps. The everlasting Alps. At this distance, they came and went, the eerie whiteness of the moon in daytime. You could never be sure you were seeing them because they were there.

The village was nowhere to be found in the guide books either. Too far from the mountains, not on the lakes, not scenic, not quaint, not historic. No fairy-tale palaces, no mist-blued ruins, no half-timbered cottages on winding cobbled lanes. Not far off, on a path through the woods, a monastery occupied a thousand-year-old site. It had been plundered and pillaged, sacked and burned, and all those things that happen in history; but a carved niche from the font, black bones in the crypt, were said to go back to Karl the Gross—Charlemagne. It was famous also for its bitter brown beer. The stone walls, however, overlooked another town: the red stars on the road maps, the sightseeing buses, the tourists shopping for flashbulb film and airmail stamps. So the village had what villages have: a *Platz*, pigeons, benches, a fountain—dry the year round and now collecting carp-colored leaves; a memorial column of greenish-bronze busts and greenish-bronze plaques; a bank, a post office, two churches, a school; a railway station, or at least a stop; a telephone booth. Most of the houses were painted stucco—gray or mustard or khaki—and the flat drab fronts and peaked orange roofs might have belonged to any age. New ones were going up, the same red brick and raw bulldozed lots as in any American suburb, and though only the main street was paved, there were more and more cars. Every morning a dairy herd plodded to pasture, stopping traffic, raising dust. Impatient German drivers leaned on their horns, the fanfare and bugle blasts of wedding processions, victory parades. The cows switched their tails, unmoved; their plaster-cast faces gazed a cow gaze.

Kitty had seen cows before. And she hadn't taken the flat, at the top of the house, the top of the hill, for its charm or romantic past or a view. She didn't have much choice; it was the cheapest she could find, on the train line to Munich, close to a kindergarten for Christopher. And the landlady seemed friendly. The Grubers lived below with a pair of smooth yellow cats, named for the brats in a nursery tale. Frau Gruber doted on her Max and Moritz.

She was the doting type; one of these heavy old souls, always fussing, always out of breath. When she came toiling up the stairs, knocking at the door, it took her a moment to stand there and catch it—her hand over her heart. She had, as she said, a *complaint*. Maybe she had guessed that something was wrong, things were not as they should be; the Americans looked shy and lonely, she only meant to cheer them up. But sometimes Kitty was actually afraid for her. The large lopsided face, the scroll of bangs under a kerchief, the big seeking eyes. They were full of *expression*. What it was might be hard to say; but it was urgent.

The landlady was not supposed to climb stairs—*streng verboten*—but the house was all stairs, nothing but stairs. It topped the hill like a steeple. One, two long flights up to the attic, half a flight down to the cellar, fifty steps at least to the garden gate. Kitty from her window could watch the landlady making her way, sidewise, one step at a time. Her head bobbing in her kerchief, her back round and stooping, her market basket jogging at her elbow. In everything she did there was a hustle and bustle, an earnest commotion. *Eile mit Weile*, the Germans said. She made haste slowly. She seemed to be heading in all directions at once. The planks were slick with flat fallen leaves.

Just inside the gate, a rusty key hung on a rusty nail. Frau Gruber never failed to lock the gate behind her; then she reached and peeped over the posts, hiding the key. That was a law of the house. Doors must be shut, or, better yet, locked. The same went for drawers, kitchen cupboards, the wardrobes in the bedrooms—so German, Kitty thought; so overbearing and gloomy—the broom closets in the hall. But next to stairs, the house was all doors. It had been a family dwelling, once upon a time, and on each floor you had to go out onto the landing to get from one room to the next. All day long Kitty heard comings and goings, scraping and slamming, hasty footsteps. To keep the cats in, Frau Gruber said; to save on heat. Now that the son, Schatzi, was away at school, the large room on the ground floor was used for storage, locked and shuttered and cold as the cellar. But no explanations were needed. This was only another of the habits and virtues of the good German hausfrau. What else were doors for?

Kitty would have liked something more; something that said Here She Was. But if pipes knocked, if lights flickered and dimmed, as in gusts of dark wind, if radiators hissed and popped and spilled their secrets—it was because the house was old, old the way things are old in America. And for all the stairs, high up as she was, her window presented nothing worth calling a view. Rusty treetops, garden steps, the gate. Where Kitty came from, not much grew taller than the corn—though that grew taller than you might think. Here there was no horizon. The sun rose with the crows, hatched from branches. You couldn't see the forest for the trees.

2.  It was September, the sky was blue smoke, warmth hung on the air like a spell. At the fountain in the *Platz*, along the paths through the woods, old women in black sat on benches, waiting turns in the sun. In German they called it old wives' summer, Frau Gruber said. It was easy to see why. Indian summer, Kitty told her. But how to explain? Was it the color of the leaves? Or their rustling? Or the smell of their burning—hidden campfires? Leaf dust glowed in the trees, sifting through branches in gold ash.

But Herr Gruber was out first thing with the crows and the cows, digging up his bulbs and shrubs before the frost. Slight, wiry, scrawny even, in his baggy overalls and fishing boots. A cigarette twitched and glimmered under his slim silvery mustache; an eye twitched and glimmered above. He was prophesying a hard winter.

He lifted his hat, dipped his head—a turtle thrust—a slack line of neck, chin, lip. Kitty was not used to such formalities—tipping of hats, thumping of heels—and she wondered if the old man might be pulling her leg. She thought him old: he was in his sixties, she knew, soon to retire as a government clerk, and she had heard him boast he had been born with the century.

An early winter!—Hard and long!—So many degrees of frost!—So many meters of snow!

It was his way of being friendly; he liked to tease. And what was there to say to the Americans? Even if they could talk? Which they couldn't. Mother and child both, gazing up, up, offering up their faces—empty white plates. The same uptipped noses and Dutch-boy bobs, though hers was shiny dark and the child's was red—flashing—and forever in his eyes. They looked the way Americans looked; everything was news.

Oh oh oh! Kitty played along, giving a shiver. Her face was more heart shaped than round, but bare and sober as the child's. When worried, puzzled, it did not contract: it expanded. The pupils of her eyes dilated, their blue became black; the very space between them seemed to widen—and it was wide to begin with. She had her troubles with the metric system. A kilo was just over two pounds, a liter was less than a quart; but a kilometer was six-tenths of a mile. Why six-tenths? And when it came to temperature—! If one hundred was boiling, if zero was freezing, where did that leave her? What did the old man mean, degrees of frost? How cold was cold?

She was lost, and she looked it.

Kitty was used to cold, real cold, the kind you could see. Ponds froze and steamed, frost crept under doors, ice licked the glass with a fiery tongue—lit the windows with frozen infernos. The wind blew and blew. There was nothing to stop it. And when it got cold enough—too cold to snow—then you could hear it. The silence that comes after the crack of a rifle.

Still she shivered. Already there was something in the air, the glimmer of the Alps. They were said to become very distinct before bad weather. Kitty knew that mountains had names: Mount Everest, Mount Rushmore... Here her brow blanked, expanded, trying to think of another. But Herr Gruber seemed on intimate terms. Every Spitz had a name. *Spitzname* was German for nickname. And *Alpdruck* was German for nightmare. Alp-pressure, Alp-squeeze. *Alp-trick* was what Kitty heard. Again, she couldn't explain the English; and again, there, for a fact, were the Alps. Or were they? Now the mountains seemed made of distance and mist, as if they might melt.

But it was the leaves, Herr Gruber said. They were in a hurry this year—fleeing, fleeing. The leaves were his almanac. He clutched the rake under his elbow, one arm always stiff at his side. He seemed to be standing knee-deep in dead leaves.

That same shivering sensation Kitty felt whenever she heard the time announced. The Grubers owned a brand-new TV—a tiny porthole of a screen, ghosts, rabbit ears and all, like American sets of ten years before—and the landlady had passed on her old radio. The signal was weak, a constant crackling, static, hail, at times a fluttering—timid, tremulous—moths beating their wings feebly among the dusty vacuum tubes. Voices faded in and out, symphonies became weather reports, operatic arias gave way to advertising jingles. Kitty didn't much care for operas or symphonies. But this was Europe—she might learn to. She had a general idea that that was what she was here for. And to study German. She had taken the language in high school, when everyone else was taking French, because Germans sounded more serious, and she wished to be serious. But the truth of the matter was, more often than not, she tuned in to the American station, broadcast from the army base in Munich:

*Luncheon in Munchen.* It rhymed.

A siren whistle.

A sonorous announcement:

High noon central European time.

Central European time!

Then Kitty felt it: a shiver, a thrill, a portent. Here she was. Here She Was! Though in fact what she felt was only far away. Very very far. Not a matter of maps or oceans or another country, another continent. Oh no, much farther. Another age.

3.  Frau Gruber knocked at the door, busily out of breath, taking an envelope out of her apron. —Just now—In the box—No postmark, no stamp. She thought it might be *wichtig*, important, she said.

Kitty wished the landlady would not deliver the mail in this way. There wasn't much, and that only junk—Kitty had not been expecting junk mail and advertising jingles in Germany—but by the time the poor old soul had huffed and puffed all the way down to the box at the gate and all the way back up, one step at a time, she was in a state; almost eagerly alarmed. She looked to be the bearer of bad news.

But Kitty did not know how to discourage her either. Who could? The landlady meant well; she always meant well. And she was always at the door. Recipes, household hints, tattling on her cats. Der Moritz, the fat one, the sleek one, snoozed on the window seat in its coat like rancid butter; but Der Maxi was her *Liebling*, skinny and scabby, in and out of scrapes. How she loved to scold him! Coaxing, clucking, setting out saucers, *Schande Maxi*! Shame! Shame! And the landlady watched all the old American movies on TV. Gangsters. Cowboys. Kitty heard them through the floor—machine-guns, cavalry charges, war whoops. The voices were dubbed, but not word for word, and soon would come a knock. The landlady—her head tucked to one side, her hand to her heart:

*Bitte.* What was this loco? Plum loco?

Kitty fluttered through her pocket dictionary, fat and black as a bible, the thin pages edged in the same red dye that used to rub off on her hands in Sunday school.

Loco: *Verrückt*

Bootleg: *Alkoholschmuggle*

Vigilante: *Sicherheitsausschusses*

Some things were lost in translation. But not with the landlady. She spoke no English, Kitty had only her high school German, but Frau Gruber had a way of making herself understood. Maybe because she expected to be understood. She spoke German to her cats, didn't she? Why not to Americans? Now she stood in the doorway, not trying to hide her difficulties. She was exhibiting them. Her chest rode recklessly under her apron.

It occurred to Kitty—a brainstorm, for her—that the landlady was waiting to be asked in.

The two rooms were pitched like a tent under the roof. In the parlor, the smaller and dimmer, with its kitchen alcove and slanting ceiling, light came through the balcony door. Such light as there was; there was too much of everything else. Unsteady end tables, pull-chain lamps with scorched paper shades, a scratched dinette set, a humpbacked sofa. All had the accumulated gloom of a secondhand shop. Kitty knew Salvation Army furniture when she saw it, and she guessed these must be the landlady's castoffs. They bore a certain resemblance to objects downstairs.

A certain resemblance, she thought now, to the landlady.

The old woman sank into the sofa. She sighed audibly—visibly. So did the cushions. They were of shiny crinkly green chintz, spackled and red veined like the leaves of a plant. Kitty could never think of which one.

*Nacht!*—In the night!—Kitty heard nothing? Such a *Lärm!*—Frau Gruber had hardly shut her eyes. Not an *Augenblick*.

Kitty by now knew enough to ask: The mother-in-law?

Frau Gruber had—of all things—a mother-in-law, the bane of her existence. It was the mother-in-law this and the mother-in-law that. She was almost another member of the household; the whole family was at her beck and call. But for the landlady the mother-in-law was a special trial, a personal affliction, the cross she had to bear. The mother-in-law was *tyrannische*. The mother-in-law was *hypochondrische*. The mother-in-law was always crying wolf.

The mother-in-law had been at death's door for twenty years.

She was Herr Gruber's mother, she was Schatzi's grandmother—but nevertheless she was *die Schwiegermutter*—the mother-in-law.

The mother-in-law would outlive them all, Frau Gruber said.

She heaved up her eyes and crossed herself. She uttered the name like someone taking an oath.

So it was the old story, the usual crisis. The landlady told her tale of woe; Kitty clattered about, making tea. The kitchen was a matter of a few shelves, a double hot plate, a sink. When she turned the tap, the pipes rebelled, grinding and pounding as if possessed. When she switched on the kettle, the lights dimmed. Any surge of electric current and a storm threatened: Frau Gruber's tiny refrigerator, the TV, the droning of the black-bagged *Staubsauger*—dust sucker—the buzz of Herr Gruber's shaver; even the train to Munich clattering over the viaduct. Meanwhile, Kitty sensed the landlady glancing all about under her kerchief and fringe, taking it all in. This was her territory, her property.

Was she inspecting for damage? Scars, burns, stains? Checking up on Kitty's housekeeping? The flat was neat enough, the floor swept, no dishes in the sink. But ah—was the windowpane polished and sparkling? Were the faucets scoured till they shone? *Armschmalz*, Frau Gruber said. Elbow grease. Was the bedding hung out to air over the balcony rail? On walks through town the landlady never failed to point out the feather quilts in their buttoned covers, draped like flags and bunting over the flat drab housefronts. It was plain she had made up her mind, in her dutiful way, to take her tenant under her wing; to advise and instruct. The American girl had much to learn.

Kitty had a mother-in-law. It surprised her to realize this: the word had such import, and she had never thought of Justin's mother as mighty and dreadful. She had never really formed an opinion; she didn't have many, she knew she ought to have more. Justin had opinions about most things, but he had never volunteered one about his mother. He rarely mentioned her at all. She lived a thousand miles away, like most people's mothers—their friends, Justin's friends, graduate students in the small university town. Kitty had met Mrs. LeBow only once, on a trip east after Christopher was born. A large woman, soft, billowy, in spite of her foundation garments, as she called them, and her permed brittle hair. She smelled of lipstick, face powder, lavender sachet, and hankies dabbed with toilet water and tucked up her sleeve, and her eyes seemed adrift in the deeps of her glasses. Mother-of-pearl frames, rhinestone-studded fins. She got lipstick on everything; coffee cups, spoons, cigarettes, her teeth, other people's cheeks—and all over the baby, his feet, his belly, his smooth white bottom. She was *in fashion*, she said. Justin had to explain: his mother did alterations in a fancy dress shop; she fitted women who were large and billowy like her.

Kitty had been nervous about meeting her; she knew she wasn't, she couldn't be, what Mrs. LeBow was expecting in a daughter-in-law. But she saw that Justin's mother didn't know what to expect; she never had, with Justin. He was so brilliant! So gifted! He could be anything he wanted. If he wanted to be a poet, well, Mrs. LeBow was sure he would succeed, if he only put his mind to it. Though she had hoped he would make something of himself in this cockeyed world. Whatever he did, he was bound to be different, and all the time he was in service she had worried that he would get shipped to some awful godforsaken place no one had ever heard of before, like Korea, and bring home a war bride. At least Kitty talked English—though she didn't talk much. She was a native of that state on the far side of the Mississippi, and the suspicion might have crossed Mrs. LeBow's mind that Justin had rescued her from one of those strange religious sects they had out there—farm folk who dressed in black and drove in buggies. She had that look. Pretty, in a scrubbed way; the turned-up nose, the prim lips. The sort of face you wouldn't be surprised to find hiding under a poke bonnet; a bed of dark lashes made even her most direct glance seem sheltered. And maybe Mrs. LeBow wouldn't have minded, either, with pins in her mouth and a tape measure dangling on her scented bust, taking Kitty in a little here and letting her out a little there. Kitty was not *in fashion*.

So her reaction to Kitty had been mainly relief. She got out the albums and scrapbooks she had been saving; Justin's report cards, all As, his test papers with the gummed gold stars, his prizes and diplomas and class pictures. Justin in the front row, squatting cross-legged on the floor—always one of the smallest boys and always the smartest. In the early 1950s, in Hackensack, New Jersey, neither was the thing to be. But even then there had been something in the set of his shoulders, the crewcut head lowered between, the pondering forehead, that suggested that no one would want to start up with him.

When they were leaving, Mrs. LeBow had turned aside, in some confusion, to dig a handkerchief out of somewhere. For the baby, she said, pushing into Kitty's hand the twenty-dollar bills, folded and refolded to the size of a matchbook. They were scented too. Her eyes in their fish-bowls swam erratically. She left a smudged print on Kitty's cheek.

After this visit, Justin spoke no more of her than he had before, and Kitty still thought of her as Mrs. LeBow—though now she called her Mother.

Justin was teaching university extension courses at the army base in Munich. Jobs were scarce, he was lucky to get one—even this one. It might not be much of a job, but it was Europe. It was experience. Justin was a poet; he needed experience. And he had never been out of the country before, not even in the service. Two years as a clerk-typist in Kansas! And then that isolated university town—dullest of the dull, flattest of the flat, the middle of nowhere, the capital of it, he said—a Land of Low Relief. That phrase he got from a drugstore calendar—Mrs. LeBow was right, Justin read everything—a caption under an aerial photograph. It showed what appeared to be bars of children's clay—red, yellow, green—and here and there a toy roof, a dribble of trees. Across the lower edge fell the shadow of a wing.

A land of low relief! / A land of low relief!

Justin chanted it for days. Found art, he called it. Of lost art Kitty had heard; she was surprised to learn it could be found.

Justin was living at the army base; there were no facilities for families. That much Kitty had told the landlady, and it was true—as far as it went. But he had never expected her to come. So why had she? Why had she? She guessed she wanted experience too. She was here on her own, here under false pretenses.

He had stopped by to take Christopher for a drive; a yellow Volkswagen was parked at the gate. A woman got out so he could get in—an Italian interpreter, Justin had said. But she was dressed more in the American style—tall boots and tight jeans—and her hair hung to her hips. Coarse, wave-warped, wheaty-blond hair. Kitty thought Italians were supposed to be dark! And that was all there was to see, as she bent, solicitous, stowing the child in back: the boots, the hair, and—in between, under pockets and rivets—two taut crescents.

The landlady must have noticed, since, it seemed, she noticed things. None of this did Kitty feel like saying. She couldn't if she had wanted to. She was as shy as she looked. Confidences—offered or sought—embarrassed her. It was about all she could do to exchange a few words with Herr Gruber about the weather—the *Atmosphäre*, as he liked to call it—or ask the landlady about the mother-in-law; topics connected in her mind. After that her store of conversation was exhausted. And yet she sensed that something of the sort was now required of her. There sat the landlady, tipping and tilting her face, tipping and tilting her teacup: her nose small, flattened at the end, as under a thumb. With her angling head and shining eye, it gave the impression of a bird bill.

The letter.

Another brainstorm. Kitty had forgotten all about it; she knew who it was from. Christopher had a runny nose, a neighbor had offered a remedy. Now Kitty understood that the landlady must know too—must have spied the neighbor stopping off at the gate, and that was what this was all about.

She opened the envelope and shook out the contents, two packets of dried roots and leaves.

The landlady set down her cup, plumping herself up among the shiny chintz greenery. Caladium? Kitty thought. Beet greens?

The neighbor, *ja?*—the Frau professor?—*Exzentrische*! The *Charakter*! Everyone knew her—she spoke English, didn't she? So Frau Gruber had thought. *Spitznasig.* Nosy. Kitty never said anything, she hoped? About the mother-in-law? Because she mustn't. Not a word. *Himmel*! If Herr Gruber knew. The landlady pulled a long face, her mother-in-law face, frowning with all her might, shooting out her lip. No one must breathe a word about the mother-in-law!

Kitty blushed. She was a blusher. Half the time she didn't know her feelings herself, until she felt her color rising; and that made her blush more. She blushed when she told a lie, she blushed when she told the truth; no matter what, she blushed. In this case it was a lie, though a very little white one. She had barely got out the name. The neighbor pounced, her voice sharp as her nose—sharp as her laugh:

What? A mother-in-law? Frau Gruber had a mother-in-law? How old must she be? Ninety? One hundred? *Erstaunlich*! *Unglaublich*! Almost too good to be true! It deserved Frau Gruber right, all her Sturming und Dranging! Who else would have a real live mother-in-law?

4.    The Frau professor lived in the next house on the hill, higher up still, hidden in the trees. Every morning she pedaled to the dairy at the end of the road, the edge of the woods, in her Loden cape and her Jaeger's cap; white faced, white haired, erect—oh very erect!—her little dog perched in the basket. She spoke English very well; better than Kitty did, Kitty thought—meaning British English. She didn't say Kiddie, like everyone else; she pronounced it Kit-ty, so you could hear both *t*s distinctly. Kitty couldn't do that.

You speak English!

That was the first thing she had said, gliding up in a clanking of gear chains. Right away the dog poked out its snout and began barking its head off. It was *spitznasig* too: a miniature something-or-other, with the fuzzy golden-brown coat of a caterpillar.

You see? Mitzi wants to speak English! Hush Mitzi. *Du*!

Like many shy people Kitty had a habit of staring—solemn, wide eyed—as if against her will. She stared now.

The neighbor knew her reputation and enjoyed it. My dear child! She called everyone my dear child. One needn't be a mind reader, or a fortune-teller with a crystal ball. She had heard of Americans in the village, a mother, a small boy. Who else could they be?

Who else indeed?

Kitty had lived in small towns all her life, and she knew that everyone knew everyone else's business. But she herself seldom did. She didn't talk about other people, and she didn't expect other people to talk about her. Besides—what business did she have? What was there to say? Now it gave her a strange feeling—almost sinister—to discover that she could be an object of gossip, curiosity; that people might be talking about her—in a foreign language.

But it was the little boy; you could see he was different. Tugging at his mother's hand, towing her along, his clumsy boots sizes too big for him, his mittens dangling from his sleeves. Boots! Mittens! In this weather! And everything loose, coming undone—the very hair popping and flashing on top of his head. Brazenly red. Flagrantly red. The bold eyes stared through it. That was American children for you—overprotected and underdisciplined.

Clouds loafed in the blowsy blue sky; underfoot, leaves were running for cover.

The Frau Professor took an interest in the mother-in-law—took her side. She was an old relic herself, she said. She liked to tell the story.

It was two winters ago now. She lived alone, no telephone, only a woodstove in the parlor. Carrying in logs, she slipped and fell. The fire was catching in the stove. She could hear the flames, snatching, snapping, as animals snap and snatch at their food. Did Kitty understand? *Essen*: to eat as humans eat. *Fressen*: to feed like animals. To devour. That was the pain: wolfish, greedy. The logs cracked like bones. She had broken her hip.

Mitzi had a favorite toy, a bundle of rags knotted together, and when it wanted to play it dragged out this rag doll. Now it stood over its mistress, the rags in its mouth, begging and whimpering and wagging its tail. The most dreadful noises.

*Schrecklich! Furchtbar!*

The dog knew when it was being talked about. It lifted its snout and, as if to demonstrate, began to squeal. It was very old, its eyes milky, iridescent, the tear ducts cruel scratches. It was weeping.

Yes. *Genau*. Squeak squeak squeak. A rubber doll getting squeezed. The Frau Professor kept passing out, she thought; the room darkened, the logs smoked and blackened, the fire died down in the stove. Every time she opened her eyes, the world had gotten colder. Older. It smelled of ashes. And worst of all—those frightful noises. It was the pain begging, the pain squeaking and squealing, the pain with a rough wet tongue licking her face. What wouldn't she have done to stop it! Strangled it, gladly, with these two hands. The next day, or the next—she had lost track of time and never been sure since—the postman, noticing that she had never collected her pension check, climbed all the way up to investigate.

But it was you that saved me, wasn't it, Mitzi? Naughty Mitzi! Mauling its head, wagging her finger. *Du Mitzi du!*

Christopher moved closer to his mother. The dog was not so little to him. The sharp claws on the basket, the poking snout, the curling pink tongue. And its bark! Its bark! He could see it springing. Another darker creature inside, trying to get out.

5.    It was raining, a clinging drizzle; lights spread a glittering mist over the Wiese. Lights on the roller coasters, lights on the Ferris wheels, lights flooding the colossal bronze statue of Bavaria. Blinking lights, whirling lights, flashing dueling lights. Beacons—white swords—clashed against the sky. The sky was heavy and low, stirring like smoke. From the beer halls came a roar of light—explosions—so big and noisy and bright you thought it had to be done with mirrors. It couldn't all be under one roof: so much noise, so much glare, so many benches and revelers and barmaids and streamers, so many arms locking and beer mugs banging and boots stomping and bands on platforms crashing out drinking songs:

*In München steht ein Hofbräuhaus...*

And giant balloons wobbling under giant beer labels and draft horses in bells and fringes dragging beer barrels and crowds—crushing crowds. Aprons and dirndls, breeches, lederhosen, ghosts, witches, red-nosed clowns, shuffling bears, Death himself—hooded Death—with a scythe over his shoulder. Only the beggars stood still. Kitty had not seen beggars before, and she thought at first they must be in grim masquerade; crutches, black glasses, flat pinned-up sleeves. In stall after stall lights dripped bleakly on shooting galleries, carnival games, stuffed toys, plastic prizes. Food. But this was not the grange fair back home: hot dogs, caramel corn, orangeade, pink hives of cotton candy that vanished on your tongue. This was the famous Oktoberfest. Everyone everywhere was eating, drinking, carrying food—wearing food; sausages, salt-studded pretzels slung from necks. And jars, tanks, barrels, cages: birds beating their wings to dust; tentacles wavering in murky seaweed; live slippery fish squirming on stakes. Whole oxen, Herr Gruber said, were roasting in pits.

Herr Gruber was in a good mood tonight, his stripes of thinning hair scented with brilliantine, his handkerchief lining his chest like a row of decorations. Time and again he turned to his guests, squinting through the smoke of his cigarette with something like a wink:

What would they like? Eels? Snails? An octopus, *ja*? His knuckles rapped the glass cases. Pigs' feet! A nice German delicacy. *Wholgreschnack!* None of your American pabulum.

Something optimistic in the little boy's face had this effect. Gazing up, up, cheeks horizontal, even the two small identical nostrils gazing. Up was the only way he could see.

Time and again Frau Gruber laid a hand on her husband's sleeve and exposed her great eyes. They had brought their own treats. Bundles in net bags swung from her coat, shifting from side to side as she walked. She breathed with an air of doing her duty.

Oops! Pardon me! I'm drunk!

He's ploughed!

He's pie eyed!

He's polluted!

Americans. College boys. Crew cuts, hairy legs, cutoff jeans. They were loaded down with souvenirs—balloons, pennants, pink plastic dolls—emptying bubbling beer into their throats. One wore two caps, low over his eyes; he was stumbling backwards, groping in front of him, apologizing left and right with a friendly foolish grin:

Hey! Where'd everybody go? I'm blind! I'm blind!

The boys gave Christopher a balloon—so you won't lose him, Lady—and Kitty fastened the string to his wrist. The balloon bobbed along above him in the crowd like a cork in a stream.

At last they found a bench among picnic tables in a grape arbor. The vines looked real, gnarled and twining, but the leaves were plastic, strung on wires like the lights. Frau Gruber began to spread the feast, unwrapping warm greasy parcels, pancakes, paprika chicken. Herr Gruber went to fetch the beer. He struck his knife into the loaf of black bread, raised his mug; they all sat down.

A little ceremony of offering and declining, and the old couple began to eat.

Christopher, as at a signal, stretched up his neck, lifted his face, and aimed his gaze across the table at the Grubers. He seemed to be staring straight into their mouths. Likely he was: he kept an eye on grownups' mouths. It was the most important part of them, the secret of their strength, the source of all their power. The hair hanging in his eyes gave him a look of perpetual discovery.

What you saw was a gleam.

Christopher was past three and didn't talk yet. He made noises. His mother had taken him for tests and been told to wait and see. His development otherwise seemed normal, and his hearing, if anything, proved exceptionally keen. That you could sense, you could see: the ears pricked up, alerted, under ragged edges of red hair. Astonishingly red, mineral red. He had the illuminated white skin that goes with. But his eyes were animal brown.

The old couple were enjoying their meal. It was what they had come for; to feast on chicken and pickles and black bread and to drink their blond beer. They didn't seem to mind his stare; they were enjoying that too. They stared back: ogling, mugging. Frau Gruber nipped and nibbled at her chicken, showing what big smooth eyes she had, what neat teeth. She tucked her head to one side, smiling encouragingly. The flat curls were a row of hooks across her forehead. She seemed to think the child needed encouraging. Herr Gruber tipped himself backwards to drink, wiggling his brows over his beer mug—slim, pointy, like the silvery emblem of his mustache. Every time he popped a morsel into his mouth, it clapped shut—snap! A trap! A hiding place!

It was all a game, a performance staged for the little boy's benefit. Tricks! A magic show! They were making food disappear.

Rain clicked on the green plastic leaves. From the flying saucers, the Tilt-A-Whirls, shrieks and swoons rose with weary mechanical regularity, as if the thrills might be part of the machinery. Bees buzzed under the lights. Christopher propped his chin on the edge of the table, the better to stare. You'd think he had never seen people eating before.

Sometimes his mother told herself it might be just as well he didn't speak. God knew what he would say.

But now—slyly, slyly—Herr Gruber was sliding a beer mug across the table. Frau Gruber had hardly touched hers; it was still foaming. Kitty hesitated—she didn't want to hurt the old man's feelings—and besides it was too late. Christopher had already observed. Up went his head, in his discovering way. He scrambled to his feet in his boots and hood and dipped his face into the beer.

It came right up. Stung. There was foam on his lip, and one taste of beer showed on it so plainly—bitterly—that everyone laughed, even his mother.

That startled him more. This was adding insult to injury. He dragged his fist across his face, wiping away the insult, the sting.

But this was what Herr Gruber did, every time he drank—thumping his mug, wiping his mustache with a wink. Everyone laughed louder. Christopher's face went blank—round and white as his balloon. He stared from one loud shocking grown-up mouth to the next, too stunned to cry.

By now others were turning to watch, loudly laughing, shooing at the drunken bees under the lights.

Christopher's eyes gleamed in his hair. In the transparency of his face light was dawning. Something clicked. His teeth caught his lip in a sharp-toothed grin. He dunked his cheeks into the mug.

A splash. A noisy swallow.

He looked up, grinning bitterly, wiping his lip.

This time there was applause. The table just across the way. A man leaned into the aisle, a cigar between his fingers, pounding the heels of his hands together:

*Echt Bayern*! A true Bavarian!

He raised his mug aloft. He had a heavy handsome face, and his hair and his eyebrows seemed sunburned.

Herr Gruber turned himself slowly to view their audience, all of him as stiff as the arm at his side:

*Eck Boyr'n.*

His thickest Bavarian. Even Kitty could tell he was laying it on. Without offering to click mugs, he stretched forth his neck to drink. The turtle thrust; his lip was quivering. Something was wrong; but what? Why? Yet another of the mysteries of a foreign country. Even the Germans, Justin said, didn't like the Germans.

And that is what they were, the party at the next table. They all looked alike: large, fair, handsome, tanned—the very glow of the sun—in their thick sweaters, their gold watches and rings. They looked the way everyone thought Germans looked; the way Germans ought to look; the way Kitty thought they should, anyhow. They might have been on holiday somewhere, just up from the sea or down from the Alps. Anywhere in the world you would know them.

Christopher splashed and swallowed, splashed and swallowed, grinning up, ever hopeful, waiting for applause, a laugh.

*Hierher!* *Hierher!*

The man was determined to be friendly. He clamped the cigar between his teeth in a wide-stretched smile and went on clapping. His smile drove the pink wedges under his eyes. All the while they were drawn toward his companion, who sat across from him, blowing smoke at the vines and the lights. She was used to being looked at. Large, of course; blond, of course—pale shimmery blond, like foil, Kitty thought; and her eyes of course were blue: strikingly light against the metallic bronze, the lids slanted, Oriental. It had never occurred to Kitty before that such a large-scale woman might be beautiful, that not being an American view. But this woman hardly cared what she thought—some mousy little tourist!—or what anyone thought. She wore her flesh as she might wear something expensive—colossal, gilded, like the statue of Bavaria.

Frau Gruber had given Christopher a chicken wing, which he polished off in no time. Now his cheeks were greasy and his nose was runny and very soon it appeared that he was tipsy. He clambered down from the bench and went wandering among the tables—stolidly planted with elbows and back—hiccuping inquiringly, swiping his mouth in a slapdash salute. His eyes just reached over the edges. The buckles of his boots clinked like spurs and the balloon tagged along behind him.

Even passersby were stopping to point out the funny little boy in the squelching boots, the half-tame hair in his eyes.

He was amusing everyone except his mother.

How to deal with a drunken three-year-old in this happy crowd?

Christopher—she heard herself calling. Her face wore its look of solemn surprise, abstraction, as if she were doing calculations in her head. Christopher—

*Criss-to-furrr*—she heard a voice in whining imitation—

*Criss-to-furrr*—

Now Christopher parked himself at the woman's large lap, staring through his hair in his bold way, his face glowing and greasy and the balloon hovering over his shoulder. Hiccups escaped him; wondering grunts. He had a deep gruff voice—croupy—comical—coming out of such a small body. People started laughing all over again. Lovesick! Moonstruck! Her face seemed upside down under the lights; her eyes tunnels of darkness like her nose, her mouth. Her mouth! Smoke seethed out of it, dribbling, drifting, fixed in the buzzing haze around her.

She clicked her cigarette case shut and rose—a waft of scent and smoke. Abruptly her companion got to his feet, and all the rest of their table with him. The polished forehead descended in a bow; they took their large departure, stooping under the leaves. All at once the people at the other tables became stunted, lumpy; their knobby red jowls and knobby red noses; their thick necks and stout backs in Bavarian black. And the dreary cries of rides and games, the burned incense from the pits and grilles; the crowds, the beery bleary lights—

Something happened. A cigarette, possibly, brushing in passing. The balloon made a rude rushing noise—crumpled up—flapped its tongue— and disappeared.

Christopher looked up, looked all about. Where was it? Where did it go? His balloon, balloon, following like the moon. He turned himself around and around, dizzily, tipsily. He never noticed the string dangling from his wrist, dragging a rag of white rubber. A belly-button knot. He tripped over it at last and sat down hard.

6.    Herr Gruber had forgotten where he had parked the car. In the dim lot raindrops sparkled like beer bubbles on the windshields of two thousand Volkswagens. Herr Gruber went one way, Frau Gruber another, calling back and forth in their search. Kitty held Christopher slumped over her shoulder, his boots sagging, his toes pointing down, his breath warm and damp on her neck. He had cried himself to sleep. Every once in a while he gave a self-righteous shudder, half-hiccup, half-sob.

Crowds straggled toward the cars. Lights and noise seemed far away. No, it wasn't the grange fair. The dense heat of prairie nights, the tinny simmering of crickets in the grass, insects fizzing under the lamps. Shadows grew long and branchy as trees; in the lights leaves shone green as bottles. Megaphones would be calling out the winning numbers of bingo games, the license plates of parked cars, the names of lost children. The air would smell of fried hamburgers, mustard, buttered popcorn, and summer.

Along came a lone tippling feather—under it a Tyrolean cap, and under that a man, staggering backward, bald kneed in lederhosen. He was dwarfed in the darkness and shadows, but you could see the beer mug swinging in his fist, the hand gripping his fly—spraying before him a hot sizzling arc. It zigzagged and sparkled.

*Ein! Zwo! G'fluss!*

Crowds laughed and made way.

7.   After Oktoberfest it rained and rained, a brewing of wind and darkness and leaves. It stripped the trees, laid the fields low, soaked, and brown. Mornings you could see your breath; boys on the way to school shivered in their lederhosen, and the muddy roads, even the cow pies, were brittle with frost. The mountains, Herr Gruber said. You could see their breath too. Day by day it would be coming closer.

Kitty had acquired a grammar—*Deutsch Frei von Schmerz*—she liked the title, *German Free of Pain*—and several paper-covered exercise books, the kind children practice penmanship in. Frau Gruber used them for recording expenses—every *pfennig*, she said. She was still eagerly instructing Kitty in the ways of the hausfrau. But on these dreary days Kitty found it hard to keep her mind on German lessons. Rain rushed the roof in sudden ambush. Wet branches snagged the glass. And the house, the old house, had a life of its own—an atmosphere of stealth, secrecy, suspense. Doors slammed. Stairs creaked. Radiators whispered. The yellow cats sneaked. Frau Gruber sighed in her dutiful way as she went about her chores. She sounded as if sighing itself was the chore.

And why study? That Kitty could do anywhere. What had she come for, if she meant to learn from books? There was the village: the train, the telephone booth, the *Platz* with its fountains and plaques. Whose were the greenish faces? And the café—patrons glimpsed through the window, turning pages of *Zeitungs* and *Tageblatts*—newspapers fastened to poles, like flags. And what about the shop signs? *Metzger*: the butcher. *Bäkerei*: the baker. *Apotheke*: that was easy—apothecary. And *Friseur* meant the hairdresser; *Gemüseladen* the chilly greengrocer's shop; *Lebensmittelladen* the supermarket—dingy shelves of American cornflakes and soap flakes. Rain was *Regen*: German rain. Fog was *Nebel*: German fog. Church bells tolled in German:

*Kling klang. Bimbam.* Horns honked, crows crowed, the white-hooded cows mooed, the wistful smoke wandered over spires and roofs—all in German. She was here. Here She Was. There were German lessons all around her. Why bother with vocabulary drills? Declensions? Conjugations? Kitty had no need of a grammar to learn German without pain.

8.  Christopher was in the tub, getting his bath—he had an eye on the soap: how would it be if he took a *bite* out of it?—when there came a *Geschrei.* Tramping hooves. The TV, Kitty thought. Cattle Rustlers. *Vieh stehlen,* it said in the dictionary. But she opened the door to have a look, and something streaked past—live, white, low to the ground.

*Halt*! *Halt*!

Frau Gruber came laboring up the stairs. She was white too; her kerchief, her curls, her flat-tipped nose-bill and lopsided cheek. What was this? A Halloween prank? Was it time for Halloween?

*Katastrophe*!

The cat—the kitchen—the flour barrel.

*Bums*! *Plumps*! *Platz*!

She clapped her hands. Poof! Powder puffs! Blackboard erasers.

The trail of neat cat tracks led across the landing through the bathroom door, under the tub. It stood on four painted iron feet. Christopher peered over the edge, the soap forgotten in his hand, his face, his body, glistening like soap. His eyes were listening, glistening, hedged round with red hair.

Frau Gruber lowered herself cautiously, with all her encumbrances—huffing dust, puffing dust—and knelt on all fours, crooking her finger. Her eyes in her white face bigger and brighter than ever, and the bigger they got the more they shone:

*Hier, Maxi*! *Mien Liebling*!

In the farthest corner crouched the cat, the same way—rump up, head between its paws.

Miauww miauww!

Another voice. A mincing mimicking falsetto. Herr Gruber in shirtsleeves, suspenders, trousers hitched high on his waist like a movie gangster's. His cigarette smoldered on his lip and his mustache was glinting a wicked glint.

Hssst! Psst!

An electrical spatter and crackle and the cat scuttled out. Herr Gruber aimed a swift soccer kick. He missed. He kicked and missed again. Kitty snatched Christopher out of the tub, Frau Gruber rose to her knees, hands clasped as in prayer. Her apron front heaved, a leaky flour sack. And it was a very small space—Herr Gruber kicking and missing, the cat hissing and spitting—spine arched, scruff up, a cardboard cutout of a witch's cat. But white, all white. Only its eyes were still yellow; candle flames—in the dead center of each narrow black wick.

There was no love lost between Herr Gruber and the landlady's cats. *Verdammnt!*

Herr Gruber's foot struck the iron foot of the tub. The cat took off between his legs and spurted down the hall, tail sizzling. A lighted fume. A firecracker.

Now Kitty was not a good German hausfrau. The door was shut, but not on the latch, and before anyone had time to wonder:

*Bums! Platz! Kracken!*

Herr Gruber hopped to the stairs, dusting himself off, muttering under his mustache, and you didn't need to know German to know he was cursing. He thrust his head, his sputtering lip, over the rail:

*Schatzi! Auf! Schnell!*

Schatzi was the son. He came home on weekends to pay his respects to the mother-in-law, but spent all his time locked up with his lawbooks. His coat hung on a hook in the hall. Kitty had scarcely laid eyes on him; she had an idea he resented her. He wasn't used to girls, Frau Gruber said. Too studious, that was the trouble. He was taking Social Dancing—*Walzer, Foxtrott*—in hopes of striking up some acquaintances. Now he came trudging up the stairs, holding a broom, bristles upright before him, as he might bear a torch. Tall, lean, high colored, dark haired—nice-looking, Kitty thought, in spite of his slouch and the fuzzy black sweater he wore faithfully as a uniform. He presented himself—a prompt click and bow, more mechanical, even, than his father's bow—staring past them, avoiding their gaze. Which wasn't easy; Frau Gruber's was so earnestly seeking his. He had her same great oval eyes—but not, alas, their expression. His didn't shine.

Herr Gruber had gone in and slammed the door. He put out his head, gave a shout; Schatzi squeezed in sideways with the broom. Something pointy and yellow peeped briefly from under the crackled green chintz: the door slammed again.

The final score was: One lamp—smashed. One table leg—cracked. One neck—nicked. Or so it seemed. Herr Gruber emerged, ginger-ly touching his collar, and stalked down the stairs, shoulders high, sus-penders crossed on his back. Schatzi followed with the broom, shoulders hunched in his black sweater; but they didn't carry the same message. There was no love lost, either, between father and son.

The next day Kitty saw the backs again, heading down the steps to the gate, on the way to the mother-in-law. Herr Gruber, as usual, carrying himself with an air of taking offense; the clipped hairs bristling under his hat brim, his stiff arm cocked at his side. Frau Gruber leaned and dragged on Schatzi's arm, clutching it possessively. She had told Kitty how he hat-ed—dreaded—these visits. The mother-in-law was such a terrible sight. *Schreckbild. Der Schwarzer* Mann. And as mean as she looked! Meaner! The landlady made a face, her mother-in-law face, doing her best to play the part: A scarecrow. The bogeyman. Her lopsided cheeks, even her flattened nose-beak, seemed to shrivel and darken. She was afraid the mother-in-law would give Schatzi a *Komplex*.

The road was splashed—splurged—yellow with leaves, slippery leaves; the last, shiftless, shrank and shivered on the branches. Schatzi certainly looked unwilling. His coat hung on his back the way it hung on the hook in the hall.

The lamp was a loss and had to be swept up. Herr Gruber repaired the table leg—more or less, he was no carpenter—pounding resoundingly, cigarette twittering. For a few days there were no greetings; no tipping of hats, no clicking of heels, no *Guten Morgens* or *Grüß Gotts*, not so much as a *Gesundheit*! His favorite joke. All the German they knew.

Why couldn't Americans learn to shut their doors and keep them shut?

The cat never did come out. I knew the house better than anyone, Frau Gruber said; escape routes, secret passageways, hiding places. It would lie low until the coast was clear, or take off on an adventure. Der Maxi was a *Herzenbrecher*—a ladies' man. And Frau Gruber delivered another lamp, a brass urn on a marble pedestal. It was very heavy; the old woman, after her climb, was breathing like a conspirator. Kitty wondered where she had dug it up. Buried in the cellar? Stored down there with Herr Gruber's bulbs and shrubs? All it needed was a little *Armschmalz*, the landlady said. Kitty thought it might take a lot. The brass was as green as the faces on the plaques.

9.    But how Kitty wished she had never spoken those fatal words—the mother-in-law.

*How old was the mother-in-law? Who was she? Where was she? Why were the Grubers hiding her? What was wrong with her?*

The neighbor had taken, as she said, a *fancy* to the subject, and whenever she came whizzing up the road, the wind in her cape and her nervous little dog frantically barking—she was at it again. The mother-in-law! The mother-in-law!

Kitty seldom asked questions; she seldom had any. The lilt of her nose was puzzled, wondering, not inquisitive. And the questions she thought of she seldom asked: they seemed too simple. She didn't want to seem simple. The fact was, she regarded questions as something on the order of sallies, witticisms, and really wished she could ask them as Justin did—as if he already knew the answers.

That was how she had met him—her brooding TA in English Comp. Kitty was a typist in the steno pool and got to take courses for credit, tuition free. Even Kitty could see that that heavy brow was pondering matters not to be found in the syllabus. The brooding had attracted her: she supposed it went with being a poet.

Kitty was a little afraid of poetry. It was a word like *experience*—she wasn't sure what it meant. So how would she know it, if she saw it? She was suspicious of any she could understand; she knew it must be, above all, something complicated. At first, when she did Justin's typing for him in his cold room at night, she worried. What if he asked questions? What if he wanted her opinion? What should she say? What should she say? Torn plastic weatherproofing rattled at the window; in the space heater red coils gnashed and glowered. It was all right. She never thought of anything and he never asked.

He had promised to stop by again for Christopher. Maybe next time they would visit the monastery, he said, since it was so close. Close! Close if you had friends with yellow Volkswagens! He had spoken of his plans—trips, sightseeing, skiing in the Alps. And yet she was not jealous of the Italian interpreter. Envious, yes; deeply greenly envious. And who wouldn't be? Those tight tight jeans! That waving stirring wheat field of hair. An Italian interpreter. An Italian interpreter. The phrase suggested to Kitty a worldliness she could never aspire to.

Maybe she didn't know what experience was—but she knew what it wasn't.

That was one question, at least, Kitty had thought of, and had even gone so far as to ask:

What was wrong with the mother-in-law?

The landlady heaved up her eyes. Her shoulders shrugged a great shrug; she sighed her most drudging demonstrative sigh:

*Alles*! she said.

Everything! The mother-in-law was *krank aber kraft*. Sick but strong. *Alles*! Everything!

The neighbor spoke English but she croaked with the crows. Her jaeger's cap angled sharply over the sharp angle of her nose. An Alpine profile—it all but glittered. Her eyes flashed in crevasses of wrinkles. She passed out literature: *Natur* remedies, *Spiritualismus*. Along with the latest newspapers and magazines, the café window displayed religious tracts, gathering dust and ten-*pfennig* donations. *Der Wachturm*! *Wach*!—Kitty was so flattered when she could read German. But the Frau professor's pamphlets couldn't be read in any language; pages stapled, hectographed, bleeding purple ink. She was a fresh-air fiend—as most Germans seemed to be—and swore by her air baths. Daily she opened all the windows and ran about in the nude, dressed in nothing but *Gänsehaut*—gooseflesh— pumping her elbows and knees to keep up her circulation. *Luft*! *Frische Luft*! Mitzi saw strange sights.

Don't you, Mitzi? Poor Mitzi?

The dog, hearing its name, poked up and barked its strident startled barks. Its white eyes throbbed.

Hush, Mitzi, hush! The Frau professor smacked its snout. We all know what you put up with. You bad dog, you!

Germans kept pets, Justin said, mainly for the fun of scolding them in public.

The Alps were up to their tricks again—hiding themselves. The sun had disappeared forever, its favors withdrawn. A raw wind herded the dead leaves, rounding them up. In the cold wind-scathed road the little dog seemed to be barking at echoes.

At last Kitty told the truth: she had been asked not to speak of the mother-in-law.

The truth, maybe; but the wrong thing to say. It seemed to be what the Frau professor had been waiting for:

She knew it! She knew it! If that wasn't the Grubers for you. Always the storm in the water glass. *Typisch*! Typical Gruber. Like that Schatzi *Geschäft*. The great secret! As if everyone didn't know. As if anyone cared.

A law student? Schatzi? Wherever did Kitty get that idea? Schatzi! A law student! If that's what they had told her! Yes yes, studying law. Doing it the hard way! Though the humor, if she knew her Grubers, must be unintentional.

She dipped a cheek to her gloved knuckle. Cold and wind made her eyes tear, and so did laughter. An icy glitter pierced her wrinkles, leaked down her steep peaks.

But my dear child, everyone knew! A school, to be sure. Make better? Make better?—the Frau professor's English wasn't as fluid as it used to be. Yes, thank you—reform. He came home on weekends for good behavior. Kitty hadn't noticed? How they kept an eye on him? Never let him out of their sight? Not a bad boy, really. Not bad-looking either, if he weren't such a Gloomy Gus. Those big glum eyes of his. A gallows bird! Oh yes, a real *Schatz*, their Schatzi. A real treasure. And you had to feel sorry for him, with parents like that. That *Zuchtmeister* Herr Gruber, carrying his arm like a stick! And Frau Gruber! *Doch*! Well well well. So the plot thickened. What next? Mark her words, there must be something. The skeleton in the *Kabinett*. If she knew her Grubers.

What was wrong with the mother-in-law?

Kitty glanced up guiltily. Now that the trees were bare you could see it more clearly, the narrow wooden house. In the midst of the tall straight trunks it stood a little off true. Chimney, shutters, scored weathered shingles: if not for the smoke you might wonder if anyone lived there. No— no face at the window. No head angling in a kerchief. No shining eye spying out. It was as if the house itself were watching.

## II.

Kitty woke in the night.

Christopher was awake; she saw his head go up, listening in the dark. By the time she had jumped out and pulled the light string, his head hung over the side of the bed and a thick yellow muck splashed the floor.

She didn't need to touch him. She could feel the heat, an aura of heat. She laid her hand to his forehead, his cheek, held her hands to her own cheeks, felt his face again. It was hot and flushed and his eyes were glittering. He lifted them to her—an appeal—gave a grunt, and threw up more.

She held his head as he went on grunting, retching—sounds wrenched out of him, guttural, indignant. The smell at first made her stomach turn, but it didn't matter now. The bare bulb glared down on the cracked linoleum, the wallpaper faded and stained. Even in the reek of vomit the pipes, the radiator were giving off an odor of burned paint.

He began to cry. He looked up, pointing to the light; his eyes seemed to reflect its glare.

What is it? What do you want? Does the light hurt your eyes?

She pulled the string. His voice rose. She put the light on again; again the cry. She kept yanking at the string, the light flashing on and off; he kept squinting, pointing, more and more indignant—outraged. Hot tears glazed his cheeks. He stood on the bed in his plastic-footed pajamas, the snap seat, the front smeared with smelly yellow paste—protesting his own helpless state.

Tell me. Please tell me. What do you want?

If only he could talk!

The lamp. Kitty had put it away in the wardrobe; she had never gotten around to polishing it. Now she plugged it in and draped a pillowcase over the bulb to shield the light.

There. Is that better?

He stopped crying. Stock still, his arm, his pointing finger, arrested, suspended—that instinctive way he had, an animal sixth sense. The tears in his eyes stood out; fixed, still, glittering filaments.

The lamp fizzled and brightened, fizzled and brightened; the brass urn shadowed in its own glow.

An electrical prickle lifted the skin of her neck.

What is it? What do you see? There's nothing there.

She thought he was going to reply. His eyes widened, astonished; his voice rose, deep as speech. He began coughing instead. Loud passionate coughs, shaking him vengefully. His chest was too small for this, couldn't contain such force. She put her arms around him, pressing him closer, closer, trying to defend him, feeling the blows. He stared at the violence of the attack—the hate.

2.    In the morning a gray Mercedes-Benz was parked at the gate, and a hand reached over the fence, feeling for the key. Kitty by now knew this sight; the doctor was a familiar of the house—as far as she could tell, its only visitor—and as a matter of course let himself in. It was a blustery day, snow flung in fitful gusts, the crows squalls of screaming leaves. The stout figure ascended. There was something immediately reassuring in his stoutness, his pinkness, the projection of his fur-lined lapels, the black bag at his side.

Frau Gruber followed him in, her hands in her apron.

The landlady's hair was still in pin curls, as it had been, earlier, when Kitty ran downstairs to ask to use the phone. She had never seen the old woman without her kerchief before, and she had an idea that the hooks and curls came attached—false—a front, was it called? But here was an eye at the door, like an eye in a peephole; then the head poking out—the twists of hair scorched, no color, white at the roots; the scalp pale, almost tender. Anxious as she was, Kitty felt a pang—embarrassment, dismay, whatever it was the landlady made her feel; as if she had caught the old woman out again, in yet another tale.

The three grown-ups stood looking down at the sick child.

Under the quilt he was shuddering, shuddering, eyes shut, teeth clicking with chills. The doctor laid a large hand across his forehead. The eyes snapped open: the lashes stiff, moth colored, with a silted silky moth sheen.

The doctor poked and thumped and listened, an ear to the high ribby chest; then, through the stethoscope, pressing here and there, the prongs in his ears, he listened more. Christopher did as he was told, breathing in, breathing out, all the while shivering shivering. Only his eyes held still: held the doctor's face. He caught his breath sharply, as if his ribs were knives.

The doctor collapsed the instrument, folded it back into its case. In loud halting English, raising his voice to make himself understood, he told the child that he was a very brave boy. To the mother he spoke in a lower tone, and in German. Kitty understood at once, without having to look up the word in her dictionary. But she did, all the same, and all the same, there it was:

*Lungenentzündung*: pneumonia.

But there was nothing to worry about, the doctor said. He gave the patient a shot, left a prescription, promised to look in the next day. The landlady stood by, turning her face from one to the other. Every word the doctor spoke—in German—she repeated: promptly, dutifully, in German. It might have been comical, but it wasn't. The girl's face was almost awed with fear.

3. Kitty hated calling the army base.

You took your chances. The German telephone system, Justin said, was primitive, mystic as the German forest. Maybe you got through, maybe you didn't; the very bleet beep of the signal sounded foreign—unreliable. Then came the switching from one extension to the next; different voices, different accents; the precise British English of the German switchboard operators, the more casual American. Somewhere along the line you might get cut off altogether, and then you had to start all over again. But mainly Kitty hated calling because she knew that Justin didn't want her to, and she couldn't help feeling that everyone must know it.

The phone got picked up at long last.

Hang on, will you? someone said—and banged it down again.

A typewriter clattered. Pins dropped. Voices faded in and out like voices over the airwaves. Other conversations, other connections.

*Atmosphäre. Interferenz.* Wires were crossed all over Germany. All the while a voice could be heard: *Wer ist das? Wer ist das?* Practicing? Grammar drills? At least Kitty wasn't calling from the coin booth. The Grubers' telephone was of an old-fashioned style; a speaker on a stem, a hook and cradle on the side. Kitty pressed the receiver to her ear, picturing the phone at the other end, facedown on a desk somewhere, a live listening thing. She felt herself helplessly attached to it.

Sorry, lady.

The voice came back. Male. American. In a bad mood. But not Justin.

LeBow? LeBow? No, no, he didn't know no LeBow. Not here. She must have—oh! If that's who she meant! Them? The college professors? Well they weren't around—not them. Not on a holiday. What holiday? Veterans' Day, naturally. What did she think?

The soldier—he must be—could tell from her voice that Kitty was no one he need reckon with. People usually could.

She pictured a triangular face, wide eared, flat topped under a visored cap. She was thinking of boys she had gone to school with; the ones in muscle shirts and tattoos and elevator shoes; cigarettes stuck behind their ears—the cigarettes that supposedly had stunted their growth. She had seen them, the American soldiers, strolling in Munich, always three or four abreast. Probably some army regulation. She was surprised how young they looked—even to her—and how small. The German women in uniform—badges on their stout busts—seemed more imposing. In Germany there were plenty of women in uniform.

No lady, he didn't know where. No lady, he didn't know when. It was some kind of semester break—that's what he heard—and they were off until after Thanksgiving. Sure sure he could take a message. Some guys had it soft, was all he could say. And they didn't have to march in no parades.

Kitty hung up slowly, reluctant to break the connection, even this connection. Armistice Day. As they still called it in her hometown; new names being slow to catch on. Armistice Day. The little paper flags in the cemetery. The rows of crosses among the moss-stained stones. The cold windy day, lonelier than Sunday. The remote November sun. The sirens. Then the silence.

4. In Frau Gruber's parlor the alarm clock ticked, the radiator hissed, feather quilts aired at the window. Ragged flakes chased past. Der Maxi stalked them—crouching, pawing the glass, a scabby red gash cocked over one eye. It must have been off on another adventure. Der Moritz snoozed in its smoky yellow fur. *Alles in Ordnung.* In the midst of the old-fashioned furnishings—ashtray stands, pull-chain lamps, a tattered faded banner of carpet—the TV seemed out of place. It sat on top of the cabinet radio, thirties vintage, like the one that had stood in Kitty's grandparents' parlor; the best piece of furniture by far, bought and delivered out of the catalog. It was shaped like a tabernacle and reminded her of illustrations in her Sunday school reader: Moses coming down from the mountain. The tables of the law. The Ten Commandments.

And the first one was: Thou shalt not touch.

Grandchildren were not allowed to fiddle with the doors, knobs, glowing dials. It was not meant for entertainment. The radio was grim grown-up business, and Kitty could still recall the grim grown-up voices coming out of it. What funny names they had. H. V. Kaltenborn. Gabriel Heatter. Weekdays you listened after supper to the news, and on Sundays after church to the sermons; and, as a special treat—if you were sick—you were permitted, lying on the sofa under blankets and plasters, to listen, one after the other, to the soap operas. Those voices got mixed up with measles and fevers, thermometers and castor oil, and smells from the kitchen—ammonia, borax, boiled starch. Oh the stringency of affection!

This tabernacle was the family shrine. Photographs in stand-up frames from the five-and-dime; the wedding pictures, the smiling sons in uniform, the grandchildren in high school caps and gowns. Also, souvenir gifts; ashtrays, dishes, painted plaster casts of skyscrapers and Indian chiefs; from the Ozarks, Lookout Mountain, the Chicago World's Fair.

There were no souvenirs in Frau Gruber's parlor. No knickknacks, no photographs, no frames. Nothing on the walls; not so much as a mirror;

though in some places the cabbage rose paper appeared rosier; so there might have been once, once upon a time. Maybe that was why the room never felt as cozy, *gemütlich*, as it should have, in spite of the quilts and the cats and the radiators hissing at the snow. No family history. No wedding pictures. No Schatzi in short pants or cap and gown. Kitty blushed, recalling what the neighbor had told her. Was that why? And what about the mother-in-law? Kitty had wondered what such a creature must look like, and thought she might want to see for herself. But then she recalled the mother-in-law face—the shrunken shriveled image sunk into the soft wax of the landlady's features—and thought she might just as soon not.

Kitty marked down the day, the hour, the length of the call in the ruled notebook Frau Gruber kept by the telephone. Armistice. The eleventh hour, the eleventh day, the eleventh month. She supposed that hadn't changed, even if they had changed the name. It made her feel very small, sitting in Frau Gruber's parlor—very far away—the clock ticking, ticking central European time.

5.   It was a county seat, sixty flat blacktop miles, straight as the crow flies, from the university. There were three stop signs on Main Street—a truck route—and buses stopped at the luncheonette twice a day, one heading east, one west. For north and south you had to change at the capital. Once the wide streets had been shaded by elms, like green fountains; they had died off from a disease and been chopped down, and now the sidewalks were broken, heaved up like tombstones, from buried roots. Shopwindows wore tinted cellophane to keep their displays from fading, and when the buses and trucks grumbled past, gushing diesel fumes, the windows rippled like dark water. The headless flat-chested mannequin in the ladies' shop, the bedpans and rubber hot-water bottles in the pharmacy. The hardware store, the five-and-dime, the shoe emporium—in an X-ray machine you could see the bones in your toes wriggling. The brick church. The stone church. The movie marquee. An electric clock over the canopy of the funeral parlor; a Roman-numeral sundial over the courthouse. The railroad car diner, the other Texaco station, the other train tracks, and then good-bye—you were past it. Farther out on the highway came the Clapboard Church, at the junction, the blinking yellow

light. On the roof the cross blinked on and off, on and off, in blue. Same as a motel sign, Justin said: Vacancy / No Vacancy.

6.    You don't even talk to yourself, he said.

He did, all the time. Glory be to God for dappled things! he shouted into the bathroom mirror, shaving, a towel around his hips. No longer the smallest kid in the class; he had taken up boxing, weight lifting, to practice self-defense; he was muscle-bound, his shoulders slung like boughs of a tree from the thick trunk of his neck. But he was still very fair, his arms, his back sprinkled with freckles like cornflakes in milk, and the face emerging in the mirror—out of shaving cream and steam—was still the face of the Boy Scout pictures. The bulging forehead, the heavy brow ridge, the crew cut so short you could see through it—an effect at once of baby fuzz and premature baldness.

Now the face sported a soft blond mustache.

It would have been only natural, only to be expected, for a child of his—a son!—to turn out gifted, precocious. Since Christopher, whatever he was, was no prodigy, it must be someone else's fault. It must be hers. Not that Justin had ever said so; no, not outright; not in so many words. They had never talked about it—period. Still, she knew he blamed her. She blamed herself; her own uncommunicative nature.

Christopher got along well enough in nursery school. The other children knew he was different: he wasn't German. After that, nothing could surprise them. And maybe, when he grunted and growled—that guttural voice—they thought the funny noises must be his own language. American. Tough-guy talk. They watched gangsters and cowboys on TV too. But there were other things. The swaggering boots. The sharp-toothed grin—like his talk, out of the side of his mouth. That candid white face, outspoken without saying a word. And he bit things. The soap! Was this normal? The American mother asked herself an American question. He liked to hide—under the covers, behind the sofa, a flash of red among the greenery. He thought you couldn't see him if he couldn't see you. He insisted, in his stubborn way, on dressing himself, squirming, resisting her help. Which was why he was forever unbuckled, unzipped, coming undone—straining at the leash. He undressed himself too. He seemed to think he had to take everything off when he sat on the toilet, even his socks and shoes. Kitty knew that sooner or later he would take it into his head to show off this particular accomplishment at school. She could see it. The pleasant room, the pans of water simmering on the radiators, the coal scuttle filled with silvery sand, the floors placid with wax. The children wore felt slippers to keep from scuffing them. There they would be, the German children, sitting up straight, as if about to get their picture taken, waiting for a story or to say their prayers. Their folded hands. Their fat red cheeks. Their clean combed hair. German children behaved and behaved. And enter Christopher: his clothes bundled underarm, his hair in his eyes, his potbelly candid and white and bold as his face.

That was how she had discovered him, once—hiding under the tub, crouched naked as the cat, rump up, head low, staring out from under red leaves or grass.

What she saw was a gleam.

In part, Kitty thought, it was because he was American. And in part, yes, it was because of her. But in part it was because—just because—he was Christopher.

7.    Christopher was a good patient. Too good, his mother thought. She sensed that he was trying to be good. He had never tried before.

He took his spoons of medicine—sticky red stuff—without any fuss, offering his mouth, swallowing mutely, his eyes always on his mother's face. She didn't know that he was imitating her. They were dark brown, serious brown, brown as a dog's. He lay very still under the covers, concentrating on keeping still, watching them shuddering over his chest. His forehead, with his hair combed back, was surprisingly high, white—palest in the center, like a face pressed to glass.

The fever dropped quickly but was slow to pass. Every day the doctor came, patted the child on the head, the mother on the hand. Always Frau Gruber came with him. The landlady set great store by the doctor. When he glanced about for a place to set down his bag, she stepped forward to take it from him. When he shrugged off his coat, pulled his arms from the sleeves, Frau Gruber was there to hold it for him. She shook it out, stroking the fur collar. He brought the snow and cold with him—in his pink jowls, his briskly rubbing hands, the snap of his white-cuffed gold-studded wrists. Rays of hair shot from the bald circle of his crown, the way children draw pictures of the sun.

The landlady watched his every move, her head to one side, her hands in her apron. And always, glancing anxiously from one to the other, she acted the interpreter; repeating—word for word—his German.

Kitty was grateful for the landlady's sympathy. But must the landlady be so sympathetic? As she was so everything else? That drama, eager alarm, in all she did? Her gestures, her faces, her dumb show; above all her eyes—their expression. It was catching. Kitty found herself wide eyed and whispering too.

But the landlady meant well. The landlady always meant well. Her whole person quivered with good intentions. She was up the stairs half a dozen times a day. *Wie geht's mit der Christoff?* Could she peep in on him? Not to wake him. *Stirbt nichts!* She brought surprises. A handful of nuts, cookies sprinkled with sugar, tiny golden oranges with green stems. *Mandarinen.* Kitty had never seen them before and thought at first they must be tree ornaments. And at last in fact here was an ornament: a glass ball, a souvenir sold in the village. A winter scene. A yellow-haired angel knelt beside a young deer. The angel's wings were stumpy, like antlers; green triangles—shields, spears—stood for trees.

Nothing much had ever happened here; no monuments or museums or relics or famous ruins. But once upon a time, so the story went, a deer pursued by a pack of hunting dogs had been saved in these very woods. To this day, it was said, the deer could still be seen, appearing suddenly on the paths to the monastery.

Christopher was concentrating under the covers. He looked older; the red hair darker, a metallic glint, the moth-colored lashes heavy, like weights. He glanced up under the covers of his lashes, listening with his eyes.

There she was. There she went again. The old woman—sneaking in, stealing up on him, her hand behind her back, her finger to her lips. Pretending. Playing hide and seek.

She always looked as if she was just about to say boo!

She held out her hand to show him the scene.

*Siehst du, Christoff?*

She took it back; huffed and puffed and blew on the glass, her eyes expanding, expanding, snug and smooth in her head. She rubbed her hand across it, tipped it over, showed it again:

Snow!

Snow thick as smoke! Swirling white smoke. Where did it come from? The angel, the deer, the tiny green trees. Where did they go?

*Siehst du? Siehst du?*

Her mouth! Her mouth! That other whispering sound inside her. The old woman talking to herself, telling secrets.

Light focused in his face like the light in the ball.

Kitty wished she had never heard the landlady's story.

She saw Frau Gruber now in a new light; saw her, she guessed, as others must see her. A ridiculous old woman, a pathetic old woman. Her cats, her complaint, her mother-in-law! Her kerchief, her foolish fringe, her lopsided cheek and flat nose beak. That walk of hers!—half-waddle, half-hobble. Her locks and keys. Her sighs and secrets.

But Kitty did not feel scornful. She felt sorry. She felt whatever it was she so often felt. That tender scalp—picked, plucked, singed like pinfeathers. The puffy hand, the gold band embedded in the right ring finger. The fearful softness of her arm when Kitty took hold of it to help her. Her heaving apron front, her expression—anxious, almost pleading—trying to catch her breath. Whenever you were anywhere near her, you had to hear: you were privy to it.

But—was it a story?

Frau Gruber showed off Schatzi's lawbooks; dumped one, actually, onto Kitty's lap. It looked like a lawbook; weighty, musty, old dark binding. There! See how heavy it was! And Schatzi had to have it all up here—in his head! And what about the *Tanz Klasse*? Frau Gruber gave reports: how he practiced the box step in the parlor, counted out loud while he waltzed with the broom. The famous broom. Kitty could picture him, stiff as the broom, grasping it grimly:

*Ein zwei drei! Ein zwei drei!*

Did they give dancing classes in reform school? And how could anyone dream up such a thing? True, she had sworn Kitty to secrecy; but she was always pledging secrecy—her hand to her heart, her finger to her lips. When she complained about the mother-in-law. When she tattled on her cats. Der Maxi had dragged a dead bird into the house. Der Maxi had done his *Gesselschaft* on the carpet. On the other hand, what reason would the neighbor, the Frau professor, have, for making up tales? *Exzentrisch*, yes, maybe even *fanatisch*; her bicycle, her air baths, her croaking crow voice and her Ouija board. Kitty thought she must have a Ouija board. But that sharp nose, that keen glittering eye—. And then there was Schatzi himself; his own worst witness. Avoiding Kitty more than ever, she thought; slinking through doors, flat as the cat, hunched to his chin in his fuzzy sweater. And his bow—so abrupt, so grudging—striking his boots together, flinging up his dark forelock. His head and heels seemed to be connected. And the way he dragged down the steps, his head sunk to his glum eyes in his coat collar, his feet scraping, trudging like his father's shovel.

He looked guilty. He looked shamed.

One day when Frau Gruber knocked, Christopher was sitting up at the table in his striped polo shirt and buckled corduroys, blowing bubbles in his milk. His heels, in gym shoes, drummed the rungs of the chair. The landlady clasped her breast in surprise and relief; her eyes expanded, her apron collapsed in a sigh.

At once Christopher looked up, ever hopeful—his hair in his eyes, a white mustache on his lip, his teeth snagged in a carnivorous grin.

His face was a small glowing cup. This was it. What he had been waiting for. This time, oh this time, for sure she had popped.

I I I.

Even the ice pictures on the window were different here.

Back home there would have been tropical scenes; palms, ferns, hothouse gardens, lush prehistoric vegetation. Strange, come to think of it, on the prairie. But here they woke one morning to something stranger: flashed in glass, burning on it, the very same image they might have glimpsed beyond. Xmas trees. Tannenbaum. The German forest grown old overnight—every branch, every needle, dipped in white acid.

Kitty called all evergreens Xmas trees. Where she came from, that was the only kind she was likely to see; artificial, propped in buckets. She didn't know many trees. Oak and maple she recognized by their leaves in the fall. Cottonwoods by their thistles. Sycamores because every farm boasted a sycamore—a half-naked trunk over the water trough. And everyone knew willows. Half a dozen old boled willows dangled over the creek in the municipal park. No Fishing Allowed. The water was polluted: chemical fertilizers or radioactive wastes dumped upstream. That was fine with the fish—giant carp, some black, some brassy, gliding the spangled shallows undisturbed. Their scales seemed to glow in the dark.

Almost every day Kitty wheeled Christopher to the playground in his stroller. Young mothers from the prefabs, the Quonset huts, in their spongy pink hair curlers and old army jackets, gossiping, smoking, pushing swings. Their husbands were also studying on the GI Bill—agriculture, accounting, engineering. Teeter-totters creaked, rusty chains squawked, children fought in the sandbox. The autumn smoke caught in your throat. From the small zoo came an awful squabble—turkeys, peafowl, guinea hens. It was a matter of a few pens and cages; a fox, dingo dogs, a pair of buffalo with moth-eaten withers, brown bear with insulted bloodshot eyes. Children pelted it with popcorn and peanut shells, which it snatched from the air the way it snapped at its lice.

Over the cage two signs were permanently bolted:
Please Do Not Feed the Animals
These Lion Cubs Presented by the Royal Order of Elks

2.    Homesick: *Heimweh*.

Homesick? Was this homesick? Was it possible? Was it permitted?

They didn't live in the prefabs or Quonset huts. They lived at Ivanhoe's. The landlord's name was Ivan Something, so they called him Ivanhoe! He looked like Humpty Dumpty, Kitty thought; his slumping chest, his skinny legs, his bald head in its fringe like an egg in a nest. He wore buckskin vests and cowboy boots and smoked cigarillos, and gave the poets, the potters, the painters something off their room rent in exchange for digging, pushing wheelbarrows. Every square foot of the house, the garage, the dilapidated barn, had been rented out. And Ivan was busy connecting them to get around the zoning ordinances. Stairways. Stepladders. Tunnels. Bridges. All one happy family, he said. The hippies, as the city fathers called them, were just invading from the West. Rumors spread: drugs, orgies, beards, bare feet. Beards and bare feet, yes; of the rest Kitty knew nothing. Though, to be sure, she wouldn't have; not necessarily. But no one cleaned the bathrooms, the communal kitchens; toilets overflowed, sinks got plugged with hippie hair; and worst of all she had to scrape the remains of other people's dinners from the pots and pans—fried eggs, dried beans, most were trying to be vegetarian—before she could cook her own.

Leaving! That was all anyone talked about. Leaving! That was what they were there for. The heartland. The hinterland. The capital of nowhere. The Land of Low Relief. No art, no music, no theater, no foreign films, no *New York Times* on Sunday, no bagels, no coffee beans. Nothing for scenery but the weather—and the land was so flat you could see it coming. The only body of water for a million miles around was a reservoir dug out by the Army Corps of Engineers. Instead they had blue laws. Bars sold 3.2 percent beer. The spaghetti joint and the chop suey joint—the only excuses for restaurants in town—served sliced white bread and butter pats between squares of waxed paper.

Kitty didn't add her voice to the chorus of complaints; not out of home loyalty, however. She would have, gladly, but she was never sure if she got the joke. She laughed along with the rest, a little in the dark. What was wrong with serving Wonder Bread and butter pats? She had never been in a restaurant that didn't. What was so funny about listening to the corn grow? Didn't they know you really could?

Still, these conversations came as revelations. They explained a good deal to her; stirred longings more aching because unnamed. Something she had been hearing all her life, in the sound of the train whistles; truck tires punching the white-ribboned highway; buses loudly double-parked outside the luncheonette—engines roaring to be off—to be away—speeding toward their destinations. Other places. Places people had heard of. Places with names.

In a way, she was grateful. She was ready to complain.

The one thing they did have in these parts was a peasantry, even a native dress. Farmers in platter-brimmed hats, buttonless pants, chin beards; farmwives in black bonnets and cloaks. They ploughed their flat tan fields with teams of oxen; sold heavy pies and funnel cakes at farmers markets and fairs; menaced the highways in clip-clopping spring buggies like Model T Fords on wooden wheels. Even the horses seemed in mourning—plunged into the gloom of their wide black blinders. Kitty had not come from such a sect, though people might have been excused for thinking so. Something somber even in the blue of her eye. She was what people were in her part of the world—a little of this, a little of that; maybe even some Indian blood—the sturdy build and black hair. People claimed the connection now that the tribes themselves had vanished. She wasn't really a farm girl either, though Justin let it out that she was. It occurred to her now that he really believed it: she was his idea of a farm girl, the closest he could get. What Mrs. LeBow feared had come to pass: he had gone to foreign parts and taken a native bride.

Kitty's grandparents owned a farm—what was left of a farm; her grandmother kept chickens and a kitchen garden. Kitty had picked weeds, scattered feed, gathered eggs from haystacks. She didn't know how to ride a horse, though she had had her picture snapped on one, and she didn't know how to milk a cow—though she had tried. It was harder than it looked. You didn't just squeeze: you had to pull! Yank! The rubbery pink teats. The hairy udders bursting with veins, scabbed with flies. The barn was still standing. Birds nested in the lofts; the doors squeaked and whinnied. The dark rafters shored up the dusty beams of light. Only the wind galloped in the pastures.

There was a house. You might have glimpsed it from a passing train; nothing special; two story, frame, needing paint. Trumpet vines climbed the porch columns, twined the gutters. The long empty windows were plundered with sun. It had broken in, robbed them blind. Most of the panes were of original glass; if you put your eye to the bubbles you were in a strange, still world; weedy green ponds, purple twilights. There was no heat or electricity upstairs, though a hole had been drilled in the kitchen ceiling for a stout extension cord. In winter they used to put on earmuffs and mittens when they went up to bed; in summer, the climate being what it was, you couldn't sleep for the heat. That was when you could hear the corn—something stealthy in the grass.

It smelled of summer. Other summers. Summers done.

Justin liked to drive out when they could borrow a car, to picnic and camp on the lumpy mattresses. He could sleep anywhere, through anything, anytime. Thanks to the United States Army, he said. And he slept late. Poets' hours. But through the window one morning came a sharp persistent tapping; someone mending fences, tacking up chicken wire. He thudded to the window, barefoot, in boxer shorts—army issue. The first thing he did when he got discharged from the service, when he got back to his mother's flat in Hackensack—the first thing he did, he said, was to lug his duffel bag down the hall to the incinerator. He tried to stuff it in; it wouldn't fit. So he lugged it back; lugged it with him halfway across the country. It came in handy thumbing rides. And when he got to the university, that was what they were all wearing—the poets, the painters, the potters—crew cuts, dog tags, camouflage pants.

The hammering persisted; the air was a lifeless corpse.

He raised the window higher—all the sashes were broken, propped up—and leaned halfway out: ponderous shoulders, ponderous forehead. His legs were bowed with muscle but still painfully fair, his neck was mottled with anger and sunburn.

He drew his head back in with a sheepish grin.

Hey Kiddie! Kiddie! Come quick. A woodpecker. No kidding. An honest-to-God redheaded woodpecker. It looks just like its pictures.

He had called from his trip. Kitty told him the crisis was past, there was no need to hurry back. His voice long distance sounded small and scared. She had pictured his eyes, his eyes in the circles of his horn-rimmed glasses, his eyes the same color as the frames. His eyes, always the last line of defense. They were small and scared too.

The small far voice never said what she was so afraid to hear; but Kitty heard it anyway:

What did you come for? What did you come for? This would never have happened if you had stayed home.

It wouldn't have. It couldn't have. She was here. Here She Was. She had lost something. She didn't know what. She couldn't name it. She didn't know if it had a name. She never knew she had had it, until she had lost it.

3.    In the woods they saw the deer.

Christopher was trudging ahead, pulling his sled—a gift from his father. He had insisted, in his stubborn way, bundled to the eyes in his boots and snowsuit, a scarf around his face. And there it was, suddenly, on the path in front of them; the young deer on its spraddled legs, its ears erect, its eyes all iris. It might have been a statue, the deer inside the glass ball, except for the vapor spraying powerfully from its nostrils.

Christopher stopped at once, almost as still, the scarf moving in and out over the bump of his nose. His eyes above were as dark as the deer's.

It was a day inside the glass ball—a crystal day—the woods sunk under snow, deep as an enchantment, the mountains like their own reflections in an Alpine lake. The trees bowed down in white silence.

The deer broke the spell.

Its ears twitched, its tail flicked, it gave a hoarse snort—fierce, for a deer, let alone for a spirit—and bounded off with rocking-horse leaps. Crashing. Cracking. Branches breaking under the weight of snow, trees sneezing snow, the white boughs, released, springing up green.

Was it a spirit? Wasn't it?

Once upon a time. In the olden times. This was how the fairy tales began. The unknown way in the unknown wood. The deer had led them astray; they had lost the path. Snow arches; snow grottoes. Blue prisms of sky, fir needles spurting light. No one had ever been there before. Their footsteps deepened the silence.

And there was the house.

The house was under an evil spell.

For an instant, Kitty thought they had come upon a shortcut to the monastery. That couldn't be; it was six or seven kilometers off. Not a ruin either; ruins were historic. A house like other houses in the village; tall, flat walls, painted plaster. But hollow, smoked, the door and windows charred, the sky pouring blue through a hole in the roof. An abandoned house, like the hearths and foundations you came upon in the fields back home; the broken-down barns, tar-paper roofs. Dump sites; rusted farm machinery, empty gasoline cans. No Trespassing signs—usually used for target practice; ragged starbursts of .22s or BB shot. What harm was left for a trespasser to do?

Voices.

Frightened. Bewildered.

Where were they hiding? There was nowhere to go. Nothing around but snow and silence. Every leaf in flight all fall must have taken refuge here; the floor was foot-deep in heaped dead leaves.

But she heard the voices. A child sobbing. A mother hushing.

Christopher heard them too; listening with his eyes, the scarf sucked flat over his nose.

Something flew into his face—whirring, slashing, claws extended—a frenzy of feathers and wings—many wings—more than one pair. Their flashing lighted his face.

Kitty struck out. *Raus*! *Raus*!

The bird rose higher, flapping.

Pigeons.

Pigeons roosting in the rafters.

Their fretful noises, shuffling wings.

Only pigeons.

But it was as if the bird had flown up inside her.

4.     It was this place. This atmosphere. It was too old. Too much had happened here. Things meant and meant: there was too much history. Even the earth smelled older. Everything was an omen: The Ice Age pictures on the window. The noises of the old house. The lights fluttering like candles. The Alps—the Alps moon white, moon cratered. The Alps as far as the moon. They were on the dark side of the Alps, Herr Gruber said; that was why you couldn't always see them. But they were there; whether you saw them or not, they were there. Now she understood why they called it Alpdruck. She woke in the night listening for Christopher's breathing. She had forgotten how high pitched, rapid it was. He snored. Was he warm enough? Was he too warm? Was his face flushed? Was his nose runny? She was forever feeling his forehead, taking his temperature.

She didn't need to know the metric system; a red nick marked the glass. Normal! Normal! She was sick of the word. And she saw he didn't like it, she was frightening him; he resisted, wriggling, making his stubborn noises. Guttural as German, Kitty thought. He clenched his teeth, even snapped at her, as if he meant to bite the glass in two.

It was bound to happen.

All at once; to Kitty there was no sequence.

He snapped at her hand.

The glass shattered.

Drops of silver, now liquid, now solid, slipped and quivered.

She slapped him.

With the same quick quiver his eyes blinked up at her.

Her hands flew to her cheeks, as if her own face was struck.

Forgive me! Forgive me!

He hid his hands behind him, shaking his head—almost involuntary, a shudder, as when he had the chills.

Please forgive me!

She sank her face into her hands, red fingers of a blush spreading under her fingers. Please? Please?

He went on hiding his hands, shaking his head; his eyes, dark to the quick, discovering her face:

Oh what was it? What was it? What did she want? He didn't have it. He never took it. It was gone. It was spilled. The floor swallowed it.

Give me! he saw her saying over and over. Her mouth moving between her fingers. Give me! Give me!

5.    Kitty pushed open the door and the first thing to greet her eyes was the landlady—on her hands and knees scrubbing the stairs. Her kerchief. Her apron. Her pink rubber gloves. Her head was nodding industriously. *Armschmalz! Armschmalz!*

It was if she had been lying in wait.

Kitty felt a squeeze at her throat.

The mother-in-law?

Frau Gruber crossed herself quickly with a pink rubber glove and went on scrubbing.

The end! *Gangräne*. The mother-in-law was black as a *Mumie*. Her mouth was grinning a mummy-grin. Her lips—*schrumpfen*. Her teeth—*glänzen*. Buttons. Seashells. The mother-in-law was *Atheistisch*, but they had sent for the priest. *Alles in Ordnung*. The last oiling.

It was early, the light leaky gray as wash water. The landlady was making her way backwards down the stairs on her knees, one at a time. Bumping and kneeling. Nodding and scrubbing.

Kitty wasn't sure she had heard right. She had an austere Sunday school fear of ritual. Of priests and robes and censers with their foggy breaths; of waxy faces, waxy candles. Extreme unction sounded bad enough. But—the last oiling! That was almost black humor. Gruesome. Inhuman. Kitty thought of junked cars, twisted scrapmetal.

Yes! The end! At last! The end! No false alarm this time. The mother-in-law smelled dead already. Paul! Paul! The doctor said she couldn't live through the morning. Only out of spite that she lived through the night. They would have the funeral at once. The landlady must get ready for the visitors.

Visitors?

*Totenwache*.

A wake? In this house?

*Natürlich*. It was the mother-in-law's house. *Alles*! The mother-in-law. *Immer*! The mother-in-law.

She slashed her brush, she splashed her bucket. Her chin quivered; her cheeks, the heavy baggage of her apron front, even the fleshy pods of her elbows—trembling. She was talking to herself now, angrier and angrier, taking it out on the stairs. Giving them a drubbing.

Kitty thought of another ritual. Washing and laying out a corpse. Even Baptists did that.

So much to do. Cleaning the house from top to bottom. Shopping. Cooking. Herr Gruber had gone to the bank—the box. *Alles in Ordnung*. The landlady had an appointment with the *Friseur*.

Kitty was hanging on her words like a lip-reader.

So it was here. In this house. Death. Stinking death. Death was coming for a visit. And this was what people did. This was how they prepared. They went to the bank—to the safety-deposit box. They scrubbed the stairs. They made appointments with the hairdresser.

The landlady had got to the bottom of the stairs. She hauled herself up, hauling her bucket, squeezing and sighing. Her eyes reached up, taking an oath:

*Bitte?* The stairs were wet? Kitty would please wait until they were dry?

Kitty nodded. All she could think of was the telephone booth at the train station.

6.      Someone else had got there first.

The telephone booth stank like a cage. Dense, sour, acrid, almost furry. More than a smell: a sensation of warmth. A tramp must have taken shelter here—waited out the worst of the night, the wind. The dirty glass was fogged with his breath. It was as if he were still inside. As if she had stepped into a rank sweaty embrace.

In spite of the cold, the dull numb whiteness of the day, she had to open the door. She shook the coins out of her glove; she had only one thought. To get Christopher out—away from that house. Now. Today. The house of death. The mother-in-law's house. She had put him to bed; he was flushed, sniffling. The phone bleated and beeped. A busy signal. She hung up. The coins didn't return.

She clicked the receiver. The box was full of coins; she could hear them jangling. Why wouldn't it spit them out? It refused to cough them up. She jiggled the phone, banged on the box.

A tramp. A tramp in clean well-ordered Germany. She recalled the beggars at the Oktoberfest; the crutches, the empty sleeves, the blind men listening for the clink of coins in their cups. And the drunk—the little man with the big shadow. The knobby knees; the sizzling stream. Omens. All omens. Things were not what they seemed. She was banging on the box, on the booth, cold sweat trickling in her scalp, down her spine, bone by bone; the glass steaming, streaming with her breath. She dropped her head against the cold wet glass. Something clanked. A faint clink and the box began cranking out coins—faster than she could catch them—coins rattling like bolts, like broken pieces.

It struck her. Here, shut inside this booth; this was the closest human contact she had had in Germany.

7.    That night a light glimmered under the landlady's door.

An eye peeped out: an eye in a peephole. The door opened. The landlady stepped forth; from head to foot she stood transformed. Powdered,
rouged, all in black, rhinestones sputtering in her ears and sparkling
round her chin. Her brows and her lips were arched and darkened and
her hair was hennaed—root-beer-color—molded to her head in a frieze
of flat bangs and clinging waves.

The brows arched higher; the lips compressed.

She regarded Kitty as from a distance, imposed in the doorway, her
hand on the latch.

Kitty had rehearsed a speech, looked up phrases in the dictionary.
Now she scarcely knew how to begin, what to say, to such a personage—
on such an occasion. So she said what people say; she said she was sorry.

Frau Gruber acknowledged this as people do; an inclination of the
head. She gave a little shrug and dropped her eyes.

Behind her all was ready. *Alles in Ordnung.* The table laid in a profusion of cut-glass and silver and tall waxy tapers—unlit. The landlady, ever
thrifty, was waiting for the visitors. But the room was hushed, shadowed
in a cold flickering glow. The box? The narrow wooden box? Would there
be flowers? Wreaths and ribbons?

The landlady pulled the door closer.

Kitty realized she was being nosy; a new sensation, for her. Staring
past, her eyes drawn against her will. She blurted it out—spoke her piece.
She was leaving. Going back home as soon as she could. The climate was
no good for Christopher. She was worried he might be sick again. His
father was coming to get him. She didn't say—to rescue him.

Again the nod, the shrug. The landlady fingered her necklace with five
stubby red nails. A *Maniküer.* She looked taller, for God's sake. A flapper.
The ankle-strap shoes, the drop-waisted dress with silken fringes at the hips,
the flat band of bangs across her forehead. Kitty was still staring past her.

The TV?

Could it be?

Yes, the TV on top of the cabinet radio. That was the source of the
tremoring glow—Alp-light or moonlight. The landlady was sneaking in
a movie. The sound was off or very low or maybe silent. Under their

ten-gallon hats the faces of the cowboy actors were deadpan with makeup. Cornstarch. They wore lipstick and mascara and black lines around their eyes. It seemed Kitty's fate to catch the landlady out in small secrets.

She had something more to say. To ask. It had taken a great deal for her to work up the nerve. It was now or never.

Behind the landlady the camera was cutting. Hands. Holsters. Pistols jutting. It was the showdown. The black lines narrowed—eyes flashed like snakes.

View her!

The landlady exposed her great eyes:

Kitty wished to view the mother-in-law? *Schon gut*!

The keys were on the hook; Frau Gruber pulled the door shut and, huffing and puffing, the hoop in her fist, headed for the stairs. Head bobbing, back stooping, fringes trembling on her hips. Through the thin black crepe—rusty under the armpits, smelling of mothballs—Kitty could see the rigid outline of corsets, like a saddle or hide.

Kitty had to ask. She had to see the mother-in-law; had to face it—this specter, this *Schreckbild*, this bogeyman—or forever after carry it with her. Still, she had hoped the answer might be no. The landlady might refuse, or say it was impossible, the mother-in-law was buried. Then at least Kitty would have made the effort. She could tell herself that. Maybe it would have been enough.

But the landlady was too surprised to refuse. And the mother-in-law was here, in this house—as, in a way, she had been all along. But where? Where were they keeping her? The cellar? Bandaged? A *Mumie*? Shrouded in burlap like the shrubs?

The storeroom. The landlady was sorting through her keys, turning the lock. She put a finger to her lips. From the darkness came a gush of damp and cold. Of course the storeroom. It made a kind of horrible sense. Kitty could hear the old woman breathing suspensefully, searching for the light string, bumping into objects in the dark. A persistent stealthy rasping and scratching. Mice? Cats? It was the black crepe scraping over corsets and stays.

Even before the light came on Kitty knew what she was going to see. She was so sure that at first it was what she saw: A table. A table long and narrow as a bier. A table laden end to end. China, silver, cutlery, glassware, lamps, vases, clocks, a chandelier—a chandelier of crystal pendants and smoked stubby candles. Stacked, piled, cluttered any old way. Lined up around it, in strict formality—a dozen chairs. Tall, straight, stiff backed, pigeon breasted. As if they were sitting there yet: the ladies in velvet and brocade and jeweled bosoms; the gentlemen in uniform, stuffed shirt-fronts, sashes and gold braid.

The whole room was like that. Boxes, crates, barrels, wardrobes, ta-bles on tables, chairs on chairs, curio cabinets gorged with bric-a-brac, bookshelves, mirrors, picture frames. Everything carved, gilded, scrolled; lion faces, claws, wreaths, ribbons, clusters of grapes—oh, grape clusters galore. An upright piano under a shawl, and, under a sheet, a harp. A harp! Did people own harps? But what else could it be? Kitty understood that this was where the brass urn was from; probably the lawbooks and the silver crystal laid out upstairs.

It all smelled of dust, dampness, cats, ashes, cold grates.

What did this mean? Where was the mother-in-law? Was she dead? Alive? Was there a mother-in-law? But what about the doctor, the priest, the last oiling? The bank, the safety-deposit box, the *friseur*?

The landlady was examining objects, holding them to the light, blow-ing off dust. The room was so cold Kitty could see her breath, huffing and puffing like dust. That was it. The landlady was breathing—anxiously, eagerly as ever—but her bosom was still. Strung like a bow. Her eyes had their old expression:

Kitty must go now. The landlady must lock up. *Alles in Ordnung. Stirbt nichts!* She planted the red nails to her breast. Kitty would say noth-ing? It was their secret?

The mother-in-law will outlive us all, Kitty said.

It was a question. Her voice sounded small, stifled, a voice in the dark, in bad dreams. Did it count? Was she absolved? Was it the end? She was more frightened than she had ever been. The wings were fluttering in her chest. The mother-in-law was here; whether or not you could see her, she was here. And all the way up the stairs—and for a long time after—Kitty could hear the landlady sighing to herself; could see her standing behind the door, a finger to her lips, an eye shining out—hiding and seeking.

# CALM SEA AND
# PROSPEROUS VOYAGE

On my way back into town I stopped off to look for you. Where were you? I couldn't find you. You weren't there. What's this? Am I losing my marbles? The deep green grove, the glazing sunlight, the breeze stirring the leaves and the red marquee. All that pageantry gone—and no sign of you? If this is a joke! Here was only a nice suburban lawn, the gravel level, the flat grass mowed. Across the road, a white church spire was sprinkling out organ tones, skating-rink music, and a bank of wreaths and ribbons decked a new grave. That's the Christian cemetery. Omit Flowers for Jews. And nothing, not even scraped earth, to show for our pains? But you have to be here, I have to find you—here, where we left you just this morning. Here? Where the grass lies uneasy? It's hiding something. Three strips of sod, dried and muddied, like coco matting. A marker as ancient, rusted, as the rest. I knelt to read it.

Victor G. C. Lazarus
1945–1995

Patchwork, Victor. Patchwork.

## TUESDAY
## JUNE 6

Your colleagues had taken up a collection of worn old books to be buried with you, as is the custom at the funeral of a scholar, and the service started off with a reading from your work. I have to apologize, Victor, I couldn't keep my mind on it. Someone was sobbing out loud. Already? I thought. And the trees, the tent top, the rug of green Astroturf, the mourners seated all in a row. Ben squirming in his necktie and skullcap, the soles of his gym shoes stuck together, his blue eyes wandering, scared. How long is this grown-up stuff gonna last? His grandmother—your mother—leans down, her lips to his ear, his fist in her fist. Easy to guess what she's saying. Her head trembles, as from a long habit of chiding. How little, how aged, she is today, her white hair brittle, her face behind dark glasses bolted and barred. Next your half brother, staring boldly in front of him, a hand on either knee, as if he's been told not to blink. Then your two stepsisters. Last, an empty chair.

None of them looks to be listening either.

Not half an hour ago, everything was white; the sky, the sun, the milky mists of the hollows. The mountains were smoking like idols. Now all is made clear. It happens that way, in our valley. Truly the light is sweet. I wish you could see it.

The young rabbi steps forward, the books close to his chest. Very young, very slight; fragile, even. The narrow black suit. The narrow black beard. The black-black eyes in the white-white face. You know those intense Jewish organs. There are one and one-half rabbis in town now, and this Rabbi Pilcher here is the half, a rabbinical student, pinch-hitting at temple while they search for a successor to Rabbi Jim. Rabbi Jim. Remember him? The one who used to dress as Queen Esther on Purim and deliver his sermons in drag? Something about how there's nothing wrong with being a woman, we're really okay, guys. You told me they were thinking of joining up with the Ethical Culture Society anyhow, tossing in the tallith. Another of your jokes, Victor? You know I never could tell with you. Oh, I catch on eventually; I almost always catch on—eventually. Eventually isn't always soon enough.

This must be Rabbi Pilcher's first funeral; he seems so nervous, almost pleading, hugging the books, as if for protection, holding on for dear life. He lifts his eyes to the hills. Whence shall come his help? For his eulogy, he means to compare the life of Victor Lazarus to the life of Moses Maimonides. There are many parallels, he says; not just that, like Maimonides, Victor Lazarus was married twice, and had a son—.

Wait, Victor. Don't turn over. You're not in your grave yet.

I wonder if the young rabbi knows he's been the eye of a storm these last few days?

It was your wish, stated in your will, to have an Orthodox Jewish burial. Easier said than done—as you, of all people, ought to know. And among the obstacles, not the least is the fact that you, Victor Lazarus—master of languages ancient and modern, mysteries mathematic and metaphysic, authority on Maimonides, at home in Hebrew and Greek, in the Arabic of Averroës and Avicenna, in the Latin of Saint Thomas Aquinas—the great medieval mystics and philosopher-healers, reconcilers of faith and reason—you, Victor Lazarus, to get to the point, were not Jewish.

Not technically.

Your grandmother—your mother's mother—was Mercedes (called Sadie) McDade, baptized in the Tombigbee River, which wends its way out of Mississippi down the length of western Alabama—Alabama, where the stars fall—and somewhere safe to sea. At sixteen she caught the eye of Benjamin Gottlieb, late of Warsaw, a successful businessman, lover of grand opera, Panama hats, and Havana cigars. Because of the difference in their ages and stations, he sent his bride-to-be to finishing school. Ah, the Jewish romance with America! Nine children were born to this union before Benjamin Gottlieb collapsed one summer morning, shaking ripe gold from the pear tree; dead on the spot of a heart attack. The way you were expecting to go yourself, weren't you, Victor, and at just about your age. Goes to show how much we know. Sadie McDade, still a young woman, was to remain his faithful widow for fifty years. That was the Depression; soon came the war. At the Jewish canteen, Belle Gottlieb—Belle of the Irish eyes and the Southern charm—met Victor Lazarus, a husky dark-browed airman stationed near Tuscaloosa. They fell in love and married, the way people do in wartime; desperate, as you said, for her to get pregnant. He was training to be a pilot; he would be flying bombing missions. They were in luck. Before he shipped overseas, your father-to-be and never-to-be spoke to his brother of the unborn child. If something happens to me, he said, take care of Victor. Something happened. So they named you, as we Jews do, after a dead relative. You became Victor Lazarus.

I like your genealogy. The American mishmash; bedrock Southern fundamentalism, pie-eyed immigrant dreams. It seemed right for you, scholar of Torah and Logos, Lover of Wisdom, Lover of Women, Man of Many Contradictions—not all of them high-flown. But we are an ancient tribe, more ancient than our history, and—though you'd never know it, from all the begats and begats in the Bible—descent is through the mother's womb and in the mother's blood. This was your dark secret, your bar sinister, the sign of that shadow over your fate and character your friends the philosophers keep telling me about. You didn't want to be half-something. All or nothing at all. Was that the Jew in you?

Let me say right now, Victor—I have no complaints. You gave good value; I never felt shortchanged. I don't see how anyone ever could—except for *her*, your former wife, a fateful exception; and, it seems, the rabbis. Still, there are plenty of reasons you can't have a strictly kosher Orthodox burial. It's not all your fault, those famous last words. Were they, Victor. The last you heard? Not only the tainted blood of Sadie McDade. Sometimes the fault is in our stars.

Well, as Belle, your mother, says, in her mother's Alabama twang: We must just do as best we can.

So here goes.

SUNDAY
JUNE 4

All morning Belle kept trying to reach the other rabbi, the Orthodox rabbi here at the university. There was no answer at his house, so I called his secretary.

Do you know if Rabbi Salmon is out of town? I said.

I don't know that, she said.

We thought he might have gone away because it's commencement?

I don't know that, she said.

Aw, come on. What gives? You've seen this woman, haven't you? Big friendly bust, big round glasses, the kind of frizzed orange hair that looks as if it just caught fire. The motherly type; a gusher. So what's with the snotty stuff? Am I fixing to slap a paternity suit on the rabbi? Out to repossess his car? All these months, the doctors, the hospitals, the social workers—O the social workers! The road to hell, you said, is paved with social workers—and I'm still not used to it. Always the collection agency. Always the adversary.

Maybe the rabbi hasn't paid up his malpractice insurance.

I said Rabbi Salmon was wanted to perform a funeral service. That fetched her. He gets respect, your pal Death.

It's Shavuot, she said quickly, almost in a whisper. Today and tomorrow. That's why the rabbi's not answering his phone.

Shavuot? What's *Shavuout*? Oh, she must mean Sh'voos! That's how we used to say it on the West Side of Chicago. By the rivers of Babylon. The Feast of Weeks. Pentecost. And bat mitzvah was *bas*, and Shabbat was *Shabb's*. The creation of the state of Israel has sure fixed up our diction.

O my heartiest! She hesitated. That didn't sound right, did it? Hearty?

That's for happy occasions. A wedding, a bar mitzvah, a bris. What's the right word for grief?

But why didn't you say so in the first place? she said.

In the first place, Victor, you're not dead. Not technically. I don't know if you're interested in details; the usual scenario. You had a second massive stroke early this morning, a young intern rushed to the rescue, jumped on your chest, and now you're hooked and wired to life support. They're keeping you going until the rest of your family gets here, and your doctor comes back from a weekend vacation. Besides, we have blue laws in our valley; we can't buy beer or pull plugs on Sunday. And what's the big hurry? Does it matter now? You'll keep. You can die tomorrow.

And in the second place—.

May I ask—who? Her voice had dropped an octave. The force of gravity. Is it anyone—we know?

She's gotta be kidding! In a town this size? The secretary is a personal friend of your second wife—your ex, as she calls herself—as I think I'll call her. X has only personal friends.

I'm going to make it, you said. I'm not going to die. I'm not going to give her the satisfaction.

Why is it, Victor, why is it? The only ones who get the satisfaction in this world are the ones who can't be satisfied?

Please convey my condolences to the family, the secretary said. Still this hushed husky voice. I'll be only too glad to speak to the rabbi for you, if you want. And? May I ask? What are you—to him?

The engines of curiosity are never idle. I could just see that orange hair sizzling. But let's be fair, everybody asks. You know how people are: they need a damage estimate before they shell out with the sympathy. I guess we're all strapped for funds.

I ask myself. A good question.

What am I to you, Victor? What are you to me?

## THURSDAY
## JUNE 1

I knocked. No answer. The door was open. The Levolor blinds were drawn, the living room a vat of stale light; I heard that rackety contraption, your air conditioner, clattering and crooning in the bedroom. You must be taking a nap. Who else could snooze to such a lullaby? But you were sitting on the edge of your bed with your back to me and you turned to look over your shoulder. Guilty things, backs. Your chin seemed impaled on it; your eyes, those night creatures, burrowing in your glasses. You took the cigarette from your lip.

Victor Lazarus.

Now don't go nagging him, I told myself. Don't do what comes naturally. Six months without a drink or a cigarette and the doctors warned, if you ever started up with all that again it would kill you—just as your friends always said it would. Sooner or later. Forgive us, Victor; we meant later. You know you're under surveillance, we're keeping an eye on you. We start sniffing as soon as we walk through the door. Belle calls every day from Tampa to remind you. Th' smok'n an' th' drink'n. Th' smok'n an' th' drink'n. God he'ps those who he'p theirselves. Belle's your mother. But I figure, since you're supposed to be so smart, with your zillion books and your umpteen languages—give or take a few—and your reputation, they say, the world over, you don't need me sticking my two cents in.

So I said, in my most dutiful voice—you know it breaks my heart to pass up a chance to preach—Didn't you want to come sit outside? Breathe the fresh air? On such a lovely day?

Lovely days, lovely days. How weary you must be of hearing about all the lovely days. How many have you lost? How many have you left?

I dragged a couple of lawn chairs out onto the piazza, as we call your six-foot-square slab of concrete overlooking the parked cars and the dumpsters and—unexpectedly—the rough raked furrows of the corn-fields. All the new construction going on in our valley; so much Sheetrock and tar paper and pink insulation; so many shantytown apartment complexes, like this one; student barracks, shopping malls, gas pumps, twenty-four-hour convenience stores. And here's the barking dog chained to the clothesline, the tire swing strung from the lonesome pine; some farmer holding out for the American Dream. Or for a price.

But mine own vineyards have I not kept.

By and by out you came, your high shoulders propped higher, halting, on crutches. Splinted wings. This was something new; you didn't have the hang of it yet. Cramps in your legs. The pain gets worse. Weakness, the doctor says; too much time in hospital beds. Learn to live with it, he says, drink quinine water. At last you managed to lean the crutches against the wall and flop yourself down into the lawn chair. Your long skinny self, your scaffold. Six foot two, slouching. One hundred and twenty pounds. Hair dark, straight, Oriental. Your knee bones poking in your trouser legs. Your skeleton was showing again.

It's harder… than… it looks…

Do I mention it now? The hole in your throat. The tracheotomy. All those months breathing on respirators, scribbling on slates and legal pads, mouthing your words, mute. And the wound never healed: a piece of gauze sucking in and out, in and out. To speak you press your fingers to your throat, force the words to your lips. In an odd way, it's as if you're blowing kisses.

Along came three young women in shorts and halters and fresh red sunburns, dragging black plastic bags. All of a sudden these containers are cropping up everywhere, like miniature portable toilets on construction sites. They are for sorting garbage. It goes like this:

Brown glass: *crack*.

Green glass: *smash*.

Clear glass: *crash*

You were wincing.

I put my hands to either side of my mouth:

Hey! You guys! Can't you make it a little louder?

They laughed and wagged their ponytails. They weren't just pitching out trash; they were performing a mitzvah, a good deed. Such are the virtues of our times; separating the pizza boxes from the beer bottles.

They're striking a blow for humanity, I said.

You touched your fingers to your throat:

Humanity... you said. Has had... enough... blows...

This is no country for old men. It's a university town; they're out there by the thousands, the scores of thousands—the young in each other's arms, the skateboards, the Frisbees, the birds and boom boxes at their song.

But what a spring! Even you took notice. After the smokestacks and blacktopped parking lots of the medical center, the mountains in their moth-eaten pelts like scruffy buffalo hides, the raw cold fogs, the high blue windows. You were half-sick of windows. And lo! The winter is past. The redbuds and cherry trees are in flower—like pink popcorn, you said—and you confessed an urge to pick dogwood, embrace the branches. That was the thing to do when you were in college, tender armloads of blossoms to your lady love.

Could this be Victor talking? Victor Lazarus? Victor who calls me a pantheist, a tree worshiper, with my sunsets and moonrises and mountaintops woolgathering under the clouds. But this is the place where His glory dwells, I say. I talk that way sometimes. As if I didn't know. The proper study of mankind is books! Five of them! It says so in the Talmud.

And Socrates himself—your pagan patron saint Socrates—allowed there's no percentage in talking to trees.

Between Torah and Logos, tell me, Victor, who stands a chance? We're finished!

The girls were waving good-bye, dragging their empty sacks and their ponytails.

I had been sitting the while considering how to begin.

The kids called last night, I said. David and Judith. Checking up on me again; they wanted to make sure I'm looking after you right. I said no, I'm not Victor's mother, I'm no watchdog. It's none of my business. I say, leave the guy alone. Let him do what he wants.

That's a… good… attitude… you said. I like… that… attitude…

I bet you do! But Judith didn't. She got indignant with me. You know Judith, she's a Quaker, she gets indignant.

Oh not with you, Victor; you are her husband's teacher, mentor, dearest friend. No, not with you. But I'm her husband's mother: she gets plenty indignant with me.

She thinks it's a bad attitude, I said. The wrong attitude. She says it's like saying it doesn't matter.

You lifted your face to me, all of a sudden interested, the way you might get all of a sudden interested, say, if someone pushed a knife against your ribs. As a matter of fact, you have felt the knife at your ribs—for months, for years—most of that time without flinching. But now you blinked: the bird fluttered.

I was afraid to go on. The subject was your mortality.

The phone began to ring.

You felt for your crutches. I was not in the habit of answering. If it was her—X—you'd never hear the end of it; and usually it was. How many years since you separated? How long divorced? And still no letup. Day after day poureth forth speech; night after night, tirades. No use shutting off the telephone: it won't take long and she'll be out there in the hall, child-size, in bathrobe and slippers, beating down your door with her tiny bare fists, her tiny bare feet.

*Wee Willie Winkie runs through the town*
*Upstairs and downstairs in her nightgown*

*Rapping at the windows*
*Crying through the locks…*

Some people just have to be the center of attention.

I used to go into the bathroom and turn on the shower full force to drown out the noise. Shame on me. The oceans will run out of water before she runs out of rage.

But I was wrong about the phone.

You came hopping back. That was… the police…

You mean the KGB? I said. That's gotta be a record. How'd you get rid of her so fast?

Oh, she's got the gift of gab, all right. X would blab for an hour if she dialed 911.

You touched your fingers to your throat, that heartfelt gesture; swearing an oath, taking a pledge.

No, honest… For real… They're on… the way…

Uh-huh, I said.

I wish you'd quit teasing me, Victor. Everyone does. I'm so earnest, a straight man born. But you? Victor Lazarus? Your brain meant for cracking the conundrums of the universe? You get a kick out of pulling my leg? That's nothing to brag about. Any Tom Dick or Harry can pull my leg.

I'm on to you now.

Yeah yeah, I said. Sure sure sure.

Crows cackled over the cornfields.

A squeal of tires, a static spatter of gravel. Two cops; two squad cars. We watched them get out, slam the doors. Let's face it: no one gets out of a car and slams the door the way a cop gets out and slams the door. What do they do? Practice? So they came waddling up, the cop waddle, the gun-slung hips. Crossing Rubicons. Burning bridges. They hitched up their pants. All right for you. They meant business.

You sat forward. You held out your hand.

In hospital beds, in skimpy string-tied gowns, flapping bottoms. That device in your throat made you mute, so the doctors spoke in loud voices, as if you might be deaf as well. Or defective. You'd think they never saw a dying man before. They gave you the news—no news was good news—cut some more here, drill a hole there—and when they had done, you sat up, you held out your hand.

That stumped them. They stared. A fakir on your bed of nails, your naked arm bone trailing needles, tapes, wires, tubes. A tin cup, a beggar bell, they could understand. But a hand? What did it mean, what did you want from them? What to do with a hand?

Ever the gentleman, weren't you, Victor? The soul of courtesy. Belle, Southern Belle, would have seen to that.

You startled the cops too. They hadn't come to shake hands. What do you think the uniforms are for? The white coats and beepers, the holsters and badges? These are not meant to be human transactions. But you insisted. Face to face. Man to man.

It took a moment for the two of them to recover; gird up their loins, heft their heft, scowl their scowls all over again.

They were investigating an incident that afternoon in the parking lot at the bowling alley. It seems a vehicle, backing out, nicked the fender of another vehicle. Witnesses got the license number and description, which happened to fit the number and description of a vehicle registered in your name and parked right there by the dumpster. The officer jerked a thumb over his shoulder. He'd stopped by earlier to inspect the fender and found, sure enough—will wonders never cease?—fresh paint. He knocked at your door but got no answer. He knew he had you though, a culprit caught red handed; knew you were inside, hiding from him.

Hiding, maybe; but not from him. What would he know of who was knocking at your door?

The cop had a case. Haven't we all? He was going to make it. He frowned down at you sternly, forebodingly, chin doubled, fists on hips. Were you at the bowling alley that afternoon? Because if you were and you denied it, he could charge you with obstruction of an official investigation. Witnesses got a good look at the suspect, last seen drinking at the bar. A tall skinny guy, like you. Long hair and glasses, like you. And even—.

He slid a finger across his throat.

You touched your hand to yours.

Yes... Yes... I'm the man...

Well that was a relief! I'd hate to think there was another one out there. This town, this whole valley, wouldn't be big enough for both of you.

Your automobile registration had expired, your inspection sticker had expired, your driver's license too. Well well well. I was impressed. How'd you ever get away with it, Victor? That must be the only thing in your life you ever got away with.

And O you looked so meek! I had to hide a smile. Your shoulders hunched, your head sunk between them up to your ears, your glasses sliding, sidling down your nose. I don't say it was your finest hour. But after your heart bypass a few years back, and these last months battling cancer, the knife at your ribs and the fog in your throat, I don't suppose you gave a good goddamn about cops, official investigations, expired stickers, and scratched fenders.

But what—just what—did Victor Lazarus give a damn about? That is the question.

I wish you could have seen him before, Simon said. Before all this. The way he was when I first saw him. He was beautiful. I hate to use that word, but it's the only word. Beautiful—that's what he was.

Simon is a philosopher. He doesn't take words like the Good, the True, the Beautiful in vain.

That was the next day, Victor. Friday afternoon. I left a message for Simon as soon as the ambulance took off. The air conditioner was still rattling in your bedroom; I shut it up, grabbed your keys from your desk, and locked the door behind me. A man was trying to start the sputtering motor of his power mower and he didn't look up to follow the flashing lights. So they haul out some guy feetfirst. So they slam the doors on him. So what. He kept tugging, tugging, the motor grunting, grudging, siren screams falling from the sky. The air smelled of gasoline and fresh-cut grass.

Now they had rolled you downstairs for a CAT scan, and we were waiting for word, sipping Diet Pepsi at the vending machine by the elevator doors. We both knew this was it; we were holding a wake of our own. The janitor was mopping circles around us.

*Caution Slippery Wet Floor*

Simon doesn't look like a philosopher, does he? The oblong brow, the gladiator nose, the ridges of kinky Vitallised metallic gray hair. The solid block of a man that is Simon. And the raw silk jackets, the snazzy neckties, the pointy-toed Italian shoes. With a tan he could pass for another kind of don. Though how should I know what philosophers look like? I don't even know what philosophers do.

I never read any of Simon's books. I checked a couple of them out of the library once and, with an armlock on the weighty tomes, ran right smack into him outside on the front steps. Simon took one look and shook his head, his big head; abrupt, dismissive, more like a shudder. No use, he said. Forget it. His thoughts were too deep for me, I'd have a hard time. So as soon as he turned the corner, I sneaked back in and dumped the books down the slot. Took a load off my mind. You never know when you'll really need a hard time.

Simon Wiseman, your best friend, your more-than-brother, the one person next to of course Ben you love most in all the world. That's how Simon describes himself. Easy to kid about Simon, the greedy ego of his genius; but you know and I know it's true.

Simon and I are virtuous, we are vigilant, after the manner of our times. We don't smoke or drink, we take our vitamins, we get our exercise, we count our calories, and we test our cholesterol. So you see, we will never be in your place, will we, Victor. Never hooked up to the oxygen, the drips; never trolling on a gurney down these antiseptic corridors, the sinister slick tiles, the popping automatic doors. Oh no. Not us. Not if we can help it.

I can't see Simon sorting out his garbage, though.

Do you want to hear what Simon says about me?

You were a good friend, Simon says. A good woman. You meant a lot to Victor.

Wow! That was nice of Simon! To say you cared for me. No, I really mean it. He never mentioned our connection before, whatever that is or was or might have been. Usually he talks about your other women— your friends being, I notice, fascinated by the subject; the secret of your success. Is it because he thinks I care? Or because he thinks I don't? He would, Simon, very much; Simon, so eager to be loved. And I get the feeling Simon is trying to tell me something, Victor. That he's the one—the only one—who knows you, really knows you; the only one, now, who ever will. Sometimes I wonder. I'm a much simpler proposition than Victor

Lazarus ever was, and Simon doesn't know me.

Maybe he only understands other philosophers.

I wish you could have seen him, Simon said. It's more than thirty years ago now. He was only eighteen. He turned up on my doorstep. He read my book, he borrowed a car, he drove five hours to see me. Just like that. Out of the blue. Who was I then? A nothing! A nobody! A lowly instructor. Smoking a pipe, phony leather patches on my sleeves. That was my first book, on the *Poetics*, it sold 439 copies. I might as well have tossed it overboard in a bottle. But this kid! This long skinny kid. He's here to talk philosophy. I thought he dropped from the skies. So we go for a stroll. If you think this town is the boondocks now—! Thirty years ago it was a cow pasture. The school of agriculture, that was our claim to fame; they threw in all that other bunk, philosophy, poli-sci, lit crit, to give the farm boys their money's worth. It was an oink-oink here and an oink-oink there. Everywhere an oink-oink. Moo-moo and baa-baa-baa all over town. You think he noticed? Not Victor. As far as he's concerned, it's the agora. I took him home. We're living in this crummy flat with the crib in the living room and the diapers drying on the radiator pipes, and everything smelly from sour milk—you know how it is with a new baby. Those were the days! Thérése feeds us and goes to bed—she was up all the night before, the kid had the colic—and we take turns walking and burping and patting it on the bum-bum. Doesn't bother Victor, he doesn't miss a beat: he's just getting going on *The Birth of Tragedy*. He keeps pouring the wine. I can still hear the jug—glug glug gulp—it's burping too. He didn't seem to notice, only a reflex, and I didn't think anything of it either. Not then. It was part of his attraction—his eagerness, his enthusiasm—getting carried away like that. He didn't need wine. He was already intoxicated, intoxicated to begin with; that was his nature. And I remembered myself; who I was, who I wanted to be. Victor had a way of reminding you. We talked until it got light. Then he had to take off; he promised to get the car back by noon. What kept him going? Don't ask me. What keeps him going now? Not physical stamina, he never had that. But he had everything else. And youth. He had youth. My God, it made you ache to look at him; that high color, his face all fired up and his cheeks burning. Oh, he was the Golden Boy all right: the

Golden Boy in all his Glory. Victor Lazarus. People were already talking about him. His future. No, it's really too bad. I'm sorry you couldn't have seen him. Before.

Before. What Simon calls the ten terrible years. Before the drinking.

Before your first wife left you—the one you loved. Before the silly scandal at Blackwood that dimmed your future, all but put out your light. Before the hellish second marriage you made on the rebound. Before the heart surgery. Before the cancer.

Before and before and before.

The strange thing is, Victor, I had seen you—and just the other day. We were sitting out on the piazza, in the lawn chairs, just as we were now. It was getting dark then too, the air thick with rumors of twilight, its blue mood upon us, an X-ray of moon in the sky. You took off your glasses and frowned. Funny, for a man of tsuris, you didn't frown much; nor for a deep thinker, either. A rare thing, your frown; the straight glossy black brows almost meeting over the plumb line of your nose, your eyes green, green as light in deep water, their gaze offshore. I never did figure out what color they really were. And there was always something of the adolescent about you, the stripling. Personally I think it was your miserable physique, your meager shoulders and underdeveloped chest. Youth? Oh yes. Victor Lazarus had youth, and would have, always, had he lived to the proverbial 120. Or half that. My age.

How beautiful you are, Victor, I wanted to say.

But I never knew when you might turn me away with your irony. That's what you called it: I think you used that word too often, Victor, even for a philosopher. And you never cared for compliments. I can see how some people might have taken this for arrogance, and some people did; Victor Lazarus considering praise no more than his due. To me, it seemed superstition.

Lover of Wisdom, Lover of Women, did you fear the evil eye?

Lover of Wisdom, Lover of Women, you had cause.

How beautiful you are, Victor! I wish I'd said it! Set that down, put it on the list. Sins of omission, that's my specialty. I wasn't about to ask what you were seeing, gazing into your cloudy crystal ball. But I knew what I had seen; what glimpse, what gift, had been given me. It was you, at eighteen, grown young and beautiful.

I must confess, it had occurred to me that you must have looked better once upon a time. Before. Before the wrecking ball took a few swings at you; not to mention the hacksaws, jackhammers, and machetes. Why do I always get them when they've been through the wringer, I asked myself. Never mind, never mind; only a rhetorical question. The glasses were new, some medication that turned out to have side effects; but my guess would be you'd always let your hair grow too long, always stooped your studious yeshiva bocher stoop. Only now, with the cleats in your ribs and the staples in your lungs, you had the look of someone hunched against an ill wind—the kind that blows nobody good—and the removal of the long vein from your thigh, to make new arteries for your heart, had left you with—if not a limp—the slightest suggestion you might be dragging a leg-iron. Still, you liked nice things; cashmere topcoats, camel hair jackets, good leather, and whose business was it, anyhow? If the shoes needed resoling, if the linings were in holes, if almost everything you owned dated back to the days of your future. You dressed with an air of formality, as you did everything else; your manner courtly, your voice gentle. I never heard you raise it, not to me, not to her, not even when you were drunk; when your eyes capsized; when I was wondering by what calibrations you were managing to remain vertical. Your overall effect, if ofttimes askew, was chivalrous, even ascetic.

Yes. That was it. A knight. *A verray parfit gentil knyght.*

It was getting late; the crows made wing to the rooky wood and the cops were getting restless. One of them was eyeing me up and down, making calculations. He cocked his head, sent a sidelong glance your way. Who was I, he wanted to know. Where did I fit in?

To tell the truth, I had never given the matter much thought.

I can remember sitting in kindergarten story hour—radiators hissing and cracking steam heat, smells of egg tempera and pee—pondering my hands folded in my lap and my shoes side by side with bells in the laces—children used to wear bells, like sheep—and thinking, for the very first time—This is Me! This is Me! And it doesn't take long, half a century, say, and here I am, sitting in a striped lawn chair, in the gloaming, looking down at my hands and my feet—rings on my fingers? bells on my toes?—and thinking—not for the first time—Is this Me? Is this Me?

And she shall have music wherever she goes.

So now a cop was asking me to state my business. Who was I? Where did I fit in?

But that was only the beginning—the beginning of your end—and I didn't see it. Didn't see the two of us sitting there, the parked cars, the dumpsters, the deepening evening scented with spring. Didn't see myself, a woman of a certain age—what better camouflage? Didn't see that this was it. I missed my chance again.

They wouldn't have know you, either. Did I? Victor Lazarus. The long list of honors, distinctions after your name in, as you called it, who zoo; and in your obituary. You didn't have much to show for it, did you? Your zillion books, your umpteen languages, your reputation, so they say, the world over. A flat in a student barracks, a mattress on the floor, secondhand furniture, a secondhand car. Not to mention your second-hand body. Rivets in your ribs. Staples in your lungs. Man-made esophagus, stitched-up stomach.

Victor Lazarus was a man of parts.

And now the cops had come to give notice: the finger across the throat. Your registration had expired, you could pay your fines by mail. But neither were you the scofflaw, the desperado, they had been hoping to nail. A paint scraping in a parking lot! So they shifted from one foot to the other, sorry they ever got themselves into this. What you were was some poor soul, stoop shouldered, on crutches, with crooked glasses and a hole in your throat and they wanted to be on their way. I think they knew. Cops know things like that. It's their job, they get their noses rubbed in it. They can see it coming. Oh yes, they'd met that gaze before, the face already pressed to the other side of the glass.

Come on. Let's get going. Let's get out of here. This guy's a goner.

Sometimes, doing the most ordinary things—pushing a grocery cart, rinsing a dish at the sink—I freeze. Solid fear. Not of death, that's nothing. Everybody dies. If it's good enough for you, it's good enough for me. Life,

Victor, life. It happened—all of it. It happened the way it happened. It happened that way and no other. I can try to say what and how—but will that change anything? We move onward, towing a cold wake behind us. What, Officer, you don't know me? Then let's keep this short and sweet. Just say I'm the witness. The witness at the scene.

## TUESDAY
## JUNE 6

It must be your friend the Israeli from Ashqelon. The woman who's sobbing, trying so hard not to sob, while the rabbi speaks. Tall and brave as a mast, the features angular, the fist of Kleenex squeezed against a long elegant thigh. Ooh la la. Never let it be said your tastes weren't eclectic, Victor. I mean no disrespect, but the rabbi looks as if he's about to get baptized himself—dunked into the Tombigbee, maybe—delicate as a maiden, as Sadie McDade, his elbows clasped modestly over his bearded breast, his eyes floating up, up on pious whites.

Her skirt is fluttering in the sweet-talking breeze.

I wish I could go up to her. Wasn't he wonderful, I would say. You were, you know. What the hell, it's time for the eulogy. Maimonides! Maimonides! You weren't all Maimonides. Even Maimonides wasn't all Maimonides. Everyone here knows about Victor Lazarus, scholar and teacher unsurpassed. I want there to be someone who knows what I knew about you. So it wasn't much? It was enough. Your eyes up close. How shy your smile when you were happy. How sweet your mouth. For a chain-smoking drunkard with stomach cancer, Victor, yea most sweet, and altogether lovely. What a waste, what a waste. All the women in the world who could use some loving.

But I guess I don't need to tell Victor Lazarus that.

This is no time for lies, Victor. Who would I lie to—to you? And who else matters? You called me with your news; you called everybody. Why wouldn't you? I'm here for you, Victor, I said. Isn't that what everyone says? I meant it, too, more than I knew—because I didn't know then what it meant. We speak Prophecy, every day of our lives, you wrote in your notes for *Ardor and Irony*, the same way we speak prose. And yet, at the same time, a blip flashed across my mental screen and a readout might have gone something like this:

I spend all these months detaching myself from this guy and he goes and gets cancer.

I meant to stay detached.

Not that I was betting against you, Victor; I never put my money on the other guy. Oh, there were times. That day we drove down to the medical center to keep your appointment with the oncology team. You were throwing up when I called for you, your face in stark relief, streaked by strobe lights, under your eyes the purple valleys of the shadow of death. Why are we going through with this? I thought. There's only one way for this story to end. Just nerves, you said. And yes, once you dragged a comb through your hair, knotted your necktie, shrugged yourself into your camel hair coat—I did love to watch you rigging yourself out, O my chevalier! bracing your cheeks with aftershave and your locks with the drops of the night—yes, you might have been back in your old haunts again, Oxford, Cambridge, running with that fast crowd of analytic philosophers. Who would have guessed you were about to learn your fate; that the large manila envelope tucked under your arm was the oracle—your X-rays; that a fist of cancer was growing in your gullet, going for your throat.

I was there, no more. You always said I was lucky. Because I cleaned you out in poker, right? Took all those penny pots? Luck indeed! Didn't anyone ever tell you not to smile your still small smile when you were bluffing? Huh? O Beautiful and Wise? Never draw to an inside straight. Luck. Luck. The lady who ever eluded you. No wonder you wooed her so recklessly.

Was it a year ago? More, by now. You were giving a paper at a conference in California and my phone rang in the middle of the day.

Do you know who this is?

It doesn't say a lot for my IQ, but the fact is, unless I was expecting a call from you, I rarely recognized your voice over the telephone. There was something in your voice—whatever it was that made your voice your voice—that wires couldn't transmit. Something more felt than heard. I can't hear it, but I can still feel it.

Do you know who this is. You could never resist pulling my leg.

I wasn't expecting a call, not from you, not anymore, but for once I had no trouble guessing who. Slurred words, weird acoustics. You sounded like a bad PA system. Your amplifier was on the fritz.

What time is it? I said.

I was squinting at the kitchen clock. Let's see: 3:00 P.M. here, that makes it noon there. High noon in California.

You were never drunk at noon.

You never got up till noon.

But what difference does time make in California, California where the night shines as bright as the day?

Oops!

A thud. What got knocked over this time, Victor? The lamp? The clock radio? What were you reaching for? As if I have to ask. I'm wising up at last. Remember the broken glass in the bathroom sink?

What time is it? you said.

The night before, you had met another participant at the conference, a nice white-haired guy. Really, Victor. You were famous for your style; lucid—for a philosopher—elegant, cadenced, and a trifle old-fashioned, like you. But when it came to descriptions! Nice guy. So this particular Nice Guy—this Nice White-Haired Guy—frowned when he heard your name. Oh yes, he said. Now I remember. Victor Lazarus. You were potentially the best philosopher of your generation.

I caught the reverberation that was your laugh.

I pictured you sitting on the bed, one of those goofy hotel-room beds, the size of islands we used to test bombs on in the Pacific; blackout curtains drawn, smoke holding séances in the murky light. You would have been up all night burning incense to your muse. Victor Lazarus liked to live dangerously. You wrote your papers at the zero hour, and in a pinch you could stand up and deliver a lecture without one; without notes, without preparation of any kind—except of course for the god in you and the wine. And if, afterward, you could recall nothing of what was said to have been a brilliant discourse, what matter? There was more where that came from; there would always be more for Victor Lazarus. And now you were three time zones away, you were light-years away; and I couldn't hear that something in your voice that made your voice your voice—though I could still feel it.

What time did you say? You had to go; a lunch date. The Nice White-Haired Guy.

Wonderful. Marvelous. Just in case he was still wondering whatever happened to potentially the Best Philosopher of Your Generation. You wouldn't keep him guessing, would you? One whiff would do. Better make that two: one to surmise, one to confirm. More likely it would be enough to catch sight of you, the legendary Victor Lazarus, navigating the treacherous shoals of the dining hall—Arctic air, ice floes of tablecloths, chilly chandeliers—avoiding obstacles made known to you alone. Your long arms, your long legs, your rigid upright drunken dignity. Not staggering, no. Oscillating—ever so slightly—your compass needle quivering toward the North Pole.

I dreaded these trips. You couldn't smoke in airplanes anymore—federal regulations—but you could drink. So you drank. You drank you drank you drank. In spacious skies you drank, over purple mountains' majesties, above the fruited plain. You drank your way from sea to shining sea.

And the grueling hours and the jet lag and the sleepless churning nights. Those scars like rows of white barbed wire, salvaged scrap metal latching your ribs. A wonder you didn't set the detecting devices squawking at the gates. You were a sick man, Victor; you had a price on your head. And you paid for it, too, couldn't keep food down for days after.

Just nerves, you said.

Just drink, I thought.

Was it that same trip? I was leaving for the airport to meet you—to catch up with that part of me, I mean, that had already gone ahead—when I got the message. You wouldn't be arriving on your connecting commuter flight; you'd been rushed to an emergency room instead. A heart attack, they'd thought at first. I sensed the airline rep was trying not to say what I was thinking. All those long lovely layovers at airport bars.

When I called the next morning you were waiting for a cab; you'd checked yourself out against medical advice. The doctors wanted to perform tests on you, your gullet, your gut. Maybe you should stay, Victor, I said. We were talking long distance, as usual. I'm a heart patient, you said. Playing the odds again, Lover of Wisdom? I can't blame you. Fair is fair! Who would kindly stop for him? That hitchhiker with his fife and drum and O! his great big grin.

And where had he been all this time, anyway, your nice white-haired guy? Hadn't he heard? Victor Lazarus. Recognition coming at last; books, papers, publications by the score; not a day's mail without some request; lectures, conferences, reviews; and—first of all, best of all—a whole generation of teachers, your students, who wanted to be you. In spite of everything; the drinking, the blackballing, the marriages, the divorces, the heart surgery—the ten terrible years—you were Victor Lazarus still. Potentially the best philosopher of your generation.

And now this.

Weeks in a coma. Months of pneumonia. Shuttling back and forth between hospitals. Feeding tubes, breathing machines. The collapsed lung. The hole in your throat. Tests and more tests. Surgery and more surgery. And more and more and more.

The plowers plowed upon your back, they made long the furrows.

It'll be all right, we said. It'll be worth it, you'll see. You'll have the time, the time you need.

Miserable comforters were we all.

No one thought you would put up such a fight for your life; no one thought you cared enough for your life. Your doctors never expected you to survive their remedies, let alone the disease. And once again you'd made it: a miraculous self-cure, they said. Victor Lazarus. Ever the prodigy, ever the wunderkind. All the invitations you had to turn down, the lectures you'd been forced to cancel, the papers you couldn't write. But there was one conference you weren't about to miss; this fall, in Las Vegas—Las Vegas, of all places—top billing in a lineup of stars, including some who turned their backs on you when you were down. Your chance, you said, to see your name in lights. You joked about this, ashamed of yourself for wanting it so much, wanting to show that you had won. The years when invitations stopped coming, when no journal would consider your work, when lectures already booked were canceled, when papers previously accepted never saw light, when a recommendation from Victor Lazarus was the kiss of death. And now in spite of everything you'd be going to Las Vegas; bound for glitz and glory and the green green tables. Spinning the wheels, rolling the dice. You were sure to hit the jackpot. What could stop you now? Victor Lazarus had beaten the odds twice.

I feel... lucky... you said. I'm on... a roll...

## SUNDAY
## JUNE 4

The yellow curtain was drawn over the glass of your fishbowl, shadows moving across it. The nurses were performing their rites. They kick us out, we're in the way. Not for us to witness these mysteries: the washing, the turning, the changing of sheets, disposing of wastes. Your perishable belongings. Brackish blood, black waters. The monitors beep. The tubes drip and drain. The respirator clicks and sighs, clicks and sighs. The tubes giveth and the tubes taketh away.

I called the secretary back.

She was sorry, but Rabbi Salmon could not in good conscience perform your funeral service, because your mother was not Jewish.

But his mother's a convert, I said.

Orthodox convert? she said swiftly.

Oh oh. Better watch out. What I know about the faith of our mothers you could put in your eye. I was afraid to ask:

Is there such a thing?

Of course, she said.

The fear of the Lord is the beginning of wisdom.

Not Orthodox, no. Conservative, maybe. More likely Reform. Yes, I'm pretty sure it must be Reform.

You see? she said.

She doesn't like me—rack my brains as I will, l can't think of one good reason why she should—and now I had sent her on a wild-goose chase. Why couldn't I say so in the first place?

And she was sorry, but Rabbi Salmon wouldn't be able to come to the hospital today, either, because today was a Jewish holiday, and the rabbi can't ride in a car on a holiday.

You were acquainted with this Rabbi Salmon. It was the business of the get.

At the last minute, just as the divorce papers were about to be signed, and you had agreed to X's final demand that you pay for her dental work and the cost of her braces—you had already agreed to pay for her visits to her therapist—over your lawyer's fax machine came a final final demand. The ultimate. She had to have a get. As a good Jewish daughter, X could not in good conscience consider herself divorced without a get.

All these people with their good consciences. Where do they dig them up? Is God holding a garage sale? I tell you, Victor, these good consciences will be the death of us.

A get? I said. Isn't that a divorce decree from the rabbinical court? That's for strictly observant Orthodox Jews. What does she need a get for? Since when is she so religious?

Since when?

You glanced down at the fax on your desk. Your lashes, lowered, seemed heavy—weighted. When you raised them, how wide eyed, Victor, how guileless, how surprised. Here it is in black and white, you said. The day, the hour, the very second. It is written. It is never too late to accomplish the return.

My grandfather used to read the *Forward*, way back when it was *Der Forvitz*. He'd rest his bifocals on the folded pages, and in the thick sedimented reservoirs of his lenses, magnified, illuminated, the wavering black symbols blurred and brimmed over. I don't know if they still ran a letters and advice column by then, but during the great migrations at the turn of the century, *Bintele Brief*, as it was called, might well have been the want ads instead. So many inquiries from wives of the Old World seeking husbands lost in the New. Husbands wanted—dead or alive. If dead, fine; leave well enough alone. If not, they could stay lost, for all the wives cared; only first—please please send a get. A woman without a get is like a man without a country; neither fish nor fowl, unmarried, unmarriageable, unprotected, without status in this world or the next. An agunah.

The golden land seemed populated with deadbeat husbands and stranded wives.

It's a joke, I said. X has such a sense of humor. She smokes pot, she eats pork, she orders from the Frederick's of Hollywood catalog and Victoria's Secret. Six-inch spikes, push-up bras, leopard skin and ostrich plumes.

The little girl, you said. The little girl dressed up in her mother's clothes.

But there are women who live by these laws. They keep kosher, they honor the Sabbath, they light the candles, they say the blessings, they go to the mikvah, the baths, they wear the wig. She's only making fun of them. A fax yet! Fax her back, why don't you? Tell her, if she wants a get, she can shave her head.

You pushed your lip into your stubborn smile, half-mischief, half-rue. What was it, Victor? Where is it? The You in you?

Nope. Nope. God forbid! Stand in the way of a religious conversion? Her share in the world to come?

Her share of your flesh, you mean.

So be it, you said. I gotta get a get.

X was just getting warmed up.

Off she stalked to Rabbi Salmon, on stiletto heels, with sequined eyes, to pour out her side. You had been joined in the bonds of holy matrimony by an Orthodox rabbi in an Orthodox ceremony, with all the trimmings. The cantor. The canopy. The reading of the marriage contract. The smashing of the glass. The margarine instead of butter, the Coffee mate instead of cream, the chickens slaughtered according to ritual, their innards inspected for bad portents; signs of corruption, disease. O birds of ill omen! They lied in their gizzards. Righteousness doesn't come cheap; everyone knows kosher tastes worse and costs more. X's stepfather paid through the nose. And what did you think? After he laid out all that dough, you could up and fly the coop, soar away free? Not so fast, Victor Lazarus. The rabbi wasn't going to let you get away with that, was he? Playing such a dirty trick on her? X—of all people! X—an agunah? X the good Jewish daughter, descendant of a noble house, a family famous in the Old World, a line of rabbis and scholars going back generation unto generation; the learned in the law, the wise, the just, the blessed.

All this is true, by the way.

A good Jewish daughter? What an understatement! X is the Flower of Our Lineage.

And X in her own way is learned in the law:

A Jewish wife should have a fur coat, she says. All the divorcées at temple have fur coats.

A woman of valor, who can find?

On your solemn promise to accompany X and Rabbi Salmon to the holy city, the divorce papers were signed.

Rabbi Salmon summoned you to his office to face the music. A lecture on your duties, your obligations, the proper way to conduct yourself before the hoary heads and briny beards of the rabbinical court. An Orthodox divorce with all the trimmings. And out it all came. Sadie McDade. The Tombigbee River. Summers up at the lake with her vast clan, your hymn-singing Bible-thumping cousins and aunts. The prayer meetings, the sweltering tents, the raging revival preachers roaring hell-fire and brimstone. The mosquitoes eating you alive: Vengeance is mine, saith the Lord. And every night after supper the clove-studded hams, the greens shining in bacon grease, the biscuits sopping pork gravy, the Jell-O wobbling in Reddi-wip. Hallelujah! "Just a Closer Walk with Thee." "Leaning on Lord Jesus." "Stand by Me." And chairs rocking and porch swings creaking and hands clapping and stars splash-splashing in still black waters, and fireflies flashing upward like sparks.

Lakes hatch snakes in Alabama.

Rabbi Salmon is a sturdy wide-set young man; strong straight nose, strong straight brows, profile of a Syrian bas-relief, and one of those topiary beards to match. Like a long black muffler his Jewish mother might have knitted for him. He doesn't go in for robes and miters, alas; he favors sneakers and jeans and fastens his yarmulke with bent wiry pins to his bent wiry hair.

Aye, a hairy man is Rabbi Salmon, a ram caught in a bramblebush, and the roots of his frown go very deep.

You're not Jewish?

Not technically, you said.

And you never told the rabbi who officiated at the wedding?

He never asked.

Then a pox on both your houses! Forget the holy city. Never mind the get. The rabbis would laugh you both out of court. The marriage would be declared null and void; according to Orthodox Jewish law, you had never been married in the first place. And how come a good Jewish daughter, descendant of a noble house, generation unto generation of the learned in the law, the wise, the just, the blessed—the Flower of Our Lineage—didn't know that?

Rabbi Salmon, you said, turned out to be a nice guy.

Too bad you never played poker with him, big bluffer. For once, just this once, Victor Lazarus had an ace up his sleeve.

So you got the last laugh, your first laugh, you said, in all these years. You just wished you could see the expression on X's face when she heard the news. Sadie McDade must be smiling down on me from heaven, you said. I was always her favorite.

You were always everybody's favorite, weren't you, Victor? You darling of the gods you. They couldn't do enough. They dandled the grapes, they poured the wine, they set the wreath of violets and ivy leaves on your head. Then they sicced the dogs on you. Gods are like that. It's their job; they're bluffers too.

Hey, Philosopher. Didn't anyone ever tell you?

Beware of Greeks bearing gifts.

Then you let the matter drop.

What? I said. You're not going to let her have it? You're not going to zap her?

I don't want to crow over her, you said.

All right all right, so I'm crowing. She asked for it, didn't she? Beating you over the head with her Orthodox baseball bats. Her deathbed conversions. Your deathbed! Her blood is true royal blue and you're only half a Jew. And the wrong half at that. I wouldn't turn up my nose at poetic justice if I were you, Victor Lazarus. It's the only justice you're likely to get.

I don't want to cause pain, you said.

At one time it would have mattered a lot to me, when your divorce came through. And now here was some fax machine somewhere spewing out the papers at long last—and it made no difference. It was all over, all off. Sure it was my fault; a preemptive first strike, you might say. Won't I ever learn? Don't burn your bridges until you come to them.

Is that what they call irony, Lover of Wisdom? Is that how it feels?

Oh, I thought. He doesn't want to cause pain.

But I see now it was as you said; because I see now what you must have seen. The agunah. A lost soul, an accursed soul—unwanted, abandoned, unloved—wandering the worlds. Wandering in search of you.

Wait a minute, Simon said. Whoa, back up. Let me get this straight. The rabbi won't come to the hospital to pay a visit to a dying man because he can't ride in a car? He won't come to the hospital to comfort the poor widowed mother, bowed and broken with grief, because he can't ride in a car? What's with the rabbi? You can break any rule for the sake of a prior obligation. He who is engaged in the performance of one precept is exempt from the performance of another. That's logic! Tseichel! Common sense!

Simon shuddered. You know Simon. Whenever he starts talking about logic, he gets carried away; his throat swells with emotion, he lays his hand over his heart. I've seen this guy, the rabbi—he's getting a gut on him. If he can't use his head, let him use his feet instead. He needs the exercise. Can't ride in a car! Can't ride in a car! That's religious, maybe, but it's not Jewish.

Simon is Jewish, maybe, but not religious. Not an atheist or an agnostic, either; that would imply there's a question. Simon doesn't believe in the question. I never gave it a thought, he says. If the skies were to crack open this very minute, a tumult of clouds, chasms of light; if a big voice boomed out behind the mountain—This is a test! This is a test!—I'd still say thanks but no thanks. Now he tells us? What kind of god would it be?

There is no question.

All this Simon says in his cantor's voice, which his father was, and his father before him, and Simon himself was meant to be. A lot of history in that voice, an immemorial timber. The destruction of the second temple.

The Babylonian captivity. Just for starters. How shall we sing the Lord's song? We have hung up our harps.

Simon and Belle were standing at opposite ends of the nurses' station, talking on the telephone. Actually, Simon was leaning on his elbow at the counter, the neatly folded triangle of his handkerchief pressed to his eyes, under his glasses, and his chin on his fist like the statue of *The Thinker*. The receiver, facedown, was droning at his elbow. Something angry was trapped inside it.

!!!??? !!!???

That noise! That noise! That hoarse buzzing. How well you know. Every sentence? Ending in a question mark? Anxious? Querulous? Hysteria rising? The same note? Again and again?

My hand gets tired, Simon says.

Simon gets the job of talking to X. He's Ben's godfather, he has to listen to her side. Take care of my little boy! Simon says. Those were Victor's last words to me. Last words. How I wish. Simon forgets, there was no time for last words. People don't die natural deaths anymore. It's not legal. Last words are a dying art. Every day he comes up with a new revised version of your last words to him. If I were to revise anything, Victor, it would be my last words to you. Too well I remember what they were—I, who of all of us, had the chance. What would I have said if I knew? If I knew? And why didn't I know? Didn't I know? Didn't I know? Whatever I said, I've learned this much from you: I would have meant it more than I knew.

???!!! ???!!!

Uh-oh. Duty calls. Simon picked up the phone. The busy signal, he says. The bumblebee with bronchitis. Yes yes! Sure I'm here! Sure I hear you! Nodding and talking through his stuffed nose. Sinuses, he says. Hay fever. He tucked the phone to his cheek, clapping his hand and his handkerchief over the mouthpiece, craftily, as he might swipe at a fly.

You know those little girls in the horror movies? he said. Those scary little girls with the livid lips and the prism eyes? Like reflector lights?

Like roadkill, I said.

Being catty is no fun anymore, I'm getting a bit long in the tooth for that sort of thing. Still, I like to keep my hand in. I try.

But what's this??? Simon watches horror movies??? Simon Wiseman??? Famous philosopher??? That... you said. Is an oxy... moron... Famous... Philosopher... That steep scored brow like granite cliffs pile-driven through expressways. Deep thinking will do that for you. Simon??? Understudy for Mount Rushmore???

You see??? It's catching???

Is it ever.

Even the Furies, Simon says. Even the Furies knew when to quit.

In the emergency room, X had me paged. Don't ask me how she knew you were there—let alone that I was—but she always does, doesn't she? Did you order the ambulance? she wanted to know. Who ordered the ambulance? Order, like a livery service. And it seems she's been on the phone ever since. When Belle called the funeral parlor, X had called there first. When Simon called the insurance office, X had called there first. X has already contacted your lawyer to demand a copy of your will—because, she says, she's going to break it. Break it? Simon says. She doesn't even know what's in it. What difference does that make? It was your will, Victor; it must be broken. Whatever, wherever, X is always there first. And that day, Victor, that day—she got there first too.

Like you say, she's on... a roll...

So that's what this is all about: Simon and Belle, with phones to their cheeks, shouting back and forth across the nurses' station.

Belle was still trying to reach the rabbis. Calling Baltimore, calling Philadelphia, calling Delaware, New Jersey, Washington, DC. The rabbis were tending their own vineyards. The rabbis have hung up their phones.

She says she's got a rabbi! Simon says. To perform the funeral service!

No! Belle says.

A Reconstructionist! Rabbi Pilcher from the temple!

No! Belle says.

Her personal friend, she says. She says he'll do it for her.

No no no! Th' hell he will! Not huh choice, dammit! Ovuh mah dead body! She ain't his wife. She ain't nuth'n t' him. She got no call runn'n his fun'rul.

Her white head seems shaken with the strength of her righteousness.

What's a Reconstructionist? I said.

Belle's a convert, she'll know.

They-uh Aww-th'-dox in some things, she said. In othuhs they make they-uh own rools.

So? What's so special about that? Isn't that what we all do?

This morning when I walked in, Belle was standing in front of your window, huddled up in an old jacket of yours, hugging herself, rubbing her elbows. The empty sleeves dangled from her shoulders. She seemed to be holding onto herself, holding her stomach, as if she'd been kicked.

She gets cold. Hospitals are cold. She's not used to this Northern climate, either; all winter long, looking out at snow and fog and the smoking chimneys of the medical center, she kept saying she just knew she'd nevuh get warm. And she's cold still, this so rare day in June.

It really was a perfect day. Through the narrow window, mountains, trees, sticks, stones, sky, the very blades of grass on the hospital grounds, seemed bottled in light, light clear as truth. It filled the little fishbowl cubicles like a transparent preservative. Even the power lines on the utility poles were tingling.

Like many women, Belle caught her second wind when poor Sam Starr, your stepfather, died. Why do I say poor Sam Starr? You never called him a nice guy. A widower with two little girls to bring up, a war widow and an infant son who bore his father's straight black brows and his father's name. I don't suppose it was a love match. Belle has become an activist, a marcher in protests, a shouter of slogans and wielder of banners. Free at last! Free at last!

The tremulous white head, small and sleek as an ermine's. The deep teak of the Florida tan. Her glasses and the eyes in them are too big for her face, an effect—with the rhinestone-finned mother-of-pearl frames—of a domino mask at a fancy dress ball. She wears sweat suits and sneakers, Day-Glo lipstick and nail polish, elastic stockings and nitroglycerin patches, and, on her wrist—her thin brittle wrist, dark as bark—a watch that pings when it's time to take her pills. Pills for lying down, pills for rising up; pills before meals, pills after meals; pills for every purpose under heaven.

Liberty and old age come at the same price; all it takes is eternal vigilance.

That time I took her shopping, trying on clothes. Behind the doors of the dressing room she stripped them off with, as it seemed to me, brutal alacrity. The wrung ropes of her arms, the withered udders and aged cheese of her flesh; blue marbled, white clotted, crumbling. Yes yes I know, this is no way to be talking about your mother, the loins that bore you; sacrilege, profanation. But Victor, please try to understand: I'm really talking about myself. She was giving me a preview of coming attractions. So that's what it's like, I thought. Ripeness is all.

Ahh'm a grandmothuh! She loves to remind me. Ahh'm a grandmothuh! Ahh'm a grandmothuh!

I do wish she'd lay off. She knows darn well Ahh'm a grandmothuh too.

I'm sorry I can't say *hell* and *damn* the way Belle does, though. The fervor, the conviction, of that old-time religion. The sweet dulcimer twang of Sadie McDade. Not a whole lotta shak'n go'n on, back in the shuls on the West Side of Chicago. The hole-in-the-corner operations, like the one down the block my father used to go to when it came time to say Kaddish. Cracked linoleum, folding chairs, the dipper in the rust-pocked sink, the squat sand-silted spittoon. That's the first thing he did in the morning—spit. Hit or miss. He drove a coal truck, rose in blue-black dark, in the somber city, clearing his throat with an Old Testament wrath. Harsh as a verdict. His prayer shawl with the stripes and zizith smelled of mothballs in bottom drawers. No sooner would the service begin than the radiator pipes got in on the act, knocking, banging, a percussive accompaniment, an iron clangor, calling hoarsely on the chthonic forces of the cellar. The rising smoke smelled of cold ashes. Fingers numbing, noses dripping, knees creaking; the sonorous monotony, the luminous ache. May my right hand forget its cunning. May my tongue cleave to the roof of my mouth.

And yea we wept when we remembered Zion.

Afterward they passed the bottle, a few drops of schnapps to warm the bones, wet the beards of the hook-backed old souls dragged in to make a minyan.

For all I knew they might have been speaking in tongues.

She has an open wound too, Victor, a wound that will never heal.

It's five days before the wedding, Simon says. Victor calls: I gotta talk. Fine. He flies down, we go for a stroll. I had a pretty good idea what was up. I was his best friend, I knew him better than anyone did, as well as anyone could. There were things about Victor even I—. Sometimes I'd ask myself what's down there? Where does he go? What would I reel in if I cast out a line? But I knew what was coming, it was no surprise to me.

What should I do? he says. I don't know what to do. How can I go through with it? I can't marry her. I don't love her, I never loved her. If Farridah were to call—one word from her, a sign—I'd pack up and go, go back to her this very minute. Pride! What's pride got to do with it?

Farridah.

Farridah was your first wife, the one you loved. One of the most beautiful women I ever saw in my life, Simon says, and a marvelous marvelous person. Nuts! So it's not enough Farridah has to be the fairest among women, the rose of Sharon, the lily of the valley, with a face that looketh forth as the morning and kisses sweeter than wine? No. On top of all that, she has to be good?

But everyone says so. She was the most precious precious gal, Belle says. They just loved each other so much. You said so yourself. She was really very nice, you said. That may sound like faint praise to anyone who never heard your voice, Lover of Wisdom, Lover of Women; the words without the music. But making allowance for Simon's hyperbole and your understatement—.

He was still in love with Farridah, you know.

Yup, thanks Simon, I know. I'd know without your telling me.

Th' smok'n an' th' drink'n, Victor. Th' smok'n an' th' drink'n. Too many boozy kisses. Too many numb-lipped I love yous. That—and the commuter line. Some zhlob, Simon says. Some zhlob she met on the 5:45.

She would have been looking for an out; it wouldn't have mattered much who—not after you.

What should I do? What should I do? Victor keeps saying it over and over. Are you sure it's not just a case of cold feet? I said. Not that I thought so, not for a minute, but I had to say something. What was there to say? He didn't bother to answer; he wasn't listening. Not to me, anyway. He keeps on going—you know that long-legged slouch of his, the hands in the pockets, the head in the collar, staring down at his feet. And this scarf two yards long trailing behind him. Say what you like, you had to hand it to him—he had style. Distinguished though emaciated. That's Oxbridge, you know. Leave it to the Jews to out-Brit the Brits. He should have posed for the centerfold in *Ectomorph Magazine*.

I can't back out now, can I? he says. It's too late now. Not after they've gone to all this trouble. X—her family—her stepfather. Not after all these preparations, these elaborate preparations.

I *dare say*, I said.

I told you: I keep trying.

Oh I *just bet*.

All right, vulgar. Simon shook his head. Vulgar vulgar vulgar. Shudder shudder shudder. Strictly kosher? Strictly Borscht Belt! Vaudeville! Burlesque! The things they do to poor little innocent chicken livers. Where do Jews get such ideas? And they played that old Orthodox rag, the whole routine, every last song and dance. You'd think they imported a piece of the Wailing Wall, with all the davening. And the beards? And the peyots? They're the only real Jews, and the rest of us—phoo! Tref! You are what you eat. Orthodoxy for orthodontists. But what could you expect? Being Jewish is the family business; that's their racket. Praise the Lord and pass the ammunition.

Then don't do it, I said to Victor. Don't marry her, not if you don't love her. You'd be making a big mistake. It wouldn't be fair to her either. That's what I said. After all, I had nothing against the woman, I hardly knew her. Not then. Not in my wildest dreams. It had nothing to do with her anyway, she never stood a chance. It was all Farridah. It was always Farridah.

Simon married for love. Who would have thought she'd give him a glance—the lovely long-legged Therése? Surrounded not by thorny hedges but by a wall of suitors—some of them ready to risk blinding in the briar patch, if she would let down her long gold hair. Simon risked it. Not our Simon, the Simon we know, Simon splendid and successful, Simon of the silvered crest and the gilt-edged brow. Not that Simon, no. Simon pudgy and Brillo haired and four eyed. Simon just another smart-ass Jew. Simon not so simple. Simon of whom professors jibed: What makes Simon run? Simon carried off the prize. A thing like that can set a man up for life. Simon knows the difference.

I've wondered since, Simon said. Ever since. If there was something I could have said, something I should have done. Like what? Smash his kneecaps? Have him kidnapped? I'm not from Chicago. She wasn't Far-ridah, that's what he saw in her; that's what he married her for. The one woman who would never touch him, never tempt him—the opposite, in every way. What could I do? What could anyone do? He wanted sackcloth and ashes, he got sackcloth and ashes.

A hard act to follow, Farridah.

Please, I'm not blaming you, Victor, I'm not feeling sorry for her.

She can feel sorry for herself—who could do that better than she can? May she beat her wings in bottles, may she live a thousand years. She wasn't the woman to do that to; it razed her soul. You scorned her? Good! She would show you a woman scorned. It would have been the same with any man; no one could have given her the satisfaction. But you, Victor, you. Never raising your voice, never responding to her rage, never playing her game. Retreating to that place inside you where no one could follow, no one could reach. You lived your life, your real life, somewhere else. We've all felt it, even now we feel it; more than ever now. Who hasn't seen you like this?—your cheek to the pillow, your eyes half-closed, their focus far off, charting your course with compass and polestar. Who knows where you go? Who knows where you are?

The monitors beep.

The tubes drip and drain.

The respirator clicks and sighs, clicks and sighs.

Woe to the lovers of the lovers of wisdom!

# FRIDAY
## JUNE 2

I know this man, the doctor in the emergency room said. I've seen him before.

He was Filipino, I think: a sad Spanish face, the face of carved Peni-tentes in back-road churches in New Mexico; the pointed beard, the hol-low cheeks, the brows propped sorrowfully beneath a crown of thorns. No crown now: a green scrub cap. The ambulance crew had failed to bring you around; they were pumping your stomach, just in case.

That was the first thing he asked me, the police officer who was standing in your kitchen. Not one of the cops from the night before. Sorry, he said, he didn't know the front door was open; he'd broken in through the sliding glass door. I started past him but he blocked me—a bare blond-haired arm, fatty freckles, tinny watchband. Don't go in there, he said. You can't go in. They're working on him, they've been at it a long time. You'll be in the way. Outside the ambulance was loudly waiting, throbbing, pumping, flooding noise. As if that was all it was there for—to drown the stunned silence in noise.

Its doors were wide open.

Was he despondent? the officer asked. Over his health? Did I think? Painkillers? Pills?

No, I said. Not after all that.

So he fetched the bottles from the bedroom. Only two; quinine tab-lets, a vial of tranquilizers. He shook them out, counting them into his palm. You'd taken fewer than prescribed.

That's what I was trying to tell you, I said.

What was I trying to tell him?

All that. All that. All the days of your death.

Out came the crew, in a hurry, one talking into a radio that hissed and crackled, the other two backing up, a stretcher between them. Their burden was light, a pile of blankets. I didn't know it was you.

So now the emergency room, the doctor a man of sorrows in his green scrub cap. He had the face: you had the body. Skinny, rib racked, sheets wringing, twisting. A tube gurgling down one nostril, a tube hooked over your lip. In the cracked black blood the imprint of your teeth. And still you looked younger, as you did at such times, the skin of your forehead glistening, exultant with effort.

The oxygen mask was over the hole in your throat.

Through the clear plastic I could see it, the tracheotomy, the open wound that never healed. You dressed it twice daily, swabbing with some fierce corrosive. I watched you once, your chin lifted, your neck up-stretched, the sword athwart your throat. You might have been shaving yourself with a very sharp razor.

You raised an eyebrow when you saw me.

It's just… a hole…

Oh no it wasn't. Not now it wasn't. Inside the oxygen mask it was open-ing, closing, frantic, sucking. Lipped with shiny scar tissue. A pink-lined primitive mouth. It had a life of its own, and it was fighting for its own.

I know this man. I've seen him before.

The doctor means he's seen you drunk, Victor. He thinks he knows you.

Funny how things work out, isn't it? That's what attracted me. Your learn-ing. Victor Lazarus. Potentially the Best Philosopher of Your Generation. That doesn't sound very romantic, does it? But you knew better, Lover of Wisdom, Lover of Women. That's what attracted everyone—the ardor that was in you. The ardor that was you.

Let me tell you his method, Simon says. Method! That's what Victor called it. Say he decides it's time to learn Italian. Who should he study? Dante. Who else? So he gets hold of all the grammars, the dictionaries, the collected works; he sits down at his desk. You know what that means: cigarette butts, coffee cups, books like leaning towers of Pisa. Coffee cups! He never touched the stuff! As if that fooled anybody. Schnapps, more likely; wine, beer, mouthwash. Give him two weeks, three, and he's reading the "Paradiso." Give him a couple more and he's writing a pa-per on the *Commedia* and medieval Islamic philosophy—one version in Arabic, the other in Italian, no less. That's the first part. Then come the invitations; Milan, Rome, Florence. *Ah, what a lad I was beside the Arno!* The great green greasy Limpopo, if you ask me. Personally, I never cared for the place. Too much pollution, hell on my sinuses. Where was I? Oh yeah, Victor. So he gives his talk. He's a sensation. The ladies go limp. No wonder, poor women. All those little Italian men skidding around on their little Italian motor scooters. A nation of Centaurs. Chivalry went out with the rape of the Sabines. But Victor! That's another story. His Italian—so flowery, so old-fashioned. His manners—ditto. They stuff him with gnocchi, scungilli, octo-pussies; buckets of pasta, puddles of grappa. And that's how he picks up the idioms.

Brains are sexy—in men. Any woman alive has brains enough to know that. And who wouldn't want to hear love poetry read aloud, for her ears alone? In the original. French, German, Spanish, Italian, Archilochus and Cavafy, Sappho and Sefardíes, medieval Arabic, the Hebrew of David and Solomon.

*Let him kiss me with the kisses of his mouth.*

Victor Lazarus could provide the translation. Nothing was lost. Three wistful hairs on your washboard chest and honey and milk under thy tongue.

I'll say this much for myself: I knew I had something to learn from you. Some of it—some of you—might rub off on me, just from being near you, maybe even in my sleep. Breath nigh to breath. Osmosis, hypnosis; I'm always up for a little learning—the easy way. Look at all those people who tuck Berlitz cassettes under their pillows and wake up speaking foreign languages.

You were a teacher, teach me. How nice to have an in with an ambulatory encyclopedia. Now I wouldn't have to keep looking up those same old words in the dictionary again and again. Ontology. Epistemology. Hermeneutics. I could get my definitions straight from the horse's mouth. Except when you drew the line.

Victor, what's deconstruction? What's semiotics?

Some things... I discuss... only... for money...

Should I tell you a secret? You really did talk in your sleep.

It might be Greek, it might be German, it might be the poets:

—*Man by nature desires to know.*

—*Überselig ist die Nacht.*

—*But in the flesh it is immortal.*

Just like that. Sentences, even paragraphs.

—*Perhaps in the end, but only then, the sheer consolations of Myth will exceed the mournful contingencies of the True.*

Victor Lazarus whispering sweet nothingness.

—*We need not concern ourselves here with the creation ex nihilo, as if God were merely a magician; the necessary question will always remain that of the prior existence of the Forms.*

What was this? Lecturing? Should I be taking notes?

You didn't twitch and jerk in your sleep anymore, the way you used to, those heart medications jiggling your limbs like a skeleton on a string; but now and then still you would jolt, give a start, catching yourself falling through dreams.

—*So you were up to your old tricks again.*

—*So you conjured another of your schemes.*

—*So you left the women in the dark.*

My eyes snapped open. I stared up at the ceiling.

He discovereth deep things out of darkness.

Yes, you were lecturing, and it wasn't Maimonides. You were lecturing yourself; Victor Lazarus on Victor Lazarus. Then this was the way you talked to yourself? The voices of your night season? The voices you had been hearing all your life.

—*Oh, they saw through you all right.*

—*So you reach for the gear—and it isn't there.*

No fair! No fair! You know what I had in mind. Plato, Aristotle, Hegel, Nietzsche. Not this, not a wiretap on your soul.

Man by nature desires to know? Maybe so. But what does woman want?

I got earplugs.

I meant to stay in the dark, in the dark.

I used to think this was the loneliest stretch of road in the world, you said.

We were driving back from the medical center. It had been one of those late fall days, snowing and melting, melting and snowing; the woods exhaling a fragile breath, the pine needles and dead leaves glowing pink, as if someone were puffing and blowing on embers. Your appointment was for one o'clock, but the waiting room was packed, a temporary barracks of plywood partitions and plastic weatherproofing that made the windows grimy and fogged; the light bleak, the outlook grim. We might have been in the midst of mining country, the smoke and chimneys of those exhausted mill towns up the river. This is the Rust and Bible Belt, though tourism, strange to say, is the major industry in these parts now. It's Xmas season and the merchants at the mall have gone all out with decorations—lights, trees, tinsel, angels, paunchy Santas, reindeers red nosed with bulbs that pulse and glow. Bells jingle, carols pipe. Billboards advertise ski slopes, golf courses, celebrity entertainment, four-star hotels; and the motel chains offer free shuttle service to the medical center—which is, after all, a kind of tourist attraction too. No need to promote the little guesthouses around the hospital, the kind with the bathroom down the hall and the phone at the foot of the stairs—the all-important pay phone—and names like Faith, Hope, Good Samaritan. Forget the charity.

A new wing was going up, parking lots getting graded and tarred, and it wasn't easy to talk over the groans of heavy machinery, bulldozers, concrete mixers in travail. Not that anyone was trying.

You kept getting up to go out.

Let me know if they call my name.

Sure, I said. I'll just tell them to wait while you finish your cigarette.

No, you said. No, don't tell them that.

But your smile was stiff, you seemed preoccupied, the sense of purpose, single-mindedness, that ever inspired you when you were drunk. I watched you making your way cautiously down the gloomy corridor, the hammers and sawhorses, dragging your leg-iron with halting dignity. Knight-errant on your high-shouldered quest.

You needed to throw up again.

Among the couples in the waiting room—no one comes to oncology alone—there was no telling which was which; which was the one. The one whose name was written on the charts; the one they had the contract out on. No one looked sick or scared or in pain. But, then again, pale rider, neither did you. What they looked was weary. They were waiting, waiting the way people wait in airports, bus terminals, other places of arrival and departure.

Faces stared at the TV screen.

All over the medical center, in every waiting room, whether anyone is watching or not, the tube is on; tuned to talk shows, game shows, and—

mostly—the soaps. Life and death stuff. *As the World Turns. General Hospital.* Doctors in lab coats and stethoscopes, nurses in white stockings and jaunty starched caps, actresses grieving in waterproof mascara. Lots of choking sobs and tears.

The voices sounded flat and far away, like voices carrying across water. Every once in a while a burst of riveting split the screen with a sword of white static and made it sizzle.

I never saw any tears. Not in corridors, elevators, cafeterias; not over hospital beds, not in waiting rooms. Not even when the families were herded into the little office with the big conference table, the social worker clutching her clipboard, the thick-stacked charts, the doctors striding in at last. A pride of beepers.

The door is shut, the gates are sealed. It won't be long now. Someone is scheduled for departure.

All the stories we don't have time for.

How is it, Victor, that it never occurred to me then that this was the way your story would end?

Pain. Pain is what it was all about. Treasonous pain. Your eyes rolling back in your head, coming up whites, blank with revelation.

He hath made you to drink the wine of astonishment.

Your cup was running over.

You never let on, not when you could help it. Matters best kept, you said, between oneself and oneself. But in the recovery room, the anesthesia wearing off after this surgery or that, there was nowhere to hide. Pain is where you were. Yourself was pain.

Once, in their revolutions, your gaze halted: an image had registered on your pupils. My image, Victor—two tiny reflections on those black cisterns—and I felt about that size, too, spying on you, dredging up your secrets. The wiretap again.

You meant us to stay in the dark, in the dark.

Why don't they show this on TV? The waiting rooms. People listening for their names. Plastic chairs, plastic geraniums, windows sheeted like dirty snow. Boots, gloves, laps burdened with wet-smelling coats, purses clutched to knees, faces staring at the screen. And on the screen—faces staring at the screen. And on and on forever, like Chinese boxes.

In real life you wait. And in real death.

Your name was called at half past three.

So you sat on the examining table, your yeshiva bocher stoop, your question-mark chest; taking, as it were, a philosophical position. It had been a while since I'd seen you stripped to your shorts—you kept a pair special for these visits—and I'd forgotten. How rutted your ribs, how rocky your spine, how prominent the hinges of your scapula, the knobs like ball joints on your shoulders.

I can tell all my bones, they look and stare upon me.

And I was so proud of the weight you'd put on when we were together. You needed flesh to pad your spare parts. But now you were right back where you started again, the way you were when I first met you, the two of you. You and X. A marriage made in heaven. Scholar of Torah and Logos; Daughter of a Noble House, Flower of Our Lineage. And indeed I beheld a perfect match, an ideal union.

I thought, Whoo whoo, kinky. A pair of necrophiliacs.

Yes yes, I know, I say the nicest things. And O Victor, when I think of the things you used to say to me.

The young resident, bright eyed, bright cheeked, bushy mustached, bustled about you, rapping here, peeping there, prying down your throat, spying on tonsils and tongue. His lab coat was snapping briskly at his knees.

Aha! he kept saying. Oh yes! Mmm hmmm.

Heart-stopping, stomach-dropping exclamations.

Since when? he said. How long has this been going on?

And thou, O Lord, how long?

He was delighted with you, you wretched specimen you. One for the books.

Bad news you were ready for. The solemn voice, the somber verdict. A firing squad you could face, and never mind the blindfold. Philosophy, the Man says, is the study of dying; and now was your chance. I could just see you shrugging your little shrug, smiling your little smile, the last cigarette twittering on your lip. But all your ironic detachment was no match for this, was it, O my chevalier?—this eager young resident, his simple enthusiasm and pink-cheeked good cheer.

He had you up on the auction block and he was knocking down your price.

It seemed to me that you were weighing your answers, playing your cards close to your chest. Isn't there a law against self-incrimination?

Anything you said might be held against you. Which was the trick question? The trap? Which admission would be one too many? The final, the fatal one. Then the gates would clang shut, the verdict be sealed. Who shall live and who shall die who by fire and who by water.

A little late in the day for bluffing, no? Yours were the X-rays on the light screen now. The auspices were handling your entrails; exposing your lurid secrets, your shadowy schemes. No more cover-ups.

*Oh, they saw through you all right.*

The doctor touched the wall switch, the lights went out. In the dark he leaned close to you, closer; his ophthalmoscope clicking. Your eye stared past him, unseeing, its pupil contracting in the tiny beam. Where is the way to the dwelling of light.

Hardening of the arteries! he said.

Again he touched the switch; one by one the fluorescent tubes in the ceiling tinkled and blinked like breaking glass. Hardening of the arteries! Just as I thought! He smiled to himself, sounding pleased. You can tell, you know. Every time.

You lifted your shoulders in your silent shrugging laugh. You could remember when oracles spoke riddles.

There were no gross indications the cancer had spread; there was still chance for a cure. But surgery would be necessary, and no time to lose. Now you couldn't swallow your food. Soon you would be unable to swallow your spittle.

But you weren't thinking of that now, were you? Not on that long lonesome road.

It was that stretch along the Juniata, the dark and shining Juniata, winding as its name; the banks deep, the mountains like night.

Night comes early in winter, in the mountains.

Ten years ago. You were teaching at Blackwood, a small liberal arts college of good repute, when an offer came from the university. A major department, graduate students, colleagues. There was no question you'd accept; this was the call you'd been waiting for, the summons, Der Ruf. So it was decided: you would go on ahead and Farridah would join you as soon as she could. For the time being you'd drive home on weekends.

This would have been the lonely part, heading in this direction, away from her.

After a while, the road got too lonely. Farridah still wasn't ready. It was hard on her, this itinerant life of the academic frau, never settling down, forever pulling up stakes. She had come to like the pretty town, the tamed gardens, the pleasant trees, the Cotswold-style cottages and cobbled square. Post office pizza parlor drugstore dentist. Sun moon stars rain. She liked her job, an easy commute to the city; she liked her friends, and it wasn't easy for her to make them. She was so shy, so gentle, so exotic; something of the veil of the goddess drawn about her—her biblical beauty, her Lilith hair.

On this same stretch, heading home at Xmas vacation, you spotted a truck stalled at the side of the road. The driver leaned against the tailgate, stamping and blowing, his hands up his sleeves. Your mechanical skills were limited, to say the least; but it was cold, the sun going down in banked red coals, and not much traffic to speak of on this road, so you stopped to ask if you could be of help. Was there ever a knight like the young Lochinvar? He was selling roses, only two bunches left and—you being his very last customer—he gave you a cut price to get rid of both.

The shivering made him look shifty: a hijacker of roses? Like the mark of a hand, a port-wine stain leaked along his cheek, and one walleye fixed itself with glum intensity on something over your shoulder. Something heading your way. When you got back into your car and glanced up at the rearview mirror, he was gone—vanished—truck, taillights, smoke, and all; so suddenly you had to look again, in case the roses had vanished with him. Two dozen tight-budded dark-blooded long-stemmed roses. American Beauties. A good omen. Your homecoming was to be a surprise.

You were driving now. It took your mind off things; off of some things. You drove slowly, cautious to a fault, which was just as well since you so often drove drunk. We had stopped at a cozy joint; vinyl booths, rowdy jukebox, a good dish of spaghetti. I ate mine, you threw up yours. Not that you mentioned it; no fanfare; a mere formality by now, excusing yourself with a stoop and a bow, your usual air of disheveled chivalry. As if you'd just thought of something you'd promised to do, a phone call, maybe, you needed to make. A matter between oneself and oneself.

On your way back from the men's room you stopped at the jukebox, punching in quarters, priming the pump. You were such a sucker for corny movies and country western. *Honkytonk Man; Guitars, Cadillacs; It Won't Hurt; I'll Be Gone.* Soda-pop lights, changing colors streamed over your face.

Maybe this disease is going to be my death, you said. But it isn't going to be my life.

You kept your eyes on the road. In the glare of oncoming cars I saw them staring ahead, like your eyes in the doctor's office. He looks into your eyes and sees hardening of the arteries. I've looked into your eyes often and often these last days, Victor, your eyes that stare and stare and don't see me. What do I see? What do I see?

You were swallowing. Testing it? This thing that had you by the throat?

Over the river the moon was rising, alone and cold sober.

## TUESDAY
## JUNE 6

A man was pacing in front of the squat stone pillars, frowning down, scraping the gravel, and he glanced up sharply when we pulled in. Short, burly; rumpled suit, gritty crew cut. A security guard, I thought, from the funeral home or the memorial park. It was early, the sun burning a hole in the fog, the sky still thick and white, like exhaust; but he looked impatient. As if he'd been waiting a long time, watching at the gate.

David turned to Judith as soon as we got out of the car.

Wasn't that—? From Blackwood?

David and Judith met at Blackwood, they have fonder memories than you do.

She was standing hip-high in children, the twins, placing the yarmulkes on their heads. I don't think they'd been to a funeral before, and they knew something was up, something in the air, so heavy-laden; they stood at attention, chins to chests, arms stiff at their sides, their fair hair slicked down sleek as their skullcaps. Their front teeth are new, big and rough edged, like Ben's. I'd just been sitting squeezed between them in the back seat, and O Victor, the consolation, the tender mercies of their flesh. My flesh.

At least he came, Judith said. That took guts.

A plane from the East must have landed; a caravan of little blue taxis, sandwich boards swaying on top, advertising Rock Stations and Fast Delivery—Fast Food. Passengers alighting, reaching for their pockets, flight bags over their shoulders. A radio was blaring, but stopped abruptly; the driver had caught on to where he was. The low boughs of the maples, the dark furled cypresses, the headstones flat as pieces of pavement. *Guests Star-scatter'd on the Grass*. I don't suppose they often discharge their fares at the pearly gates.

The man went on scraping, frowning—quick squinting inspections. He didn't seem to see what he was looking for.

The injustice, Judith said suddenly.

At once the twins looked up, her hands on their heads, their eyes raised like altar boys to their mother's face. She was wearing one of those Quaker or Pilgrim maternity smocks with the wide white collar and cuffs, and her Pilgrim face; round, scrubbed, in shining earnest. Even the tip of her nose is earnest; and the perch of her lips; and her pale Buster Brown bob, chiming emphatically when she speaks. I swear the three of them could pass for triplets.

The boys opened their mouths, scared, awed. Was their mother going to cry?

But no, she shook her head, bit her lip, swallowing tears. Oh what an injustice!

I hope you notice I'm not talking about David. You didn't like that, did you? You loved him, you prized him—your student, your friend; you could talk about him all you wanted. But not I. You sound like a doting mother, you said. But I *am* a doting mother, I said. Please don't, you said. I guess one doting mother was enough for you.

I asked him once if he believed in God, Judith said. He said yes. And I thought, what if—who knows?—there might be something to it after all. If he believed, if a man like Victor Lazarus.

I was surprised. What would they say, what would they say, all those frock-coated knee-breeched ancestors of hers, with their buckled pumps and tricorner hats? The nature preserve on the Blackwood campus stands on land deeded by some branch or other of her family, long long ago, when they didn't need to worry about taxes, either. Blue spruce, purple beech, rhododendron bushes tall as trees. Castles in the air, you said. I didn't know faith was optional for them; didn't think they needed to ask. But question or no question, her tribe believes in good works. They put their money where their mouth is. Blood drives, fund drives, food drives, clothing drives—whatever anyone is taking, they're giving. They do their duty by their communities, their churches, their parties, their schools; put in sixty-to-seventy-hour weeks at the office, volunteer in hospitals, tutor in illiteracy programs, read to the blind. In their spare time, they serve in soup kitchens. They play hard too: serious tennis and soccer, and for fun touch football, and they wouldn't dream of stepping out for a leisurely stroll without taking along something to toss around, so everyone can get a shot at catching or ducking. They discuss serious topics when they sit down to table—capital punishment, abortion, right to die—and afterward they stand up and sing. Hymns. Madrigals. "The Silver Swan." "Amazing Grace." How sweet the sound. How virtuous, how dutiful, people look when they sing! Oh the shining light of those WASP faces. None more virtuous, more dutiful than the twins; their blond bobs and full cheeks, the pug pulpits of their noses.

I love to hear them all theeing and thouing.

In short, they share the close intense family ties people who don't know any better think Jews enjoy. And this strenuous existence does them no harm: death before ninety is an untimely event, and they keep their marbles to the end. I notice they don't travel together, though. Every Thanksgiving, at the gathering of the clan, the Boston cousins come and go on separate schedules. Three trains down, three trains up, six trips for Judith, driving back and forth to the grimy Amtrak station half an hour away. Thee keeps thy cool, Judith, I heard one say.

Now how do I tell my excellent daughter-in-law that just because Victor Lazarus said he believed in God, that doesn't mean you expected to find yourself anytime soon chasing buffalo with bow and arrow on the happy hunting grounds or clanking sword and shield in Valhalla. Ours is not a religion of rewards; ours is a religion of obligations.

Six hundred thirteen, to be exact.

You liked to tell the story of how we got them.

It goes like this. The Lord descends upon nation after nation, offering this book of his, with all the rules. Just do what he says, keep your nose clean, don't get out of line, and he'll take care of you. In other words, he's running a protection racket. But all these other folks want to take a look at the book first, read the fine print, find out what's in it for them. Maybe they can cut a better deal with Moloch or Baal, the fire gods, the volcano gods, their sound and light shows of hot ashes and lava. So the Lord, as a last resort, makes his pitch to the Jews. They don't ask.

We shall obey, they say, and we shall hearken.

And the Lord, he throws the book at them.

Okay, so this wasn't your version, not exactly.

—*God gave us a book, He promised a story. And God is keeping His promise. The Scenario is the sign of the Covenant, the Bow in the Cloud. All sorrows can be borne, if they belong to the story.*

And we have to keep our end of the bargain, you wrote, because our end is all of the bargain we know.

This morning, after breakfast, Judith was sitting over her coffee cup, her belly between herself and the table, and she looked up when I walked in. Her conscientious face, her childlike gravity:

What happens when the Messiah comes?

Outside, the kids were running around in the tall slippery grass, wearing cowboy hats and blowing whistles.

What happens when the Messiah comes.

We all get to obey the 613 commandments, I said.

Promises promises! Will you look at what the competition is offering? Tickets to paradise! True, advance purchase is required—but, hey, it's only one way. And Jews are supposed to be such shrewd businessmen! You'd think *they'd* be the ones checking IDs, turning away the standbys; you'd think *we'd* be the guys offering rebates and giving out green stamps.

But no. Missionaries beat a path to my door; a mile down the dead-end road, half a mile of goat path and gopher holes, blowsy milkweed pods and the blank blue gaze of wild chicory. They come bouncing along rocks and ruts, heedless of their shocks and tires in their zeal for my soul, alighting from vans—they come in vans, by the wagonload, except for the nice clean-cut Mormon lads who juggle briefcases and pedal bicycles—two by two, with their smiles, their Bibles, and their umbrellas.

The rain is driving rusty nails into the mud. It never rains but it pours in our valley.

I stick my head out the door:

We're Jews here!

This saves time for all concerned.

We are a stiff-necked people.

I suspect the other grandparents get nervous about the twins being raised as Jews. I get nervous too; one Jewish grandparent is all it takes. These are people of the New World, the New Jerusalem, and the New Book—the second installment, the part where God gets religion. We never bought that one. Not for us the red-letter Bibles with the good news; still too much of exile in us, the *Blut und Boden* of the Old World clinging to our roots. For them the rainbow, for us the cloud. So sometimes I think their story, their script—the new covenant, the new scenario—serves them better than ours serves us. They once were lost, but now are found. We may be chosen—but they are saved.

Fear and the snare and the pit and the steep sides bitten by the teeth of the backhoe; that hard-packed mound of yellow-gray clay—your rough-hewn altar, your high new house. You back there in the curtained hearse, the grim wooden box.

They say it's you.

Victor, if we're not lost—what are we doing here?

I should have lived back then.

That's what you used to say. One hundred, two hundred years ago. The good old days, the glory days, the golden age of East European Jewry. The Old World, the lost world.

Before.

In that world you would have been the prize. Victor Lazarus, ever the prodigy, ever the wunderkind. From Kovno to Kraków, from Berdichev to Białystok, the word would spread far and wide. Wise men with their bird-nest brows journeying to get a look at you, putting their questions and pondering your wisdom; shadchans, matchmakers, smacking their lips while visions of fat commissions danced in their heads; rich merchants in their gabardines and shtreimels vying for the honor of acquiring such a son-in-law, the privilege of supporting you in the lap of luxury all the days of your life. Jewish laps! Jewish luxury! Nothing to sneeze at. Spikenard and saffron, calamus and cinnamon, carrot tzimmes and kugel. For you the softest feather quilts and the juiciest chickens; the purest wax for your candles, the choicest wines for your kiddush, the sweetest pomegranates for your table, the most fragrant citrons, and only the ripest persimmons.

Nor would they forget the poor widowed mother, either. Somehow I see a poor widowed mother always in the background, Victor—don't you?

Think of it! Victor Lazarus. Potentially the Greatest Chochem of Your Generation.

And for this—all this—all you would have to do is all you ever wanted to do, O beautiful and wise. By night and by day, waxing and waning, sitting sunken shouldered and nearsighted over your books while wicks skipped raptly in the lamp oil. The life of the study house. The life you were born for.

A life sanctified by ritual.

Prayers for lying down, prayers for rising up; prayers before meals, prayers after meals. Prayers on the new moon and the first star. Prayers for putting on the tefillin and for kissing the zizith. Prayers thanking God for not making the Jews as other nations, and for not making you a slave, a bondsman—or a woman. And—lest anything be overlooked—the blessings for special occasions.

On seeing lightning flash, or a shooting star.

On beholding the first blossoms in spring, or a rainbow in the sky.

On hearing the roll of thunder, or the roar of the sea.

On hurricanes, on earthquakes, on strange creatures and sweet trees. Jews think of everything.

There is even a blessing to be said on encountering a great philosopher. You must know it, Victor; you knew them all:

*Blessed art thou O Lord our God King of the Universe who has given of His wisdom to the mortal.*

Easy to be a Jew then.

Easy to sing the Lord's song.

Easy to obey the commandments:

*Thou shalt have no other Question before me.*

Easy to keep the rules when the rules keep you.

There was just one thing. Weren't you forgetting? Your end of the bargain, I mean. The rich merchant's daughter, remember? Your beloved, your betrothed, your bride? You, the groom, I can picture waiting under the canopy. That's easy. Your shining brow of the anointed, the splendor of your garments, and the ardor of your eyes. The very candle flames would be quailing before you: the Golden Boy in all his Glory. Victor Lazarus, grown young and beautiful.

But who would it be, trembling at your side? Whose heart beating palpably, visibly, under the bridal gown? Whose face, whose, would you see when you lifted the veil?

Farridah? Farridah, your first wife, the one you loved? Dove-eyed, spice-lipped Farridah? Farridah with hair black as an eclipse and skin like the light of the moon? A Shulamite indeed was Farridah, a daughter of Jerusalem. The old city, with its archways dark as secrets, its steps like stones in vandalized graveyards. Her family fled in '48. Her brother, a self-made man, grown rich as Ali Baba in the oil jars and open sesames of America, gives pots of gold to Hamas and the Hezbollah. That might have gone over in the time of Maimonides—Maimonides, chief rabbi of Cairo, physician to Saladin, husband to the sister of the sultan's scribe. But Victor—how would it play in Lodz?

Me then? Me? For the sake of example? I'm not the leading lady type;

not even the heroine of my own life, let alone yours. Infant mortality, death in childbirth—you can keep your good old days. I'll take my chances, thank you, in the here and now.

No, I don't think so. No, not me.

Who then? Who? Who would it be?

Oh come on, Victor. Who do you think?

She is of that world. The old world the lost world the dead world the death world, the great centers of God and learning known to us now as places of the pits and chimneys, valleys of the bones. Of all that host—the long line of rabbis and scholars, generation unto generation of the learned in the law, the wise, the just, the blessed—X's mother alone survived the war. Her grandmother is a lampshade, Her sainted grandfather, soap.

She was born there. It was the early fifties; Jews were still coming out of hiding, coming out of the woods. That's how X's mother managed to stay alive; a small band, hunted, in hiding. Not guerrillas, not resistance fighters: Jews, just Jews, Jews trying to live another day. The fire gods were stoking the ashes. Rumors reached them but who could believe? Over? The war? Why should the war be over? There seemed no reason for it ever to end. At last, a few of the youngest and strongest—X's father among them—set out to find what was left, to see for themselves. Months passed before word came. The good old days were back; all had been slaughtered the old-fashioned way—rocks, ropes, pitchforks—in a pogrom. This was one rumor at least that had the ring of truth.

I don't know if X's mother died then, or after the remnants made their way to the refugee camp.

A well-to-do American businessman and his wife were thinking of adopting a child. They had served on various boards, committees, relief agencies, collected money for the cause. Now they wished to perform a mitzvah. Why not a war orphan, a brand saved from the burning?

X would have been two or three by then, but no one would have called her a toddler; that sounds plump and rosy and cherubic. She was small for her age, all ribs and stick legs and sharp little face and bald skull, scarified from scratching lice and the sores of malnutrition, her hair growing in like a tattoo; and her eyes—her eyes—seemed to belong to someone else. As if a soul still in hiding had taken possession, haunting the windows of her house. As we say, an old head.

She didn't speak, she didn't smile, and in the camps she had to be taught to chew. She had never been fed solid food. She had been starving since she was born—since before she was born—before she was ever conceived.

I'm not making this up. I wish I were.

There must have been others like her in the camp; the grainy-pale faces of black-and-white news photographs, the lips bloodless as knuckles, the eyes extinguished in ashy hollows. The preternatural child, the feral child, the old child who has played with dead dolls. But this child, this frail twig, half-girl, half-bird, bore an illustrious name. The American couple could hardly believe their luck. They weren't just adopting a child: they were acquiring a sacred relic, a living symbol, like those Torah scrolls recovered from the smoke and rubble of cremated synagogues. The Last of Her Line. The Flower of Our Lineage.

There are mitzvahs and there are mitzvahs. This was really piling up the bonus points. And they weren't the only ones. It was the fancy pedigree, wasn't it, Victor? You were in the market for credentials, too.

Let the heart of him rejoice who seeks the Lord.

You could have converted, made it official anytime; but that would have been to concede: that you weren't what you were, what you knew yourself to be. A matter between oneself and oneself. So something of the sort happened after all, only this time the bride's dowry wasn't the rich merchant's wealth—her stepfather's money. It was her mother's blood.

Did the rabbis ask whose question you prayed to? What commandments you kept? If you ate tref—which you did—or wore the tefillin—which you didn't? No. Was your mother Jewish? Your mother's mother. Sadie McDade, Sadie McDade, from everlasting to everlasting, Sadie McDade. Just a bit of a thing, Belle says, a wee little bit of a thing. Ninety pounds wring'n wet. I bet. And the drowned hair dripping and the white dress clinging to the rosy tints of her flesh in the living waters.

*Shall we gather by the river? The beautiful the beautiful river?*

You wanted a child, and it was all right, you weren't particular, anything would do—as long as it was a boy. A man-child, a son, an heir. Like that other Victor Lazarus, your father-to-be and never-to-be. All the begats and begats in the Bible; all the injunctions to be fruitful and multiply and replenish the earth; all the promises that your seed would be as the sands of the desert, as the star-strewn sky.

Oh Victor, who sez you weren't Jewish!

And over your son, your man-child, your heir, would hover no shadows, no doubts, no black marks. For him the scroll of honor inscribed in letters of gold. Wait—just wait!—until they questioned his credentials. Wait until they asked if his mother was Jewish! The whole genealogy, chapter and verse: the Yitzhaks and Yossels, Avrams and Sholems, Simeons and Gideons, Hayyims and Hillels, selections and transports, gold teeth and ashes.

*Son of man, shall these bones live?*
*O dem bones dem bones dem dry bones.*
*With harp and flute and timbrel. Selah.*

You look up from your newspaper at the restaurant table and here, clutching Ben by the elbow, comes X. She's not that much taller than he is, and the spike heels make her look smaller. The pale face, the braces; the hair hanging and dragging, the skirts hanging and dragging. She's gone in mourning ever since the divorce; even her hair turned black overnight.

The agunah.

The little girl dressed up in her mother's clothes.

A man hastily picks up his check and slaps down a tip. An elderly couple about to seat themselves at the next table—he's already pulling out her chair—change their minds, decide to move on. Other diners look away, look anywhere else: studying their plates, the menus, the handwriting on the wall.

She hikes up Ben's arm, yanking him closer. He stands awkwardly, crookedly, hooked by the elbow, glancing warily from one to the other. Ben the hostage. On exhibit. Not sure whom to trust. His big ears, his chopped hair, his new chipmunk front teeth. He takes after you both: your straight nose and straight brows, your eyes wide with wily innocence. But his are blue, blue as the wild blue yonder, as broken mirrors of sky, and his arms and legs are frail and narrow, like hers.

When I get through with you! she says. When I get through with you!

She seems to be eating her own mouth.

Victor Victor will she ever be through with you?

All those months, asking for Ben, needing him, Ben—the last of her line, and the last of yours. X refused. Too traumatic, she said. Bad enough the child had an alcoholic for a father; bad enough his parents were divorced. That wasn't enough for you? Now you wanted to show yourself to him? Look at you! A scarecrow, a stick. Hooked, wired up, needles, tubes, breathing on machines, a hole in your throat. An empty craw, a hungry bird crop.

Weren't you ashamed? Didn't Victor Lazarus ever think of anyone but Victor Lazarus.

You asked the social worker if there wasn't something she could do.

I can't make him come to me, she said.

You mean you can't make her bring him, I said.

I can't make him come to me, she said.

The kid's only six. You expect him to hop a cab?

She spread her fingertips over her breasts:

I can't make him come to me.

It's no use, you wrote on your legal pad. X speaks their language. She's raising my son to be a victim.

Like her.

X goes to all the meetings. The pink Kool-Aid and cookie clubs. AA for you, because you won't go. Children of Alcoholics and Children of Divorce for Ben, because he's too young. The rap groups, support groups, consciousness raising, twelve stepping; the survivors of this and the recovering from that; the dysfunctional, the codependent, the abused and the abusing.

On that circuit, X is the star; a familiar spirit in every church basement in our valley. Sleepy Hollow, as it is called, without irony; and the state prison, whose walls and watchtowers can be seen from your hospital window, swords of searchlights clashing by night, is called, without irony, Hard Rock.

X stands up and *shares*. She tells her side. She punches her breast, reciting the litany, the sins inflicted upon her, the high heels, the slit skirts like black flags flapping, the hair at half-mast. Her little fist tightened over her little heart:

*They have trespassed, they have been faithless, they have robbed, they have spoken basely, they have committed iniquity, they have wrought unrighteousness, they have forged lies, spoken falsely, scoffed, blasphemed, transgressed, committed abominations, they have gone astray and they have led astray.*

The agunah.

The little girl dressed up in her mother's clothes.

Okay, so it's not funny, harping on her; her pint size, her braces, her widows' weeds, her hair dyed black to look like Farridah. Her mouth devouring itself in a smile: I know something you don't know. No, she's not funny. The New Age New World victim. Does she ever speak of it? The other? The Old World, the lost world, the dead world, the death world, the great centers of God and learning, of barbed wire and electric fences and the dark forests of the night. The forests of fairy tales, of evil spirits and enchantments, of giants and ogres and wicked witches, of orphans and ovens and beasts with the power of speech.

Day after day X called the social worker, hour after tearful hour pouring out her side. She named her conditions; it was like negotiating for the divorce all over again. You were an alcoholic, a heart patient; she was the mother of your child. You never had a leg to stand on; you would have agreed to anything.

At last you gave in. The one thing X really wanted all along was to see you herself.

She held Ben in her lap, held his face against her, his one eye shining out through the bars of her fingers. You held up messages chalked on your slate:

HELLO

HOW ARE YOU

I LOVE YOU BEN

Your breathing machine was bubbling like a fish tank. When you opened your mouth, mute, the shadow words, he turned his face aside and hid it in her dress.

Then it's true, you thought. My son is afraid of me. I've done him harm. X was right all along and I was wrong. Or, to use the language of your dreams:

*—It was all your fault.*
*—You brought it on yourself.*
*—You were to blame.*

Hospital routines don't stop for visitors. Messy business, bedpans and bloodletting, suctioning your throat. X got up to find a bathroom; Ben followed with his eyes, reaching after. But he stood stock still, holding his breath; with his chopped hair and big teeth and wide wild stare, like some small furry creature frozen in the grass. You were afraid to breathe, too, but the machine that breathed for you went on hissing and clicking; the noise in your throat keeping time with your heart. Then Ben scrambled up onto your bed on his knees and spread his arms over you; not to embrace you, not to touch you, but carefully carefully guarding, shielding— afraid you might spill. He laid his ear to your chest and listened.

The grange fair. The dense hushed heat of the summer night. Squeaky lamentations of carnival rides, crickets coming to the boil, insects fizzing at the lamps. Under their light the leaves glowed, translucent; the stained-glass leaves, their greenness, as the poet says, a kind of grief. You bought a roll of tickets for the Ferris wheel, mounting the ramp with Ben again and again. His stick legs were so thin they frightened me, and your shadows hand-in-hand looked like trees. I guarded the loot: pennants, baseball caps, helium balloons, troll dolls, dinosaurs. You'd blow ten bucks pitching horseshoes or shooting at duck decoys just to bag such a prize; always grabbing for the brass ring. Hot dogs, hamburgers, mustard, french fries, root beer and orange Crush, caramel corn and cotton candy, funnel cakes and piccalilli. All the delicious smells of America. Someone nearby was smoking a cigar, and from the stalls, the reek and stink of acrid hay, drifted odors of Aqua Velva. The pigs were getting their tender ears shaved. Meanwhile megaphones were barking out the winning numbers in bingo games and the names of lost children.

All of a sudden the lights went out.

The lights went out, the lights came on. A painting on black velvet. The glow-in-the-dark T-shirts and decals. The candles and lanterns and live coals on grills. The luminous dials, the smoking sparklers and punks and red-tipped cigarettes. The fireflies sending up phosphorus flares, deep calling to deep. Body heat. Our gaudy life. Our brief glow in the dark, in the dark.

The stars were keeping their distance.

TUESDAY
JUNE 6

All the people all the people. Browsing in shopwindows, crowding into restaurants, laughing at curbstones, crossing against the light. It hasn't started yet; it will, soon enough. Someone waiting in front of me at the checkout counter, or browsing through pages at a bookstall, or heading away from me on the other side of the street. Something about his back, his high-propped shoulders, something hesitant in his step. The way his hair grows, too long and straight over his collar; or the way he looks up, a sudden light in his glasses. Sometimes he'll be too young and sometimes too old and sometimes there'll be no resemblance, none at all, not when I look again. But again will be too late. There will always be someone waiting in ambush. All the people all the people who will never be you.

A strange place for him to have ended up, Arnie Rheingold said.

A strange way of putting it, Arnie! I said.

Oh, I didn't mean it the way it sounded. I just meant—he flung out an arm—the glory that was Greece? The grandeur that was Rome? And Victor Lazarus picks this place? A place like this?

It was happy hour in Happy Hollow, time for celebration. The streets were mobbed. Every bar, every balcony, every boom box and open window detonating with the ear-imploding brain-exploding beat of heavy metal. The cruising cars were earthquakes. It's a company town, a garrison town; the architecture runs to cinder block and siding, what you called American temporary. Circle the wagons. Subdivisions sprouting on newly bald hills look like thickets of campfires and stumps. But thanks to the School of Agriculture, downtown and campus have kept their sacred groves, the ancient trees; the Druid oaks, ecstatic sycamores, the Protestant elms that line the walks like hymns. This time of year, this time of day, light swims in leaves, and the streets become sleepy lagoons. I like this place, Victor. It's where I knew you.

But I was thinking of that other place. Your suburban lawn, the reaped grass, the earth patched up and healing over.

*He maketh me to lie down in green pastures.*

It's always greener on the other side.

Arnie wasn't looking where he was going, slinging off his jacket, his neck-tie, with wide-flung gestures, rolling up his sleeves. Lampposts, fireplugs, parking meters were dodging him. You haven't seen your old friend in a long time, ten years. I don't suppose he's changed that much; he doesn't strike me as a man who changes much. Still the Security Guard. The wrinkled suit, the grizzled crew cut, the squinting impatience. His eyes are like minnows. He's gone gray, nearly white. Did he have a beard then? Well he has one now; he could be unshaven or shorn in mourning. The splinters glisten, crystallized in sunlight. And he still has that accent, the Bronx cheer:

*Lady of Spain I adaww-you*
*Right from the time I first sore-you*

Victor never talked about me? He never told you anything about Blackwood? He sounded disappointed. It wouldn't have been flattering, I gathered, if you had; but we all have our own versions of the tale, and nobody likes to get left out. Maybe it never mattered much to Victor, he said; if anything ever mattered much to Victor. But it mattered to me: I've been thinking about it for the last ten years. Victor called it a failyuh of friendship. Sounds like him, doesn't it? So Victor-ian. But don't get me wrong, I don't come as a supplicant. I'm not taking that rap, you can't pin it on me. It was all his fault. He brought it on himself.

I said that's what I used to think too, but I had learned to my sorrow it wasn't so.

Arnie frowned. It was that word *sorrow*. He didn't like it, no good could come of it. He wasn't here to talk about sorrow. Next thing you know, I'll be crying on his shoulder, blowing my nose in his handkerchief. Next thing you know, I'll be talking about myself.

All of a sudden the air is whizzing and whirring with big winged things that spatter and clack like windup toys. Tarnished, iridescent, like dark oily rainbows, like glass long buried in the earth. Empty shells turn up everywhere, discarded selves. The eye bubbles, the antennae, the tiny nymph wings, even the cilia on the insect legs. And the trees are in an uproar, a shrill shimmering din. Every leaf metallic; tinkling cymbals, tinny disks on tambourines.

Cicadas, I said. You know—seventeen-year locusts? It's the year of the great hatching.

Arnie had been brushing bugs off his sleeves without noticing. They don't look where they're going, either.

A strange life cycle, I said. I looked it up in the encyclopedia. They lay their eggs deep, the roots of trees. They spend most of their lives underground, in the pupal stage. Then they hatch, they mate, they collide and die. It's a suicide mission. That's their mating call.

*Cicaders?*

The wincing inspection. His frown was becoming a twitch, a tic. What's with this dame? First it's sorrow, now it's cicadas? What did insects have to do with it? The trees want to talk, let them talk. A man after your own heart, Victor. For all he cared they could be yakking Greek.

*And the trees of the wood sing for joy!*

You think I'm being a snob about his accent, don't you? And why not? Provincials make the best snobs. But, see, I know about accents like that: they're hard to keep. It's been a long while since people used to snap their finger and point at me—West Side of Chicago, right? If I forget thee, O Jerusalem! And you didn't sound like a boy from Alabama anymore. No banjo on your knee. So what's the story? Arnie Rheingold playing stickball in the alley? Ash cans, squawking clotheslines, the old lady's knickers and the old man's long johns up there kicking in the breeze? Please. You told me the rule yourself. It's simple, you said. Politicians keep their accents, academics lose theirs. Unless it's a foreign accent. Then it works the other way around.

Last night there were five of us in the house, and one on the way. The kids get all excited, laying their hands, their ears, to Mama's belly, listening for bumps and thumps and heart-kicks. They do everything in unison; they even tell one another's dreams. It touched our hand! We felt it! And now they've hit the road again, gone their separate ways. Plenty of time to look for the missing gym shoe, the toy truck that might have got lost down the bathroom sink. For now the house is empty, the refrigerator is empty, everything—empty. And I'm empty too. Tell me, Victor, where should I go? Where do I belong? I'm not your student, not a colleague, not family; no longer a lover. I don't want to be alone, not just yet; and the only one I want to talk to is you.

Will I ever be alone again?

What am I to you, Victor? What are you to me?

He lied! Arnie Rheingold said. He lied on his résumé. Victor Lazarus. The great Victor Lazarus. The rising star. Everybody's fair-haired boy. Makes most of us look like a bunch of undergraduates fooling around in a bull session. And guess what? No PhD. That's right, you heard me; he never finished his dissertation. Sure! Sure he could have. Victor Lazarus could have written a dissertation anytime; a dissertation in classical philosophy, a dissertation in analytical philosophy—you name it. Only that's not good enough, not for Victor Lazarus. He has to do both. He'll show 'em, he's the one, the one who'll pull it all together. The Grand Unified Theory. Well he couldn't bring it off, no one could—Einstein himself couldn't do it, could he?—and I don't care if his name *was* Victor Lazarus. Because there is no unity. But that was Victor, wasn't it? Had to have it all. If you've given me so much why not more? Hubris! Good old-fashioned hubris. Jewish hubris! The worst kind.

There were two things you held against these little liberal arts colleges, you said. One was the word *hubris*. The other was the word *catharsis*.

It was a fluke, too. No one ever checks up on these things. We're on the honor system, academic integrity and all that. It happened when he came back to Blackwood. We hired a new secretary in the meantime; she's the one who found out. Sent for his records, his good old Almer Matta. No no, not the bureaucratic type; a kid, a sweet kid, didn't know any better. Trying to do her job. One of these redheads, frizzy hair, freckles, blushing to the eyes, can't hide a thing. She asked me what she should do; she knew we were pals. What did I say? What could I say? I told her take it up with the chairman. What did she have to ask me for? I wish to hell she never picked on me. And the worst of it is, if you want to talk about irony—I think she had a crush on him. Victor. That's how come she was so interested, checking up on him, looking in his files. They all did, they all fell for him. The women! The women!

Victor liked women, I said.

You're telling me? That was his other claim to fame. Lazarus the Lady Killer. Lazarus the Lover.

No, I said. I mean he really liked them.

What did I tell you, Victor? Your secret is safe; wear it on your sleeve. He came running up to me after your funeral; he needed to talk to someone, he said, someone who knew you. I said I wasn't so sure that meant me. Why not talk to Simon, to David; your students, your colleagues? But he meant one of us, your women—as he took us to be. She was your wife, but never your woman, and I don't fill the bill, either. Though I'll have to do. So I'd say he's a ladies' man himself, Arnie, though not like you. The loosened necktie, the open shirt collar and rolled-up sleeves. And the impatience; something aggressive in that wincing glinting irritable glimmer, the pale irises riddled with little black pupils. No, not like you, Victor, thank your unlucky stars. Not like you.

All the world loves a Lover.

I taught a class that night, I thought it would never end. I knew I had to see Victor, tell him myself, get it off my chest. Listen to me, will you? Get it off my chest! Like I was the guilty one, the one in the wrong. Victor could make you feel that way. That little shrug, that little smile. How could I look him in the eye and come straight out with it—pulling a stunt, a dumb stunt like that? And look at the position he was putting me in. What you don't know won't hurt you—but once the cat's outter the bag.

The door was open, wide open. It's winter, mind you, the sidewalks are slippery, patches of ice, gloomy blue snow. The furnace is roaring. And the place is a mess, everything turned upside down; not that it was ever an advertisement for *House & Garden*, not with Victor around. You could always tell where he'd been working; he'd build himself a nest—books, butts, and booze. They could've hired a butler just to follow him around dumping the glasses and ashtrays. I hear this thudding and slamming in the bedroom. A burglary in progress, that's my first thought. Something tells me, don't go in there, Arnie, keep your nose out of it. So, naturally, I go.

It's Victor. He's groping in the closet, yanking everything out, tossing it all on the bed, not looking, not seeing, feeling his way. His head is angling, listening for something, like a blind man. All the lights are on and he's in the dark.

He hears me. He looks up. It's funny; Victor was the tall one, the long skinny one—they used to call us Mutt and Jeff—but the way I think of him, the way I see him, he's always looking up. Expecting something. But just then—his face! His expression. I can't describe it, I shouldn't try. *Glad*. Glaring with gladness. Too bright to look at. It wasn't meant for me, not for me to see.

But that's only for a split second, though; then he realizes who it is. The light goes out.

By this time I'm sniffing liquor.

I knew he drank, everyone knew that, it was no secret. The big question was how much. He kept you guessing—Is he drunk, isn't he? You could never tell, never be sure, not of anything, not with Victor. Only I never saw him like this before. The guy was paralyzed. Pie-eyed, plastered. He's blind, all right—blind drunk.

Hey! Cut it out! I said. Whadderyer doing?

He's standing there, swaying, with this puzzled look, like he's about to speak only he's not sure what he'll say. Then his legs give way. They slide out from under him and down he goes. There's a little wastebasket by the bed, this little straw basket. He crawls over to it. He pukes.

Stop me if you don't want to hear this. I don't know how much you really care to know about Victor Lazarus.

She'd left you, Farridah. That very evening. At dinner she told you. She laid down her fork, she blurted it out. I've met someone, she said. There's someone else. She said she needed to think. She'd been removing her things, little by little, the short time you'd been home. Her personal belongings; her charms and potions, perfumes and powders, robes and veils. You wouldn't have noticed, not while she was there. Now you were ran-

sacking the closets and drawers for something that belonged to her, something left of her, something overlooked; something, anything—she might
come back for. That's why you left the door open—for her, for Farridah.
In case she came back.

At dinner, Arnie said. I try to picture the scene. The loaf of bread?
The jug of wine? The book of verse? Scheherazade beside you, singing in
the wilderness. They say you could have passed for sister and brother, you
looked so much alike, as beautiful young couples do. As gazelles and young
harts upon the mountain of spices. Thou hast ravished my heart, my sister,
my bride. Thou hast ravished my heart with one look of thine eyes.

How lovely are her cheeks with circlets and her neck with chains
of gold.

Arnie says he hauled you to bed, took off your shoes, threw a quilt
over you. He put out the lights and shut the door. By the next morning it
was already too late; the dean woke you first thing with a call.

The credentials. I might have known.

Just last week—can that be? Only a week ago? Just last week?—and the
door is shut, the gates are sealed. Just last week a student was giving a
defense of his dissertation. No one expected you, it was out of the question; and no one could look at you, either, when you walked in. That's the
oldest building on campus, Simon says, good enough for the philosophy
department. Did you see the new Ag building? The little lambsie-divies
get air-conditioning, and we don't even rate elevators. Victor had to climb
four flights, double flights; he wasn't fit to climb four steps. A physical
impossibility. But you know how stubborn he was, the most stubborn,
stiff-necked, obstinate, obdurate! Too stubborn to die. That's what kept
him going, that's why they had to throw the switch on him. Go figure
it out; when it came to drink, the guy had all the will power of a tsetse
fly. But once he made his mind up. He never missed one of these things
before, never let a student down, and he wasn't about to start now. So
he hauls himself up arm over arm, hanging onto the rail like a life rope.
The thing's half over by the time he makes it. The door creaks, the floor
creaks—everything in that goddamn building creaks—all the heads go

up. Talk about an entrance. Count Dracula: the lip peeled back, the teeth wired together, the death rictus. The mummy grin. And the death rattle. That piece of cheesecloth sucking in and out in and out over his throat. So he puts his hand over it, covers it up—you know the gesture, touching, really. I hereby do solemnly swear. The truth the whole truth. And nothing but. He apologizes for being late. Late! Black humor, I wouldn't put it past him. He knew he'd won only a stay of execution. I saw it then, we all saw it. We had to look away. The late Victor Lazarus.

You did it, you said, because you thought… You ought…

I know what you're thinking, I know what you're going to say. The real thing? Sure, Victor Lazarus was the real thing. He knew it, we knew it, everybody knew it. We're talking about a principle here. An apology! That's all we wanted. An apology. Let him admit it, say he did wrong, say he's sorry. Oh no, not him. He refused to humble himself, he wouldn't give us the satisfaction.

You wanted Victor to humble himself? I said.

Why? What's so funny? Was he Gawd Awwmighty? Kings have done it before. Emperors! Who was the one, stood barefoot in the snow begging the pope to forgive him? Three whole days! Some kind of penance. And he was the ruler of the whole blinking bloody Holy Roman Empire.

Yeah, and I bet he made the pope pay for it, too. Breast-beating, chest-thumping, it's all the same, you said. Just another form of self-promotion.

Victor wasn't into confession, I said. Maybe he wasn't sorry. Not the way you wanted him to be.

Then he damn well should've been. He could've played the game for a change, for once in his life. A little pleading wouldn't've killed him. You'd think we were the ones on trial. He never said a word. No apologies, no excuses, no denials, no self-defense. No nothing. He wasn't even listening, he wasn't even there. Humble himself! Lotsa luck. Nothing and no one could humiliate Victor Lazarus. Too stubborn—or too drunk. Same difference. And that look, that look on his face, in his eyes; the way they got when I walked in on him, when he saw it was me, only me. Me instead of her.

Yes, I know. I've seen it too, your dark-adapted eye.

Look, I'm not trying to whitewash myself. I was up for ten-yuh—and I'm no Victor Lazarus. I'm one of these guys, your ordinary mortals, who needs the PhD. Okay? I have to play the game. The sixties—remember them? The sit-ins, the demonstrations, the draft card burning? I was a radical, a political, a war protester; kicked out of grad school, thrown in jail. Nothing to be ashamed of, but it didn't look so hot on the résumé, not back then. That's another thing Victor never had to worry about. The draft. I'm not talking about the physical, though it's a cinch that's one test he'd flunk for sure. The guy was built like the gallows. Is that supposed to be romantic or something? The dead poet look? I'm just asking. No, I mean his father, a war hero, gave his life for his country. That's what was left of him; a couple of ribbons and medals and a pair of broken sunglasses in a box. Victor had an exemption. He would, wouldn't he. Just like him. Always the exemption, always the exception; and he thought it was always going to be that way. He didn't have to play by the rules. Rules were only for the rest of us. He could get away with it, he could get away with anything; all would be forgiven, just because he was Victor Lazarus.

It was his attitude, it was always his attitude. He just didn't give a damn. Name me one thing, only one thing. Her? Sure? Let's leave love out of it, okay? That's no excuse, not in my book. He ups and chucks his appointment at the university in the middle of the year, at Xmas, because he's lonely. Lonely! Can you beat that? Any one of us would've given our eyeteeth for his chances. But I guess he figured there'd be more; there was bound to be more; there would always be more for Victor Lazarus. You say he was planning to write something called *Ardor and Irony*? Sounds like Victor. Let me tell you something myself, if you don't mind listening to my mundane opinion. Ardor and irony don't mix, there's your answer. You saw me toss a stone into his grave, but that doesn't mean I'm contrite. He had it all and he blew it all, that's his story. That's as far as I go. You can't forgive someone who isn't sorry.

So he saw me watching? I'd better watch that. I thought he was impatient, but he *is* contrite. He's playing himself—badly, the way we all do. It's like Simon says: We didn't know you, Man of Many Contradictions, Man of Parts, but we knew ourselves when we were with you.

The ten terrible years. The drinking, the divorces, the blackballing, the heart surgery. The cancer. He knows, he must know; he's just been to your funeral—there's a clue. He can take a hint. And yet none of it matters, nothing has changed, not between the two of you, not for him; and it never will. You are still Victor Lazarus, you will always be Victor Lazarus. And he will always be Arnie Rheingold.

Okay, let's leave love out of it.

I want you to know that it wasn't easy. Ironic detachment isn't for everyone, I'm no philosopher. The unexamined life was all right with me. A nice normal life. Is it my fault there's no such thing? I was willing to do what people do: imitate. For you that could never be an option. You were a sick man. You were a drunkard. You had given hostages to Fortune. You had a bum heart. And the Furies were after you—O the kind ones! The venerable goddesses!—the white-faced Furies with their smoldering eyes and seething lips and the black curses of their wings.

Stay away from this guy, I told myself. This is going to hurt. It took no soothsayer to divine. The gods held a lien on you. Prior claims.

How many times—day after day, night after night—does X drive by? To make sure you're there, to find out who's with you. How many times— day after day, night after night does she call? Calling and haranguing by the hour. Calling and hanging up. Calling in the middle of the night. She trails you, tracks you down, waylaying you in parking lots, waiting in your hallway, pounding on your door dressed in feathers. You hear her footsteps behind you, high heels clop-clopping under bony hooves. And how many times have you pulled the cord on the Levolor blinds and looked into that face, that face, pressed against the glass. The blade edge of the hand to the forehead, the eyes ignited, lip gnawing lip. I know something you don't know. That pale face seeking its own paler reflection; only a pane between you—and the foggy omens of her breath.

When you're out of town she leaves threatening messages on your friends' answering machines.

She wasn't always like this, you said, she can be plausible. Plausible! Victor! How am I supposed to put words in your mouth, if you're going to select them so stringently? But I thought I detected a note of regret in your voice: as if you sensed you had been her fate, as she was yours.

You said yourself it was never going to end. There was more where that came from; there would always be more for Victor Lazarus. Gods will be gods. Like they say, love is as strong as death. And Victor? She must have heard you talking in your sleep too.

I couldn't take it, I turned on you. There is such a thing as self-defense; you must have heard of it, even you. You *want* this, I said. You *ask* for it, you *need* it. The term *self-destructive* may have been used; yes, that sounds familiar. Everyone's a psychologist nowadays. She's the only woman in your life, I said. There's no room for another.

You raised your brows, considering. You may be right about that, you said.

And what difference does it make, what I said; all the usual stuff, the hurtful stuff. I wasn't trying to be original. It was that voice, that Voice— Das Ewige Weiblich. Eternal Blame, Eternal Retribution. You'd heard it before; you heard it in your dreams. I must have changed from Farridah to X before your very eyes. Every woman is some of each. Where does it come from, the rage? The rage we feed on, that feeds on us? We devour ourselves. The game, the dangerous game, you wouldn't play. The danger isn't losing, it's winning. So you let us win.

Self-destructive, Victor? It all depends on what we take to be the Self.

I know you loved me because I know when you stopped: there were some things Victor Lazarus wouldn't lie about. So I'm sorry for the pain I caused you, the pain of disillusion—no small thing, for a romantic like you. It meant a lot to you to feel that way again. Me too, Victor; me too. But compared to the gang that was working you over, the loan sharks, the hired thugs with their brass knuckles and shivs—. Anyway, like they say, it hurt me more than it hurt you. And let's face it: who was I fooling? How long could I keep it up? Since the idea was to be young and beautiful. That was you, Lover of Wisdom, Lover of Women, what you were, what you will always be. But it's not me. I never cared for being young, it didn't suit me; I'll take middle age any day. Too bad it can't last.

I guess I shouldn't have said that. You will never be my age.

Just like old times, isn't it, Victor? I'm doing all the talking.

## THURSDAY
## JUNE 8

32 LANES 32 the sign outside read. Thirty-two bowling lanes loudly lac-quered and gleaming; and every last gutter and tunnel deserted. The place was empty as echoes. Way back in the shadows behind the pins someone was crawling around trying to fix a setting machine, a pair of knees bald in torn jeans, and overhead on the TV screen four pretty maids all in a row bounced and clapped while balls rolled in the background. Sequined bras, flat tanned midriffs, ten-gallon hats. Cheerleaders at a bowling tour-nament? What won't they think of next? The sound was off, the pins exploding in slow motion and silence.

This couldn't be the right place. I tried next door.

### THE LAST RIDER

A vast dim barn, a stage set. The husky young bartender polishing the glasses; the solitary drinker sunk over his elbows and beer. A couple of lettermen were tossing darts at a board, and a man alone at a table turned to get a better look at me when I walked in. Overhead paddle fans were mixing the lazing shapes and shades.

The bartender approached, taking his time.

Can I help you? He sounded doubtful. Behind him ranks of bottles—green, brown, amber, gold—glowed against the tarnished glass with oth-erworldly bar light.

Were you on this time last week? I said. Last Thursday? Just about this time?

He thought. He looked like a football player, somber with muscle. No, he said. No, I don't think so. May I ask—why you want to know?

A certain man, I said. He was in here then. I'd like to know what he was doing. It doesn't matter, he's dead now. I just want to know.

He blinked. I'm sorry!

I'm sorry. It was the first time anyone said that to me.

Maybe if you could describe him, he said. I might remember him.

I laughed. Oh you'd remember him all right, I said. If I could describe him.

I would describe you, Victor, if I could.

Tall? I said. Skinny? Kind of stooping? Dark hair. Glasses. Crutches, maybe. A bandage, for sure. I touched my throat. A bandage? Here?

He thought some more, an earnest effort, then shook his head slowly, regretfully. No. No. No one like that.

Oh yes, I said. One other thing. There would have been a ruckus. The cops? You'd remember that. Something about a fender in the parking lot?

The man at the end of the bar looked up from his beer. I know the guy you're talking about, he said. The guy you mean. Yeah, the quiet guy. I spotted him the first time he come in; the bandage. A trache, right? I used to work down at the state hospital. I seen plenty of those. That's what I said to myself when I saw him. I said—that's a trache.

He was feeling in his shirt pocket for a cigarette. His fingers stiffened. So he died? he said. That man died? I'm sorry to hear that.

He was, too. Aren't we all? The tap over the breast pocket, the brief reminder. *The thing most terrible and most true.*

I was wondering. What happened to him. He used to come in every day. Every day?

Since I been here, anyways.

That would be what? Three weeks?

Just about. The middle of May. He comes in around the same time, sits in the same place—that table over there—orders himself a hamburger, reads his newspaper, drinks his beer. Like I say, a Quiet Guy. Never bothered nobody. Never gave no trouble.

It took me a moment to catch on: this was a professional assessment. He's the bouncer. Did you know that, Victor? The lean leathery guy down at the end of the bar? Bootheels. Stovepipe jeans? Nursing his beer? My age, I'd say; a Nice White-Haired Guy. Is this a stage set after all? The spirit world. Smoke and mirrors. Then what does that make us? The props?

Yeah, he said. I remember that day. I watched him get up and leave. He was weaving. Crutches? No, but he sure could of used them. I looked at my watch—it was ten of five. I called Chrissie over, she's the waitress, she was on then. Whad'd you serve him? I said. Whad'd he have to drink. Two beers, same as always, she says. That's what I thought. Two beers. So I'm sitting here kind of scratching my head. How could he be drunk? How could anyone get drunk on just two beers? Not unless he never drank before.

Or unless he was an alcoholic with half a stomach.

Well it don't take long and this guy comes running in, this old guy. Call the cops! Call the cops! Some goddamn sunuvabitchen drunk out there just run me over. I got witnesses. So I go out, I take a look. It's nothing, a fender, a paint scratch, not even a dent. But there's a whole pack of them out there, these old guys, old geezers; I don't know where they all come from. The bowling alley, I guess. Senior citizens day. They're all squawking at once, getting worked up. We seen him! We seen him! He couldn't even walk, that's how drunk he was. Pickled! The stumblebum! He went and banged up my car too. You know how some people are, they see a chance to collect on the insurance. They're just hoping something like this would happen. People. Don't worry, I can tell you about people. If it was me, I would never—. But these guys are ready to tear him to pieces. They're out for blood. I guess they figured—.

I know what they figured, I said.

He brought it on himself.

That's right, I said. He brought it on himself.

It's too bad. Like I say, he seemed a nice gentleman.

All at once I wanted him to know. Not about your zillion books and your umpteen languages, and your reputation—so they say—the world over. Victor Lazarus. Potentially the Best Philosopher of Your Generation. Author of *Torah and Logos*, *The One and the Many*, *The Cure of Philosophy*, *Beyond Dialectics*, *Ardor and Irony*—unfinished and illegible—and dozens of papers on everything from Pythagorean mysteries to mathematical physics. More will be coming out now; much more never will. The file folders labeled To Be Continued. You lived that life, that other life, after all, Victor; lived it all the while, right under our noses. The life you were born for. But that's not what I mean. I mean you, Victor, you. The You in you.

Let me see thy countenance. Let me hear thy voice.

If I could. If I only could.

It's too late now. You slipped through our fingers. What's the use? There was a man. He sat over there. A Quiet Guy. Never bothered nobody. Never gave no trouble. Now he's gone. They yanked him off the stage—gave him the hook.

Oh yes, I said. A very gentle gentle man.

*I'm sorry.* What a relief! *I'm sorry.* All these months—the hospitals, the doctors, the nurses, the social workers, the orderlies, the aides. The powers that be. We're only amateurs at this business of dying. They're the professionals, they know how it's done. Happens all the time. Leave it to them. Dirty business, this mortality; hush it up, handle it with rubber gloves. We're in the way. *I'm sorry!* That's all it takes. What else is there to say? And I hope I remember to say it myself, Victor, from now on. Now that I know what it means.

So I hunted you down. I tracked you to your refuge, your lair. THE LAST RIDER. It was close to your flat, you could keep out of traffic, park in that lot out back—most people don't know it's there. She wouldn't be likely to discover it, looking for you on her eternal rounds. For a while you would be safe—from her, from us, from all that. All that.

Sanctuary, Victor, sanctuary. Shadowless as the next world. And now you knew you could never go back there again.

You must have stopped to buy cigarettes at the vending machine in the lobby on your way out. I think you wanted to see if they gave you any pleasure; I think they didn't. You'd been lighting them up and grinding them out one after the other. That's how I found them, in the trash, yesterday— the day after your funeral. Belle and your brother were going through your things, and I showed up to help. Only I wouldn't—I couldn't—go inside, so they handed the trash bags and boxes to me through the sliding doors. Ben's toys alone took up the back of my truck. There was scarcely room to squeeze under the shower for all the frogs, ducks, masks, flippers, sailboats, sprinkling cans, in your tub. Those were your best times, you said, giving Ben his bath; kneeling beside him, your man-child, your son, your shrine. Should I tell you something else? I snitched one of his toys. The eight ball. Ask? Sure I could have asked. And for sure she'd find out, wouldn't she, when she grilled Ben after and put him through the third degree. My son tells me everything, she says. My son has no secrets from me. I wonder if anyone does. She'd demand it back, She's demanding everything. The papers in your files, the letters in your desk, a bundle from the girl in college you picked the dogwoods for. A wedding band engraved Victor and Farridah.

I coveted that eight ball, I had my eye on it from the start. Ben never played with it, and we did. You demonstrated the proper technique for me. You touched it, Victor; I saw you hold it in your hands; polishing, rubbing, coaxing, cajoling; rolling your eyes, rolling your *rrr*s:

I can call… spirits… from the vasty… deep…

Eight ball O eight ball: should we go to the movies?

OUTLOOK HAZY ASK AGAIN LATER

But do they come, when you do call them?

The fellow at the table was still twisting his head, craning his neck at me, not trying to conceal his disappointment; resentment, even. Suit, necktie, horn-rims, hair slicked back in swales of mousse; attaché case at his knee. A salesman? Computers? How long has he been sitting here, waiting for some action? This is a university town. It's happy hour. Twenty thousand coeds, at least. So what gives? Where'd everybody go? Why aren't they rolling out the barrels, firing up the grills? The light-footed lads tossing Frisbees. The rose-lip't maids quaffing beer. He doesn't know the town is dead now, a Ghost Town. Graduation is over, school is out, moving is done. Lamps and carpets and chairs on the lawn all day. Busted furniture waiting for the trash collection. And brightest things that were theirs. A couple of foxes, that's what he's hoping for. A couple of foxes—is that too much to ask? And will you look what walks in? Would you believe? An old gray mare.

Darts thudded peacefully. Fan blades stirred.

I'll tell Chrissie. She'll be sorry. He was her favorite customer. Real polite, she said. Always asks nice, like you're doing him a favor; always leaves a nice tip. You say the cops came to the house? Tough break, everyone hounding him like that. Him being so sick and all, I mean.

Well, I said. He was not a lucky man.

## THURSDAY
## JUNE 1

You were drinking in the bowling alley? I said.

I was... served... drinks...

Oh, I didn't mean it the way it sounded, I said.

How will that look on my epitaph, Victor? *She didn't mean it the way it sounded.* I did, though; I meant it just the way it sounded, and you knew just what I meant. It wasn't often Victor Lazarus let his goat get got.

It must have been pretty noisy, I said.

No... not... noisy...

You were gazing out at the cornfields, the stubbled husks giving up the ghost, the last glowering light. Streetlamps were quivering on, distant traffic winking and glimmering. So the rumors were true. Time to be tending to the soul's business, lighting the guttering candles, muttering the blessings. Jews and dusk: we go way back.

The gloom of night was in your glasses and the bird was on the wing.

Ever since the police took off, I'd been sniffing liquor. What was this? The power of suggestion? The cops—God forbid? You, Victor, you, the usual suspect? But there you sat in the lawn chair, all your angles acute, sipping quinine water from a plastic cup. Quinine water; I poured it myself. Quinine water—for the cramps in your legs. For the blood clot swimming upstream toward your brain.

Is he drunk? I thought.

We've all seen you like this, not drinking and getting drunker; your lips numb, the antifreeze rising to flood tides in your eyes.

You were admitted to the hospital a week before the first surgery. At least he's dried out now, that's what we thought. The operation was a success. Then came the coma, the pneumonia, the struggling, the raving. The DTs. One foot in the grave and it took two orderlies to pin you down. After that, IVs dripped alcohol into your veins. We know more about it now, this disease, this miserable disease that ruined your life; things undreamed of in our philosophy. Was that all it amounted to, your fatal flaw, your fate? A missing enzyme? A mutant gene? But biology isn't irony, O Beautiful and Wise. Or is it?

The phone began to ring.

You reached for your crutches, dragging them after; another burden, a cross you had to bear. You were done jousting with crutches. It was time to get going anyway, so I carried the tray inside. You were leaning against the wall, your shoulders hunched—your running-the-gauntlet look—gripping the phone in your fist. Lest one precious drop of poison spill. Clumps of soft moth wings were clotting the screen. Then your head jerked back, as from a sudden blow, clubbed from behind; your eyes went blank, you slid along the wall and sat down—surprised.

Are you all right? I said. That's what I said. What happened?

Dunno... legs...

The phone was dangling from the cord. I grabbed it, clicking the button, trying to get a dial tone. I think I'd better call the doctor, I said.

No... no more... doctors...

You were shaking your head. Help... get up... get... to bed...

Is he drunk?

The phone seemed to have gone dead. I wasn't getting a signal.

You began to crawl, pulling yourself along stubbornly on your elbows, your head outthrust, your gaze fixed in your glasses. With your long legs dragging, you looked like a grasshopper. You were chanting:

To bed... To sleep...

So he is drunk, I thought. He must be drunk.

To bed... To sleep...

Perchance to dream.

It was hard to tell when you were drunk, Victor, because drunk is what you were.

One of these days, Simon says. One of these nights. You'll wake up, you'll stare at the ceiling, your mind will start running on rewind. All the things you might have done. I could have—. I should have—. Why didn't I—. What if—. Whoa! Hold on! Stop right there! Because you'll be wrong. Wrong wrong wrong. Take it from me. There was nothing you could have done, nothing you or I or anyone could have done, nothing that would have made the slightest difference. Not as far as he was concerned. Couldn't you see from the beginning how the story would end? What's the good of running those scenes over again? We get what we pay for and we pay up front; that's the price of admission. He went into shock. Believe me, I know what I'm talking about. I've been going through this for thirty years.

So Simon wakes in the night? Simon too? In the dark, in the dark.

One month in the hospital, they said; six weeks recovering at home. That was the timetable. And you'd prepared for your convalescence with an un-accustomed indulgence toward yourself, your bodily self—a tenderness, almost, as if for another person; as an expectant mother might assemble a layette. For you this meant a supply of detective novels and opera tapes, and—in deference to this other, this unfamiliar person, yourself—you had actually purchased a bed. It had taken not one month, but six instead, and you'd lost your taste for leisure.

The air conditioner was hacking and wheezing.

To bed... To sleep...

I was expecting you to be deadweight, drunken weight, wondering how I would manage to heave you up; but, with very little help from me, a tug under your arms—with a spurt of strength and a nimbleness and light-ness that startled me—you vaulted up and tumbled over onto your bed.

It wasn't the first time I ever suspected you of putting me on, Victor Lazarus, and, alas, not even the last.

Sleep... Sleep...

That sounds like a good idea, I said.

I reached for the buttons on your shirt, but you raised your hand. Your eyes held my face.

All... cut... up... you said.

You were mouthing the words, less than a whisper, not troubling to cover the feeble fluttering at your throat.

All... cut... up... all... cut... up...

Now for sure I knew you were drunk, puddling drunk. I'd never known you maudlin before, never; no matter how rigid your back, how cautious your step, dragging your leg-irons on your high-shouldered quest.

Oh, are we feeling sorry for ourself? I said.

Mother... you said. Mother Teresa... of... Calcutta... is... the only girl... for me...

"The Yellow Rose of Texas." You never could carry a tune.

The phone began to ring.

I don't think you understand, Victor, I said. It doesn't matter, it makes no difference. No one cares about that. We'll still love you, every last one of us, all the same.

All the maidens love thee. Rightly do they love thee.

It didn't seem tactful to mention it just then, O Beautiful and Wise, but that miserable body of yours was never your strong suit. In another life you must have modeled for El Greco, his phosphorescent nudes with the potbellies and the surplus vertebrae.

That reminds me, I said. I've been meaning to ask. Did they ever get rid of that belly for you, your big beer belly, those scalpel-happy hotshots down at the medical center?

You nodded gravely, your eyes still holding my face: your last line of defense.

I'll have to take your word for it, Victor. I never saw your belly; I never saw it for the scars.

White scars, pink scars, purple scars, blue scars. Old barbed-wire scars, fresh fat wormy scars, wriggly ones and narrow ones, and puncture wounds like tattoos. Those diagrams of cow cadavers in the butcher shop, showing where the different cuts of beef come from. Rib roast.

Loin chop. Eye of round. Only the crews that cut up this carcass of yours must have been practicing their trade in blindfolds. What were they thinking of? How could they have done this to you? In the name of healing.

Patchwork, Victor, patchwork. What a piece of work is man.

The phone went on ringing. You gave no sign you heard. I tried... to warn... you...

We counted your scars, matching them up, which went with which. The surgeries. The procedures. And still not enough scars to go around. Do they recycle incisions?

You had no choice, I said.

No... choice...

If it had been anywhere else, anything else, any other site—.

No... choice...

We'd talked about that. You could decide to do nothing, let the disease take its course. There must be some doctor somewhere willing to give you a prescription to kill the pain. It's illegal, of course, to kill pain; some do it for mercy, some for money. You could choose death. What you couldn't choose—what no one could choose—was to choke to death, strangling on your own spittle.

And this wasn't the end, it wasn't over yet. You were scheduled for more surgery: the wound that never healed. And then what? What next?

Victor Victor, would they ever be through with you?

No more… you said. No more… hospitals… No more… doctors… No more… cutting… And no more… Never… that voice… again…

I fixed the pillow under your head, pulled the covers over your chest.

Do you want me to leave the door unlocked? I said.

You shut your eyes, you nodded.

We knew what it meant.

I pecked your lips; they slid into a smile.

You opened your eyes. Sleep… you said.

Yes, sleep, I said. Sleep it off.

*Sleep, Big Baby, sleep your fill.*

I put out the lamp by the bed, left the dim hall light burning. At the door I stuck my head back in and called into the darkness, the wheezing clatter of the air conditioner.

Then I'm leaving the door open, I said.

Last words. How I wish. You didn't need to say them, Victor—but I did. O turn thine eyes away from me. For they have overwhelmed me. What's the good, what's the good, if I can tell the world and I can't tell you.

Eight ball O eight ball should I have phoned for an ambulance?

SIGNS POINT TO YES

Eight ball O eight ball would it have made any difference?

MY SOURCES SAY NO

Tell me—Lover of Wisdom, Lover of Women, Scholar of Torah and Logos, Man of Many Contradictions, not all of them high-flown—could your rabbis and your philosophers do any better than that?

## MONDAY
## JUNE 5

At midnight a zombie voice sounded over the intercom.

*The power will be out for five minutes.*

The nurses giggled. They were eating sack lunches at the nurses' station; plastic spoons, paper napkins, Styrofoam cups. There he goes again, one of them said. He keeps saying that.

*Repeat: the power will be out for five minutes.*

I wasn't meaning to stay so long. I drove back to the hospital tonight to meet the rest of your family, your stepsisters and your half-brother, flying in from both coasts; and just in time too. They say the airport has shut down now, socked in by fog; and on my way out, on the road that runs through the grounds of the prison, the watchtowers seemed to be on fire, going up in the blaze of searchlights, the fog thick as smoke.

Everyone else left hours ago; they'll be coming back in the morning, but I won't. I glanced up once again at the clock on your wall. Just another half hour, I thought.

The nurses' station is brightly whitely lighted. Your room is dark, except for the gleam of the night light low on the wall, an eerie effect. The plastic tubes seem illuminated from within, bubbling with greenish neon. You are getting antibiotics for the infection, acetaminophen for the fever, blood thinner for the clots, sugar water for dehydration, and oxygen. Your temperature has risen to 106, your heart rate to 180; your blood pressure fluctuates between 50 and 30 systolic. All this I can watch in spikes zigzagging the monitor screens, but your diastolic pressure is too low to chart. Your legs are icy to the knee, your feet and ankles blotched deep hemorrhagic purple. In the fluids draining from your body, rust flakes of blood gurgle and skitter, and under your bed a bag fills with a dark foaming tea. You are composting; you won't leave much work for the worms.

The tubes drip and drain.

The monitors beep.

The respirator clicks and sighs, clicks and sighs.

No heroic measures!

That's the first thing we said, Simon and I, when we saw the doctor coming back at last, passing through a succession of popping glass doors. His bald head was beaming under the lights, a perfect circle, like a skullcap. Oh, I thought—a rabbi. And his lab coat—a kittel. Isn't that what you call the short white robes the rabbis wear on Yom Kippur? The burial shroud; symbolic of purity, the angel of death. They make me think of butchers' aprons—kosher, of course. And his hands clasped so solicitously in front of him, his brows over rimless glasses tilted in surprise. So they sent for a rabbi! A messenger, a go-between, a matchmaker passing through the portals of the worlds.

The janitor was still mopping the floors.

How would it be, Victor, how would it be? If they changed places, the healers? If the doctors let the rabbis remove their gallbladders, and the rabbis asked surgeons to look after their souls? Would we ever know the difference?

Is there no balm in Gilead? Is there no physician here?

At least they've promised to quit drawing your blood, every hour on the hour, filling up their little red vials. The one thing I've been able to do for you, Victor. Even the lab technician was sick of it. She was Japanese, I think, a face with the perfection of a piece of enameled jewelry. She dropped her emerald eyelids: I don't want to, she said. Doctor's orders, the nurse said, the records, the tests. Records. Tests. Always the credentials.

You are going to die in the morning, this morning; you are scheduled to die. It is written. The neurologist says you are already dead, your circuits shorted, your fuses blown. Your lights are out. Yesterday—it will always be yesterday now—when I laid my hand across your forehead I could feel the fireworks: neurons blasting, rockets' red glare. Lightning flashes? Shooting stars? The human head, your Man says, is the image of the world. So this is the way the world ends. The dark night of the skull.

*The power will be out for five minutes.*

I looked at the clock. Twelve thirty. I'll stay till one.

I went to the window. Over the parking lot the sodium-vapor lamps were exhaling an amber blur, a misted breath. A car was pulling in, its yellow lights pushing the fog ahead like sulfurous snow, its wipers bleakly licking, licking. A fog plow. The windows in this unit are narrow slits, like medieval battlements. How can we say what's out there now? Drawbridges? Moats? Foot soldiers armed with pikestaff and crossbow? For all we know we are surrounded, besieged by fog, night and fog, up here in our high tower, our castle keep.

Strange prisoners are we, and strange witnesses.

*Repeat: the power will be out. The power will be out.*

How many times did I look up at the clock before it struck me. A clock? Why a clock? In each of these rooms, these glass cases—the monitors, the respirators, the greenish beeping lights—a clock is mounted on the wall. They keep time by rote: all the hands on all the faces on all the clocks on all the walls skip the same beat at the same instant. But why? What for? The nurses don't need clocks; they look at their wrists, the sweeping second hands on their watches. The same must go for the doctors, there must be doctors, though I've yet to see any here. So why the clocks? Who's watching them? The sick? In case they wake in the dark, in the dark. The numb lights, the zombie voices, the dread. Ignorant armies of the night. But never fear: they are not alone. The clock on the wall will keep them company. The clock ticking clicking the identical mechanical inalterable minutes. We all know the consolations of a clock. Till the day breathe and the shadows flee away.

But Watchman, what of the night? Watchman watchman, what of the night?

Next door, in the next cubicle, an old man lies beached on his back, swollen to the size of a monster sea creature. His arms are flippers, his lip sags under the grappling weight of a hook, the breathing tube, exposing the roof of his mouth, his tongue, crusted with open sores and black scabs. He might be any race, all races, his skin dyed the color of tobacco juice from jaundice; the saddle brow and strong nose, the white hairs in his nostrils thick as cobwebs. He's been here so long, trying to die, they've forgotten him by now, wired up to his machines like a papier-mâché window display collecting dust and dead flies.

I'm the only one watching the clock.

Is it for me? For me, then? Sitting here holding your hand through

the bars of the guardrail. Your fingers, anyway; your hand is taped stiff to
a board and stuck with needles. For me—not leaving, not knowing how to
leave; but all the while in the back of my mind worrying about the time:
how late it's getting to be, how dangerous the driving in the night and
fog, fifteen miles on unlit country roads, and no matter which way I go,
all roads lead past the walls of the prison.

I just heard the nurses say that the visibility is zero.

So the clock is for me. And when the clock clicks one, I'll leave—because the clock clicked one. What's a clock got to do with it? The god out
of the machine. The graven image. We all have our idols.

Why do I have to leave you now? There will never be any more leaving you now. There's nothing out there, nothing. A land of thick darkness, as darkness itself, without form and void. The mist spirits have risen
in our valley and hidden his holy mountain. The world is not dead, it is
just away.

This is the place where his glory dwells.

You are lying on your side, your cheek to the pillow, your eyes half-
closed. Your eyes that stare and stare and don't see me. What do they see?
What do they see? Your pupils are not dilated in darkness, but constricted, stricken by a startling brightness. The light at the end of the tunnel,
Victor? In thy light shall we see the light.

Shall we see the light? Shall we see?

*From the hour that death has him in its grip, the dying man must not be
left alone, lest the soul, when it departs the body, be astounded.*

I know you're not going to die tonight. I've figured out that much,
I'm catching on at last. That's not the scenario, not how it goes. You knew
it from the start, I think.

—*All or nothing at all.*

—*If you've given me so much why not more.*

—*All sorrows can be borne if they belong to the story.*

Do you think so, Victor. Do you really think so.

So you'll have to wait; this business of yours will keep until morning:
the doctors, the social workers, the clipboards, the charts. The papers will
be signed, the plugs will be pulled. It will become official. And you'll die
choking for breath after all, strangling on spittle.

The sun had come up, the fog melting in light, shadows were moving across your drawn curtains. The nurses, getting you ready for the next shift, the last. Your body, your blood, your wounds, your wastes, the humiliations of your flesh, your green goings. Not for me to see. As if I don't know your body better than they do! Is that what you thought, Victor, when I saw your scars, your eyes holding my face? Were you watching to see what other women might see? And I said nothing. Nothing. Did you think your wrecked flesh ugly, repulsive? How could that be? Not to me. Not with you inside it.

*But in the flesh it is immortal.*

A lab technician was going into your room, carrying a basket of needles, siphons, and dark red vials.

## FRIDAY
## JUNE 2

She knocks. No answer. He's there—she knows. She always knows. His car is parked outside by the dumpster, she can hear the air conditioner making noise in his bedroom, and something is pushing crowding her chest, the way it does whenever she stands here waiting. Waiting. The dim hallway. The smells of last night's hot dogs and french fries and pizzas. The row of mailboxes, the names scratched out and scribbled over. His name. His. Is it too early for the mail? She stretches up on tiptoe, puts her eye to the slot. Nothing. Empty. That metallic taste in her mouth. She couldn't wait this morning to get Ben off to school. Last night over the phone he sounded so weak, so weary, she just wanted. All she wanted. He would come limping to the door, his fingers to his throat, and when he opened. When he. No one ever loved him, not the way she loves him. But the bitch was there, the old witch, the witch bitch with that wolf pack of white hair. And he hung up. On her! Who did he think? Hanging up on her. Just to show him she left the phone off the hook. Let the line go dead. If that's what he wanted. See how he liked it. She could hear the receiver clicking. Who was he trying to call? Who? Never let him get away with. Hanging up. On her. And all night long dialing dialing the phone buzzing in her fist and as soon as he answered.

Answer! Answer! If he knows what's good. But he never did. And he's not answering now. He's alone. She knows. She has ways of knowing. Alone on the other side of the door. Open! Let her in! Let her! But he never does. Once and once only, she was wet, it was raining, a cold spiteful rain, rain cut to ribbons streaking the lamplight, and she asked him if. He pointed to the place where she should stand. This far and no farther. Did he think she would drip? On his carpet, his mangy carpet. If that's the kind of person. Serve him right. Drip on it, drip blood on it. Her blood. Hers. No one ever. Not the way. The great scholar. Brilliant. Oh yes, brilliant. She liked that. Who wouldn't? All his books his walls of books. His long lashes lowered under the lamp. Looking at his books, who never looked at her. I hope they fall on you, she said. Fall down and bury you. Bury you alive. I'll bury you in books. Pulling books off the shelves, hurling books. How did he like them now? His books. He looked up, surprised, an arm raised in front of his face. That's right! Hide! Hide why don't you! Hide! Who always hides from her. No one! Ever! Not! The way! He frowned past her, a cut open over one eye, leaking dark blood, glossy, like his brows. You may be right about that, he said. His little shrug, his little smile. And only the door between them. Always the door. She wants to beat on it, beat on it, pound it down with both fists, the way her chest is pounding against it, the way the door is pounding under her ear. And now she knows. She's always known. The door is open. She's always seen herself stepping onto the dingy carpet, glancing down, fearful. Is there some sign of her? A stain? It has happened before, it will happen again. He will be asleep, curled on his side, like a baby, a big baby, his two hands under his cheek, and she will slide in beside him and press herself against him. The smell of his hair. His breath warmed by his body. His body. His breath. His. She will kiss his shoulder, nip at his ear, put her mouth on his neck. All she wants, all she ever wanted. Because no one. Never. And he will turn, his still small smile, his lips moving. Talking in his sleep! Who never talks to her. Saying in his sleep. Who never says to her. Listening listening her eyes open in the dark, up against the dark, its weight its deadweight pressing down on her chest. Buried alive. Buried to the eyes. She knows. She's always known. The air conditioner is humming. A faucet is dripping. Tick tick tick. It sounds like a clock. And makes the room so still. The vertical stripes of light from the Levolor blinds. Like the woods, the deep woods. The tall trees. The rotting leaves. Someone is listening. Someone afraid to breathe. Her blood is pumping backward, draining her fingers. The taste, the terrible tin taste in her mouth. And the still-ness the stillness crushing her chest. In the hallway the numb bulb is burning. He's on his back on his bed his forehead glistening his eyes glimmering glimmering under his lids. The dead bolts of his eyes. His ribs are rising steeply climbing the gauze struggling over his throat. And his stomach! His chest! Who did this? Who dared? No right no right! He's hers, he belongs to her forever and ever and no one never. The cold gushing from the air conditioner. A fly snarling against the glass. The sun slicing through the blinds its light searing her fingers. Her hands over her face. The worms the worms are eating him. The snake scars squirming. And the laughter bubbling up bubbling from her lips. Not her laughing not her own self. The other. Inside her. Quivering under her blouse. Its paws on her chest. Stop! Let her breathe! But it won't, it will never. It has happened before, it will happen again. She will always see herself backing away, afraid to take her eyes from the eyes on the bed. What if? Watching her? The white moons of his eyes. Footsteps, stealthy footsteps. Someone walking on grass. Walking on graves. The darkness lurking. It's here. It's hers. It belongs to her now. Where is it? What is it? Will she ever find it?

TUESDAY
JUNE 6

Well, Victor.

No sound now but the trudge of the shovel, the dull clods dropping on your box with a plodding tread. The heart's drudgery.

Like you say—it's harder than it looks.

It took a full five minutes, Simon says. He says you put up a fight. They switched off the machines, they pulled the plugs, they disconnected you piece by piece, part by part. Your heart beat violently, your blood pressure spiked, your chest rose—galvanized—as if you might rise with it, as if your ribs would crack. Your rivets held. On monitors and graphs they watched you die.

It was 1:25 in the afternoon, hours late, as usual; the powers that be kept you waiting till the end.

I was at the park, feeding the fish, casting crumbs on the quibbling water. It was brown-green, the color of algae—the color, I think, of your eyes—and sunlight reflecting on the shallow creek bed forged a pattern of links and chains. On the slimy banks the ducks came waddling up, quacking their wisecrack quacks.

Not many stop to toss a stone into your grave. Your brother, staring in front of him as if he might never blink again. Ben, with some coaxing from your mother. X, stooping to scoop up a fistful, flinging them swiftly behind her. That man with the scrubby beard, wincing, hasty, the sun in his eyes. I take my turn. A prayer for forgiveness. Any unkind words or deeds, pain or anguish I may have caused you, sins of commission or omission toward you. Yes yes, all of the above. But Victor, it seems to me I wronged you most in never knowing you. Hear ye and hear but do not understand; see ye and see but do not perceive.

I didn't want to know and I know.

I didn't want the pain and I have the pain.

So that's how it's done. Hard cases take hard knocks.

I'm learning, Victor, I'm learning.

It doesn't matter so much if I didn't know you, we didn't know you. There's time. I think I know you better now. But did you? Did you know Victor Lazarus? Or did you die with that voice, that voice in your ear? Nothing and no one can humiliate Victor. Victor, I'm here to tell you: nothing and no one ever did. Aren't there enough of them yet? The noble, the exemplary, the perfected dead. Who needs more? You, Victor, you; alive, as you were, living your own life, Lover of Wisdom, Lover of Women. Let them keep their consolation prize.

Victor, I said. What difference does it make? What kind of life we live? Short life, long life, good life, bad life. After we're gone, we'll never know. It'll be all the same to us.

You touched your fingers to your throat; you forced the words to your lips.

For those... who come... after... you said.

So be it.

This is the way you wanted it, isn't it? More or less. Not an Orthodox rabbi—but a rabbi. Not a pine box—but a plain one. No autopsy, no organs donated. What a laugh. You and your jokes. What was left? Who would have it? Your refuse, your retreads, your staples and rivets, your remaindered heart. No embalming, no cosmetics, no cutaway suit, no cold-waved hair. Not all dolled up. No false front. A simple shroud.

The old words, the good words, the words I don't know, the words everyone knows.

Did a watcher pass the night with you to drive off the evening wolves?

So it's all over. Time to go. The congregation is forming an aisle for the mourners to pass through, back into the world of the living. How far away they seem, the wrong end of a telescope. The sobs, the bowed heads, the handkerchiefs; the clairvoyant sunlight, the speaking leaves. Nigh is the land that they call life. This world so much more real than we realize. What am I waiting for? The workmen stand ready to pull up stakes, fold the chairs and the tent top, roll the rag of green rubber; the backhoe is grinding over the dazzled grass. They'll finish the job. I'm keeping them waiting too. And here he comes again, that guy who was watching at the gate. His short gray beard and glittering eye. Who's he looking for now? Not me, I hope. Just now I'd rather talk to trees. They're burnished with sound, you can all but see it. I don't know what they're saying, but it seems urgent.

And Victor? I just thought. It's all over—and it's only the beginning.

# AFTERWORD

In nice chairs on a stage sit five North American writers born in the 1930s—three are dead, but only one was lost, Bette Howland, born in 1937. They're seated younger to older, which has Bette flanked by Raymond Carver and Joyce Carol Oates, both born in 1938, and Margaret Atwood and Toni Cade Bambara, born in 1939. Neither of the two others dead is as out of print as Bette Howland was until this volume. I love the very literary story: In 2015, Brigid Hughes, editor of the magazine *A Public Space*, finds *W-3*, Bette's 1974 memoir, in a sale bin at a used bookstore, reads everything she wrote, and plans for the present collection result. A press is founded, A Public Space Books. Publication of *W-3* will be next—placing Bette next to Maxine Hong Kingston and Vivian Gornick as progenitors of the resurgence of memoir.

Wherever you position Bette Howland's absence, the vacancy is glaring—she has the kind of large presence on the page that reconfigures the literary history of its moment, as, for instance, the revival of Jean Rhys did in the 1960s. Both were mentored by an A-list great male novelist—Jean Rhys by Ford Madox Ford; Bette by Saul Bellow, whom she met at a writers conference on Staten Island in the early sixties. Like Rhys and FMF, Bette and Bellow were "lovers for a time." He continued as her friend until the end of his life, giving her advice that's solid gold for a blocked, often depressed writer lacking in self-confidence: "I think you ought to write, in bed, and make use of your unhappiness. I do it. Many do. One should cook and eat one's misery. Chain it like a dog. Harness it like Niagara Falls to generate light and supply voltage for electric chairs."

That Bette is being revived now makes her a member of a cohort who have benefited from the forty-year gap between the end of a woman's youth and beauty when, at say forty, one's reputation goes dark, until eighty or so, when one becomes a discovery! Think Marie Ponsot, American poet, the above-mentioned Rhys, the recently deceased Diana Athill, "discovered" in her late nineties. When Bette came into this company she was some years into dementia and multiple sclerosis; but the likenesses reproduced were of a 1960s babe in bathing suit and sunglasses, a 1970s beauty in a fedora. Not recognizing her in the photos, I was drawn to the exhausting formulaic epithet, "a lost woman writer"—then I saw the name: So it's finally happened, I said to myself, I actually knew one of them.

My friendship with Bette Howland began in January 1977 at the MacDowell Colony in New Hampshire. There were feet of snow, and she had invited a group of us for a drink. The three stairs down to her studio were covered with new snow, beneath it a slick casing of ice. My feet went out from under me and I fell hard onto the right upper quadrant of my back. It is actually true that whenever I feel that ache, which I often do, I think of Bette Howland, writing there in the dark, her typewriter in a pool of light. As I sat quiet that evening, she held court with the men and I watched, intrigued. This woman did not have the luster of the women poets I knew who were already called "great," nor did she have the sheen and confidence of the men she was entertaining, who despite their accomplishment or lack thereof lurched through colony dinners with confident boasting. She had a resonant alto voice and an intensity and kindness that pulled me in. We became friends.

I remember long talks in that very dark writing studio—what we discussed is long gone, but my preoccupations at the time were "am I really a writer" and that I lived with one man and wanted to have an affair with another, one of the colonists. What a waste, I think now, when we might have talked about sentences, the density of words, or how imagination works when you are writing from your own life. We were both writing from our lives, and we were both wounded but she was older. "Make use of your unhappiness," Saul Bellow had told her. Did she tell me that? We corresponded and visited for a few years, but then at the end of the 1970s my life exploded and we lost touch, though when it was published in 1983, she sent me *Things to Come and Go*, a collection of three novellas, and the following year she won her MacArthur. At the time, my writing life was fully supported by an inheritance, and Bette had often been broke, even homeless, relying on artists' colonies and the apartments of friends. Now she had money. I'm sure I wrote congratulating her. But she never published another book. In accounts of her life, lack of self-confidence is the general diagnosis for her silence. The loss of her in those years when I might have returned her favor of encouragement still hurts.

There is a way in which all of Bette Howland's characters seem like visitors from a parallel universe, where they are freed rather than confined. This is the eponymous visitor in the opening story of this collection: *I was catching on at last. The bad roads, the crash, the minor injury. This petty bureaucrat. This place. Sir? I'm dead? Is that it? I'm dead?... That's what they all want to know! he said. But that's the whole show! I can't give that away, can I?* An uncle's young wife is *a big handsome Southern girl, rawboned, rock jawed, her pale head dropped over her knitting. Peculiarly pale; translucent, like rock candy, and almost as brittle.* It is as if they step into a room accompanied by their own lighting. *"When are you going to get married?" Uncle Rudy asked, towering over me.* Imagination is what she calls what she does with them, imaginative selection from the panoply of life. *He's a scofflaw. He'll go out of his way to park illegally. He'll drive around the block looking for a No Parking sign or a nice little fire hydrant.* Reading the prose brings a Bette I'd forgotten—a glass of Scotch, how she threw back her head and uproariously laughed. Ah, yes; here's the one with verve, the woman in the fedora photo.

Story is the melody, but the art is in improvisation, the voicing. As in her native city, lines of blues give way to jazz, in the progression from *Blue in Chicago* to "Calm Sea and Prosperous Voyage." Experimental, someone called that novella somewhere, but I say no, just the workings of the mind. Anything to rough up the calm of mere narrative—music born within the bounce of her language. She's at the grave of Victor Lazarus, who cheats death, as much a victor as the New Testament character he's named for. She'd want you to get that joke. *Here? Where the grass lies uneasy? It's hiding something. Three strips of sod, dried and muddied, like coco-matting. A marker as ancient, rusted, as the rest. I knelt to read it.*

She withholds the identity of the speaker. She's the final lover of Victor, her telling toggling between the Jewish funeral of this non-Jew and his pre-death in a hospital. *Cut some more here, drill a hole there—and when they had done, you sat up, you held out your hand. That stumped them. They stared. A fakir on your bed of nails, your naked arm bone trailing needles, tapes, wires, tubes. A tin cup, a beggar bell, they could understand. But a hand?*

"And always the prose with which she searches is arrhythmical, nervous, self-questioning, passionate," wrote Christopher Lehmann-Haupt in the *New York Times*. "You can't fall into step with her, because the moment you do she shifts her cadence and takes off for another part of town..."

In an article in *StoryQuarterly*, the interviewer, Roslyn Rosen Lund, introduced Bette as "a strong featured volatile woman who maintains her own balance between reticence and assertiveness." She goes on to say that she also found Bette "intuitive, easy to interview," as if that were a relief.

> For a start I reminded her that her book has been called "non-fiction," "a series of sketches," "an autobiography." She added that it has also been called "a short-story collection," "a first-class novel," "a chronicle." She shrugged and said she is not concerned with labels. Yet the question of form, which has been thrust upon her, dominated our conversation.

The controversy was then just as dreary as now for those who write that way. Here is the brilliant Bette:

> What form did I use? Well you don't *use* a form. That's the whole trouble. You *find* a form. When people ask is this non-fiction or fiction, they mean: is it fact or fiction, is it true or not.

For Bette, this was not a frivolous question.

> But when people worry about whether something is fiction or non-fiction, they are worrying about how much *invention* there is. They should be worrying about how much *imagination* there is. Imagination is the only way of experiencing life.

I'm walking a street in Chicago and I feel the surge of energy that I always identify with that city, wind blowing toward me, bracing, inspiring, literally filling my lungs with an air different from New York. "We are not in the same line of business as Paris, London, or New York," Bette quoted from *Blue in Chicago*.

And here is the opening of this book: *I was driving an expressway through a large city. Interchanges, on-off ramps, bridges, underpasses. Traffic glittered, roadwork stretched ahead forever. I kept heading the wrong way. You know how it is: the wrong lane, the wrong turn, and you're stuck; nothing to do but just keep going, on and on, until the next exit.* Once you get onto those roads and into the night, she seems to be saying, you're stuck unless you admit the possibility of alternative realities. *You know how it is.* Well, yes, I do know how it is, but I have not before encountered the experience in literature. A woman driver, no despair, just observation, recitation of reality. The traffic does not roar or undermine, it glitters, offering the reader not obstruction but "forever." The "wrong way" it seems is not so wrong, just leads to the next exit, the next departure from reality.

—*Honor Moore, March 2019*

# ACKNOWLEDGMENTS

The dedication and efforts of many people made this book possible. Thank you to Jacob Howland and Frank Howland and their families, for entrusting us with their mother's legacy. To A Public Space's board and contributing editors, Charles Buice, Annie Coggan, Martha Cooley, Elizabeth Gaffney, Mark Hage, John Haskell, Brett Fletcher Lauer, Yiyun Li, Ayana Mathis, Kristen Mitchell, Robert Sullivan, and Antoine Wilson, for their abiding commitment and belief. Julie and Jay Lindsey, Joshua and Marcella Rolnick, Julia Shea, Jan and Marica Vilcek, for their early support. Thank you to the staff of A Public Space, in particular Megan Cummins and Laura Preston, as well as Sarah Blakley-Cartwright, Will Cabaniss, Anne McPeak, Jesse Shuman, and Lena Valencia, who add to the joy of the work. Lauren Cerand, Allison Devers, Nicole Dewey, and Renée Zuckerbrot for their exceptional advocacy. Honor Moore for her superb words. The Hughes family, fighters for fiction. The community of CLMP.

Most of all, thank you to Bette.

**A PUBLIC SPACE** is an independent nonprofit publisher
of a literary and arts magazine and A Public Space Books.